THE THIRD GENERATION . . .

From the homestead rushes of Indian Territory to the statehood of Oklahoma, the Heron family challenged the primitive American wilderness to wrest their fortune . . .

Now, with half a century of struggle and strife behind them, the third generation of the clan face far greater crises following World War II as they become involved in political intrigues and international affairs that will test not only their strength but the legacy their forebears had so nobly forged.

And once again, their indomitable spirits will prevail in this powerful saga of passion, pride, and perserverance that is a triumphant testament to human endurance and everlasting faith.

Whitney Stine, a native of Garber, Oklahoma, who now lives in Upland, California, has had many best-selling books, including *Mother Goddam*, the story of the screen career of Bette Davis; *The Hurrell Style*, for which he wrote the text accompanying glamour photographer George Hurrell's famous portraits; and *Stardust*, the three-generation saga of a famous acting family.

Other Books by Whitney Stine:

THE OKLAHOMANS
THE OKLAHOMANS: THE SECOND GENERATION

THE OKLAHOMANS:
The Third Generation

Whitney
Stine

PINNACLE BOOKS NEW YORK

This is a work of fiction. All of the main characters and events portrayed in this book are fictional. In some instances, however, the names of real people, without whom no history could be told, have been used to authenticate the storyline.

THE OKLAHOMANS: THE THIRD GENERATION

An original Pinnacle Books edition, published for the first time anywhere.

First printing, October 1982

ISBN: 0-523-41662-8

Cover illustration by Norm Eastman

Printed in the United States of America

PINNACLE BOOKS, INC.
1430 Broadway
New York, New York 10018

To Oklahomans everywhere—who have not forgotten the old values . . .

THE OKLAHOMANS:

THE THIRD GENERATION

1

The Enactment

The flame, at first, was small—no bigger than an au-
burn spitcurl.

But in the tightly closed atmosphere of the tiny place,
with all windows and doors closed and the temperature
outside climbing to one hundred degrees in the hot
noonday sun, Sunday papers stacked near the grill turned
amber, then dark brown. A whisper of smoke curled
upward, and soon the pile of papers ignited. Yet the fire
was slow to spread, content, it seemed, to blaze from
paper to paper, to wicker napkin holder to oilcloth,
dancing along the countertop. There were no billowing
clouds of smoke to warn those taking part in the parade
on Main Street in Angel, Oklahoma, that the Red Bird
Café was on fire.

High school marching bands from Medford, Pond
Creek, Covington, and Garber circled dramatically in
front of the drugstore, and the Angel band, instruments
flashing in the sun, practiced short order drill in the
center. The effect, supposed to resemble a Hollywood
musical number, was lost on the spectators who lined
Main Street, because the band leader, who had choreo-
graphed the movements on the high school football
field, had forgotten that no bleachers were to be set up

on either side of the street. Two drum majorettes held a long banner that read:

LIBRARY DEDICATION DAY—APRIL 8, 1946

While the crowd grew restless, waiting for the parade to resume, Letty Heron Story Trenton and her husband, Bosley, sat perched atop a buckboard, circa 1893, identical to the model that had carried her from Hennessey to Enid when she had participated in the Land Rush, fourteen years before Oklahoma achieved statehood in 1907. People from all over the United States had gathered on the borders of what was then known as Indian Territory, to take part in the Run and stake the one hundred and sixty acres that the government had set aside for claiming.

Letty, a naive young girl in those days, was now a spry seventy-five, with white hair upswept in an old-fashioned pompadour that even at her age was becoming. Bosley, more frail than she, was six years older, but his face looked almost young, flushed as it was with the excitement of the occasion. He appreciated the fact that the town had gone to so much trouble to stage the event. Most of the young dudes wore four-month-old beards and others had glued false goatees, sideburns, mustaches, and muttonchops to their freshly shaved faces, with the result that the assortment of appendages were in various stages of disarray, caused from perspiration, which was melting the glue. Teenage girls wore old-fashioned calico dresses and sported poke bonnets.

Finally the bands whipped out of the circle into formation, reins were tapped over horses' backs, and the parade began to move again. Cherokee Indians proudly displayed their feathers and turbans as their horses marched smartly down the freshly asphalted street. Although their brown faces were impassive, Letty wondered if they were thinking that this very ground where Angel was built had once been their unhappy hunting grounds, in the days before the white man had mercilessly wrenched the territory from them, sending men, women, and children to reservations, which in time had become as worthless as the Confederate money that had been doled out to them for taking up arms against the North.

Truthfully, the Indians were bored. This was just another parade, another public appearance, another show. They could scarcely wait until the canvas tepees could be wrapped around tent poles and the collection of arrowheads, clay pots, tobacco pipes, beaded moccasins, and other unsold souvenirs—made in prewar Japan—were loaded into the backs of pickup trucks and taken back to Tahlequah, the old tribal Cherokee headquarters located in the lush green country beyond Tulsa. Their formal regalia would be placed into cellophane garment bags among mothballs, to be relegated to back closets until they were once more asked to provide window dressing for another public event.

Directly behind Letty's buckboard, a brown stagecoach, expensively restored to its original luster, played host to Luke Heron, fifty-two, the president of the oil company that bore his name. He was the son of Letty and her first husband, Luke, senior, and was accompanied by his wife, Jeanette, and their two sons, Luke Three, age nineteen and Murdock, age four.

"Mommee, Mommee, gimme, gimme!" the child shouted as they passed a balloon vender.

"Later, after we finish the ride," she replied. "Now, dear, wave to all the nice people!" She felt like giving him a smack across his bottom. At her age, she was inclined to be impatient. It was a strange experience, she conceded, to have both sons in the same carriage, when Luke Three was old enough to be Murdock's father—one of the joys, she reflected wryly, of having a change-of-life baby.

"Mommee, Mommee, peepee." Murdock lisped.

Luke was smiling widely to the crowd, turning this way and that, doffing his white ten-gallon hat every few feet, and Jeanette counted to ten under her breath while she waved to Belle Trune, who had taken the day off from the Red Bird Café and was standing, a little bow-legged, by a fire hydrant. What was the term that Luke had once used in connection with Belle? *Pleasure bent.* It was the first time that she had ever heard the old expression.

"Mommee, mommee, peepee!" Murdock exclaimed distinctly.

"Luke, if you'd stop behaving like a movie star long enough to pay attention to your son, he has to go to the bathroom!" Jeanette said furiously out of the corner of her mouth.

"Son, can't you wait a little longer?" Luke bent down and whispered in his ear.

"PEEPEE!" Murdock screamed.

Luke Three, attired in the famous blue uniform trimmed with white piping that all Heron Service Station personnel wore, with the perky blue cap raked over his left eye, stopped saluting the crowd with hands and fingernails that were none too clean. Although he habitually scrubbed up with the dexterity of a surgeon, he was never quite able to remove all of the engine grease. "Mother," he said with resignation, "I'll take him over to the Heron Station, we're almost there. If the baby has to go, he has to *go!*"

"Driver," Luke called, "Would you pull over for a moment? The baby has to go to the bathroom."

"Have him use the funnel under the back seat," came the gruff reply.

Luke shrugged his shoulders and gingerly felt under the seat, and finally brought out a small copper spout with an attached hose that snaked through the floorboards of the vehicle. He blithely handed the contraption to his wife. "Here, woman"—he smiled and waved to the crowd again—"do your duty!"

"This is ridiculous," Jeanette retorted, helping Murdock undo his pants and holding the funnel for him. "This is my last parade, Luke!" she cried under her breath. "Here we're got up to look like extras in some old cowboy and Indian movie, wedged into these silly carriages and stagecoaches, waving to a lot of people we don't know, and for what? Just because your folks and some of the other oil millionaires decided to build a library . . ."

Luke laughed. "We're celebrities to these people," he answered quietly, "and we may not know them, but they know *us*." He smiled, looking at Murdock and the funnel. "It's a good thing this stagecoach has doors!" And, the baby, for the first time that day, laughed and waved his pudgy little fingers at the people lined up on the sidewalk.

Next in the parade lineup was a huge flatbed truck decorated in red, white, and blue crepe paper—the nearest resemblance to a formalized float that the procession sported. The design background, a sunburst, effectively hid the entire Clement Story Swing Band and the leader himself from the spectators that lined the left side of the street—a mistake not noticed until the vehicles were at the assembly point. Clement, Letty's forty-three-year-old son by her second husband, the mixed-blood Cherokee tribal lawyer George Story, had thrown his baton at Eben Baker, who had organized the parade. "Dammit!" he had shouted, "I gave up a perfectly good concert date to come back to my home town to appear in this fucking parade, and half the people can't even see the orchestra!"

But now, in a calmer mood, Clement nodded to Tracy Newcomb, who was seated uncomfortably at the sawed-off piano, and ambled to the microphone to bleat:

Come along, boys, and listen to my tale.
I'll tell you of my troubles on the Old
Chisholm Trail. . . .

And the orchestra members came in dutifully with the chorus:

Coma ti yi youpy, youpy ya, Youpy ya. . . .

The portable sound system, which Clement had especially designed for outdoor appearances, reproduced the music so loudly that children seated on the curbstones held their hands over their ears. Several babies began to mewl, and the sound was picked up by every dog within four blocks of the parade, until the old cowboy song carried its own curious echo.

At the Red Bird Café, the flames were now spreading up the sheet of linoleum that backed the wall of the grill, and plumes of black, acrid smoke were billowing toward the ceiling, gathering under the pressed tin nailed directly to the attic timbers.

At the rear of the cumbersome flatbed truck, Clement's twenty-two-year-old daughter, Patricia Anne, dressed in blue gingham and a poke bonnet, sat as easily as she could in the polished oak barouche, considering the fact that she was six months pregnant. Her husband, Lars Hanson, M.D., was involved with endocrinology research at Walter Reed Hospital, and when he had complained that he could not take time away from his work to come back for the celebration of the opening of Angel's first library, Patricia had been firm. "Grandma's counting on us, dear. After all, she named the town!"

He had given in reluctantly and told her, "All right, but we're not coming back for the Cherokee Strip Celebration in Enid in September. Enough is enough!"

Behind the Christian Choral group from Vrona Valley, Letty's forty-eight-year-old nephew, Mitchell Heron, rode in a fringed surrey with other members of the Chamber

of Commerce. He was slightly embarrassed, because
the trap was originally supposed to accommodate his
cousin Luke, Jeanette, and their children, but changes
had been made at the last moment, and there was no
time to remove the famed blue Heron logo from the
canopy of the vehicle. That same bird-in-flight was emblazoned on fifteen hundred gasoline service stations,
forty tank farms, eight hundred drilling rigs, three hundred field houses, and countless other Heron Oil Company holdings. The proud bird had nothing to do with
his own modest holdings—three Heron furniture stores—
with headquarters in Enid.

John and Fontine Dice were the only older members
of the community, who had made the Run in 1893,
brave enough to ride horsesback in the parade. John, a
former Republican Senator, and owner of the Dice Bank
in Angel, was sixty-eight, long and lean, and he wore his
gold and blue cowboy outfit and ten-gallon Stetson with
an easy grace. What was bothering him at the moment,
was his sterling silver-trimmed saddle, which attracted
the sun's rays like a witch's melting pot, burning his
thighs.

Fontine's custom-tailored riding habit was ringed with
perspiration, and her weight of one hundred and fifty-
five pounds slid precariously over the slippery saddle
studded with sterling silver stars. Although she had rid-
den since the age of four, she plopped up and down on
the saddle like a greenhorn, her platinum curls dancing
around her face like silver springs. "Dammit, Jaundice,"
she screamed above Clement's rendition of "Mexicali
Rose," "I'm like a pancake on a grill, hotter'n hell!" In
her discomfort, she had reverted to her old Texas speech
patterns, discarded except in times of stress, because
her husband and she had not learned to read and write
until the age of twenty-six, and had no formal education.

"What did you say, Fourteen?" he shouted.

She threw him a furious look, but his face was blank,

mirroring the far-away look that she only knew too well. He was thinking of the old days when he had come up from Santone with Poppa Dice to make a new home in Indian Territory. Her heart welled up, and tears came into her eyes. Jaundice was a good man and a caring husband. Even at their age, she knew that they would go back home that afternoon, take long, warm tub baths, followed by cool showers; then the shades would be pulled down in the huge master bedroom of the Federal Restoration mansion, and he would make gentle and passionate love to her that just might last until suppertime.

"Jaundice!" she cried, "look what's happening at the Red Bird Café!"

He turned to look at the small frame structure they were passing and drew his Appaloosa up strongly, then broke rank and trotted the horse out of the procession and up to the mayor's landau. "Fire! Fire!" he shouted above the choral group's strains of "Nearer, My God, to Thee."

Now that smoke was billowing under the roof of the Red Bird Café, other participants in the parade began to turn out of the procession, the flatbed truck stopped, horses were reined up, and the members of Angel's volunteer fire department jumped down from their various vehicles and ran down Second Avenue to the Fire Station.

At first the crowd lining the sidewalks did not know what had happened: one moment the parade was progressing in a structured manner down Main Street, and the next, utter confusion reigned. Then the shouts of *Fire, fire!* were passed down the procession, which then completely broke up, some vehicles darting out to the right, and others speeding out to the left. Parents snatched children from curbstones, mothers held screaming infants to their breasts, old people staggered back onto the sidewalks, and shouts and screams were punctuated by oaths and curses as the crowd surged toward the Red Bird Café, which was now a brightly burning box.

Belle Trune, the owner, cook, and chief bottle washer of the café, dressed in a tight blue satin dress and leghorn hat with a cerise feather, was running down the sidewalk, holding her skirt up around her ankles and tottering on high-heeled button shoes. Midway she lost her hat and, gasping for breath from a too tightly laced corset, and with tears streaking her face, reached the site just as the volunteer fire department drove up in its 1935 wagon. "Do something!" she screamed, mascara running down her cheeks. *"Do something!"*

"Hold on, Belle," the chief shouted from the cab. "We can't do anything, the Red Bird's gone. We got to try to save the Stevens Hotel next door, and the hardware store on the other side." And the firemen, red slickers hurriedly pulled over their Western gear and still in cowboy boots, pulled the long canvas hoses from the truck and attached them to a fire hydrant in front of the hotel. Soon streams of muddy water were feebly shooting into the flames and watering down adjacent buildings. Belle, her auburn hair glinting in the sun, and showing all of her forty-four years, wept openly. Mitchell Heron climbed out of the fringed surrey and put his arm around her; a few of the townspeople who remembered that far back cast sidelong glances at each other, and women tittered and turned away, Mitchell, when he was caring for his mother's farm in the late 1930s, had paid a weekly Friday night visit to Belle's shack on the other side of Angel. Of course, that was before Mitchell opened up his furniture stores and Belle took out a mortgage on her house to buy the Red Bird Café.

"It's not the end of the world, Belle," Mitchell comforted.

Letty and Bosley, coming down the sidewalk, stepping over the fire hoses, looked askance at the strange couple holding on tightly to each other in front of the conflagration. They arrived in time to see the building collapse, which brought further cries from Belle, whose daughter, Darlene, also in tears, had just run across the street.

Letty turned to Bosley. "You don't suppose they're taking up again where they left off, do you?" she asked under her breath.

"No," Bosley replied, "but old friends count in times of trouble."

Letty nodded and took Belle's hand. "Now, I don't want you to worry one little bit," she soothed. "I hold the mortgage on the place, and I'll see it's rebuilt, and if any of my other property here in town is damaged, I'll do likewise." She shook her head. "Bosley, it's time Angel had a new fire truck, too."

The crowd had grown very large, and as a prairie wind blew in from the south, the mayor climbed up on a fire hydrant and held up his hands. "Folks, I'm going to ask you all to go home. We've got a powerful job to do here, and we can't do it with all you onlookers." No one moved, as clouds of smoke drifted over the scene. "Goddammit," he cried, "I said skedaddle!"

The crowd began to disperse, and the parade vehicles started to line up to return to the assembly point on Second Avenue, behind the Sugar Bowl.

The mayor turned to the fire chief. "I'm going to call for reinforcements from Covington."

"Forget Covington," the fire chief replied, looking at the smoldering roof of the hardware store. "Call Enid. If the wind whips up, we'll damn near lose the whole town of Angel!" He shook his head, "And we better start evacuating the Stevens Hotel."

Clement Story rushed up to the fire chief. "My band members are staying at the hotel. I'll have them pack their gear."

The Herons and the Storys and the Dices stood in a group in front of the Red Bird Café, which was now only a pile of smoking embers, and were joined by Bella and Torgo Chenovick, who had driven up in a white wicker surrey. Dressed in colorful Bohemian "good calling" clothing, they looked like life-sized puppets: Bella was short and fat, and Torgo wore thick pop-bottle glasses. In their seventies, they were not as spry as the others in their age group who had made the Run in '93. Bella was crying into her starched white handkerchief embroidered with peach blossoms. "It's the end of the world, Letty!" she wailed.

"No, it's not the end of the world, Bella, not by a long shot, and as far as buildings are concerned, they can be rebuilt." Letty paused, her face lined with worry. "Let's just hope that human life is spared—that can't be replaced."

Every available man had been pressed into service; several took turns manning the water pumps on the old fire wagon, and others had formed a bucket brigade from Baker's Emporium across the street. At last two fire trucks roared in from Enid, bells clanging; a roar went up from the crowd, and the men alighted to applause. Soon hoses stretched out from a block away to the nearest hydrants, and someone was dispatched to the water tower located by the railroad tracks.

An hour later the fires were brought under control. The Stevens Hotel had lost its roof and upper story, and the hardware store, as big as a warehouse and just as airy, had collapsed into a smoky ruin.

Now that the excitement had died down, the Angel grade school reopened its hot dog stand, and a line of hungry citizens lined up to buy soggy buns and half-cooked frankfurters spread with runny yellow mustard, for fifteen cents. Ice cream cones were also much in demand, and the only flavor available, vanilla, was scooped up in soft mounds by none-too-clean hands, the nickel being pocketed by the same grubby fingers.

By the end of the afternoon, thirty dollars and fifteen cents had been raised for the New Band Uniform Fund.

John Dice had consumed half a cone when Fontine came through the little knot of people in front of the Red Bird Café. "Jaundice!" she screamed. "What are you doing?" Her silver spurs whirled in indignation. "How dare you spoil your supper! A body'd need a cast-iron stomach to digest what you've had to eat today. Hot dogs this morning, cotton candy, and now—"

"Just cool off, Fourteen. Now that all the excitement is over, let's get cracking. I'm a mite tired and I'm going to lay down."

Her anger faded as she flushed at his obvious invitation. "Well," she admitted, "I guess a little ice cream won't hurt." She looked at him sheepishly out of the corners of her eyes. "I'm sorry about making such a to-do out of everything. If I get to acting up again, you've got my full permission to slap me silly!"

"Ah, I'd never do that to my honey," he replied with a slow grin. He turned to the horses tethered at the curb to the old-fashioned iron posts still left from the old days. "Come on, let's ride home."

She burst out laughing as he helped her mount up and she caressed the silver stars on her saddle. "It's just like the territory days, Jaundice."

"Yep," he said, getting on his horse.

"Of course, in those days we didn't have two Cadillacs, a motor scooter, or a bicycle in the garage." Fontine paused a moment. "Well, come to think about it, we didn't even have a garage!"

Luke Three was helping unhitch teams of horses at the assembly area when Darlene Trune parked her roadster at the curb. He noticed that she had a new red hair rinse that complemented her white complexion and the freckles on her nose. "I'm awfully sorry about what your mother had to go through this afternoon," he said.

"She's got insurance, and then your grandmother is going to help with the money, so it's not as bad as it could be. I guess we'll get a new building out of it." She paused and smiled pertly. "I need some gas, Luke Three. I must take Mama into Enid first thing tomorrow morning to file the insurance claim, and we'll be leaving before the station is open. Will you let me have some gas now?" Her eyes were very large, and he could see her sweater in front moving up and down as she breathed. He felt a pang of regret that he had broken off their affair.

Even now, sometimes late at night, when he was in bed, running his hands up and down his thighs and over his stomach, he would have given almost anything if she were lying beside him. She had a soft, supple body that he coveted. Many times he had closed his eyes and thought of her soft, moist warmth, reliving again the many times when they had been together, joined as two people who love each other should be joined. But that was the catch, he thought as he came up to the front door of the car and looked through the window at her legs. He did not love her really, not her personality, not her mind—only her body, and that was not enough.

"The station's closed." He gave a long sigh. "But I suppose I can open it up for you."

She looked into his eyes. "Oh, would you, Luke Three, would you?"

He almost asked her what she would do for him if he did help her out in an emergency; then he thought better of it.... No, the affair was over. He had ended their relationship when she had brought up the subject of marriage. Even if she offered to make love with him this very afternoon, he would refuse. He disliked conditions, especially strings attached to sexual gratification. One either did it for pleasure, he reasoned, or not at all.

Luke Three climbed into the front seat, and Darlene

drove the two blocks to the station, where he unlocked the pump, removed the lid from the gas tank, and thrust the nozzle deep into the tank. A surge of power came over him as the gasoline spurted out of the hose. He methodically pumped the lever back and forth. He was physically aroused, and he almost moved to the side of the car so that Darlene could see the bulge in his trousers. Then he decided not to draw attention to his condition, because she would think that he wanted to resume their relationship, and he could not, or would not marry her. Filling the tank to the top, he wiped his hands on a towel and came up to the car door. "I'll have to charge this, Darlene," he said. "I don't want to go to the trouble of opening the cash register. Would you start the motor again?"

She switched on the ignition, pushed down the starter, and the motor sprang to life. "That's what I thought I heard." He clicked his tongue. "Spark plugs need changing. Can you bring it in tomorrow morning after you finish with that insurance business in Enid?"

She shook her head. "I've got to do an interview with your Uncle Clem for the *Angel Wing*, and he's supposed to be leaving for New York tomorrow afternoon. How about Thursday?"

"No, I'm booked up all day, and besides, those plugs need changing now." He paused and looked at his wristwatch. "It won't take long. How about doing it now?"

She gave him a long look, while a smile played around the corners of her mouth. He colored. "I mean ... changing the plugs."

"All right," she replied soberly, "but you'll have to put it on Mother's bill. I don't get paid until Friday."

An hour later, Darlene Trune deposited Luke Three in front of the Trenton clapboard and waved, then sped down the road, red dust spewing out behind the road-ster. He could not have invited her in for supper, or the whole town would be buzzing that they had started dating again.

"Where have you been, Luke Three?" Letty said from the kitchen, wiping her hands on her apron. "We were about to sit down without you."

"I had to open the station for a customer, that's all."

She was dismayed. "Oh, Luke Three, this is a *holiday*."

"I know, Grandma, but when people need gas, they need *gas*!"

She nodded. "You're a good boy, and a kind boy, Luke Three, but look at your fingernails!"

He placed his hands behind his back and to distract her, asked: "Did you bake an Angel cake?"

She smiled crookedly, brushing a strand of silver hair back from her forehead. "Now, you know that I'd never hear the end of it if I hadn't! What kind of an Oklahoma feed would it be, not having Angel cake?"

He kissed her on the cheek. "I love you, Grandma," he said.

She drew back and looked at him with surprise, because the Herons and the Storys and the Trentons did not often show outward affection. "Now what was all that about?"

He was suddenly shy. "It just occurred to me, Grandma, that I don't think the family appreciates you. The other day I went out to the section road to read that plaque again about the Discovery Well that you had a hand in bringing in in 1903. I thought to myself that you must have gone through a lot since then. What was it like—I mean that first gusher?"

"Oh, Luke Three," Letty exclaimed, "you must have heard that story a thousand times."

"Would you tell it again?"

She flushed with pleasure. "Well, it was Easter Sunday—we were coming home from church in our horses and buggies, and I had on a white dress with a hat with cornflowers and a parasol, and all of a sudden there was a roar deep down in the earth and the ground trembled. The crude oil shot out of that wooden derrick with such force it threw four hundred and twenty-six feet of pipe casing up through the crown block. That rig just flew apart, and when I looked down at my dress, it was gray, and we were all soaked with that green crude. But the funniest thing was that your dad, who was about seven years old and wearing a new blue and white sailor suit, ran up and down the fence, shouting, 'We're rich, we're rich, we're rich!'!"

Luke Three grinned. "And were we, Grandma?"

She sighed with remembrance, then raised an eyebrow. "No, not then, for a long while; that came much later after Oklahoma became a state." She threw a long look at him and admonished, "And as far as being rich, young man, you shouldn't even think in those terms, because everything we have is invested in the Heron Oil Company. There's not much to spend on everyday things." She paused and looked at him suspiciously. "Why this sudden talk of money?"

"Well, Grandma," he replied seriously, "it's just that I haven't had a raise in six months, and the station's receipts are way up since I got back from Okinawa, and I do work awfully hard, and ..."

She patted him on the back. "I'll speak to your father. How much are you making now?"

"A dollar and a half an hour."

She nodded thoughtfully. "I think that under the circumstances, a twenty-five-cents-an-hour raise would be sufficient, don't you?"

"Yes, ma'am!"

"Very well, we'll see what we can do—but right now you'd better wash your hands. It wouldn't hurt to use a nail file, either!"

"Yes, ma'am!" And as he went up the stairs to the bathroom, he threw back his shoulders and congratulated himself. If you wanted something from the family, it didn't do any good at all to ask, but if you brought up the old days—and the Discovery Well never failed—and stirred up memories, you could get almost anything within reason. Yes, he smiled to himself, he would get his raise, and in another six months, if he worked it right, he'd be getting a percentage of the station's profits.

Letty stood for a moment at the foot of the stairs and smiled. Luke Three was a wheeler-dealer all right, just like his grandfather. Whenever he brought up the Discovery Well, you could bet your bottom dollar he wanted something. . . .

After supper, Letty and Bosley went out into the yard. The smell of the fire was still in the air, and he took her hand and led her gently down the street. It was dusk, and the only street light that Angel possessed was glowing in front of the Blue Moon Theater. A few firemen from Enid were still watering down the debris, and one of them tipped his hat at Letty, who nodded.

"I'll go see John Dice at the bank tomorrow, Bos," she said softly, "and since I own so much of this property down here, I'm going to instigate some improvements." She paused meaningfully. "You know, Bos, when those three buildings were flaming up this afternoon, I shocked myself. I found that I was thinking: Let the whole town burn, it's all old and wooden, and some of the buildings weren't constructed right in the first place. All but about four or five were erected well before nineteen hundred." She turned to him, taking his hand. "Bos, we're going to rebuild Angel so that it won't look like all the other prairie cow towns. We're going to make Angel look as pretty as our new library!"

Bosley squeezed her hand. "That will take some doing, my dear, and a lot of money."

"What's money, Bos? Luke Three got me to thinking this afternoon. Angel *has* never really recovered from the Great Depression, and in a way, it's our fault. When we opened the refinery during the war, we had a prosperous boom, then when it closed, we lost a lot of young folk. We've got to put our thinking caps on, Bos, and create a reason for people to come to Angel to shop, and the first thing on the agenda is a town as clean and white and new and sparkling—as an Angel cake!"

2

The Assignments

Luke came into his office, yawned, and glanced down at the stack of mail on his desk.

He and Jeanette had driven in from Angel the evening before, exhausted because of the parade and the fire. He hadn't fallen asleep until 2 A.M. He rubbed his eyes. He must be getting old, he decided, because if he didn't get to sleep before twelve, it took a long time in the morning before he could function at capacity.

His secretary, Bernice, knocked on the door and then entered. "Here's a letter that concerns Clement that I thought you should see."

Luke smiled. "A fan letter?"

She shook her head. "No, Mr. H. Here, take a look at it."

He glanced at the message:

April 9, 1946
Willawa, Oklahoma

Dear Mr. Heron:

   I am a teacher at a small school and I hope that
you will pass along this information to your brother,
Clement Story, who I understand from the Tulsa
newspaper advertisements will be performing locally.
I know a eighteen-year-old part-Cherokee by the
name of William Nestor, who is a brilliant musician.
Would it be possible for your brother to meet the
boy?
   In all of my years in the school system, I have
never encountered such a naturally gifted student,
and I feel that at least he should be given a chance to
be heard. I am enclosing my telephone number on
an index card.
   I sincerely hope that your brother will contact me.
I am,

                              Yours truly,

                              Louisa Tarbell

Luke looked up and shrugged. "Should I bother Clem
with this, I wonder? Where is Willawa, anyway?"

   "I think it's near Tahlequah." Bernice paused. "The
letter seems sincere."

   "We'll give it to Clem, but it sounds to me as if the
teacher is hinting for some kind of handout for the
family." He paused. "I know Clem gets a lot of mail
from people who want something."

   "Well," she replied reluctantly, "maybe this should be
thrown in the 'revolving file.'" She went back to her
office.

   Still troubled, Luke went to the window and looked
down unto the street below. Something about the letter
triggered his conscience. For some reason he thought
of his trusted Cherokee friend Sam Born-Before-Sunrise.
He could see him as a boy, trudging up the incline
towards The Widows, his slim form lonely and detached

from the real world. What bothered him, he supposed, was that the boy the schoolteacher had written about was part Cherokee. On a hunch, he pushed the intercom button. "Bernice, save that letter. At least we should show it to Clem and let him make up his own mind whether he wants to pursue the matter or not."

"I think you've made the right decision, Mr. H," she replied, and it was only later that he realized that this was the first time in the ten years that Bernice had been his secretary that she had ever offered a personal opinion.

The six-thousand-seat auditorium had been sold out for a month. As the big bus that housed Clement and the orchestra pulled into a parking lot the afternoon of the Tulsa concert, there was a large crowd, mostly made up of teenagers of the zoot-suit variety, milling around the stage-door area. Mac, the bus driver, turned to Clement, who was in the seat directly behind him. "Should I get a police cordon?"

Clement looked out the window at the crowd. "Oh, I don't think so. Probably all they want is some autographs. They don't look unruly to me. Go ahead and give your usual spiel."

Mac opened the door and stood on the second step of the bus, raised his hands, and projected his voice. "Thank you for coming down here this afternoon," he said with a smile. "Clement Story has an extra half-hour when he should be rehearsing with the band inside, but if you'll call out numbers and line up, you'll each get an autograph." He indicated a middle-aged woman in a red sweater in front, obviously an old-time fan. "Ma'am," he continued politely, "Will you start?"

"One!" she shouted.

"Two!" a boy beside her trebled, and the countdown continued. The last number was eighty-five.

While the other members of the band filed out of the bus and unloaded the instruments, Clement leaned up against the front fender of the bus and signed his name; then, when he grew tired, Mac brought out a folding camp stool with a small umbrella, and Clement lowered himself into the seat. He looked up at each person, asked the name, and if the person was under thirty, inscribed "Regards" or "My best" before he signed his name. If they were in a middle-aged group, he wrote "Sincerely" or "Best Wishes," but if the fan was an older lady, he always smiled as he wrote "With affection." If they were teenagers, he scribbled "I dig you."

Inside the auditorium, while the band members were removing their instruments from the cases and the stage manager was arranging the music stands in proper order to be set up by the stage hands, Tracy Newcomb checked out the sound system and tested the microphones. When all was in readiness, he gave the downbeat from his position at the piano, and rehearsed the orchestra to see what the acoustics were like. This same routine was followed in all the cities on the tour, except in those areas where there were no fans lined up outside; then Clement took up his baton and led the men through their paces.

That night, after the concert proper was over, Clement, wet with perspiration under the hot spotlight that shone directly on the podium, raced through four encores, each to wild applause. It was late, and yet the huge crowd would not let the orchestra leave the stage. The handclapping, whistling, and stomping continued after two more encores: "Tangerine" and "Red Sails in the Sunset." Then Clement gave the signal for "Lady Luck," with which he signed off his radio shows.

Still the crowd continued to applaud. It was obvious to him what they wanted. He nodded to Tracy, who picked up a guitar, and as the orchestra broke into "Tumbling Tumbleweed," a joyous cry rose up from the crowd. Clement grinned, took the guitar, and ambled to the front of the stage. The throng quieted. He sat down on the apron in front of the footlights, and as the spotlight narrowed until only his form was illuminated, he paused, looked up into the balcony, and sang plaintively:

Come along, boys, and listen to my tale . . .

There was a wave of affectionate applause; he could feel the love and admiration emanating from the crowd as he continued "The Old Chisholm Trail." And his talent was such that he seemed to give new meaning to the famous old lyrics. But as relaxed as he appeared to be, he automatically mouthed the words while thinking: *I'm so tired I could drop. . . . Hopefully, I won't have to sing all the verses. . . . If there are fans outside the dressing room, I just can't sign any more autographs. . . . I'm beat . . . hungry. . . . I hope the kitchen isn't closed before we get back to the hotel. . . . Wish I'd brought Sarah along. . . .*

He finished the last line, lowered his head as he always did; the spotlight faded to black, plunging the auditorium into total darkness, and he heard a quiet rustle and knew that the crowd was giving him the usual standing ovation. Only once, in San Francisco, one cold rainy night, had the audience failed to stand for him at the finish. He never played San Francisco again.

The lights came up to full. Clement stood up, laughed, and waved happily to the band. The crowd applauded. Simultaneously the orchestra bowed. The lights were switched off. Clement rushed into the wings in the darkness. The curtain swished quickly across the stage. The lights came up to full. The audience was still on its feet applauding, but the evening was over.

Luke and Jeanette were waiting in the dressing room. Clement embraced Jeanette and shook Luke's hand and, smiling apologetically, sank down on the sofa. "I'm getting too old for one-night stands," he said wearily, "but this is where the money is. Not in nightclubs anymore.... The last time I was in Hollywood I went to the Mocambo and Ciro's, and all the guests were practically middle-aged. I guess young couples can't afford the tab. Oh, there are still a few places in New York and other big cities, and of course there's the hotels, thank God, but concerts are where the future's going—as far as the big bands go." He looked up and grinned. "I don't know why I've been on a soapbox, I guess it's just the mood I'm in.... I'm so sick of "Chisholm" I may throw up! But by now, they won't let me go until I do it."

"I thought it was particularly touching tonight," Jeanette said softly. "What were you thinking about while you were singing the song?"

Clement stood up and stretched his arms to the ceiling. "Don't ask. But I assure you it had nothing to do with the lyrics!" He took off his coat and tie. "I think I know what goes through the minds of prostitutes who have to look up at the ceiling all the time. I don't think they're involved at all...." He went into the bathroom, but left the door ajar.

Luke cleared his throat. "I don't think that analogy applies in your case." His lips were set in a straight line.

"You're wrong, Luke, very wrong," Clement called, and then they heard the water running.

Luke turned to Jeanette. "I've never really understood him, you know," he said quietly.

She smiled. "It's probably because you don't have a great sense of humor."

He looked at her strangely. "I suppose you think I'm an old stick?"

She shook her head. "No. I'm glad that you're you, Luke. I'd never want to be in Sarah's shoes, for instance. Show business is a life unto itself. It's too restricting. I've got to have freedom—and so do you."

Clement came out of the bathroom, toweling his head. "What's all this talk?"

"We're speaking about freedom," Luke replied, "and how structured your life is."

"No more than yours," Clement replied quickly. "You work nine to five, I work seven to twelve—unless I'm doing concerts; then it's eight to eleven."

Jeanette nodded. "But that's not what we mean. The pressures—your way of life is far different than ours."

"True," Clement replied softly, "but I don't have to worry about new cracking plants, offshore drilling, competitive gas prices, busted tires, or lousy mechanics."

Luke shrugged his shoulders and smiled grimly. "Your point is well taken."

"All I have to worry about is getting my halfbreeds together."

"Which reminds me," Luke said, "I received a letter about a part-Cherokee boy from a Miss Louisa Tarbell, schoolteacher in Willawa."

"Where the hell is that?"

"Not far. It's a little hamlet near Tahlequah. She'd like you to meet him."

Clement waved his hand in front of his face in an old Indian gesture. "Spare me the details. I get inquiries every day, some of them quite heartrending. Apparently there are budding musicians all over the country—some of them mere tots who are so loaded with talent that every one of the little beasts is going to be the star of tomorrow. If I auditioned all of them, I'd never have time to rehearse the orchestra, let alone make public appearances. Sarah answers the fan mail. Give me the letter, and I'll pass it on to her."

Luke flushed and handed him the letter. "I wouldn't have bothered you about this, Clem," he said stiffly, "except for the fact that the boy is part Indian. Sorry I troubled you." He turned away.

"Hey, don't get mad, Luke, but you really should see my mail. You wouldn't believe ..." He paused. "Does she say how old he is?"

"Read the letter yourself," Luke said gruffly.

Clement unfolded the paper and glanced at the message. "Seventeen, eh?" He mused. "I wonder what he plays? At least she could have put that in the letter." He placed the envelope in his pocket. "I'm starved." He looked directly at his brother. "Would you and Jeanette like to join me at the hotel for something to eat?"

Luke shook his head. "No, thanks." He paused. "When's your next play date?"

"Let me see. Oklahoma City tomorrow night, then Topeka, and then back to Kansas City for a week of loafing. Why?"

"I was just thinking that I could cancel my golf game tomorrow morning and we could drive down to Willawa."

Clement looked at his older brother, and a sudden wave of affection washed over him. "This is something that you feel strongly about, isn't it?"

Luke nodded. "Yes, and I don't know why." He reddened. "When I read that letter, I got the strangest feeling ... as if ... well ... I know this sounds silly, but it was as if Sam were in the room with me, and I hadn't thought of Sam in a long, long time. I don't have hunches very often, but it just seemed to me that somehow that boy ..."

Clement placed his hand on Luke's shoulder. "Okay, I'll call Miss Whatzername in the morning and tell her we'll be over, but not until I finish the Oklahoma City date." He drew in his breath. "But I've been to thousands of auditions during my career, and you should be prepared. Talk about hunches, brother dear, I have a feeling this boy—William Nestor—is going to turn out to be a real stinker."

Mitchell Heron had been dreaming and was conscious of having spoken out loud, or perhaps he had only called someone's name. A cold sweat broke out on the back of his neck. He disliked dreams when he couldn't remember his journeys, because he always preferred to be in control of his mind and body, just the way that he had to be in control of his furniture stores. Yet if he had been on assignment, his "cover" could have been broken if he had mumbled some important bit of information in his sleep—providing someone was beside him!

He eased himself up in bed and leaned back on the pillow. He was being melodramatic, and he smiled sheepishly because he was never melodramatic in real life, and besides he had been on only one mission in his entire life and that was during the last part of the war. But those months in France, after he had been parachuted into the Plaisance-du-Gers area in the South, often came back, suffused with a rosy hue. He was apt to regard himself, during these daydreams, as a glamorized, mysterious figure, not the stalwart businessman that his cohorts in Enid were accustomed to seeing every day.

Actually, he had only delivered and returned a bit of information; that was his entire experience. Yet when he thought about those days it did seem that he had risked life and limb, dashing hither and yon over the French countryside. He must not dwell on what actually had happened; he did not fantasize in any other area of life. His furniture stores depended upon his realistic appraisal of the market, and no one could question his success. Yet in that one, short excursion into a cloak-and-dagger existence, he remained a romanticist.

Soon he heard the teakettle whistling and knew that Mrs. Briggs was preparing breakfast. That meant it was seven-forty-five. He must get up, bathe, have his coffee, followed by bacon, eggs, and toast, and be at the store at eight-thirty, a good twenty-five minutes before the employees arrived.

Mitchell Heron was always punctual and had been punctual for the ten years that he had been an upright, stable citizen of Enid, Oklahoma. Before then, he had spent more than fifteen years traveling in France and Germany, selling figurines that no one wanted to buy, and another three years in a variety of small jobs that had ended up in the harvest fields, before returning home to Angel to farm his mother's claim. He had wasted his youth, some said, yet after all those years on the road he had at last come to terms with himself.

It was true that he had wasted his young years and had been indiscriminate of time. Yet as he punched his time clock, visited his other stores, consulted with CPA's and advertising agencies, and carried on other duties, shouldering all interests with a manly concern, he nevertheless occasionally—like now—wished that he were once more irresponsibly on the road. At the end of the day he always came home to an empty house and, more important, to an empty bed. He supposed that he was still a loner in those areas of life that were the least—and the most—important.

At nine-forty-five the telephone rang, and the new receptionist pushed the intercom. "It's that foreign gentleman about that Queen Anne chair."

Mitchell's heart beat faster. He had been waiting for this call for several months, ever since he had been advised to purchase a new wardrobe of English-cut suits. "Yes?" he answered, keeping his voice down.

"Ah, can you have luncheon with me?" a French voice inquired softly. "I'm at the Youngblood Hotel."

"Of course."

"The dining room should not be full at eleven-thirty."

"Very well. See you then."

The morning seemed to slow down to such a turtle pace that Mitchell found himself looking at his wristwatch every ten minutes. Then, at eleven-twenty-five, he sauntered nonchalantly out of the store in the direction of the hotel.

His usual booth near the front window was empty, Mitchell saw as he came into the dining room. As he took a seat, he observed with relief that his luncheon companion was purchasing a cigar from the stand in the lobby. He took a deep breath, composed his face, studied the menu with an air of complete detachment, and when he heard a throat being cleared, looked up at the man who resembled nothing so much as a French civil servant.

"Oh, Monsieur Darlan," Mitchell said, unsmiling. "How many months has it been since you told me to be prepared to leave on a moment's notice?"

The little man opened his mouth in a friendly smile, partially hidden by a set of marvelous mustaches. His eyes were penetrating and bright, but his hand, which Mitchell shook, seemed more bony and fragile than he had remembered.

"My apologies," Pierre replied in French. "I was, I believe you would say, unavoidably detained." His eyes took on a glow as he glanced over the menu. "What I would give for a good quiche!" he exclaimed. "There used to be a little restaurant in the rue Montague that served the most abundant quiches, filled with truffles and mushrooms and pâté de foie gras. I salivate at the memory." He looked up. "What would you suggest, Herr Professor Schneider?"

"Herr Schneider?"

"*Ja*, from this day forward, until you return to these"— he gestured vacantly around the room—"bucolic climes, that is your new identity."

"What about Michel Bayard?" Mitchell asked, referring to his old cover name.

"Oh?" Pierre Darlan evinced surprise. "Had you not heard? He met with a most fortunate demise." His eyes sparkled. "I do not know how true it is, we will probably never learn the truth, but it seems that he took up with a *demimondaine* and collapsed while making passionate love early one morning." Pierre nodded dramatically.

"The gendarmes were forced to remove him from the embrace."

"The gendarmes?"

"*Oui.* They heard her screams from the street." Pierre threw his head back and laughed until tears smarted his eyes. "It is good to laugh with you again. So many of our ... employees ... do not possess a sense of humor." His manner changed abruptly. "Have your people been properly prepared for your vacation?"

Mitchell was not amused. "Yes," he replied darkly. "As it is, I have not been away from the store for well over a year. I have even been afraid to take a weekend off, never knowing when you would call."

Pierre clicked his tongue in sympathy. "Again, I must apologize, but the assignment that we first had in mind is no longer viable. We sent a woman instead. It seems we needed a femme fatale after all." He paused. "She has now returned with the necessary groundwork accomplished. She has, as it were, made way for you."

Mitchell smiled wryly, and Pierre Darlan thought him handsome, almost too handsome for what they were going to do to him. "If it were only that way in real life!"

"You think, then, that you were destined to remain forever a—bachelor?"

"At this stage of the game, my friend," Mitchell replied philosophically, "I doubt that anyone could put up with me, or vice versa."

"Good!" Pierre gestured aimlessly. "What I mean is— it is *good* for us. We do not like to employ men with wives." He sighed. "Life changes when you are married. Do you have a will?"

Mitchell laughed. "The same one that I made out before my last assignment."

"If changes are to be made," Pierre put in gently, "then you have a bit of time. We won't need you right away. You have time to practice German. Please read aloud everyday. Watch your accent." He looked at the menu. "Giblets and rice, Herr Professor?"

"I am not in the mood for offal," Mitchell said. "I have a feeling that where you are sending me there will be very little beef. Therefore, I will order a steak."

"How would you like it cooked?"

"Well done, please."

Pierre smiled at the waitress. "I will have the giblets and rice, please. Mr. Heron will have a sirloin steak, very rare."

When she departed with the order, Pierre looked over his glasses at Mitchell. "Should you order a steak on this trip, it must be blood rare." He paused. "A German gentleman of your deportment, background, and education would never order anything well done. You will be traveling in rarefied circles, so you should also brush up on years of vintage champagne. Which," he added, "should not be too difficult, because of the war."

"Then nineteen-thirty-eight, 'thirty-nine, 'forty are still the best?"

Pierre nodded. "Indubitably." He paused. "I assume you have been keeping in touch with your German as well as your French?"

"*Ja, mein Herr*, I have been reading *Mein Kampf* aloud every evening after the housekeeper leaves; then in the morning, if I do not oversleep, I read *Paris Match*."

"Good boy!"

When the steak arrived, charred on the outside, with a tiny pool of blood on the plate, Mitchell shuddered. "I don't think that I can even look at this," he said with a grimace.

"Of course you can. It is almost as good as a wood-chuck that has been ripening in the larder for seven days, and served very rare indeed."

Mitchell pushed the plate away. "I have just lost my appetite, Pierre."

"It will return when you eat the first bite," was the smooth reply. "The trick is to cut up the meat in small pieces, then, without looking, spear each tidbit and place it in your mouth. You will discover that it is the appearance, at first, that is so disturbing."

Mitchell did as he was told, and followed the bite of steak with a forkful of au gratin potatoes. He did not know for what he was prepared, gastronomically speaking, but was pleasantly surprised. "Why," he exclaimed, "it is delicious, only it doesn't taste like steak!"

Pierre smiled mirthlessly. "It is only because you have been consuming burnt meat for so long that your taste buds have not become acclimated properly to the finer delicacies." He shrugged. "But perhaps you are not ready for the woodchuck, even so."

When he had finished eating, Mitchell placed a paper napkin over his plate to camouflage the red residue from the meat and laughed self-consciously. "I will become accustomed to that too, I suppose—in time." He paused and looked earnestly at his companion. "When did you say that I would formally embark on my journey?"

"I didn't say, *mon cher*," Pierre replied.

"Will there be a training period like last time?"

"Training, no; indoctrination, yes."

"There is a difference?"

Pierre evinced surprise. "Oh, *mais oui!*"

"What should I do with all of those English-cut suits that you asked me to order?"

"Keep them."

"I was never reimbursed, and they really aren't my style, Pierre."

The little Frenchman sighed. "Very well, you shall be paid for them, but I must have a chit."

"I'll make you out a bill, then."

Pierre held up his hand. "Not on the Heron Furniture Stores letterhead. I could not explain that. We always pay cash, in the tender of the country, but I assure you that you will be paid in dollars, not in Deutschmarks, which are worth one hundred Pfennigs, two hundred-twenty-one point six hundred-fifty-nine mg. of fine gold, or the princely sum of twenty-five cents."

"Speaking about pay, Pierre," Mitchell said soberly, "I was not paid for my mission before, and I do not expect to be paid for this one, either."

"Ah," Pierre replied with a smile, "*before* was a patriotic expression. This mission, shall we say, has international scope. You will be paid."

Mitchell shook his head. "No, my friend, I do what I do free, or I will not do it at all."

3

The Discovery

Luke headed the new white Cadillac convertible into the heart of the Oklahoma green country toward Willawa.

Clement had asked Tracy Newcomb to accompany them, and although Tracy protested that he wanted to visit his girlfriend and went into lengthy details of what he would be missing, Clement knew that he was secretly pleased. He had been his assistant for so long and was such a capable musician that he was flattered to attend auditions.

As the road wound into hills that almost became mountainous, Clement looked out with wonder on the verdant foliage. "When I'm in Angel, I forget that a good part of the state is so lush and green."

Luke agreed. "Even so, I still like the prairie, Clem. I like to know where I'm going. It's a comfort to be able to see for twenty-five miles in every direction, especially when I'm driving."

"You should have a chauffeur," Tracy said.

"If I did"—Luke smiled—"Jeanette would say that I'm putting on the dog. Aren't women strange? She doesn't object to the plane, and she thinks that Currier and Ives are great pilots. In a way, I suppose, she thinks of them as nice boys who take her for rides." He paused. "Also, she won't have a full-time housekeeper. Mrs. Reynolds only comes in two mornings a week. At Jeanette's age, you'd think she'd want to take it easy, but she's even uneasy when we have a babysitter for Murdock. She was on pins and needles all during the night of your concert— sure that the kid had gotten into trouble. He hadn't, of course."

Listening to Luke talk about his wife and son, Clement realized, as they sped through the countryside, that this was the first time in years that he had been alone with his brother for any length of time. And the thought occurred to him that Luke was really very middle-class. Obviously he ran the Heron Oil Company with some success, though he had little imagination. Truthfully, he was a rather likable but dull individual. Years ago Clement had given up trying to fathom the strange instincts that drew, or did not draw, people together; brothers were no different. His Indian blood was the difference, he was certain.

His mind was wandering far from the business at hand, and he did not rouse from his ruminations until Luke slowed down on the outskirts of the town, where a faded sign read: WILLAWA POP. 1,202.

For a moment, Luke thought that they had been catapulted back into the Old West. Main Street was one block long. Rusting iron hitching posts were still embedded in the high cement sidewalks that rose two feet above the stained macadam street. False wooden fronts, gray with deterioration, were two-storied. Pounded-tin-faced stores featured smudged glass windows, and the others were boarded-up block structures. Only the Willawa National Bank on the corner, circa 1907, fashioned of red sandstone brick, held an aura of permanence: a dowager among lower-class buildings.

"My God," Clement said, looking at the many boarded-up windows, "I thought Angel was getting decrepit, but it looks like a thriving metropolis compared to this place. There isn't even a drugstore or a movie theater, and that water tower and the grain elevator date from the First World War."

"It's sad seeing a town go downhill," Luke agreed. "Willawa really has to be on its last legs not to have a gasoline service station."

Beyond the business district a series of small houses without street numbers could be seen. Porches sagged, decayed shingle roofs needed repair, clapboard facades were badly stained with rust rivered down from old roof gutters; only the huge trees, overgrown hedges and shrubs, and a profusion of flowers gave the area an inhabited feeling.

Luke stopped at the fourth house on the left, following the instructions given over the telephone. The neat clapboard residence stood out from its dingy surroundings, sporting a freshly mowed lawn, a large rose garden on the north side, and a white picket fence. Windowpanes gleamed in the sunlight, and blood-red geraniums overflowed huge window boxes. There was an unmistakable air of gentility about the place that was at once warm and friendly, but still slightly reserved for a small town the size of Willawa.

A pinched-faced woman in a straw hat, dull brown hair gathered up under the brim, was cutting roses, which she painstakingly arranged in a shallow basket over her arm. When she saw the Cadillac, she waved her shears. There was something theatrical about the scene, Clement thought, as if it had been recreated out of an old movie. The neatly kept house, the fragile spinster, the basket of roses ... She came forward as graciously as a hostess at a garden party, a smile lighting up her thin, gaunt face. She *was* acting a role, he felt, and when she said, "How do you do? I am Miss Tarbell," in rounded, measured tones, he knew that she had most carefully rehearsed her part.

After they had introduced themselves, she asked, "Would you gentlemen care for some refreshment?"

It was on the tip of Clement's tongue to answer, "Gin and bitters, if you please," but of course he did not. "No, thank you, Miss Tarbell, but our day is rather full," he replied. "Where is the lad?"

"Two doors down, at the church."

Luke leaned forward, to be certain that he had heard her correctly. "The *church*?"

She smiled apologetically and adjusted her straw hat, angling the brim to keep her face in shadow, and it occurred to Clement that she was trying to appear younger. "The minister has been very gracious about allowing William to rehearse. The Baptist church," she explained quietly, "has the only pipe organ in town."

Tracy exchanged glances with Clement and hissed in his ear. "You brought me all the way out here to the sticks to listen to an *organist*?"

Luke took the woman's elbow as she led them across the lawn of the house next door, then to the front door of the church. From her manner, he realized that his polite gesture was probably unique to her; obviously she was unused to being escorted. His mind went back to his own schooldays in Angel. Miss Rochelle Patterson, his home room teacher, could have been Louisa Tarbell's sister. They were both drab-looking, but their IQ's were probably in the 160's.

Tracy opened the heavy oak doors, and they were

treated to the opening bars of "The Afternoon of a Faun." Again, Clement knew that the scene had been painstakingly staged. Miss Tarbell indicated the stairway to the right of the foyer and, as they climbed the stairs, the music swelled. The boy was *good*. By the time they had reached the organ loft, the music had changed deftly. The boy, Clement knew, was playing the melody with his left hand, while his right hand was starting a variation that became a subtle boogie beat. When the trio reached the organ, the boy's hands were flying over the three-tiered keyboard. With the wild, pulsating beat of the music, the boy improvised until the melody was all but emasculated: it was a true *tour de force*.

The boy's black, ducktailed head, which had been bent low as his fingers flew over the keys, abruptly turned up to them, revealing a well-formed, handsome face that bore an unmistakable Cherokee nose, along with a jutting chin. The rather sensuous mouth opened in a smile that showed a brilliant row of white teeth. The boy pulled out four stops in rapid succession, then worked the foot pedals frantically as he placed his hands in his lap. The music faded away, with the boogie beat echoing incongruously in the sacred confines of the church.

Clement found himself applauding enthusiastically along with the others. "William Nestor, I would like you to meet Clement Story," Louisa Tarbell said, enunciating each word as if she were communicating with deaf persons accomplished at lip-reading. They shook hands. "William, say hello to Mr. Story's brother, Luke Heron."

"Hello!" the boy said, offering his hand, and Clement smiled. He was doing *exactly* as he had been coached. He admired the lady for her tenacity, her courage, and her attention to detail. She would feel quite at home on a Hollywood sound stage.

Feeling Tracy's reserve, Clement realized that his assistant was experiencing pangs of jealousy. His strained face gave him away. How extraordinary that this brilliant man should be envious of the boy! Did he feel his talent would eventually supersede his own?

"What would you like to hear, sir?" William asked, wide-eyed, but without apparent embarrassment at meeting his famous guest. Clement appreciated the fact that the boy was on home ground and perhaps in another sort of atmosphere might not seem so self-assured or confident.

"Anything you feel," he replied easily, drawn to the boy's friendly attitude.

The ducktail bent over the keyboard again, and the sounds of an improvised Latin beat pulsated from the old instrument as the boy worked in the melody of "The Old Chisholm Trail." Clement laughed out loud. The result was enormously comical; never had it even occurred to him that the old Western number would lend itself to a samba rhythm.

William adroitly maneuvered the improvisation into the clippity-clop of horses' hooves, while still keeping the South American beat, and ended the number with a wild fanfare, punctuated by what sounded like the neighing of a horse. Clement had never heard such a variety of sounds emanate from any musical instrument before; his admiration for the boy and the effects that he could produce from the wheezy old organ grew, and he felt himself applauding long before the magnificently turbulent finish. Tracy reluctantly followed suit.

The boy turned to Clement, his eyes filled with a fervor that was almost religious in intensity. He grinned. "Did I shake you up, sir?"

"Indeed you did, William"—Clement nodded—"appreciably so. Where did you learn to play?"

"Here." The boy gestured at the interior of the church.

"But you must have had a teacher!" Tracy exclaimed.

He shook his head. "No, I picked it up all by myself."

Clement leaned forward, his elbows on the riser. "You don't read music?"

William's open face was suffused with a glow. "I hear a piece and then just go to town! When I play for the choir, the leader sings me the song, and I pick it up from there. I learned quite a few modern and classical numbers from records, but my largest repertoire is naturally made up of hymns. I must know five hundred. In church I can't fool around much, although I try to do a little modernization." He paused. "I hate to play funerals." He looked up. "I think a person's personal likes and dislikes should be noted. I don't know why people shouldn't be allowed popular songs played while they're laid out. Anyway, weddings are fun. I can make Mendelssohn's 'Wedding March' sound like an Angel choir." He laughed. "I use tinkling bells to contrast the melody."

"Sounds like fun," Clement said. "By the way, when two melodies are played in conjunction, it's called contrapuntal playing." He paused. "If I whistle a tune, could you play it?"

"Sure."

"Do you know my radio theme song, 'Lady Luck'?"

The boy shook his head. "I've never heard you on the air. I only know your records. How does it go?"

Clement whistled the first four bars of "Lady Luck," while the boy listened intently.

"I didn't get that last part. Give it to me again?"

So as not to confuse the boy, Clement whistled the four bars again, more slowly this time. It was apparent that William's brain was working, memorizing. He paused a moment, lifted his hands, and began to caress the organ keys. Clement had difficulty in believing the sounds that were being coaxed from the old instrument. The boy began in a classical style, in the manner of a harpsichord—the way that Debussy might have played the band's signature tune. To test the boy further, Clement leaned forward and whistled the next phrase in his ear, and the one that followed, while William continued with the current phrase. He never missed a note.

The boy ended the tune with a subdued fanfare, embellishing the notes with what sounded like the muted tones of ancient monastery bells. It was a revealing moment. Clement exchanged glances with Luke, who he saw was as excited as he was at the virtuosity displayed. "How have you become so familiar with classical style?"

"I'm grateful to Miss Tarbell for that," he exclaimed happily, "She lets me listen to her records."

"It's the least I can do," she replied quickly. "William's parents ..." She stopped abruptly, and it was obvious that she had not intended to include them in the conversation.

"Yes? What about William's parents?" Clement asked.

The woman sighed audibly. "You might as well tell them, William," she said with an air of resignation.

He nervously fingered an F stop on the organ. "They'll only let me play for church services," he explained in a barely audible voice. "They never go anywhere or do anything. They don't believe in attending a picture show or any other kind of entertainment. They won't even let me go to a school dance." He looked up, his eyes wide. "My folks live on a farm about a mile out of town. I walk to school. They only come into town twice a week. Saturdays they go to the grocery store, and on Sundays they go to church. All this religious business came up five years ago at a big revival meeting. When the evangelist asked for people to come to the Lord and be saved at the end of the meeting, Mama got up and raised her hands above her head and called for Jesus. She was saved that night, and Dad was saved the next night, and that's the way it's been." He looked down at his hands. "I believe in God, but not like they do."

"But are they Baptists?" Luke asked.

William shook his head. "No. They go to the Church

of the Redeemer." He sighed gently. "That's a place where the congregation speaks in tongues."

Clement set his jaw. "But how come you are a member of the Baptist Church?"

"I'm *not*. I only play here. Reverend Menzies pays me two dollars for Sunday service, fifty cents for choir practice, and seventy-five cents for Wednesday night prayer meeting. My folks wouldn't let me, except we need the money so badly." He shrugged his shoulders. "And it is *church*, even if it isn't theirs."

Clement automatically reached in his pocket for a cigarette, realized where he was, and forcibly placed his hands flat on top of the organ. He needed to calm his nerves. As he pressed his hands down, he tried to compose a summation that would express his own thoughts without insulting the boy. "You have a lot of talent, William," he said with conviction, "and I'd like to help, but I don't know how. You're not out of high school yet, and with your folks being so religious ..." He looked at Tracy out of the corners of his eyes and turned to Louisa Tarbell. "But I want to thank you for asking me over today. I'm very glad that I came."

Louisa Tarbell straightened her back, and suddenly Clement could see her in the classroom, a tall, gaunt form from which authority emanated like a bright beam of light. "Mr. Story," she said in a firm voice, "you can't go back to Tulsa without helping William."

"What can I do?" he answered plaintively. "No one appreciates talent more than I do, but ..."

"Won't you see the Nestors?"

"What good would it do?"

"If you could convince them ..." She paused. "You see, they recognize that William has talent, it's just that they have no inkling that he has an interest in modern music. But if you ..."

Clement set his jaw again. "I really can't see any point in meeting them," he replied gently. "What could I say? I can't change their minds. They probably don't even know who I am."

William Nestor nodded. "They know that you're a mixed-blood Cherokee. That has weight."

Clement looked at Tracy, who shrugged his shoulders and turned away. Obviously he wanted no part of the proceedings, but on the other hand, he was a pianist who had been playing since he was seven years old, and William was an organist. Tracy obviously felt resentment at the boy's virtuosity. "All right," Clement said against his better judgment. "It won't hurt to talk to them."

Louisa Tarbell smiled with relief. "I'll get my old clunker," she said. "They don't live far, but do follow me, because these country roads wind around like a snake and there are no markers or signs."

"I know," Clement smiled and suddenly looked almost handsome. "I was born on a farm, remember?"

She nodded. "That's right. You know, it's so strange, meeting a celebrity whom you've heard about for so many years." Her face filled with admiration. "It's difficult to realize that Clement Story is right *here*, and that he's an Oklahoman, too—one of us. I'll get my car."

"Can I ride with you?" William asked Clement.

"No," the schoolteacher put in quickly, "please come with me." Obviously she was going to rehearse him on what to say to his family.

Luke followed Louisa Tarbell's old Ford Coupe, which headed down a dirt road out into the country. There was a strained silence among Clement, Luke, and Tracy. "I suppose," Clement said at last, "that this is a wild goose chase." He smiled feebly. "How do I get myself into these messes? And, what can I do for the boy?"

"I dunno, boss," Tracy replied, glancing out the window at the swirling red mist that billowed out by the side of the car, created by the exhaust from the Ford ahead.

"The kid has talent all right, but I don't think he's found his medium."

"Oh," Clement scoffed, "he's a natural and you know it." He grinned. "I got the impression back there in the church that you just might be a mite jealous."

"I am," Tracy acknowledged, wrinkling his forehead and resembling for a moment an adult version of a redheaded, freckle-faced Huck Finn. "I'm forty-four years old, boss, and as a kid at the eighty-eighter I was considered a whiz. I mean I hit all the right notes, but I never had the *command* that William has right now." He paused. "Hell, you were a child prodigy, you know what I mean."

Luke broke in quickly. "*I* know! The family had to put up with his practicing the piano, which was bad enough, but it even got too much for them when he switched to the saxophone. Mama exiled him to the pecan grove to practice. Even then, he created so much racket that he chased all the birds off the claim."

"You're exaggerating, Luke," Clement replied humorously. "I might have offended a couple of whippoorwills and a few wild canaries, but it was the mockingbirds providing the chorus."

"Yes," Luke answered grimly, "I remember." He followed the Ford down a dry dirt road that was actually no more than a wide path, and then both cars parked near a ramshackle barn. Amid the screeching of guinea hens and the barking of a yellow mongrel dog, the occupants climbed out of the Cadillac and followed William and Louisa down a path near a white, weatherbeaten privy and a falling-down toolshed.

"Come this way," William called, leading them past several automobile tires cut in half, which had been filled with some pink liquid, from which a flock of white Leghorn hens were drinking. "They have a sore throat," he explained. "Dust gets down into their gullets, and they can suffocate. The medicine keeps them breathing."

Clement nodded. Suddenly he was a little boy back on the farm claim at Angel. He could see Fontine Dice sitting on a log in the back of the clapboard, a chicken in her lap. Her hands were busy with a piece of cotton wrapped securely around a long, slim twig. Her voice came back to him. "Gotta git the phlegm outa their craws, or they'll perish!" She had swabbed the throats of the entire brood of chickens. John Dice, sitting next to her, had grasped each hen, turned it over, and applied a dab of Black Leaf 40 to its bottom. "That's for mites," he had explained to the young Clement. "Now we should have a healthy flock, with both ends taken care of!" And he had laughed and laughed.

"Why are you smiling, Mr. Story?" Louisa Tarbell asked.

"I was just thinking of the olden days in Oklahoma."

William opened the door of a shack shingled with small pieces of metal. It occurred to Clement that number 10 tin cans had been cut, pounded flat, and applied to the exterior. "Mama, Poppa," William called, "we've got company."

"Jest a minute," a high treble voice answered. Then around the side of the house came a thin dark-haired, sharp-nosed woman in a faded, pink-flowered cotton dress and a Mother Hubbard apron, which had once been white. Seeing the visitors, she brought her left hand up to shade her eyes. When she came forward, her bare feet caused little eddies of red dust to rise up around her ankles. Unsmilingly she jerked her head toward the house. "Well, do come in. Caught me unawares, but you're . . . welcome." She threw a meaningful look at her son. "Well, Billy-boy, just don't stand there, open the door for the folks!"

He obeyed, then stood back as Louisa, Clement, Luke, and Tracy filed into the house. The living room, bare floorboards scrubbed white, contained four straightback, pressed-wood chairs, a card table which Clement was certain was never used for even playing Whist, a wooden lamp with a crooked shade, and one overstuffed horse-hair chair. There was only one picture on the wall: a gaudy print of Jesus kneeling in the garden of Gethsemane.

William Nestor made quick introductions. His mother pumped each visitor's hand energetically, then stood back, shy and reserved. "Please sit down. How about some tea? We ain't got any ice. Maybe I should put on the teakettle."

Clement threw the others a quick look and replied, "No, thank you, Mrs. Nestor, we can only stay a moment."

She rested against the doorframe leading to the kitchen and looked down at her bare feet, stained from the red dust. "What's the occasion?" She asked, face flushed, eyes wary. "Has it got somethin' to do with you, Mr. Story?"

"In a way, Mrs. Nestor, but it's mostly William we've come to speak about."

"If it deals with him, I better call in his pap." She disappeared for a moment and called, "Finney, Finney, git yourself in here, we's got company!" She ambled back into the room, her hands in constant movement. "He'll be here in a minute. It's his day for fixin' harness." There was a long, strained pause while she tried to think of something to say.

"He plows with horses?" Luke asked gently.

She looked down at her rough, red hands. "Can't afford no tractor, and even if we could, we couldn't buy anythin' to fire it up with." She looked him straight in the eye. "Gas being so dear."

Luke reddened. "We do everything to keep Heron gasoline reasonable in price, Mrs. Nestor," he defended, "and our diesel fuel is a bargain. During the Depression . . ."

She looked at him dully and absently pulled a mat of hair back on the crown of her head. "Depression? Nothin's changed much hereabouts since the 'thirties," she said slowly. "People are still on relief. All the war did was take away our boys, and the few that came back had a couple of meals with their families and took off again." Her shoulders slumped, and she picked at the faded flowers on her dress. "Can't say I blame 'em. No one has any cash money. It takes us all year long to scrape up enough scratch for Billy-boy's schoolbooks, and even they're second-hand. . . . If he didn't have that job with the Baptists . . ."

A screen door slammed; a large man shuffled into the room and stood awkwardly by his wife. Finney Nestor had a fat Dutch face, brown hair shot with gray, and a large abdomen that hung over his ill-fitting work trousers, pinched in and patched at the waist. "Howdy," he greeted, his tone of voice far more cordial than his petulant facial expression.

Louisa Tarbell made the introductions, which Finney Nestor acknowledged with a nod of his head, but he made no move to shake hands with the men. "I know some rich people had to be here," he said slowly, "when I spied the Caddie." He looked uncomfortable. "What can we do for you folks?"

Clement cleared his throat, conscious of his expensive casual clothing and Luke's three-piece suit. "We came to talk about William. As you may know, I have an orchestra made up of mixed-blood Cherokees, and it's always been my belief that our brothers should stick together."

Mrs. Nestor looked at him incredulously. "Stick together? Why bring Indian blood into it? I'm American. Why, all we Nestors have in common is the Lord!"

Finney Nestor slid down on one of the pressed-wood chairs with a grunt. "You see this farm we're sittin' on?" His voice was quiet, bled of emotion, but a stricken look passed over his wife's face. "Her grandpap owned this farm once upon a time. It was his one-hundred-and-sixty-acre allotment. He had his corn all up and ready for harvesting in the summer of 'ought-eight. Some rich man with influence from up north, up in the Hampshires, came down here, and the government kicked him and her grandma and the kids off the land. They could read and write both Cherokee and English, too!"

Mrs. Nestor leaned forward, eyes wide. "Grandpap had gone through the eighth grade, and in them days that was like graduatin' from high school. He coulda been a teacher with a certificate and all." She looked at Louisa Tarbell. "Anyway, he lost the battle to save his land, and a lot of other tribal members who'd come up from Georgia on the Trail of Tears forfeited their lands, too. There was all kinds of schemes. Some shysters got 'em drunk. Some bought the timber on their land, cut it all down, and hightailed away." She coughed, with her hands over her chest. When the spasm ended, she continued in a voice as dry as the wind. "My pap and the rest of the family just went downhill, lost all their courage. He kinda went crazy then, I guess you'd say. He didn't do much to try to improve his lot, and when we third generation came along, in the 'twenties, we just holed up in the hills in a dugout." She looked around the room. "This is a palace compared to that place. We all grew up in one room."

She sighed, remembering the ordeal, and the skin on her high cheekbones tightened, and she looked very Indian. "None of us went to school beyond the fourth grade. I still have trouble writin'. The Depression come along, and I married Finn here, and we could barely keep body and soul together ..." She turned away.

Her husband went on with the story. "Then, when Billy-boy was born, we heard this Mr. Devlin who'd bought this here land from a Hampshire man, needed someone to sharecrop, and we came back to the old place."

Mrs. Nestor turned back to them, tears dried on her face, and looked around the room with a sad smile.

"This place used to be what they called a 'guest cottage.'" She jerked her thumb over her shoulder. "The big house was over there. It burned in 'thirty-six, and the Devlins moved to Clay Center." She sighed. "One of these days this old farm is goin' to be put on the auction block. We barely make enough to tithe and eat. The Devlins have to make enough to pay the taxes, or the savings 'n' loan'll git it. So, Mr. Story, I don't see how we Cherokees have stuck together much."

"My father, George Story, was a tribal lawyer," Clement put in quietly, "and tried to help, but the government was against him."

She nodded. "I've heard my grandpap talk about him. He said he was an honest man—for an Indian."

"He was," Luke admitted. "My own father was killed before I was born, so he was the only dad I ever knew. He spent most of his life fighting Washington. Even with all of his eloquence and education, he couldn't accomplish his aims."

Finney Nestor looked at Luke slyly out of the corners of his eyes. "Yes, but he got the oil, didn't he? He had sense enough to marry a Heron, didn't he?"

Luke flexed his short fingers. "Yes," he said, after a long pause, "he did. But when he married my mother, oil hadn't been discovered yet."

Finney Nestor's fat face was sullen with resentment. "It's all comin' back to me now. I guess you couldn't say that he married your mother for her money," he conceded.

Mrs. Nestor sucked her teeth. "Still and all, you had advantages. At least you didn't get kicked off the land."

"That's true," Clement agreed. "But we mixed-bloods must do what we can for our children. That's why I'm here today, Mrs. Nestor." He leaned forward earnestly and looked directly into her eyes. "William has a rare musical gift."

"Yes, he does play right good. He can hear somethin' once and sit right down and play it perfect."

"It goes beyond that, Mrs. Nestor. Playing isn't his only talent."

"What?" Her forehead was covered with tiny lines as she peered nearsightedly at him.

"You see," Clement explained gently, looking at her intently, "William's talent really hasn't been tapped yet. He has the kind of mind that can take a ... tune ... and ..." he fought for words that she would understand "... play it quite differently than the way he heard it. We call this transposing. Most musicians must work with notes on paper to be able to do this. He does it in his head." He went on, choosing his words very carefully, this time addressing Finney Nestor. "But if William had more schooling, he could learn the proper tools of his trade."

Finney Nestor was obviously impressed. "There'd be good money in this ... transposin'?"

Clement nodded. "We call it *arranging.* But, more than making money, he would be a credit to you. He might even become very well known in musical circles."

"I don't know." Mrs. Nestor smiled shyly. "That sounds far-fetched to me."

William's father shuffled his worn boots. "He'll always have a job here. Reverend Menzies, even though he ain't our parson, says he'll give him a job playing the organ in church full time after he graduates, and he'd also lead the choir." He considered the question further. "That he can be sure of, and he won't have to go back to school either. Billy-boy would know that he'd be getting twenty dollars a week, with choir practice and all."

Mrs. Nestor drew in her breath. "Besides, we can't send him to college, could barely get him in high school."

"I know that, Mrs. Nestor." Clement had a decision to make, and he disliked coming to a conclusion without significant preparation, but he plunged ahead, certain that the time was right at the moment. "What I'm prepared to do is this, Mrs. Nestor. I, personally, will send Billy to the Barrett Conservatory of Music for three years after he finishes high school this spring—with the understanding, of course, that he'll go to work for me after he graduates."

She regarded him suspiciously. "I've never heard any of your music, but I've been told it's jazzy. My boy belongs in the service to the Lord."

"I understand that, Mrs. Nestor," Clement replied quickly. It occurred to him that he had only listened to the boy play an hour ago, and he was now offering to take over his life! Events were progressing far too rapidly, yet Clement knew that he had to take a stand. Suddenly he knew that his father would have approved and encouraged him. "I don't want to hire Billy as a musician," he explained patiently. "You see, orchestras like mine don't have an organ." He continued as quietly as he could, trying to quell the beating in his breast. He had taken up a cause which he had to see through. "I would employ him as an *arranger*. But in order to do that, he must learn to *read* music, so he can do what we call *orchestrations*."

She shook her head. "This is all so strange to me. The thought of him working out there—with you, playing in places that condone drinking, where people get up and dance and carry on . . ."

"He wouldn't be traveling with me. He would be home most of the time."

Finney Nestor got up from the chair slowly, shifting his bulk to his legs. "I don't see why he can't be content to stay here with a job that the Lord knows is good and proper. It seems to me that he'd be doin' the devil's work." He stuck out his lower lip. "How much would you pay Billy-boy?"

William Nestor stood up. "Mama, Poppa, I've sat here

and listened to this conversation long enough." His voice was strained, but his emotions were under control. "You've been talking—discussing my life as if I was a piece of bacon just waiting for the frying pan. I don't like that. I'm a person." He shook his head. "I'm not going to be playing the organ the rest of my life. To me, that's just something to do that I enjoy, but it's not enough to satisfy me."

Mrs. Nestor looked up at him in amazement. "What kind of a word is that—satisfy? What has that got to do with livin' and raisin' a family and workin' for the Lord?"

"Whatever I'll be doing, it's going to be for the Lord, Mama. I don't believe in lying and cheating. I mean to go on living by the Ten Commandments. To me, that's what religion is, Mama, not going to church and speaking in foreign tongues. Look at the folks around here who sin all week long, and then go to church on Sundays and pray louder than anybody else. They wouldn't have to pray so hard if they didn't lie and cheat all week long."

She nodded. "I know people maybe who don't do right all the time, but the Nestors are different. We live right ever' day."

"You're safe here, son, *safe*," Finney Nestor put in persuasively. "You'll work with the land and rehearse the choir, and play your music ..."

William set his jaw. "And what happens if the Devlins auction this place off? What would you and Mama do then? At twenty dollars a week, I couldn't support you both."

His mother looked down at her bare feet, and tears gathered in the corners of her eyes. "We'd go on relief, I guess."

Finney Nestor straightened his back and turned to Clement. "If you do send him to school and pay all of his expenses so that he learns to read music and do this arranging you've been talking about, how long would he have to work for you to pay you back?"

Clement shook his head. "It's not that kind of a deal. I wouldn't put him in peonage. I hope, of course, that he'd stay with me, but if he got a better opportunity, I'd wish him the best of luck. I'd feel proud that I'd been able to help a fellow Cherokee."

Finney Nestor puffed out his chest and held out his huge hands in front of him, twisting his fingers. "You mean to say, Mr. Story, that you'd spend all that money and still let him go? He wouldn't have to pay you back? When we sharecrop ..."

Clement held his anger back. "It's not the same thing at all. We're dealing with *talent*, something special that the Lord gave Billy. He should be given the opportunity to become what he is inside."

Louisa Tarbell's voice was very gentle. "You see, William's gifts can make you all very proud. You can't give him his chance because of your circumstances, but Mr. Story is willing to sponsor him. You should be proud and happy that your boy is being given an opportunity now that'll never come again." Her voice was so low she could hardly be heard. "No one must stand in his way."

Mrs. Nestor looked up at the rain-stained ceiling. "I don't know. Lord, what should we do? I want Billy-boy to have a chance, and you did give him the gift, as Mr. Story says, yet the world's so wicked ..."

"Mama," Billy interjected, "I'll be eighteen in June— about the time that I get my high school diploma. That's not very far away. I want your and Poppa's support more than anything else in the whole wide world." He paused, and his voice broke. "But if you won't let me go willingly, then I'll take off right after the school term is over. I'll leave and I'll never come back."

Mrs. Nestor looked at him with a new realization. "Billy-boy, is that *you* talkin', or the devil?"

"It's me, Mama, I've got to do what I've got to do!"

Mrs. Nestor looked down at her red-stained feet and got up slowly. "I guess that's a decision we've all got to make at one time or t'other." She turned at the door. "I wish that I could say that I'm glad that all of you come out here today and explained what's on your mind, but I can't." Her voice was drained of emotion. "Before you came, Billy-boy was ours, safe here on the place, but now you've put foreign ideas in his brain and words in his mouth. You've been talking about what it means to be Cherokee. I'd forgotten all about that until you brought it up. My Indian blood never did anything for me." Her voice was flat. "Maybe it did for you because you blowed it all over in the newspapers how's you got up that musical band made up of people with our blood. You were smart enough to make your mixed blood work for you—not against you." She paused, her voice weary. "But I still think you're doin' the work of the devil."

Finney Nestor nodded. "I agree. Now, we been polite to all of you, when you really came out here today to take Billy-boy away. You've done that, and I don't know why the Lord let you do it, but he did. I suppose sooner or later we'll find out why." His voice grew petulant. "At least he ain't goin' away today." He paused. "But, I'd be much obliged if you'd all leave us to our grief."

William opened the door, and Louise Tarbell, Clement, Luke, and Tracy went out into the barnyard. There was complete silence as they got into their cars. William leaned over, his face close to the open door of the Cadillac. "We won," he said slowly. "You changed my life today, Mr. Story."

Clement motioned to the house. "Will it go badly for you in there?"

William shook his head. "No, because I've finally made a stand." There were tears in his eyes.

"We'll be in touch," Clement said, "as soon as you get your high school diploma."

*　　*　　*

That night William Nestor waited until his parents went into their bedroom at shortly after seven o'clock; then he heated water in the teakettle and washed the supper dishes in the pitted cast-iron sink, using the dark yellow homemade soap that his mother made twice a year in the kettle in the yard.

He dried the dishes with a limp threadbare towel made out of a flour sack, and stacked the chipped plates and cups neatly in the cupboard, then put out more roach powder. He glanced around the old kitchen, illuminated by a single light bulb hanging from the ceiling, and he whispered, "O Lord, thank you for delivering me from this place." He remembered his benefactor. "I'm also grateful that you sent Clement Story today to take me out of bondage to the Promised Land."

He went into his small bedroom and sat down on the lumpy mattress covered with unbleached muslin, and put on his tennis shoes. He turned out the light, closed the back door behind him, and went through the cornfields, the smell of fresh growing things in his nostrils. The moon lighted the pathway toward Willawa. On the outskirts of the tiny community he took a shortcut, which brought him, unseen, to the rear yard of the cottage.

He scratched lightly at the side door, was admitted, and went immediately to the bathroom, where a warm tub had been drawn. He took a leisurely bath and rubbed his body vigorously with a soft, furry towel. He loved the luxury of the hand-milled soap and the green-colored aftershave that he always used as a cologne. He checked his face in the oval mirror above the porcelain washbasin. He had to shave only once a week, and his cheeks were still soft and pink from the last time.

As he began to think about what lay beyond the bathroom door, his body responded to his active imagination, and his iron bar became rigid with excitement. He turned off the bathroom light and went into the darkened bedroom and climbed between the cool percale sheets that smelled faintly of a mixture of rose scents, which, combined with the tart, astringent odor of the aftershave lotion, created a sensuous mood to which he always looked forward.

He took her in his arms, and their kisses, which had at first been very light, became deeper as their tongues met. He thought to himself that this expression of love made everyday living, even with all of its hardships, somehow more bearable. This warmth, this softness, this incredible feeling of ultimate fulfillment, was what kept him sane, left him free to concentrate on his music. In these moments of intimacy, he knew that he was special, in the same way that he was special when he sat down at the organ and his hands caressed the keys. He had always been different from the other boys in school; had always known that he had a purpose, that somehow he would be delivered from the hell of mediocrity that flourished around him.

She was supple, yielding, willing to indulge him, but it had always been this way from the very beginning. He was seventeen and a half now. The first time this had happened was ... how could he forget his fourteenth birthday?

His excitement increased as he thought of that first time. He had eaten too much rich homemade ice cream at the party in the basement of the church. She had taken him home to lie down on the daybed on the back porch. He had slept for two hours, and when he awakened, she was changing the damp washcloth on his forehead. He had been dreaming, and his iron bar was very rigid and showed through his trousers. Embarrassed, he had sought to turn away, but she had looked at him with such love and understanding that he impulsively held out his arms.

He was hungry for affection. Never once in his memory, even when he had been very small, could he recall his mother taking him in her arms, and his father had never held him on his lap or said a kind word to him. He had held her awkwardly, and then, as they kissed, it happened for him before he undressed. That had been the beginning. Now he felt he was an accomplished lover; his bar of iron was always ready. He sighed again and changed positions, and she was under him and everything was going to be all right now because he was enclosed in her protective arms. They were going to explore this special world that they always created for themselves until the room was enclosed in witchery. His heartbeat increased, and they trembled deliciously together while he felt all of his energy rush out, and he lay still.

As he dozed, cozy and warm, ringed still in her intimate embrace, he fell asleep. He dreamed of warm embraces and sighed. Louisa Tarbell kissed the cheek and stroked the brow of her boy lover, her musical genius.

4

The Operator

Robert Desmond knocked twice on the door that separated his office from Luke's on the top floor of the Heron Building in Tulsa.

He had to play the scene very persuasively, he knew,

or it would fall flat. He tried to picture how an actor of Laurence Olivier's stature would involve himself emotionally, and decided he would play the gamut, from bright young businessman to tycoon, and if that didn't work, he could dive into his bag of gutter language, a ploy which did not appeal to his sensitivities. Yet all was fair in love and war, or so he liked to think.

"Come in," Luke said automatically, not looking up from a stack of field reports. It was a Monday morning. He had been up since five and had not even opened his briefcase, which was filled with second-quarter statements that he had not had an opportunity to read on the weekend.

"Give me five minutes?" Desmond asked.

Luke looked up wearily. He motioned him to a chair by the side of his desk, so that he could look at his cohort on an equal basis and not across the wide expanse of desk. "Sure, Bob, shoot."

"Several months ago, when Heron bought out my company and made me a vice president of Heron, you asked me to study the substructure of the company and submit a report."

"Yes, yes," Luke put in hurriedly, "but I've got to get the agenda ready for the executive meeting this morning at eleven, we break for lunch at twelve, then back at two. There's so much to discuss, I don't think we'll be finished by five." He paused and ran his hand through his gray hair. "I'd like to table your report now. We'll discuss it later in the week."

Robert Desmond straightened his back. He was, as always, immaculately dressed. He wore a pale beige sharkskin suit, a white shantung shirt with a brown and gold necktie, and brown leather shoes with round toes, which he was examining with great care. "You said five minutes, Luke," he said reproachfully.

Luke was conscious that his clothing was not put together in any particular order. The green wool herringbone suit was too warm for the weather, and his new black boots pinched his instep. He was also aware that he needed a haircut; perspiration dripped down from his nape, dampening his collar, which was too snug for his jowls. The necktie, a present from Bosley, was blue-and-gray-striped, and did not go with his suit. Jeanette always selected his daily wardrobe, but she and Murdock were in Kansas City visiting Clement and Sarah. The morning was not shaping up well at all. "Okay, shoot," he said again lamely, and placed folded hands over the unread reports.

Robert Desmond cleared his throat. "It's my opinion that the *entire* company needs restructuring, including the Wildcat Bit Division, the trucking department, and British Heron. Bosley is a great public relations man, and when he makes trips into the field, the older men's performance ratio always accelerates five to eight points after he's gone. He provides needed lift, I suspect, with a subtle form of flattery. Because he's chairman of the board, the men feel he has his eye on them personally, but the younger men do not seem to respond to him at all. There's no difference in their sales performance after a visit by him."

His Oxford accent became more clipped. "Now the next step is delicate, Luke, and I hope you take this the way that it is intended. My father always said that Bosley Trenton was a crack geologist, and I'm certain that up to about nineteen-forty, he led the field. I understand that he was on the verge of retiring when the Japs attacked Pearl Harbor. But now, with the new exploration that must be done in the North Sea, we've got to bring in some fresh blood from outside the company if we are to keep pace with the world of petroleum. Geologists must be employed who know more about offshore drilling, for one thing." He gave Luke a penetrating glance, "We need an executive type as chairman, someone who is fully conversant with modern business practices, including the new automation, as well as the oil business itself. Frankly, I think we should raid Standard Oil or Mobile, hire away one of their top men, and officially retire Bosley. Keep him on the payroll, of course, as an ambassador-at-large."

Luke's face was mottled red. "Now, hold on one damn minute, Bob!"

Robert Desmond held up a well-manicured hand and looked at his wristwatch. "My time isn't up yet!"

Luke set his massive jaw. "All right. Continue," he snapped. "You've got exactly two minutes."

"We should also hire an executive assistant. You should not be reading field reports—that's like a chief of staff at a hospital giving blood tests. Breakdown data should be given you *after* someone else has 'graded the papers.'

"Heron," he went on quickly, warming to his subject, "has six regional managers: North, Northeast, South, Southeast, Midwest, and the West—which incorporates the eleven western states. An additional man should be hired to head up the Pacific Northwest, and a new VP elected to be in charge of these men. Canada has two men, but with the paltry amount of business, one is enough. Conversely, there are only three men in the international division, and if we do business in the North Sea or the Middle East, we're going to need more managers and several lesser supervisors. A VP should be placed in charge over there too, someone who's bilingual.

"Also, Luke, we need a new training program for service station personnel, and a crack mechanics' school. Luke Three thinks Jerrard Jones should conduct the school. Another thing, the Heron advertising program has no direction, in my opinion. Noble and Harrison—which was a good firm in the nineteen-thirties and did well by Heron then—hasn't had any new ideas in a long time. If we're going into credit cards, a whole campaign should be built."

"Your two minutes are up, Bob," Luke announced flatly. He kept his tone low, but his clenched hands, with white knuckles, spoke more plainly than his voice. "I don't have time to treat all of the points that you've brought up this morning. I'll look at the report in detail later. First of all, of course, we can't even consider moving out Bosley. After being president for so many years, this is his due. As far as using him more in the field, that's impossible, too. He can't be running all over the country at his age. So that's out. I wouldn't even consider bringing an executive in from the opposition. Heron's always moved up its men from inside the company."

The intercom buzzed. "Yes, Bernice?" Luke said.

"It's Mr. Trenton."

"Yes, Uncle Bos?" Luke said into the mouth piece.

"I'm still here in Angel. Would you handle the meeting for me this morning? Letty wants to go shopping in Enid, and then, I don't relish that long drive to Tulsa in this weather."

Luke frowned. "Sure, don't worry about it. When do you think you'll be into the office?"

"Wednesday or Thursday."

"I see." Luke kept his voice calm. "Just dictate the agenda for the meeting this morning to Bernice on the phone, so she can make carbon copies for the men."

"I didn't get around to making one, Luke"—Bosley was apologetic—"but there's not too much to go over. We've already agreed on the advertising budget for the next six months, and we should discuss where the banquet for the Man of the Year Award will be held, maybe at the Skirvin Tower Hotel in Oklahoma City. Timson, the head chemist at the refinery in Lubbock, is retiring, he's got to be replaced, and that's about it."

"Okay, Uncle Bos, I'll see you later in the week." Luke hung up and glanced at Desmond thoughtfully. "I'll conduct the meeting this morning. Bos has some errands to do."

Robert Desmond examined his round-toed shoes again. "What about the agenda?"

"I'll make one up. Old Timson is retiring, the advertising budget must be okayed, and the Man of the Year—"

"All penny-ante, Luke, and you know it!" Robert Desmond was furious. "What about putting out feelers about soliciting more accounts for our trucking line, which is only breaking even now?"

Luke looked uncomfortable. "Well, yes, we should take that up sometime or other."

"When you bought out my company last year," Robert Desmond said coldly, "it was agreed that my management expertise would be utilized in conjunction with the Heron operation. So far, I've been left out in the cold. It's very difficult for me to sit back and see projects that I worked so hard to build up over the years go by the wayside. I came in with you because the future looked brighter. With the added capital that you were going to infuse into my operation, the sky was the limit. But so far, we've gone backward instead of forward, and frankly, I'm sick of it."

"You got your vice presidency and two hundred thousand dollars a year on a ten-year contract, didn't you?" Luke shouted, finally losing his temper. "Now you want to change the whole goddamn company!"

Robert Desmond got up stiffly, his small eyes spitting fire, "I should have bought you out when I had the chance. If old John Dice . . ."

Luke smiled coolly. "Thank God he didn't sell you either his shares or the Barrett Conservatory holdings!"

"Yes," Robert Desmond replied smoothly, "or I'd be sitting where you are—in the catbird seat!" He went into his office and slammed the door.

Luke was shaken, but his anger gradually receded. Much of what Desmond had said was true, only he didn't want to admit it. He absently shuffled the papers on his desk, then looked out over the Tulsa skyline. It was already nine-thirty in the morning, and he had accomplished very little. Furthermore, his back ached. He got up slowly and knocked on Robert Desmond's door.

"Yes?"

He opened the door and stood uncomfortably on the threshold. "Bob, come back in, will you, please? I apologize for what I said earlier. I'm not in the best of moods." He shrugged his shoulders. "The Monday morning blues, I guess. Let's make up the agenda together, huh?"

"Certainly." Robert Desmond, without rancor, casually picked up a portfolio and followed Luke into his office, speaking as he walked. "There's a lot to go over. First of all, I think we should send out for lunch—a two-hour break is pure luxury—then we've got to have a full report about marketing our new knock-free gas ..." He paused. "Which really isn't totally knock-free at all." He pursed his thin lips. "If it was me, Luke, I'd send the formula back to research and development for a series of other tests. With Timson out, perhaps the new man will have some thoughts about other additives."

When Luke called the Monday morning conference of executives together in the large boardroom next to his office, he utilized the complete agenda worked out by Robert Desmond. The ten men sitting around the table responded with rapt attention, and it occurred to Luke that it had been months since a meeting had progressed so well. There was a murmur of approval when huge club sandwiches from the nearby Calico Restaurant arrived precisely at twelve o'clock. Bernice, who brought in freshly brewed coffee, had ordered a sandwich for herself in the event that she was called to take dictation.

At a quarter past five, all items had been discussed, and the men left in a high state of exhilaration. Luke turned to Robert Desmond and shook his hand. "I must congratulate you," he said grudgingly, "for putting together a brilliant meeting. The results were far more than I expected. These men are going to be thinking tonight, and I think we'll see a tremendous change in attitude tomorrow morning. We've given them many areas to think about."

"I was pleased," Robert Desmond agreed, with a modesty that surprised Luke. "It is difficult to inspire men who've been in the same posts for many years. I think we—I mean you—have given them a new sense of *purpose*." He paused. "Now, I have a suggestion. I'd like to visit the field offices abroad, and take Luke Three with me."

Luke frowned. "I don't know what he'll learn from the trip. To me it will only mean he'll get an expense-paid vacation."

"I was thinking," Robert Desmond replied smoothly, "more what the field men would get out of it. After all, he's going to become increasingly important in the business. I think it would be a tremendous psychological boost for those men to meet and talk with the heir apparent."

Luke snapped his briefcase shut. "I don't think it's wise just yet, Bob. In the first place, you don't know what the kid's going to say. These guys are apt to ask questions that he can't answer. I know from experience that it's never good for an executive to horse around with ad libs. Give him time to acquire a little more polish before we throw him to the wolves."

Robert Desmond smiled wryly. "Forgive me for bringing it up, Luke, but your statement, I think, reveals more about your attitude than you realize. The men in the field *aren't* wolves at all. They deserve special attention occasionally. When was the last time you were in Europe?"

Luke glared at him. "A year ago, but Bos went to

Switzerland six months ago with Mother, and stopped at a couple of offices."

"A token visit?"

"Don't be sarcastic, Bob, he makes a very fine appearance."

"I'm not impugning his integrity. He's like a gentle college professor, and there's certainly nothing wrong with that, but the younger men respond to youth and ..."

"Youth, yes," Luke grimaced, "but not to some smart-ass kid like Luke Three."

"Is that how you really think of him?"

"Fifty percent of the time," Luke answered. "The other fifty percent don't count at all."

"Luke, would you leave the trip to me? I'll coach him, prompt him, and set him up in each situation so that he'll come off looking good. I promise you. Three months away will do him good."

Luke shook his head. "I don't know, Bob, it's not that I don't trust you in this area, but the kid ..."

"The 'kid,' as you keep calling him, served in the East China seas."

"Yes, and ran away from home ..."

Robert Desmond came back quickly. "Just like you did in World War One."

Luke turned away. "There's a good deal of difference."

"I don't think so. Probably Luke Three has more of your qualities than you'd like to admit." He paused to let his words sink in, then went on sincerely, "I promise, Luke, that if he doesn't take direction, and does less than expected on the first stop, we'll turn tail and come home. What say?"

Luke's back was beginning to throb painfully again. "All right, Bob, I'll give in this time because I think you're right about a couple of things. Will you be taking anyone else along?"

"Only Jorge, my valet. I'll arrange for Luke Three and

myself to occupy a townhouse in London, which will serve as headquarters." He smiled. "An old girlfriend of mine has graciously offered her place."

"Leave her name and address with the controller. I'll see that she gets a check."

Robert Desmond smiled. "It's free, Luke."

Luke shook his head. "I never permit complimentary lodging. Stay at the Savoy, if you like. The River Suite is nice."

"I can hardly refuse her offer, Luke. We went to college together."

"It sounds like she may be staying there too."

"Perhaps one weekend."

"That's even worse," Luke expostulated, "No, thank you. Reserve the River Suite. If you want to fool around with her at the townhouse, that's all right, but I don't want Luke Three involved. Get me? Otherwise the deal is off. I won't let him go."

Robert Desmond nodded, realizing he had lost a point. Luke was right. "Okay, it's the Savoy."

"And don't be introducing Luke Three to your ... girlfriend."

"You're being overly defensive again." Robert Desmond smiled. "I'm not about to set up competition. Why should a thirty-two-year-old man introduce the nineteen-year-old heir to the Heron millions to an impoverished gentlelady who screws only for pleasure?"

Luke Three parked the pink Cadillac in front of the Heron Building in Tulsa.

He climbed out of the front seat and took a chamois skin from the trunk and wiped the surface of the hood. He still could not believe his good fortune. He took the car keys out of his pocket and kissed the Cadillac insignia. The car was now his; Bosley had purchased a new black Lincoln from Detroit, and had driven into the station for a fill-up and remarked in that gruff voice that he used when he was being extra nice, "Have you got a penny?" And when he'd said yes, Bosley had held out his hand, pocketed the coin, and then quipped, "You just bought yourself the last Caddie off the assembly line before the war!" Luke Three couldn't believe his ears and had hugged his grandfather. "Don't start carrying on," Bosley had retorted. "Remember, it's six years old!"

Luke Three flexed his arms and looked at the sun. His beige trousers and white shirt clung to his body. The humidity was very high, and the temperature was ninety-eight degrees.

Upstairs in Robert Desmond's office, two huge fans moved the air about, but even with the windows open, the place was very warm. "Mr. Luke Heron ... Three is here, Mr. Desmond," Bernice's crisp voice came over the intercom.

"Tell him to come in, please," he replied, and a moment later Luke Three strode into the room. The men shook hands. "Is it hot enough for you?" Robert Desmond asked.

"I swear that Okinawa wasn't this bad," Luke Three exclaimed. "At least we had the ocean to dip in once in a while, and after we kicked out the Japs, we went around in just our skivvies."

Robert Desmond pointed the fan in Luke Three's direction. "It's supposed to be cool in New York. I thought we'd take a trip."

Luke Three frowned. "I'm supposed to be back at the station in Angel on Friday. I just came for three days."

Robert Desmond gave him a long look. "You didn't let me finish. Don't you know it's impolite to interrupt an elder?"

Luke Three smiled. "I never think of *you* as an elder, Bob."

"I suppose I should be flattered. At any rate, bub"—he pronounced the nickname he had given Luke Three with relish—"I was going to say that we'd stop by New

York on our way to visit the field offices in Europe. Your dad has given permission."

"But what about the station?"

"We'll find a replacement."

Luke Three shook his head. "I don't know, Bob, people count on me for so much. Jerrard is a fabulous mechanic, but he can never keep the cash deposits straight."

Robert Desmond fiddled with his expensive yellow Sulka tie while looking intently at Luke Three. He noticed Luke's hands were not very clean; the fingernails were rimmed with black grease. He cleared his throat. "This business of working in a station was fine while you were going to high school, it gave you a feel of the business, but now that you've been out of the service for eight months, and the station is going well, what do you want to do with the rest of your life?"

Luke Three thought of Darlene, and his senses stirred. He could see her walking down Main Street, the tight sweater hugging her magnificent breasts and the pleated skirt outlining her wide hips. . . .

"Do you want to go back to school?"

Luke roused himself. "No, Dad wants me to go to college, but I'm not interested. I want to know a lot more about cars. Jerrard says that I have real mechanical ability."

Robert Desmond threw back his head and laughed. "You don't really want to be a mechanic!" he said, his Oxford accent more clipped than before. "After all, you'll inherit an empire one day."

"It's kind of frightening." Luke Three leaned forward, his face flushed with excitement. "What's always intrigued me, since I was a little boy, was the *operation* of the service stations. I used to go out with Dad in the field when he opened up new outlets. He'd pose for pictures and do interviews, which was a smart idea. He took care of that part of the business really well. But, at the same time, it always seemed to me that the company didn't really look out after the guys who held the Heron franchises. They were left pretty much on their own, and a lot of them floundered around, and still do!"

Robert Desmond nodded. "I'm of the same opinion. I'd like to create a division that would stress the service aspect. I've already spoken to your dad about it. We should establish a school with a training program. During the war, the public didn't expect much, with most of the men in the armed forces, but now it's different. We must become really competitive to Mobil, Shell, Conoco, and Standard and the others, if all the Heron stations are going to make money—for both the franchisees and the company, too. That's why I want you to go on this trip to meet the regional managers." He lowered his voice confidentially. "There is already reorganization underway. This is one reason that I consented to be brought out by your dad." He pursed his thin lips. "Heron's been run like a family business for much too long. Frankly, how it has survived is beyond me. If the war hadn't come along, I think the company would have probably gone under."

"Was it as bad as that?"

Robert Desmond coughed discreetly. "Well, perhaps it wouldn't have gone bankrupt, but some retrenchment would have been necessary. Your dad and Bosley have always been content with a small piece of the pie." He got up and went to the window. "We'll talk further about these training seminars, but first of all, you must take a course in Business Administration."

"I've got my G.I. Bill," Luke Three replied eagerly.

Robert Desmond smiled softly. "What you just said sums up a lot of what we've been talking about this morning. *G.I. BILL!* Stop thinking small. Don't you realize that your dad is a *millionaire?*"

Luke Three shrugged his shoulders. "What good does it do if the money is tied up in the company?"

Robert Desmond sat down on the edge of his desk and looked him straight in the eye. "No, Luke Three, it is *not* all tied up in the company. Your dad has over one million dollars in a savings account at the Dice National Bank in Angel, and there's a half-million in the Hanover Trust in New York, so it's time that you began to think about how that money can be managed. You must start looking like what you are—an heir apparent. And, young man, I think you can start with a manicure."

Letty was sitting on the porch of the clapboard house in the twilight, fanning her face with the embossed ivory fan that Lou Hoover had given her in 1929 on one of her visits to the White House. She thought briefly of George Story, her second husband, and sighed gently. Where had time gone? It seemed just like yesterday that she had brought him back to this very house to die. The weather, she remembered, had been warm—just like today— roses climbed over the trellis outside the upstairs window, and there were honeybees working over the roses. She thought of the strange visit to Hyde Park with Bosley in 1944, at Mrs. Roosevelt's invitation, only a few months before the President's death.

Why was she thinking about those years when so much had gone before and after? But this was 1946, and the war was over.... She looked down at her hands, which had become fragile; there were swollen veins under the transparent skin slightly spotted with brown pigment. She suddenly realized that she was an old woman; her back was not very straight anymore, and yet she did not feel old inside.

Her thoughts went back to a Saturday night dance at the Chenovicks'—when? It had been in the days when the parties were still held in the barn. She had just met George Story. She could see him bow slightly before her and ask for the next dance. It must have been 1901 or 1902. She could feel his eyes boring into hers—those incredible blue eyes that always sent her pulse dancing. Then, he had held her—not *too* close, because he was a gentleman, but even so, the electricity that emanated from their palms as they waltzed to the tremor of Torgo's violin had made her very warm, although it had been a winter evening. This magnificent man whom she had loved so much had glided her over the floor and her feet were as light as cornhusks. She remembered fondly their honeymoon at the Prince Hotel in Guthrie and his tender lovemaking. Her first husband, Luke, had been a very sweet man, but they were both virgins when they married. They had discovered love together and they had made a happy life up north, long before he had been murdered staking this very claim. The pain came back to her, then was washed away by George Story again. He had made love to her almost every day, all of their married life. When he was away, she ached for him.

She smiled softly, recalling when the first telephone had been installed and he would call from Enid. "I just came in on the train. I'll catch the four-thirty and be home at four-fifty-five." She would meet him at the railway station in Angel with the carriage, and they would hold hands all the way home in anticipation of what would shortly be taking place in the upstairs bedroom.

When George purchased his first automobile, she would wait impatiently for the sound of the horn—he would often have a breakdown on the road. He was a precious man and—she might as well admit it—the love of her life. He had thrilled her physically more than either Luke or Bosley. She sighed. Bosley was a kindly person, and their life together, even today, was certainly satisfactory. Perhaps it was wrong to compare husbands; each man was different, and each man had changed her life. But George . . .

"Grandma, what are you doing sitting out here in the dark?"

The voice cut through the years, interrupting her memories. Had someone called *Grandma*? Grandma had been dead for years, long before she and Luke Heron had come down from Minneapolis to take part in the Cherokee Strip Land Rush. Suddenly she laughed. Of course, someone was referring to *her*! She was a grandmother several times over. She looked up and saw Luke Three standing on the steps of the porch. "I was just watching the fireflies," she said.

"A penny for your thoughts." He turned on the porch light.

"I was long ago and far away." She smiled crookedly. "Come and give me a kiss."

He leaned over and brushed his lips to her cheek. She took his hand, saw that his fingernails were clean, and looked up into his face. Her eyes twinkled. "Are these the hands of my favorite mechanic?"

He placed his hands in his pockets. He was shy. "I've been looking like a bum for too long," he replied, then stepped back. "How do you like my new suit, Grandma?"

She studied him carefully. "It's very handsome. What's the color?"

"Fawn," he answered proudly. "It's tailor-made in Tulsa."

"Your appearance has improved five hundred percent. I'm glad your dad has finally taken an interest in you."

"It wasn't Dad," he said. "It's Robert Desmond. He said that I've got to start looking prosperous and not like some dumb grease monkey."

She gave him a long look. "Yes, of course," she replied and thought: You'll be president of the company someday. Of course Luke Senior was still young. But, she reflected, he wasn't all *that* young—fifty-two.... She could remember so well the night that he was born. Sam, the Cherokee Indian boy, had brought him into the world in the old sod house in 1894. He was a spring baby. With difficulty she forced herself to look at her grandson. He stood there on the porch, tall, handsome, somewhat awkward in his new suit, and it was as if she did not know him. So much time had gone by, yet inside she felt as young as the day that she and the original Luke had come to the territory. "Do you like Robert Desmond?" she asked plaintively.

Luke Three nodded. "Very much. He's like a wise, sophisticated brother. He's a new breed, Grandma, not like us. He always looks into the future. He won't sit back and wait for events to happen like Dad does. He's what I guess you'd call a *doer*."

Letty nodded. "George Story was a doer, too." She paused. 'I've been thinking about him lately. Do you remember your grandfather?"

"I only recall that he used to take me on his lap and tell me stories ... not fairy tales ... stories about Indians. Why?"

"Oh, I just wondered, that's all." She brightened. "How about a dish of ice cream? It's homemade chocolate."

He grinned. "You know it's my favorite."

He helped her out of the swing. "There's lots of news," he said. "First of all, I'm going to Europe with Bob, and then, when I get back, I'm going to be moving to my own apartment in Tulsa." He paused awkwardly. "I'll miss you, Grandma."

She scooped out a large portion of ice cream and returned the metal container to the refrigerator. "I'll miss you, too. But it's time you were on your own, and besides, we'll be opening up the house in Washington. You can visit us there, so you see, everything is working out for the best."

"I suppose so," he answered, and then grew silent as he enjoyed the treat. Finally he looked up. "I don't know whether I like ... growing up—did you?"

"Why, what a question!" She paused. "You know, Luke Three, I don't think I remember. I only know that age has its compensations. I often think of the past, but I wouldn't want to relive any of it."

"I don't have a past, Grandma," he replied thoughtfully, "but you know what?" He took the last bit of ice cream, and then licked the spoon. "I'm going to start *living.* Next year at this time, I'll have a past—or know the reason why!" He knew an exit line when he heard one, and bounded up the stairs to his room.

Letty smiled to herself, and as a small wind sprang up, she thought she smelled the smoke in the air from the recent fire in Angel. It was possible, but improbable, because the rubble had been cleared away. The Red Bird Café was housed in a new building that sported twelve seats at the counter and four tables, and it gave her heart a lift every time she walked by and saw Belle Trune cooking on the new grill and opening that new stainless-steel refrigerator. Darlene had even made cottage curtains for the windows.

The Stevens Hotel had a new roof, and the hardware store was under construction. Also, an architect had come over from Enid to give estimates on how much it would take to redesign storefronts on the buildings she owned that faced Main Street, and the other merchants had said they'd cooperate, too. Out of chaos would come a new prosperity.

She looked over at the Conservatory of Music building that had once housed the most famous bordello in the territory, and thought of the lovely Leona Barrett, who had at first opened her house as a café, and she sighed. Leona was dead and gone, as were so many other pioneers. Well, if she had her way, and she always did, the town of Angel, Oklahoma, would look as brand, spanking new as it did in those early years when it had sprung up from dry prairie.

5

The Journey

"I dislike commercial airlines," Pierre complained as the plane touched down at National Airport in Washington.

Mitchell shook his hand reluctantly. "You're not going with me to Royal Gorge?"

Pierre smiled. "That old farmhouse was deactivated years ago, after your mission in southern France." He paused. "You will be met by a friend in the lobby."

"Then I won't see you again?"

The Frenchman laughed. "You cannot dispense with me so quickly! Go now."

Mitchell bade him farewell, exited down the metal steps of the airliner, and walked quickly across the airstrip and into Washington's National Airport.

"Hello!" a familiar voice exclaimed, and Mitchell turned and looked into the face of his old boss, H.R. Leary. He had aged since their last encounter two years before.

Mitchell grinned. "It has been a long time." They did not speak again until they approached a cream-colored prewar Citroën. "A strange vehicle for an undercover car," Mitchell remarked.

"You may be driving an identical make and year. Here are the keys." Leary yawned. "It's best if we speak German. You must practice."

Mitchell fit his long legs uncomfortably into the front seat, accepted a few terse driving pointers, then turned out of the parking lot, with Leary giving him instructions when to move into the heavy traffic flow.

"You must be prepared to drive away in case something goes wrong, because there is a war over there, as Mr. Bernard Baruch has noted. He has named it the 'cold war.' Fighting does not take place in the streets, but by diplomats around the conference table and neo-Nazis in the alleys. But it is a war all the same!"

"One of these years," Mitchell said conversationally, finding his German quite fluent, "I would like to get an assignment in April here in Washington, so that I could see the cherry blossoms in bloom. It is a wonder the trees weren't cut down during the war, considering they were gifts from Japan."

"Turn to the right, over the bridge, at the stop sign," Leary instructed, then paused. "We're not that barbaric. Please keep your eye on the road!" he cautioned.

"I remember the first day of the war," Mitchell said. "Bella Chenovick, the wife of Torgo, our Bohemian farmer in Angel, was shopping at Baker's Mercantile Store. She saw a set of dishes that were made in Japan. Bella, who's one of the sweetest, most nonviolent people imaginable, took each piece out into the street and smashed every last one against the curb. Some of the townspeople thought that she was overreacting, but that night the Bakers took 'inventory.' In the morning, a quarter of their wares had disappeared. My Aunt Letty told me recently that suddenly the store has quite a lot of new Japanese merchandise. Evidently they have trotted that merchandise out again. Don't you think people are funny, Leary?"

"No. Turn left at the crossroads." Leary lighted a cigarette thoughtfully. "In our business nothing is funny. Strange, peculiar, irrational, sometimes hysterical, but never funny. How about your trade?"

Mitchell shook his head. "There are not many laughs to be had in furniture."

"Then you don't belong to the Optimist Club?"

Mitchell smiled grimly. "Only the Kiwanis, which I think is good for business. I go to the First Methodist Church because some of my best customers are Methodists, and I'm a member of the Chamber of Commerce, but the meetings are dull, compared to—this. Yet when this assignment is over, I'll go back to Enid and immerse myself in supervising my shops and taking orders and making contacts, and I won't mind a bit. I've had my fun. I've led my double life. In a way, it is like the old days on the road."

"Don't you have to catch yourself sometimes about making comments? Wasn't it on the tip of your tongue to talk about France when the war came up in conversation?"

Mitchell shook his head. "No, because I was always guarded in my speech, even as a boy. No one in the family was as close-mouthed. In fact, the Herons and the Storys could never keep any secrets. My reluctance to communicate comes about because I lived in a small town where everyone knew everyone else's business. I escaped all of that, if you remember my dossier, because I never came back from the First War for twenty years. When you've lived by your wits for so long, you don't open up easily—even to family members." He paused. "We're in Georgetown. Where do we go?"

"At the second stop sign, turn to the left and park in front of the last house on the right. Is that why you've never married, because you have difficulty sharing?"

"No, but I've finally come to the conclusion that I'm not very sexually oriented. When you've been on the road, there are many ships in the night, but no relationships. Then, also, I don't think that I'm a very tender man." He threw him a quick look. "Are you?"

Leary smiled. "I have four children."

"But that doesn't mean that you're *tender*!"

"I'd never thought about it that way before," Leary replied. "I may not be. I do know that the best operatives that we've had over the long haul have been single. It's always been my theory that a man who's getting it all the time is rather complacent. He eats well, gets fat, and mellows as his children grow up. In the end, he becomes somewhat feminine. He loses his balls."

Mitchell parked the car in front of a three-story townhouse with green shutters and a wrought-iron fence that separated the tree-lined street from the small patch of front lawn. "Well, I hope I haven't lost mine!"

Leary laughed. "Not yet, anyway!"

The doorbell was answered by a stout woman in a cotton housedress.

"You remember Felicia?" Leary asked in English.

"Of course." Mitchell smiled. "You look well."

She laughed. "Fatter, anyway, but thank you. It's a pleasure to see you again. I so seldom work with the same people." She looked at his hair. "The first item on the agenda is a shampoo. You're not nearly gray enough, so we'll add silver. We have to take your photo for a new passport."

Mitchell shook his head in mock concern. "I've always been proud that I entered middle age without a lot of white in my hair. It runs in the family. What do I do when it grows out? Are you going to show me how to apply the dye?"

"You won't be gone that long," Felicia said cheerfully.

"And what happens if I get stuck over there like I did the last time?"

"You won't be," Leary replied suavely. "After all, the hot war is over. Transportation is not difficult now. And this time you'll be going in style—first class on a commercial airline and traveling during the day. Nothing so plebeian as parachuting in at night."

Mitchell gave a mock yawn. "As usual, you're outdoing yourself in giving out information."

H.R. Leary raised his eyebrows. "Do I detect a *soupçon* —as Pierre would say—of sarcasm?"

Felicia patted Leary on the shoulder. "Be nice to him when I give him back to you in an hour and a half." She turned to Mitchell. "Follow me, please." She led him up a curved oak staircase. He caressed the balustrade. "This is lovely work. At home, if my craftsmen were called in to construct a piece like this, the railing would cost twenty-five dollars a running foot, and the hand-turned spindles would be dearer." At the landing, he turned to survey the simply furnished living room below. "All early American antiques," he remarked, "worth a fortune today." He nodded soberly. "They're very similar to those which a friend of ours in Oklahoma, Fontine Dice, ditched into the creek when they hit oil. She replaced all the solid oak furniture with birds-eye maple veneer—which lasted about five years."

"I'd forgotten that you're in the furniture business," Felicia replied. "Let me look at your hands."

He made a little helpless gesture, and she laughed and turned his palms upward. "Thank God," she said, "there are no calluses."

"Of course not," he replied smoothly. "I don't do cabinet work myself. Never have. I'm an order taker. I sit in an office or visit the other stores. I employ craftsmen!"

"Good. Otherwise, we would have had to conscript someone else for the job. Our man can't have the hands of a laborer. He's a gent!"

An hour and a half later, Felicia handed him a hand mirror. Mitchell stared at his reflection in disbelief. "Why didn't you tell me that my hair was going to be *completely* silver? It's a little disconcerting to know what you'll look like in ten or fifteen years. By the way, why are my forehead and scalp so red?"

"That'll fade by tomorrow. Salt-and-pepper brunettes

are difficult to dye. The bleach can be very harsh to the skin."

He nodded. "I was just thinking of that same friend who ditched the furniture. She dyed her hair platinum. The beautician goofed on the chemicals one day, and all of her hair fell out. It took a year for it to grow back. She had to wear a wig." He looked at Felicia. "Mine won't fall out, will it?"

She put her tongue in her cheek. "We'll know by dinnertime."

He laughed. "I have no desire to look like Daddy Warbucks!"

"Oh, I don't know," she kidded back. "I think you'd look rather sexy!" Then she turned serious. "Tomorrow I'll give you a haircut, very close around the temples, with a deep permanent wave on top."

"You're going to roll my hair up on one of those electric thingamabobs?"

"That's primitive. I'll use something very new, called a 'cold wave.' The new cut will give you height." She looked at his waist. "You're also ten pounds overweight. . . ."

"I am *not*!" he retorted. "I'm perfect for my height of six one and a half inches. I weigh a hundred and sixty-five."

She gave him a long, maternal look. "For our purposes, you exceed the limit. Europeans learned to eat differently during the war because food was scarce. Most ended up as vegetarians, whether they liked it or not. Herr Professor Schneider is lean and gaunt—very svelte. You must lose one pound a day for the next ten days, so your new wardrobe can't be fitted until then. Needless to say, you won't be dining on Chateaubriand and chocolate mousse."

"Anything else I should know?" he asked cryptically.

"Do you shave with a safety razor?" When he nodded, she went on quickly. "Pierre will show you how to use a straight-edge." She paused, and then clapped her hands to her mouth. "Damn! I forgot your eyebrows and chest! I either must be getting old, or this job is finally getting to me! I'll tell them to wait dinner—not that it's going to be that much, mind you, but I'll need you for another hour. You must match all over."

He colored. "*All* over?"

She shrugged her shoulders like a soubrette and turned coquettish. "I'll mix the chemical for you, which you can apply in privacy to that part of your anatomy not usually on view!"

"Damn!" he replied and snapped his fingers. "Just when we were getting to the good part!" And Felicia joined in his laughter.

H.R. Leary came into the room. "What's all the levity about?"

"Nothing," Mitchell replied quickly. "How do you like my hair color?"

"Stunning, absolutely stunning!" H.R. Leary pursed his lips.

"Incidentally, why must my body hair be white? Am I to be seen nude? Just what exactly have you planned for me?"

"It's not what you think," Leary replied. "We need a photograph of you at the beach in a swimsuit to place in your wallet. Herr Professor Schneider's only recreation is swimming. That's another reason why you must lose weight."

"You really think of everything, don't you?"

"We try," Leary replied. "We try."

"Actually," Felicia countered, "when you are properly attired, you'll look very much like the respected psycho-analyst that you're supposed to be."

"If there is one thing in this world that I know less about," Mitchell exclaimed, "it's psychiatry! I didn't even know the meaning of the word until a few years ago."

H.R. Leary held up his hand. "Not to worry. You won't be practicing your art. You'll learn a few technical phrases—to drop in idle conversation if need be. People will change the subject quickly enough when you begin to speak about dementia praecox, the id, the libido, schizophrenia, or the Oedipus Complex."

"You make it sound so simple," Mitchell replied tensely. "It won't be, because it never is! Now, may I ask a little more about the assignment?"

"Ask away! Not that I'm inclined to answer inquiries that are meaningless." Leary raised his eyebrows. "But there is no reason that you can't be given some background information."

"What am I to do?"

"It is very simple," H.R. Leary replied in low German. "You are to impersonate a renowned psychiatrist who is to certify that an old man in a hospital is insane." He handed him a newspaper photograph of a distinguished white-haired gentleman wearing horn-rimmed glasses and a homburg. "This is Professor Ludwig Schneider, a renowned pupil of Herr Sigmund Freud. There is a resemblance. . . ."

"Yes, but the goatee!"

H.R. Leary pursed his lips. "This is an old photograph. Fortunately he has since shaved it off, and there is no time for you to grow one anyway. And I do not approve of false appendages. Wigs and beards, even if they have been crafted by a master wigmaker, are inclined to blow off in a wind or become loose. One of our men lost his cover because, during a strenuous bout of lovemaking, he left his sideburns on the pillow. That was in nineteen-thirty-seven. We haven't used false hair since."

"What in the hell was he doing making love in the first place if he was on duty?"

H.R. Leary raised his eyebrows. "Because that was part of the assignment!" He paused and lighted a cigarette, blew out a circle of smoke, and then looked up. "Actually, your mission is simple. You go to Berlin, see the old man, and return. You'll be back in your furniture factory before you can say 'Jack Robinson.' "

"Jack Robinson!" Mitchell said with a grin.

"Now, take a nap," H.R. Leary said. "When you get up you will eat, and then the work really begins."

The *Blue Heron* landed at Newark Airport in a heavy ground fog. Currier and Ives, Luke Three thought, had made one of the smoothest touchdowns he had ever experienced. Not that he flew that often, but he knew a good landing from a bad one. The trip had gone so well that he hoped the rest of the journey to Europe aboard a commercial airliner would be just as magical.

He felt carefree because he was not forced to worry about finding baggage stubs, picking up luggage, or renting a limousine—details within the bailiwick of Jorge, Robert Desmond's extremely capable valet, who could do everything from driving a motorcycle to pressing a pair of trousers to scrambling eggs. Luke smiled to himself. The last time he was in Newark, he had been carrying a sixty-five-pound duffel bag! Jorge was a wiry little man of forty who had been with the Desmond family since he was eighteen. And if Jorge was somewhat formidable, Luke Three realized that instead of one master to humor now, he had two—at least for the length of the European sojourn.

The private landing strip at Newark was also playing host to the *Sacred Cow*, the presidential plane, which was apparently undergoing repairs. Just outside the gate, a new Cadillac limousine was parked; its uniformed driver stood stiffly by the open door. In what seemed like three minutes, Jorge had the luggage stowed away and Robert Desmond and Luke Three ensconced in the back seat, and he himself was sitting very properly in front with the driver.

Luke Three was impressed. "Bob," he said to his elegant companion, "you know I've never been to New

York. I know we're only going to be in town for five days, but I hope there'll be time to see a few landmarks."

Robert Desmond threw him an amused look. "That depends, bub, on what you mean by landmarks. If you are referring to shooting up to the top of the Empire State Building, taking the ferry over to Staten Island so you can pass the Statue of Liberty, or clomping around Greenwich Village, I'd say no." He examined the perfectly pressed pleats in his trousers, "But if you mean shopping on Fifth Avenue, lunching at Voisin, seeing Hildegarde at the Persian Room, or going to a couple of Broadway plays, well, yes, we will be seeing a few of the landmarks."

Luke Three regarded his companion with amazement. "I don't know how I'm going to fit in with all of this," he said, shaking his head. "I haven't had much social experience. When I was going to military school in Tulsa, I dated a little bit, went to a lot of movies, and saw a few stage plays. Sometimes I'd go up to Kansas City when Uncle Clem was playing at the Wyandotte Hotel, but that was about the extent of my social life." He scratched his head. "Then, when I came back to Angel to finish high school and work at the Heron station, the biggest event of the day was to have dinner—excuse me, lunch—at the Red Bird Café across the street."

"Don't worry," Robert Desmond replied, looking out of the window at the distant New York skyline. "You know what fork to use with what course, and you're certainly personable. You'll get by very well indeed—with a few pointers."

"If we go to all those places you mentioned, won't we need girls?"

Robert Desmond sighed. "Don't you have anything else on your mind these days?" Then he continued lightly, "To answer your question, dates will be no problem. There are always a couple of charming young ladies seeking entertainment." He looked at Luke earnestly. "Luke Three, you will discover as you grow older that women, per se, are seldom a problem socially. Personally may be another matter—depending upon the type you attract—but generally speaking, females are readily available to be escorted to topflight restaurants or fancy nightclubs, or more than willing to spend a weekend on a yacht. In a small town like Angel, the supply of girls is necessarily limited, that's why you must set your sights high. Otherwise you'll end up with someone who won't be a credit later on, when you really need someone complementary at your side."

"Well, I'm fairly grown up now, I think, as far as that goes," Luke Three replied testily. "I know the difference between good girls and bad girls."

"Oh, Luke Three, I'm not talking about good and bad! I'm talking about suitable and unsuitable!"

"I'm not an idiot, Bob," Luke Three defended himself. "I've already made one decision. There was a girl back home who wanted me to marry her in the worst way, and I suppose I did lead her on before I went into the service. But when I got back from Okinawa I saw that she was pretty and ambitious, but"—he colored—"she taught me a lot. Still, I couldn't see spending the rest of my life with her." He paused. "She wouldn't fit in with the family."

"Darlene Trune?"

Luke Three looked at Robert Desmond with surprise. "Well, yes. . . . How did you know?"

"Bosley told me about her. He said the Trunes were bound and determined to marry into the Heron family, one way or the other. Her mother had a relationship with your Uncle Mitchell not so long ago."

Luke Three laughed. "Old Belle? No wonder she's always asking about him." He sniffed. "Another thing that decided me, Bob, Belle's no more than fifty, and she's worn out, fat, and funny-looking. It occurred to me that Darlene might turn out the same way."

Robert Desmond nodded. "Genes—like mother, like daughter? That's another thing, Luke Three, the morals of this country are changing. Boys don't need to get married right out of high school or the service, especially if they're going to be traveling in higher circles. Most people get married because they see each other every day. It's called propinquity. Grooms marry housemaids, movie stars marry movie stars, city boys marry city girls, farmers marry farm girls . . ."

Luke Three grinned. "Who should I marry, Bob?"

"*Whom*? Someone suitable."

"How come you haven't found 'someone suitable'?"

Robert Desmond set his jaw in a hard line. His eyes were gray and flinty. "I'm thirty-two years old, Luke Three, and I have very high standards. I've dated some very eligible women, and I have had two long relationships, but I guess you can say that I'm a snob."

Luke Three raised his eyebrows. "You said it, Bob, I didn't."

Robert Desmond ignored the remark and changed the subject. "First we must get you a new wardrobe. While I think it is ridiculous for men to have thirty pieces of luggage without women around, for this trip you'll need four suits, a tuxedo, two hats, and some decent-looking accessories. Also, new underwear." He lighted an English Oval cigarette. "Cotton may be all right for Angel . . ." He threw Luke Three a mocking look. "What *do* you wear?"

"BVD's."

"Not those one-piece jobs?"

"Yep. I missed them when I was in the service. They're more comfortable too, working around the station."

Robert Desmond threw him a long look. "You won't be working around a station in Europe!"

That afternoon Luke Three came out of the Sulka shop two hundred dollars poorer. "But monogrammed silk p.j.'s?" He glanced at Robert Desmond and shook his head. "And a dozen silk ties?"

"You are acting like a country boy in the city for the first time," Robert Desmond retorted, straightening his Windsor-knotted tie. "Didn't you pick up any sophistication when you were in the service?"

"In *Okinawa*?"

"Well, in order to get over there, you must have had weekend passes and furloughs."

"Just a couple of days off here and there. I mostly hung around the USO's, when I wasn't looking for girls. I like to jitterbug."

Robert Desmond coughed delicately. "What dances have you mastered?"

"In Angel we do a kind of modified two-step. I can waltz, but not very well ..." He paused, then brightened. "Darlene Trune taught me to Conga."

"Yes, but"—Robert Desmond coughed again, not so delicately this time—"can you do the basic steps like the fox trot, the samba, the rumba?"

"Hold on"—Luke Three laughed—"we didn't have a dancing school in Angel."

"In Europe, you know, they waltz to the right as well as to the left. I think we better find someone to give you a few lessons. You just might be invited to a party where you have to show off your prowess. There used to be a studio in the Carnegie Hall building run by a Mr. Ayres ..."

Mr. Ayres was tall and thin, and, except for pop-bottle spectacles, looked rather like Arthur Murray. There were three other people besides Luke Three taking the class: a sweet-faced girl, Debbie; a middle-aged woman, Francie, and a sixteen-year-old boy, Gerald. It was a cardinal rule that only first names were used.

"Never look down at your feet!" Mr. Ayres was saying. "Also, 'touch dancing' does not mean to *feel*. Stay a respectable distance from your partner. Men, when you grasp her around the waist, do so very lightly, otherwise you'll leave perspiration stains on her gown. Girls, hold your right palm straight up in his hand. Do not permit your wrist to go limp or you'll look like a wilted lily.

"Remember, until you become accustomed to moving in concert with your partner, remain limber! Only the Virginia reel and the minuet should be performed stiffly." He gave a bored smile, and Luke Three wondered how many thousands of times he had given that same spiel.

"Also," Mr. Ayres was saying, "we'll devote about fifteen minutes to the art of 'dipping,' which has mainly to do with balance and is never wise to attempt if you've had more than two drinks. You could both end up sprawled on the floor."

Luke Three knew all about dipping. He could always tell by one dip if his dancing partner was going to bed with him later or not. If there was pressure in the right places when he bent her back steeply, the evening was destined to end in fireworks. If she remained rigid in his arms, he knew that he would face the important part of the night quite by himself.

The fox trot was the most difficult for Luke Three, and the European waltz the trickiest. The second lesson included the samba, which he found the most appealing dance of all, especially when performed to Clement Story recordings.

At the end of the third class, he found himself dancing with the sweet-faced Debbie, who looked up at him and grinned. "I only enrolled for the samba lessons, but I've been away to a girls' school, and I thought it might be a good idea to brush up all the way around."

Luke nodded, busy counting under his breath. "My coordination is pretty bad," he admitted, "but you're a swell partner."

She looked up at him gratefully, and when the number ended, Mr. Ayres raised his eyebrows and clapped his hands. "Now I'm going to show you men how to cut in smoothly." He sighed with exasperation. "So help me, I've seen men get in altercations, trying to cut in gracefully. Now, girls, do *not* hang on to your partner when a man seeks to cut in, but allow your partner's left hand to slide away from you easily. Now, start the music, please. Luke and Debbie, I'll cut in." He glided over to them. "Come here and help me illustrate, Francie. Notice this is done by counting to three. First we match steps with the other couple. I tap Luke on the right shoulder (*one*), move in quickly (*two*), and grasp Debbie's hand lightly (*three*). Luke, surrender her gracefully and use the same procedure when you take over my position with Francie. Yes, I know it will appear awkward at first. Let's try it once more. Start the recording again, please. Now, *one, two, three*. See how easy it is?"

By the end of the fourth class, Luke Three felt quite confident on the floor, although he still found himself counting under his breath. What would the girls in Angel think about his new expertise? He looked fondly at Debbie as they started the samba again to a new Clement Story recording called "Heaven," and it *was*, he reflected, dancing with her; he loved the way she moved her hips.

"Before we say good-bye," Mr. Ayres said, clapping his hands again, "I suppose I must demonstrate a new dance that you younger people will be expected to know. I hesitate to utter the name of it, but it is sweeping the country." He pursed his lips, and a pained expression came over his delicate features. "It is called"—he sighed theatrically "—the mop!"

The Heron suite at the Sherry Netherlands Hotel in Manhattan was peopled on this Friday morning by a haberdasher, a hatter, a bootmaker, a manicurist, and a barber, plying their trades.

Luke Three lounged on a chair in the center of the room while the barber clipped nonchalantly at his sideburns.

The tailor, who looked rather like an elf, was sitting cross-legged on the floor, adding a crotch piece to a pair of wool trousers and chuckling to himself. It was not often that one of his customers needed more material in that particular area. He glanced appreciatively at Luke Three and thought: And all that money, *too*!

The hatter was adding an inch-high grosgrain band to the crown of a cream-colored Stetson, his needle flying over the wide bow.

The bootmaker was surrounded by footgear of all colors and designs, touting the merits of each pair.

The manicurist, portable tray placed precariously on her lap, was sitting on a stool, giving Luke Three a hand and knuckle massage that was sending chills up and down his spine. He was trying to look casual and was not succeeding, mainly because the manicurist's elbow was resting on his right knee, and he was fearful that the barber's white drape would turn into a tent at any moment. Robert Desmond was seated on the sofa, regarding the proceedings like an indulgent, affluent uncle.

Luke Three tried to concentrate on green meadows, babbling brooks, and snow-capped peaks, but only when the waiter wheeled in an ecru-clothed table with pots of coffee and pastries was he distracted. When the manicurist, a blonde of about twenty-five, departed, she slipped her card up his sleeve and winked.

By eleven, the suite, excepting for Luke Three, Robert Desmond, and several tissue-papered boxes which the efficient Jorge was stacking neatly in the closet, was empty. "What do you suppose," Luke said, sighing contentedly, "the poor people out there are doing right now?"

Robert Desmond shrugged his shoulders in mock concern. "They're wondering what we rich people in here are doing!"

"When the bills start piling in, Dad's going to faint dead away."

"I think not, bub," Robert Desmond replied smoothly. "After all, you obviously can't visit the field officers wearing overalls, a gingham shirt, and work boots. The Heron image must be maintained."

"Yeah? I'm not sure what that is, Bob. Dad's so conservative, the last time he was in Europe he rented a Renault and got lost every time he visited a field office."

"He should have had a private car and driver. I've arranged for a Rolls and a chauffeur for us in London."

"You *have*?"

"Certainly. I went to school at Oxford, you know, and after four years in England, I still wouldn't trust myself on those country roads." He gave him a long look. "There are times to economize and times not to economize. Traveling is difficult enough as it is, without worrying about amenities—especially when everything is tax deductible anyway."

"Well, Dad always says ..." Luke Three brushed a blond forelock back from his forehead.

"He's probably still carrying some of the guilt left over from the family oil strike. Many people who become affluent overnight never really enjoy their money."

Luke Three indicated the room with a wave of his hand. "Oh, I don't know, this place is pretty luxurious, and the Heron plane is not exactly poorsville."

Robert Desmond regarded him paternally. "This suite and the other one in the Beverly Wilshire Hotel in Beverly Hills are *conveniences*. If a customer has to be entertained, then it must be done properly. As far as the *Blue Heron* goes, it merely allows a person to get from one place to another quickly and with as little wear and tear as possible."

"The only one in the family who seems to enjoy himself is Uncle Clement, and he's in show business."

"Which is a great deal different than being in oil.

Perhaps it's because he's made his own fortune." He picked up an appointment book. "We'll have lunch at '21,' some additional shopping this afternoon—you've got to get a new raincoat, it'll be wet in London—an early dinner in the Edwardian Room of the Plaza across the street, and then we can see a play this evening. There's *St. Louis Woman*, a musical, at the Martin Beck Theatre, with Pearl Bailey, or *Born Yesterday*, with Paul Douglas and Judy Holliday.

"Is there something with a lot of—girls?"

Robert Desmond hid his smile with his hand. "In that case, there's only one show in town for us, *Call Me Mister*, not all music, some comedy too, but it does have some beautiful chorines."

"You've seen all of these plays?" Luke Three asked pensively.

"No, but I read the reviews. There are many good straight plays, *The Magnificent Yankee*, and *I Remember Mama*. But tonight *Call Me Mister* is made to order."

"How do we get tickets?"

Robert Desmond laughed. "I have a broker. For a price, he'll get me any show in town."

Luke Three got up, stretched his arms behind his back in a Charles Atlas pose, yawned, and the manicurist's card fell out of his sleeve. Before he could react, Robert Desmond reached down, made a ball out of the card, which he threw across the room, where it landed precisely in the wastebasket. "You won't be needing another manicure. We'll be leaving for London tomorrow."

A look of quick embarrassment flashed across Luke Three's face, and he turned to the window. "I'll probably be in town again and"—he held out his hands behind his back—"she certainly did a good job."

Robert Desmond stood up. "I was trying to be subtle," he said quietly. "Look out the window. What do you see?"

"A lot of big buildings."

"In those big buildings are hundreds of thousands of working girls, mostly from poor families. Most of those females would never go to bed with the Joe on the street, but a great many would go to bed with *you.*"

A patch of crimson crept up from Luke Three's collar as he studied the Central Park West skyline across the park.

"President Truman once said something very pertinent that has a bearing on what I'm saying," Desmond continued. "I'm paraphrasing, but he indicated that the honors and all the folderol that's a part of White House life isn't for *him*, it's for the *presidency*, and that it's always crucial to keep the two separate." He paused meaningfully. "You see, Luke Three, you'll be meeting a great many people who will want to manipulate you in a social or business way. There will be many attractive women who will, if you'll excuse the vulgar street expression, 'drop their panties' for you." He regarded him intently. "It's not that you're not good-looking, but ninety-nine times out of a hundred you'll have to remember that they are going to bed with the Heron name, the fortune, the influence; they are not going to bed with *you*, no matter what you have tucked into your shorts." Then, lest the discussion become heavyhanded, he laughed and waved at the buildings that could be seen through the window. "Besides, Luke Three, even if you tried, one lifetime is too short to screw them all!"

The National Theatre was packed to the peanut gallery. Robert Desmond and Luke Three, dressed in tuxedos, were seated in fourth row center with their dates, Sylvia Richards, in blue chiffon, and Joyce Robbins, in pink net, who had been introduced to them that afternoon by Boz Hendricks, Eastern Manager for the Heron Oil Company. The women would have preferred to see Peggy Wood in *I Remember Mama*, and were, frankly, looking forward to being escorted to the Stork Club after the performance. Sylvia, a thirty-year-old divorcee with blond hair and green eyes, kept casting sidelong glances at Robert Desmond whenever he laughed at servicemen's jokes that were not all that funny. Between musical numbers he occasionally looked at her, wondering absently if she would go to bed with him in the shank of the evening. He decided that it would probably depend upon how much bubbly she consumed. Vintage French champagne could make whores out of virgins!

Luke Three was very conscious of the soft, warm form beside him. When they touched elbows, changing positions in their seats, electric shocks traveled up his arms to his shoulders. It was hell, he concluded, to be hot all the time. Joyce Robbins was not pretty in the same way that Darlene Trune was pretty, but she was striking-looking. Her dark hair was swept up on her head, which gave her a look of sophistication beyond her years. She was nineteen, she had told him in a breathless whisper when he mentioned that they'd like to go nightclubbing later. He was trying to be a man of the world and he was not certain that he was succeeding.

The waiting limousine took them to the Stork Club, which was very crowded and noisy, and the proprietor, a rotund man named Sherman Billingsley, who hailed from Oklahoma, greeted Robert Desmond warmly and, when introduced to Luke Three, whispered in his ear, "I know your daddy."

They were soon seated in a booth upholstered in a plain dark fabric—the Stork Club was not like El Morocco, which featured banquettes covered in zebra skins. Luke Three was disappointed; he had expected more glitter, but Sylvia and Joyce appeared suitably impressed. Robert Desmond ordered a demijohn of Dom Perignon, and when the orchestra started to play a samba, Luke Three asked Joyce to dance. He performed the steps flawlessly but was concentrating on counting so much that he was not having a good time.

"Why are you frowning, Luke?" asked Joyce, looking worshipfully up into his face.

He grinned sheepishly. "Was I? I guess I get that from my dad. He frowns all the time."

Luke was momentarily distracted by a girl in a flame-colored chiffon dress gliding smoothly over the floor, held casually by her escort, a tall, dark, good-looking Mexican. She was his favorite partner from the dancing academy and had mastered perfectly the slightly bored facial expression of a weary debutante. She glanced at him out of the corners of her eyes and winked.

"Hi, Debbie," he said, cutting in, changing partners so smoothly that even Mr. Ayres would have applauded.

Breaking her pose, she laughed and swayed her hips in perfect time to the music. At that moment two flash-bulbs in rapid succession went off in their faces. "I hate being photographed," she whispered fiercely.

"Why should they take our pictures?" Luke asked. "Are you anyone important?"

"No. Are you?"

"No."

At that moment the dark Mexican boldly cut in, and Luke Three thought his technique very rusty.

"That was fun," Joyce said, once again in his arms. "His name is Valdez. He plays tennis."

"*Tony* Valdez?"

"We didn't dance long enough for me to find out! Who is she?"

"Oh, just a girl that I used to whirl around a lot." He chuckled.

"What's so funny?"

"Private joke."

The orchestra segued into a tango, a dance that Luke Three had not mastered. "Let's rest," he said and spirited Joyce back to their table. Robert Desmond was staring straight ahead, his jaw set resolutely, and Luke Three knew that he was angry. When the girls left to go to the powder room, Luke Three remembered to place two fifty-cent pieces on the table so that they would have tips for the attendant.

"That was a very foolish thing you did," Robert Desmond exclaimed furiously as soon as the girls were out of earshot.

"You told me I was to give them money for the powder room woman!"

"No, knucklehead, I meant out there on the floor!"

"I didn't stumble once, and it's a very intricate dance. I counted under my breath all the time."

"My God, you're dense tonight!" Robert Desmond exclaimed, his anger making his Oxford accent even more clipped. "It'll be in all the newspapers tomorrow, you know that, of course."

"What do you mean?"

"Where did you meet her?"

"Who?" He paused. "Oh, you mean Debbie?"

Robert Desmond snubbed out his English Oval cigarette, punctuating every word. "Yes, *Deborah Overstreet.* Who else?"

"In dancing class, if it's any of your business. Don't you think she's cute?"

"Cute? You mean you don't know who she is? Jesus Christ, Luke Three, you were dancing with the daughter of the Chairman of the Board of Standard Oil of New Jersey!"

Luke Three laughed as the girls returned to the table, but managed to quiet himself.

"What's so hilarious?" Joyce asked. "Who told a funny?"

Robert Desmond glared at Luke Three. "The joke, Joyce, is on your friend here, only he doesn't know it." He turned to Sylvia. "Shall we dance?"

It was the last number of the set, a fox trot, and when they returned, Desmond placed a folded-up bill on the table. "Shall we go?" he asked tersely. Upon reaching the hatcheck stand, he excused himself. "I'll meet you out front."

It took a few moments for the doorman to get the attention of their limousine driver, parked down the street, and by the time the girls and Luke were ensconced in the back seat, Robert Desmond had rejoined the group. The girls were taken home first; Sylvia lived on Fifty-second Street, and Joyce on Eighty-fifth, and when Luke Three came back to the car after opening Joyce's apartment door for her, Robert Desmond thrust a small envelope at him. "Here they are. I saved your ass."

"What is this? What do you mean?"

"I bought the photographic negatives."

"Gee, that was nice of you, Bob," Luke Three said appreciatively. "I'll have them developed and put in my album."

Robert Desmond looked at him incredulously. "Are you so naive, so dumb, that you don't know what you did?" He hit his fists together. "Don't you realize that if those photos of you dancing with Deborah Overstreet were published, it would immediately start a dangerous speculation that Standard Oil was interested in buying out Heron?"

"I didn't even know who she was!"

"That's not the point," Desmond expostulated. "Do I have to draw you a picture? Being photographed in the Stork Club is tantamount to announcing an engagement. If you were dating, it must mean that you had been introduced by your parents. After all, you live in Oklahoma and she lives in New York. The scandal rags would love it, and strange things would be happening to the oil issues on the stock exchange."

"Oh, my God." Luke frowned. "I never realized that a little thing like ..."

"It's time you behaved more responsibly, bub. You are no longer a private person when you travel in these leagues." Desmond quieted down and was no longer angry. "Besides, you spoiled a perfectly great evening." He grinned in spite of himself. "If it wasn't for you, I would now probably be bedding the delectable Sylvia."

"Talk about me lousing up *your* evening, Bob! If it weren't for you, I *know* that I'd be in bed with Joyce right now."

"How are you so certain?"

"Because," Luke said with a slow smile, "she was playing with me under the table all evening."

6

Up and Away

Mitchell sat down at the beautifully appointed table, set in the European manner.

Eschewing the American custom of changing forks from hand to hand, delicately dabbing at his mouth with a napkin, and dipping the cold borsch *away* from himself, he ate his sparse meal European style. Besides the first course, he slowly chewed one ounce of cottage cheese, one slice of tomato, four soda crackers, and one-half an apple. Leary sat opposite and sipped a glass of wine. "I will eat later," he said smoothly.

"A big salad with Roquefort dressing, a rare steak, baked potato, hot rolls with plenty of butter, and lemon meringue pie. With ice cream for dessert?"

Leary was not amused. "Don't torture yourself. It's too early in the game. By next week you will be the most miserable man alive—consumed with nothing but thoughts of food." He spoke slowly because his German did not come back to him easily.

"Possibly," Mitchell replied laconically, then looked up, soda cracker in hand. "Why, may I ask, am I to certify that old man insane? Or is it any of my business?" When he received no reply, he asked, "Is that all I have to do?"

Leary nodded.

"But why doesn't the real Professor Schneider accommodate you?"

"Because," Leary replied, "he wouldn't do it!"

A light dawned. "You mean because the old man still has all of his marbles?"

"Exactly."

"Can't you tell me anything more?"

"Well, you have to know certain things, I suppose." Leary replied grudgingly, patting his white crew cut. "For instance, the old man, whom I should now think we can identify as Herr Leopold Steinmetz, is in a hospital recovering from a severe case of pneumonia, which, incidentally, he caught in a drafty cell. He will be released soon and taken to a remote security prison; that is, if he does not die."

"What happens if he does kick off?"

"The mission will be aborted, and you'll come back, never having impersonated the famed Herr Professor."

"But where is the good doctor while I'm doing the certification?"

"In the first place, he's not good. He's a neo-Nazi." H.R. Leary cleared his throat. "He knows nothing of his summons to the Berlin Hospital because we ... intercepted the letter."

"But he could find out in other ways also." Mitchell was troubled. "There could be other letters, a telephone call, a friend visiting from Berlin. I will feel very uncomfortable knowing that he is free while I am impersonating him."

"I appreciate and admire your professional concern, but there have been no letters, or telephone calls, or visitors." Leary coughed lightly behind his palm. "We have a receptionist in his office. Besides, these trips are routine, no big deal. As to his being free, if it would make you feel better, while you are on the mission he will be sleeping rather later than usual, courtesy of a bit of magic powder placed in his schnapps the night before. You will be in and out of the hospital before he wakes up." Leary lighted a cigarette and puffed energetically. "But actually, these little details are only to make us happy. The Herr Doctor will probably never realize that he was supposed to make the journey. If he is called back to the hospital, it is unlikely that they would remember him that well. Berlin is in chaos. Remember it was not long ago that there was fighting in the streets."

"The payment," Mitchell cried, "the payment."

Leary smiled softly. "The good receptionist will simply make the deposit in the Herr Doctor's account. Do you think we are amateurs? One mission, and you . . ."

Mitchell finished his soda cracker. "I'm sorry, H. R."

Leary looked at him over his spectacles, "But with all the red tape, and the lack of communication, it will take time for even the most brilliant official to put two and two together and come up with twenty-four—which they must, in order to piece the whole thing together." He paused. "There are times when I really appreciate bureaucracy."

"I understand about Steinmetz, and I don't understatnd." Mitchell took a sip of black coffee.

"If it isn't clear to you, with all the clues I've given you, then it can't be clear to them either! Very simply, the story's this: The old Jew has first-hand information about a Nazi concentration camp that must be given publicly.

We think he was sent to prison so that he cannot testify in Nuremberg. Fortunately, he contracted pneumonia and was sent to the hospital. If we have him declared insane, he'll be transferred to an asylum. It'll be easier to spring him from there than from the maximum-security prison."

"But there must be pieces still missing in the puzzle."

"Of course!"

"Tell me, then," Mitchell asked, his voice tinged with sarcasm, "if it's not a state secret, what prompted the Herr Professor's visit?"

"One of the night nurses, who is one of us, is actually a skilled psychiatrist. She's been instructing the old man in certain behavioral patterns so other hospital personnel have reported that the old Jew is mentally slipping away and is becoming no more than a vegetable."

"All of this is very convoluted!" Mitchell exclaimed. "So much plot and so few characters."

Leary nodded. "These things always are. If you men in the field knew all of the ramifications every time you were sent on a mission, you'd be so squashy mentally, your 'performances' would be affected. You'd blow your cover. We tell each person only when he or she fits into the immediate design, but not *how* or *why*! The final outcome is unimportant to *you*—and I'm speaking collectively."

His voice became impatient. "The only reason I'm disclosing so much of this plot to you—and there are points, believe you me, that do not concern you—is that in order to undertake this job, you've got to know the background. But once you examine the old Jew and sign the Herr Professor Doctor's name to the certification, you can go back to the airport for your flight back to Vienna and then home."

"Is it important that I come back immediately?"

Leary's eyes narrowed. "What do you mean, *immediately*?"

"If it wouldn't screw up the assignment, I'd like to stay in France for a while, unless I have to be debriefed."

"A few hours after you leave Berlin, the old Jew will be safe at the asylum. There won't be anything to tell us that we don't already know." He paused, "But as far as you taking a Grand Tour at our expense, that's not possible. It's not in the budget."

Mitchell scowled. "Naturally I'd pay my own way! All that would be required is changing my return flights."

Leary shook his head. "You don't know the red tape I'll have to go through to allow you even a week in France."

"Will you let me have that week?"

Leary considered the question for a long moment, then brightened. "Oh, hell, why not? We'll be done with you."

"Thank you."

Leary ignored the remark. "Now that you've had your superb no-calorie dinner, we have things to do. Work more on your accent. Thank God the Herr Professor is a Berliner, and his accent is strong and harsh, like yours."

After having read German aloud all afternoon, Mitchell padded into the tiny library on the second floor. In an antique oak lawyer's glassed-in bookcase that would have done his father proud, he found an old, uncut copy of *Carl Jung versus Sigmund Freud*, and he decided to take these two brilliant men, who had started out as friends and ended up enemies, along to bed with him.

Mitchell was very hungry. He looked at the grapefruit sections in front of him and the cup of black coffee. How he missed Mrs. Briggs' bacon, eggs, and toast!

Felicia sat down opposite him at the table. "When did you have your left eyetooth capped?" she asked by way of a greeting.

He had trained himself not to be surprised at any

question. "A year ago. A dentist friend of my brother's in Oklahoma City did the job. Most people don't even realize it's a falsie." He raised his eyebrows. "And, for what it cost me, it *should* be undetectable."

"He matched the color of your teeth perfectly," she said. "In fact, too perfectly."

"What do you mean?"

"The Herr Professor had a gum problem, probably caused from poor nutrition during the war, and a couple of years ago had four of his front teeth removed and replaced with a bridge. Good porcelain was hard to come by during those times, and he ended up with slightly yellowed teeth. This morning we will send you to a dentist who will take an impression of your mouth. He will design very thin removable porcelain caps to fit over your own teeth. They'll be ready tomorrow morning. You must wear them from now until your assignment is over, so your speech patterns won't be affected. You won't be able to eat steak, corn on the cob, or even a hamburger—nothing chewy, even a brownie—until you become accustomed to them. The dentist will show you how to glue them on—which should be done every day. They are very easy to swallow."

"With a diet like this, you won't have to worry about me losing my caps! May I have another cup of coffee?"

"The pot is always on the stove. You can drink as much as you like." The doorbell rang and she excused herself and a moment later brought Pierre into the room. "Good morning, Herr Professor," he said in German. "How are you?"

"Hungry."

Pierre placed a small bottle of capsules on the table. "Take two, one half-hour before eating," he announced triumphantly. "This is a substance that swells up and fools the stomach into believing it is digesting a seven-course meal." He paused and smoothed his mustaches. "I feel very good today, *mon cher.* I have film to show you. We were fortunate enough to procure—at a very great expense, I might add—very rare footage of the real Herr Professor Schneider. In nineteen-forty-three he won an award from an academy in Vienna, which was filmed for their archives." He beamed and brought his hands together in a prayerful attitude. "This mission is truly rubbed with gold. Usually we have very little to go upon except intuition, which is often right, but also often wrong! Your job will be easier because you can, so to speak, look at and hear yourself!"

Later, Mitchell sat in the darkened committee room and viewed the grainy, badly scratched film. The camera had been set directly in front of the podium so that the audience could not be seen, only heard, and there was a noisy crackling on the soundtrack.

Mitchell studied the man's face. They did not actually resemble each other, yet with silvered hair, hornrimmed glasses, and false teeth—Felicia was right, he could pass for him. The Herr Professor's dental work was very bad, so bad that Mitchell wondered if someone was getting even with him by turning out such poor work.

The film was run a second time, and Mitchell paid close attention to the man's mannerisms. There was a certain patronizing graciousness, but the smile was reserved, the voice flat. He kept his mouth half-closed as he spoke, and his eyes were not as large as Mitchell's. When he walked away from the camera there was a stiffness about his shoulders, spine, and thighs.

Mitchell stood beside the screen and copied the movements of his nemesis the third time the film was run. "I can't get his *walk*," he complained.

"I think, Herr Professor, it would be simpler," Pierre suggested, "if you imagine there is a folded-up umbrella up your anus that might be opened at any moment!"

Mitchell guffawed. "That's graphic enough!" He straightened his back, arched his neck, brought his buttocks snugly together, his scrotum tightened, and he took a few guarded steps.

Pierre clapped his hands. "You've got it perfectly." He paused. "Now we've got to work on your facial expression. Did you notice that even in his acceptance speech, when he's obviously trying to be civilized, his arrogance comes through? It might help if you regard everyone as a dunce. You are the Herr Doktor, the Herr Professor, and you have worked with both Freud and Jung, and there is very little, in your opinion, that you do not know."

Pierre paused. "I have met, during my career, a few psychoanalysts, and they are, by and large, men of wit and compassion. There is almost always a certain delicacy about them."

"Of course, they can be very understanding, because they are paid to be understanding!" Mitchell retorted.

Pierre nodded. "But Herr Professor Schneider sees very few patients anymore. He lectures and consults and writes books. The war, in that respect, has played havoc with his career. Now, I suppose, he will be widely published in English-speaking countries and will probably become a famous man. I am certain, even at this stage of his career, he would think it is quite beneath him to fly to Berlin to certify an old Jew. Please run the film again, Felicia."

Mitchell put on a pair of hornrimmed spectacles, and his silver hair shone. He stood beside the screen and spoke and postured as the closeup of the man spoke and postured. A chill ran up and down Pierre's spine. This was an uncanny experience. It was as if he were seeing twin performers, a giant one on a screen and a small one, giving the same inflections in speech and the same language of the body. His admiration for Mitchell grew. The man was not only a mimic, but a "quick study" as well. After hearing the speech only three times, he had memorized the text completely. Pierre glanced back at Felicia. She was standing at the projection machine, her eyes fixed on Mitchell, completely overcome by the eloquence of his performance. The last footage of film flipped around and around on the reel, bringing her back to reality. She switched off the machine and turned on the lights.

Pierre came up to Mitchell and embraced him. "Exactly right!" he said enthusiastically.

"Please take your hands off me," Mitchell replied icily, still in character. "I dislike being touched." He narrowed his eyes characteristically; his flat nasal voice rang out. "Besides, your fingernails are filthy. I should think that a man of your eminent position could certainly afford a manicure. I suppose that your toenails are also in the same disgusting condition. I will give you the name of my personal pedicurist." Then Mitchell broke character and began to chortle, proud of his joke.

Pierre and Felicia joined in the merriment. "You really should become an actor!" Felicia exclaimed.

"No," he replied, "I'd be extremely limited, but this Herr Professor is such an ass." He turned to Felicia. "Did you notice that he wears *nail polish*?"

She looked guilty. "No, I didn't."

Mitchell once again became Herr Professor Schneider. "Then what are you doing in this job?" His lip curled. "A detail like that should have caught your eye immediately. For that slip-up, Fräulein, which could have aborted the entire mission, you shall have fifty lashes administered to the most tender portion of your generous bottom when the sun rises over the Leipzigerstrasse tomorrow morning!"

Leary, who had stood at the door watching the performance, coughed delicately. "Have your fun now, Mitchell, and you too, Pierre and Felicia, because we must go back to work. I have more film."

Mitchell laughed, happy with himself. "Lana Turner or Jane Russell?"

"I wish!" Leary replied soberly. "No, we are going to see films of the death of a great city. Captured Nazi films, showing the destruction of Berlin."

Felicia threaded up the projector with the reel of film that Leary had brought, and they all fell silent as she lowered the lights.

Everywhere the camera turned, there was devastation. Some streets, especially those surrounding the Reichstag, were completely leveled; everywhere buildings were reduced to rubble, leaving gaping holes in the street. Railway stations were in stages of rebuilding and various other constructions were under way, but Berlin had obviously been ruined.

"I can't recognize anything!" Mitchell cried. "It could be any bombed city."

Leary nodded in agreement. "Some of these scenes are a few months old, but none have been shown in movie theaters." He indicated a map on the screen. "Now, as you know, Berlin is completely surrounded by the Soviet-controlled East Germany, but the city itself is divided into two sectors. The Soviet Zone includes most of the downtown area, and the Western Zone has three commanders, American, French, and British."

Mitchell drew in his breath. "Somehow I did not realize that Berlin is, in reality, a trapped city."

Leary nodded. "Yes, but there are entry points, accessible to the West, of course, and three air corridors, Frankfurt, Hanover, and Hamburg, as well. You will be arriving at Tempelhof Airport from Frankfurt. The hospital, or what's left of it, is located near Bernauerstrasse on the other side of Berlin."

There was an aerial shot of the city which revealed utter devastation. He switched off the projector. "It's a depressing mess, isn't it?" He turned on the light, then sat down again beside Mitchell. "I don't like to send you in there, but one thing, your job is fairly clean-cut. You will have protection, not obvious, of course, but the

American sector is under good control. You must never be frightened, no matter what happens."

The little tailor off Connecticut Avenue had performed admirably, Mitchell thought as he turned to the right and to the left in front of the mirror. The man had accentuated his new thinness by sculpturing the shoulders of the suit, narrowing the lapels, and bringing in the rib cage in European style. The outfit would look out of place in Enid, but not in a cosmopolitan city like Washington. Mitchell arranged the deep wave in his hair that gave him added height, checked the heels of his new shoes that also added an extra inch of stature. Bending over the mirrored sink, he adjusted the slightly yellow tooth caps and ran his tongue over the now familiar surface. He polished the window glass in his tortoise-shell frames and placed the bows resolutely behind his ears. He took a breath and stood back to examine his reflection in the glass. His posture was wrong. He straightened his back, drew his buttocks together, and smiled at himself superciliously.

At the top of the stairs, he called out in the Herr Professor's flat voice, "Pierre, if you continue to procrastinate further, we will most certainly miss the airplane. And my luggage? Is it in the automobile? And my briefcase?"

Pierre came in from the kitchen. *"Ja, Herr Professor,"* he replied, going along with the game, but appraising Mitchell's appearance closely. "All is in readiness for your departure."

"Excellent, *mein Herr.*" Mitchell replied peevishly, still in character. "I would not like to think that another example of your stupidity has delayed us even more!" He stiffly came down the stairs, examining his highly polished fingernails, which Felicia had filed into perfect ovals. Pierre handed him a gray homburg with matching suede gloves. Mitchell narrowed his eyes. "I suppose that you've forgotten to fill the automobile with petrol again?"

"Nein, Herr Professor," Pierre answered, assuming the role of a subordinate and presenting him with a brown packet. "Here is your passport; Deutschmarks; International driver's license; wallet, complete with pictures of your mother and father, and a photograph of you at the seashore; a platinum wristwatch; a diamond ring; and last, but not least, a sterling silver toothpick."

"Have you forgotten nothing?" Mitchell asked in a bored tone.

"Nein, Herr Professor."

"How about a photograph of my sweetheart?"

Pierre gave him a long look, disappeared into the kitchen, and returned a moment later with a wallet-sized photograph. "Put this in your billfold; it will very nicely suffice, but we must remember to return the snap to Felicia."

Mitchell glanced at the picture. His shoulders slumped. A look of complete surprise took away the last vestiges of his impersonation of Herr Professor Schneider. The photograph showed a sixteen-year-old blond boy smiling innocently into the camera.

7

London Bridge is Falling Down

The street was damp and misty, but instead of feeling depressed, Luke Three sniffed the air appreciatively.

"This is the way that London always looks in the Sherlock Holmes movies," he exclaimed as Robert Desmond and he got out of the limousine in front of the Savoy Hotel. "I keep expecting Dr. Watson to walk out of the fog."

Robert Desmond looked about with concern. "Let's hope this pea soup clears up by teatime, because we have to go down to Bainbridge House to the Huxley-Drummonds."

Luke Three made a face. "*Tea?*"

"Tea is different here than back home," Desmond explained patiently. "It's always served at four o'clock. It is what I expect you'd call a 'snack' in Angel. There will be sandwiches and pastries. Sometimes the food is quite substantial. That's why the English have dinner so late. That's also why many are so plump. They go to bed on a full stomach."

They crossed the impressive paneled lobby, teeming with an international crowd. A group of men in dark suits, wearing bright red fezzes, were speaking to an Arab diplomat in robes, and a group of Western-dressed

Chinese tourists were jabbering in what sounded like Pekinese; there was a smattering of the usual business-men, dowagers in out-of-style prewar clothing, and several grim-faced, well-behaved children. A group of teenagers surrounded a tall gentleman by the dining room. Luke Three's eyes popped open. "That's Michael Wilding!"

"Who?"

"The English movie star. Aren't we going to sign in?" Luke Three asked, looking anxiously toward the desk.

"Jorge will take care of the formalities. We're what is referred to as 'pre-registered.' "

"Say, Bob"—Luke Three sighed, as if overcome by the luxury of the place—"this is really the ritz!"

"No, Luke Three," Robert Desmond retorted laconically, "it's the *Savoy*."

The limousine glided to a stop before Number 14 Bentley Square; Bainbridge was a three-story house opposite a wrought-iron fence that surrounded a small park in front. Robert Desmond, in a smart gray raincoat, and Luke Three, in a new tan trenchcoat that he had purchased at Abercrombie and Fitch in New York, walked up the steps to the huge double front door. The fog had turned to mist, and the old house looked ghostly. "I feel exactly like Humphrey Bogart," Luke Three said, turning up the collar to his trenchcoat and throwing a menacing look at an amused Robert Desmond.

The door was opened by a beetle-browed butler, who took their wraps. "Follow me, please," he said, taking their cards. He led them through a massive foyer that featured a winding staircase to the left, and into the library on the right, in which a fire burned brightly on the grate.

"Mr. Luke Heron and Mr. Robert Desmond," the butler said unctuously. The ceilings were so high that his voice echoed, creating an eerie feeling that made the room seem even more cavernous.

A tall, beautifully dressed dark-haired woman of about forty came forward with outstretched hands. "Welcome to Bainbridge House," she said graciously. "I'm Sheila, and this is my husband, Eric."

Luke Three nodded politely. "Good afternoon, Lady Sheila," he said as he had been coached to do, and managed not to burst out laughing. The customs of English aristocracy, which Robert Desmond had drummed into him, seemed the stuff out of which movies were made and had nothing to do with real life. Now he was finding that there were actually people who talked that way.

"How do you do, Sir Eric." Robert Desmond smiled thinly, and they shook hands.

Sir Eric Huxley-Drummond was a big man, with broad shoulders and a barrel chest, which he puffed out like a pigeon when he shook Luke Three's hand. "Young man," he said cordially, "you are the second-generation Heron who's been at Bainbridge. Your grandparents lived here for several months before World War One was declared, and they came back for a visit in nineteen-twenty-seven or nineteen-twenty-eight. The first time, I was away in boarding school in Switzerland, and the second time, I was in India, so I did not meet them, but my mother and father said they were capital."

"I didn't know that," Luke Three replied, looking at the acres of books on the shelves. "Your house is very grand."

Sir Eric chuckled. "I don't think they thought so! In those days the old place was dark and gloomy. I hated it as a child. We suffered bomb damage to the left wing during the war, and when I inherited the old place, Sheila brought in decorators who draped everything from the fourth-floor turret to the basement." He pursed his lips. "It is quite livable, except for the plumbing, which is abominable."

The butler wheeled in a huge silver-and-glass tea cart.

"Miss Ardith will be down in a moment," he said. "She decided not to go out this afternoon, after all."

"Good," Lady Sheila replied, looking out of the window, "it is nasty out." She turned to her guests. "I am so sorry we can't offer you better weather. We've had a change of seasons since the buzz bombings. Perhaps all that smoke and debris affected the atmosphere, somehow."

"Nonsense, my dear," Sir Eric expostulated, and chuckled. "We've always had perfectly dreadful weather, but it did come in handy during the blitz when the bombers flew over. The bombardiers couldn't make out the landmark targets. Hitler was so furious that he had the V-2 developed, which had no proper guidance systems. The Germans just pointed them toward London."

He paused and opened his mouth in a grimace, looking somewhat like Theodore Roosevelt in the history-book pictures, Luke Three thought. "Sorry about the war talk, I don't know how we got on the subject." He turned. "Oh, hello, my dear." He embraced a tall, tawny-haired girl with a spectacular figure who was standing on the threshold of the library. "I'd like to introduce our daughter, Ardith. This is Luke Heron, the Third, and, of course you know Robert Desmond."

They shook hands, and it occurred to Luke Three that Ardith was very pretty in a different sort of way than any American girl that he had ever met. She had very high cheekbones, but they were finely sculptured, not the high, flat-bone structure Uncle Clément's Indian heritage had passed on to him. Her complexion was as fine as the ivory China poppies that his grandmother grew with such pride and care. Her lips were generous, and her eyes held a bit of devilment, when she replied, "Very well, thank you," to his question of "How do you do?" He saw that although her comment escaped Lady Sheila and Sir Eric, it was not lost on Robert Desmond, who looked quite smug.

"May I serve tea?" Lady Sheila asked, presiding at the silver service that bore the ornate family coat of arms.

Luke sipped the warm brew appreciatively and took several tiny cakes that were filled with raspberry jam. "Aren't they messy?" Ardith remarked, sitting beside him on the down-filled sofa. She handed him an extra napkin. "I sometimes think that cook squirts them to overflowing out of spite, because they're our favorites. She hates to make them with a passion." She threw him a sidelong glance. "Is this your first trip to Great Britain?"

He nodded, dabbing his chin with the napkin, noticing that Ardith and he were approximately the same age. "Yes. We have to visit the field office tomorrow."

"Oh!" she exclaimed. "Daddy will take you over in the morning. There's nothing much to see. Perhaps, you'd like to do a bit of sightseeing tomorrow afternoon?"

"I've got to go along with protocol," Luke hedged. "I may not be able to do some of the things I'd like to do on this trip. Mr. Desmond is more or less in charge."

Ardith lowered her voice and spoke conspiritorially. "I'll speak to Daddy. He'll have stacks of reports on Heron British to go over with Bob that shouldn't involve you. There are some things you've just got to see in London, although Piccadilly Circus is still dark, and there's not much gaiety because of economic problems. I'm a good guide, even if I do say so myself." She paused. "Do you like to dance? They have a new underground place in Soho that's very hot at the moment, called The Four Seasons. It's very—bohemian."

Luke Three thought about Bella and Torgo, but he was certain that she wasn't referring to anything ethnic.

And he was right. The Four Seasons had formerly been a huge warehouse. Each of the four floors was decorated differently—as a different season. The ground floor was Summer, painted in yellow and green; the second was Spring, lavender and red; the third was

Autumn, orange and gold; the fourth was Winter, blue and white. They decided to begin the evening with Summer and took a small table in the corner located under a false weeping willow tree.

"What would you like to drink?" Luke Three asked.

"Oh, something terribly American."

"I wonder if the bartender knows how to make stingers?"

"Do they really have a *sting*?"

"Some people think so." Luke Three felt grown up and worldly wise. "They're made with white crème de menthe and brandy," he explained.

"Sounds positively obscene."

"It is." He gave the order to the waiter, who didn't turn a hair. "I guess we're in—like Flynn," Luke Three remarked, when the waiter had left.

"Oh, I think most of the bartenders know how to make all the American drinks from the GI's who were stationed here during the war," Ardith said with a slightly superior air. "They even began icing the beer for them."

The combo was playing jazz, and the music grew frantic with the wail of a trombone, which the bass violist put down his instrument to play. Luke Three and Ardith sipped their drinks and watched the crowd of youthful jazz addicts. After a half-hour, she pressed his arm. "Let's try Autumn, they feature swing up there."

He paid for the drinks, slowly counting out the English notes. Although Robert Desmond had apprised him of the current rate of exchange and they had completed a couple of mock transactions so that he would be more familiar with the currency, Luke Three did not want to make a mistake. He took her hand, and they climbed up the curved stairs to the third floor.

"This place used to be the center for Red Cross activities, so there is still a disinfectant smell on the stairs," she explained, turning around to look down into his face.

He pressed her hand. "All I'm aware of at the moment is your scent," he replied. "What is it?"

"Something called *Fleur*; it's from Belgium."

Autumn, they discovered, was even more crowded than Summer. The slightly larger dance floor was worked into a clearing of spectacularly colored fake bushes. The waiter found a table near the center of the room, but not before Luke Three pressed a five-pound note into his palm. It was a great deal of money for a tip, he realized, but the remainder of his pound notes had paid the check below. Besides, Ardith was proving to be so cooperative that even if he spent what would be a week's salary at the Heron station in Angel, the evening was a good value, he decided. The decor alone was worth more than he had in his pockets. They ordered stingers again, and when the music started, he led her confidently onto the dance floor. After three swing numbers in succession, they returned to their table and sipped the drinks, and when the waiter remarked that the combo in Winter played everything from ragtime to boogie, they went upstairs.

For another five-pound note, the waiter cleared a table on the rim of the dance floor. Suddenly the stark white walls lighted up in moving rainbow hues, in a perfect reproduction of the aurora borealis. The atmosphere became warm and intimate, establishing a romantic mood that neither Summer nor Autumn had encouraged. Luke Three held Ardith's hand and looked into her eyes, and suddenly felt of surge of affection for her—the same feeling that he always experienced when he looked at Darlene Trune.

The combo, which was very loud, began a languid samba. "Shall we?" Luke Three asked.

"What is it?"

"I'll show you," Luke Three replied authoritatively. "It's from South America. There's nothing to it, but the woman must do all the work." He guided her to the crowded floor and demonstrated the footwork. "It's really simple. Watch how that lady over there moves her hips."

Ardith caught on immediately and was soon sambaing smoothly. "This is fun," she said, swaying her hips to the sensuous-sounding music, and suddenly Luke Three realized that he was unexpectedly having a good time. He felt very special somehow, in the outlandishly decorated atmosphere, and he was certainly complimented by the beautiful, responsive girl in his arms. Was she regarding him in a different light because he was an American? Was that why she was intrigued? He frowned; then a peculiar thought struck him. Was she merely being nice to him because Sir Eric worked for him?

"Why are you frowning?" she asked laughingly.

"Was I? It's a family trait. My dad is the champion frowner of all time."

She giggled, and when the samba switched to a two-step, she came up close to him; the heat of her body filtered through the thin material of her dress. He pulled away slightly because he felt himself becoming aroused, but when another couple brushed by them, she pressed her breasts lightly against his chest. He drew back again.

The tiny dance floor was now becoming crowded as men and women in evening clothes, obviously the after-theater crowd, came onto the dance floor to pass time until tables were available. Luke Three felt very warm and uncomfortable as Ardith and he were forced to draw together in what was actually a close embrace. A thousand thoughts crossed his mind. He liked her very much, but he had to remember his position. He obviously could not take her back to the Savoy because of Robert Desmond, and she could not invite him to Bainbridge because of her parents. They had taken a taxi to the nightclub; at home, in the privacy of his car, he could have operated with accustomed grace. But where could one go in London?

He managed to keep in step, and then decided to find out if she was serious or merely teasing him. He took a deep breath, and as the music ended he leaned her backward in a deep dip, placing himself firmly against her mound of Venus.

"You're a marvelous dancer," she said matter-of-factly as he smoothly brought her up out of the dip.

"Thank you," he replied, somehow managing not to shout his happiness on this night of nights. "Shall we sit down"—he kept his voice low and intimate—"and order another stinger?"

"I don't know if I should." She smiled. "I'm already feeling a bit tiddly."

"Shall we go for a walk, then?"

"Not in this district. But there's a lovely park across from Bainbridge that's secure." She smiled softly and brought her hand to his cheek in an affectionate gesture. "The jasmine will be in bloom."

"I have some under my window in Angel."

"Angel?"

"My home town in Oklahoma."

"It sounds enchanting."

"The jasmine is, but Angel isn't!" he fired back. "It's just a prairie town—with one main street."

"Dusty?"

"Oh, not particularly." He glanced at her. "That seems a funny question."

"I've read about the Dust Bowl in books," she answered.

"Oh, I see. Well, Ardith, the Dust Bowl is located in an area called the Panhandle. We call it that," he explained, because Oklahoma is shaped like a pot or a pan, with a long handle. Before it was given that nickname, they called it No Man's Land. Both Oklahoma and Texas claimed it."

"I've read about the Okies."

He held his breath a moment. If she went on, she would spoil what eroticism had been created. "That name was made famous by John Steinbeck in *The Grapes of Wrath*," he explained quickly. "Those were people from all over the Midwest—not only Oklahomans—who took off for California during the thirties, in old cars and trucks loaded down with all kinds of furniture and appliances. There was no money in America during the depression."

She gave him a long look. "Did I make a gaffe?"

"A *gaffe*?"

"You know, a booboo?"

"Well, not exactly, Ardith," he explained, "but we people from Oklahoma are sensitive about being called Okies. Many Californians called us white trash."

"I *am* sorry, Luke Three." Her eyes were concerned. "I didn't mean to infer ... We don't think anything about being called Londoners."

"How about *Limeys*?"

She swallowed quickly. "I see what you mean!"

"Do you want another drink?"

"I don't think I should. Do you?"

"Shall we leave?" And when she nodded, he called the waiter, who gave him the check. He took her arm, and they made their way through the mass of tables to the stairs.

"I'll go to the loo and be back in a moment," she said with a smile, and, seeing his blank look, whispered in his ear, "That's the bathroom."

He took the opportunity to do the same, although he had something more important to accomplish than a call of nature. He stood over the washbasin and carefully removed the tinfoil wrapping from a rolled-up latex protector, which had been sequestered in his wallet for six months. He placed the article in his right sock, where it could be removed easily and without fanfare. He had perfected this strategy because there was always a fumbling moment of embarrassment at the crucial time, which could shatter the most romantic mood.

They met at the cashier's table, and by the time they had walked down four flights of steps, with the effect of the stingers and the rapid descent, they paused for breath. He leaned her back against the doorframe and kissed her lightly on the lips.

Outside, Michael Wilding was getting out of a limousine at the curb, and flashbulbs were going off everywhere. The doorman whistled down a hack, and they were soon on their way to Bainbridge Park. While they sat very close together in the back seat, Luke Three thought the ride would have been far more romantic had the taxi not needed a new axle. He also discovered, as they bumped along the street, that the vehicle could also use a new muffler, a lube job, and, from the pungent odor arising from the floorboards, an oil change.

They alighted from the hack on the opposite side from Bainbridge House, at the entrance of the park enclosed with an iron fence. Luke Three pressed several notes into the cabbie's hands and did not wait for change. The tip was astronomical, but he was feeling generous. It would simply not do to appear miserly to Ardith. In a way, he was the boss. He felt very much like a man of the world in this new setting. There was a beautiful girl on his arm, a spacious park with walkways that meandered under huge trees, the sound of crickets, and the scent of night-blooming jasmine gave the atmosphere a magical touch. A sense of peace washed over him as he placed his arm around her waist and they strolled up a dimly lighted path. The moon could have been drawn by an artist; it was an orange hook that radiated just enough light to make the shadows interesting.

Was this what the word *companionship* meant? He had never felt this particular way when he had been with Darlene, with whom the warm feeling always led to frantic movements in the back seat of the car. When the panting was all over, he always gunned up the motor and took her home quickly. But he would not want to abandon Ardith; he loved being near her, feeling her body against his. He wanted to protect her because she was so vulnerable. Then a strange thought occurred to him: was this experience with her unique? The evening had been filled with music, dancing, close camaraderie. Did she go often to The Four Seasons with other men? Did she dance as close to them as she had with him? Did she always press her breasts up to their chests? Did she always bring her thighs up so close that she could feel their manhood when they danced?

"The moon," she was saying softly, "look at the moon. It's new."

"The farmers at home will be planting vegetables that grow on top of the ground." He glanced at her. "Crops that grow below the ground must be planted when the moon is old."

"Is that all it means to you, Luke Three?" Her voice was very low.

"A new moon always means new life, a new beginning." He felt very old and very wise, and it occurred to him that no other evening that he had experienced had been quite like this one. He was so relaxed, so much in command, and he was thankful to the stingers for releasing his inhibitions.

He drew her under the overhanging branches of a huge oak tree and deep in the shadows, placed his arms around her and gave her a lingering kiss. She opened her mouth even wider and he found her warm tongue. As he kissed her again and again, he drew himself up to her—in the same way that he had pressed himself against the fenders of countless automobiles while washing windshields.

She broke away from him, and since they had walked almost all the way through the park, she looked up at the dark facade of Bainbridge House. "We must be very quiet," she said softly. "Come, I'll show you the way."

He drew in his breath. He could hardly believe his good fortune! Foolishly, he had been content only to be with her, realizing that although she wanted him, they would remain unfulfilled. Now he wanted to whistle, to shout, to let everyone know that the evening was going to have a perfect ending.

They softened their footfalls as they crossed the dark street. She guided him down a few steps by the side of the house, opened the door with a key, and, taking his hand, led him down a long, pitch-black hall, where there was the smell of cooked cabbage. She switched on a light in the pantry and then opened a small door to the left. "This used to be the upstairs parlormaid's room," she whispered. "but we caught her pilfering flatware." She turned off the light in the pantry and lighted a candle, which she placed beside the bed.

"Don't make a sound," she warned, sitting down on the bed, "because the other servants occupy the bed-rooms above."

He sat down beside her, kissed her lightly on the lips, and then pressed her back on the bedspread. She re-sponded quickly. He would have liked to think that she believed him to be someone very special, but she was so willing and so cooperative that he wondered briefly if this was a familiar process to her. The seduction had proceeded from when they had eaten dinner at the small restaurant next to The Four Seasons, through the dancing, the stingers, and the walk through the park; it appeared now that she had known from the beginning that they would end the evening in the maid's bedroom.

He had not been required to exert his masculinity to get where he was at this moment—breathing heavily on top of her—but he did miss the cat-and-mouse game that he always played with women, even with Darlene Trune. When he started to unbotton her blouse, she whispered in his ear, "Let's get undressed."

He got up at once and removed his coat. The spell

was broken, now he felt alien in this bare, institutionalized room. If there had been a bare lightbulb hanging down in the center of the room, he would have fled. But there was some mystery; the flickering candle flame threw their bodies into indistinct shadows on the white walls as they disrobed, which removed some of the clinical aspects of the place. Did she realize that she was denying him the pleasure of removing her clothing, piece by piece, until her warm flesh was moving under him? That had always been an important part of his foreplay. He elaborately folded his shirt and trousers, which he placed on a chair, then removed his socks and palmed the unwrapped oval protector.

Did married couples go through this cold, unromantic ritual every night? When he looked up, she was standing quite nude, proudly displaying her body. From her gently sloping shoulders to her small, beautifully shaped breasts, to her flat stomach and gently swelling thighs, she was a healthy specimen that an artist would be delighted to paint. She looked both golden and ghostly in the meager light from the candle. Suddenly he could not remove his new jockey shorts; incongruously, he felt that she would laugh if he revealed himself.

Why am I behaving this way? he thought, panic-stricken. *What is the matter with me?* He was not in the least aroused now. Was it the the stingers? Was it because they were in the maid's room in a strange old mansion? Did he feel, in a certain way, that he was performing for her? Or was this how adults played the game of sexuality? Did a date with a woman whom you liked, and who liked you, most usually culminate in going to bed?

You stupid ass, he told himself angrily. What's holding you back? Get with it! He moved toward her, took her in his arms, and kissed her fiercely. Her pointed breasts pressed up against him until it felt as if they were an extension of his own body. He lost his appre-

hension and sighed with contentment. He was on home
ground now. He felt her heartbeat; the erratic rhythm
seemed to echo the beat of the jazz music played on
the Summer floor of The Four Seasons.

With her so close, he found that there was nothing
wrong with him after all! It was time to get on the bed,
but how did one accomplish the feat and remove one's
shorts at the same time, without appearing foolish? He
solved the problem by extinguishing the candle with
one hand, pulling down his shorts with the other, and
pressing her body back on the bedspread in a gesture
that Mr. Ayres would have verbally counted as *one, two,
three.*

Kissing her lightly, he raised up and with his right
hand rolled on the protection; at least he had perfected
this bit of strategy so that they would not be required to
pause in a tense, pleasurable moment while he performed the little operation.

She was warm, so glowing that her body was dewed
with perspiration. The scent of *Fleur* wafted up from her
breasts. He placed the length of his arm under her
shoulders until the flat of his hand was resting on her
upper buttocks, and then, holding her lightly, kissed her
deeply. In contrast, her breathing was very shallow. She
clung to him, opening herself like a pink hibiscus.

He changed his position slightly and felt a wave of
gentle euphoria. The taste of the crème de menthe and
brandy came up in his throat. He moved forward slowly
and paused because he was unable to proceed. It had
always taken time to accomplish the mission, but now
he had to face the fact that Ardith's body was constructed differently from Darlene's. Since she did not
seem aware of his problem, he tried to move in such a
manner that she would not be conscious of the fact that
he could not enter her fully.

As they swayed together in wonderment, becoming
accustomed to the ebb and flow of each other's bodies,

he tried to remember certain line drawings in the marriage manual that he had leafed through while in service. There must be a position that would help remedy the situation. Damn, why hadn't he paid more attention to those illustrations? He breathed audibly, and she moved up toward him as if thinking that perhaps his moment had come, but he paused to let her know that this was not the case. He maneuvered himself carefully as he felt her heartbeat quicken; then she sighed and mewed like a kitten.

He swayed his hips lightly from side to side, which was all that he could think to do in his predicament, and the movement brought about his own fulfillment. It was a very gentle release for him, and he frankly missed the bone-jarring, nerve-tingling orgasm to which he was accustomed. She swayed under him once more and then, when they broke apart, she fell asleep.

He waited for a few moments, then carefully withdrew from her embrace and went into the tiny bathroom to splash himself with cold water. He was at a loss as to how to dispose of his protection. Obviously he would have to take it with him; no evidence of their tryst could be left in the room. He dressed quickly, kissed her on the cheek lightly, and turned out the bulb in the bathroom, then he made his way down the long dark hall where the smell of cabbage still lingered.

He was out into the street before he realized that it would probably be difficult to find a taxi at this hour of the morning in a strictly residential district. He remembered a few shops located several blocks away, and set out on foot. The old Victorian mansions on either side of the street were all mournfully silent, so tall they seemed to reach far into the sky. Bentley Square had long been in bed.

Obviously he had proceeded in the wrong direction, because there were no shops on streets that became more narrow. A heavy mist began to settle, which at last became so dense that the shrouded streetlamps gave off paltry illumination. His feet hurt. His apprehension grew with each block. He would not have been surprised to find Sherlock Holmes or even the evil Moriarty looming menacingly out of the fog. As he rounded a corner, a huge figure came at him out of the opaque atmosphere, and he dodged just in time. "Very nasty night indeed, sir," the bobby said.

"I'm glad to see you," Luke Three said cordially. "I've lost my way. I'm staying at the Savoy."

"Ah," the bobby replied, "you're surely goin' in the opposite direction, sir. One more block down the street, there's a phone box. The hotel will send a cabbie quick as a wink."

"I'm very much obliged," Luke Three replied.

He entered the lobby of the hotel at five-thirty, and was in bed fifteen minutes later. At seven o'clock, Robert Desmond shook him awake. "Time to get up, bub, we've a long day ahead of us."

Luke Three roused fitfully. The sweet-sour taste of the stingers lingered in his throat and bore no resemblance to their attraction of the night before. He raised up on his elbow and tried to focus his eyes on the man bending over him.

"My God, Luke Three." Robert Desmond grimaced. "You look like the wrath of God."

"Thank you," Luke replied, as if receiving a compliment.

Five minutes later, over a cup of very strong coffee, Luke Three managed to keep his eyes open, although his brain was not yet functioning properly.

"I take it, from your fragile condition, you had a great time last night," Robert Desmond remarked, his voice tinged with sarcasm.

Luke Three managed a weak smile. "It was interesting, to say the least."

"And Ardith?"

"All I can say, Bob, is"—Luke Three gave him a quick look—"her mother may be a *lady*, but she isn't."

Robert Desmond said nothing at all, because he had once gone sightseeing with the beauteous Ardith. He wondered idly if the upstairs parlormaid's room was still in the same location.

8

The Invitation

Letty and Bosley opened the Connecticut Avenue house for the summer and engaged temporary help from an agency.

Letty regarded Bosley over the breakfast table after the move from Angel and smiled crookedly. "I don't know how you feel," she sighed, "but Washington seems to have lost its glitter. I'm beginning to feel like a displaced person."

"I was thinking almost the same thing," Bosley agreed. "I've come to the conclusion that Washington is for young people, working politicians and fund-raisers. There doesn't seem to be any spit and polish anymore. If Evalyn Walsh McLean is living at Friendship, we may get an invitation. She usually gives fine parties."

"No, she's in Newport, but she'll probably be back in October." Letty took a bite of a Sally Lunn roll covered with butter and strawberry jam and chewed thoughtfully.

"The trouble with us, Bos, is that we've been around so long that we're not impressed anymore. I suppose age is a mellowing process—or at least supposed to be—but I don't feel mellow at all. Do you?"

He shook his head. "No, only when my bursitis kicks up; then I wish I was fifty again." He opened the *Washington Post* and scanned the first page. "Perle Mesta gave a luncheon yesterday for the English Ambassador." He looked up and grinned. "She's come a long way from her Oklahoma roots."

Letty sniffed. "Yes, but remember she was a Skirvin, and she had a good education, and then there was all that oil money—and then she married George Mesta, and he's a nice man." She paused. "Bos?"

"Yes?"

"Do you think the family history would have changed had some of us Herons gone to college?"

"What a question! What brought that up?"

"Oh, I don't know, I've been thinking about the early days when we made the Cherokee Strip Run. We were all so naive."

He laughed gently. "If the Herons had been better educated, they would probably have gone into one of the professions in Minneapolis and when the Oklahoma Territory was opened up, wouldn't have budged from their comfortable jobs. They wouldn't have had enough adventuresome spirit to claim free land. Would you have made the Run if you'd known what hard times were ahead?"

She laughed wryly. "But we were barely out of our teens, remember, and foolish." She clicked her tongue softly and looked at him fondly. "Let's not think about the past anymore, and after this season, let's go back to Angel and 'pack it all in' as the English say, and let the children stay here when they're in town. Couldn't this house be a tax write-off?"

"I suppose so. It could be utilized for company business—a sort of surrogate headquarters." He started at the sound of the telephone. "Who could be calling at"—he looked at his watch—"at eight o'clock on a Sunday morning?" He picked up the telephone. "Good morning," he said, with more enthusiasm than he felt.

"Bosley Trenton, please." The voice had a dry Midwestern flavor, which he almost recognized.

"Speaking."

"This is Harry Truman."

For a moment Bosley did not know what to say; then he drew in his breath. "How do you do, Mr. President."

Letty, who had been standing near the telephone, thinking it was one of the children calling, eased down on the kitchen chair, an expression of bewilderment on her face.

"Excuse me for calling so early in the morning," the President went on smoothly. "I didn't wait for the switchboard to open. Being from the Midwest, I assumed you'd be up bright and early, the same as me."

"Up at dawn, Mr. President. It's very difficult to break old habits."

Harry Turman laughed wryly and got to the point of his call. "I just read in the *Post* this morning that you've set up housekeeping again in Washington. I was talking to President Hoover the other day—I've appointed him Honorary Chairman of the Famine Emergency Committee—and he brought up your name."

Bosley cleared his throat. "Yes, Mr. President, I've had a nodding acquaintance with him for many years. Letty was a friend of Lou Hoover's. I believe they met during World War One, in London, when Mr. Hoover headed the U.S. Commission for Relief in Belgium."

"I told him that I'd known you casually from the time that I had that haberdashery store in Kansas City." Harry Truman chuckled. "And a lot of water has gone under the bridge since then."

"Yes indeed, Mr. President."

"I don't want to intrude on your Sunday, but if you and Mrs. Trenton aren't busy this morning, Bess and I would like very much to see you for an hour. I know this is on short notice. I hope you don't have other plans."

"Thank you, Mr. President, we'd be honored. All we were doing was reading the funny papers."

Harry Truman chuckled. "Well, we've got them all over here—including the *Kansas City Star* and *The Oklahoman.* I'll send a limousine over to pick you up at ten. Is that convenient?"

"Yes, thank you, Mr. President, we'll be ready."

Because one didn't hang up on the President of the United States, he waited for the line to go dead; then he sat down, legs shaking. "How do you like that, Letty? We've just been invited to the White House right this minute."

A stricken look came over her face. "My hair looks a mess, and what'll I wear?"

He laughed and patted her hand. "Don't get all gussied up now, Bess Truman is not a clothes horse."

"She may look simply dressed, Bos," Letty retorted, "because she always underplays everything, but you can bet your bottom dollar it's *expensive.* I guess my flowered silk is all right. I'll press it."

"Call Jessie."

"No," Letty replied firmly. "She worked late last night, unpacking. I'm sure it was after midnight when she went to bed. I'll heat up the iron and do it myself."

While Letty combed her hair, Bosley shaved. "One thing about growing older, dear," he remarked casually, "a white beard doesn't show much face, but white hair seems stiffer and more difficult to manage, and then hair grows out of your ears, and your shoulders slope and your rear drops and you're lean in the shanks and clothes don't look good."

She looked at him fondly. "Stop complaining. You

were a handsome man when I married you, and you're a handsome man now. I'm very proud of you."

He looked at her in amazement. "What brought that on?"

"Nothing, except it just occurred to me that I haven't complimented you in a long time, and compliments are in order."

He kissed her cheek. "I love you, Letty, and I don't tell you that often enough either, I guess. We shouldn't take each other for granted. I promise to mend my ways." He paused. "By the way, when were you in the White House the last time?"

She paused, comb in midair. "Well, let me see ..." A look of sadness came over her face. "It was nineteen-twenty-nine, when you were in Venezuela at the Maracaibo Lake Basin. Henry Ford was there, and Walter F. Brown, the Postmaster General, and quite a few other important business people. George wasn't really up to going. Lou Hoover told me confidentially that the president was going to ask him to head a committee on foreign trade, and I asked her to inform her husband that he wouldn't be up to it." She paused and passed a hand over her eyes. "As it turned out, Bos, that was George's last public appearance. He died eight weeks later, on Sunday, the day before Blue Monday when the stock market collapsed. He was only fifty-six."

Bosley nodded. "I'll never forget his funeral." He cleared his throat. "Now, we'd better finish dressing. We can't be late. Whatever's wrong with Truman, he appreciates punctuality." He toweled his face and reached for a white shirt. "You know, Letty, we did the right thing when we switched over to the Democratic ticket before Roosevelt's fourth term. It was played up in the press, and there are still some good Republican friends who don't speak to us anymore, but I had the feeling then, and I have the feeling now, that we can work with the

Truman administration." He grinned. "And I guess Harry feels the same way!"

The butler was standing at the doorway of the South Portico. Letty looked up and smiled. She was almost overcome with nostalgia. "It's Fields, isn't it?"

His face broke into a wide grin. "Yes, Mrs. . . . Trenton." He became immediately sober. The very proper Fields, who was serving his third administration in the White House, had almost called her Mrs. Story!

As they followed the butler down the white marble foyer, Letty looked about with a critical eye. "Everything seems the same," she whispered, "but the carpet looks new."

Bosley gave her a long look as they took the elevator to the second floor to the First Family's private quarters, where Letty had never been before. Fields ushered them into the lounge at the end of the hall, which was furnished with comfortable chairs and sofas and looked more homey than the imposing rooms on the first floor, with which Letty was more familiar. Fields announced them. Harry Truman arose from an easy chair, a grin on his face, and shook Bosley's hand. "Good of you to come on such short notice."

"My pleasure, Mr. President."

Bess Truman came forward and took Letty's hand. "It's certainly nice to see you," she said in the slightly reserved way that was her trademark. Her handshake was steady and firm. She was wearing a blue dress that matched her brilliant, porcelain-blue eyes, and her rather short blond hair, slightly graying, was curled around her face.

"I don't believe you've met my wife, Letty, Mr. President," Bosley said.

Harry Truman shook Letty's hand, and for one insane moment, she felt like curtsying, and she had the feeling that he picked up her thought because his hazel eyes sparkled behind steel-rimmed glasses.

"Let me see," Harry Truman mused, "the last time I saw you, Bosley, I think I hit you up for a check for some cause or other. I just want you to know that I'm not going to ask you for any money today." He paused. "But I am going to ask you for a greater contribution—your time."

"Harry," his wife put in kindly, "don't you think that we can at least sit down before discussing business?"

He laughed. "I've already prepared Mr. Trenton for what's coming, on the telephone."

"In that case, Letty," Bess Truman said, taking her arm, "let's go down to my sitting room for a chat." She guided Letty down the large central hall, which was painted Nile green, and into a pleasant room done in gray. Through an open door, Letty saw that the large bedroom beyond was lavender. She made up her mind then and there that she would redo her own bedroom in Angel in the same color; besides being quiet and peaceful, it would complement her silver hair.

"This is such a pleasant room," Letty said conversationally.

Bess Truman nodded. "We tried to redo these private rooms so they wouldn't look so formal, but it's still a far cry from our home on North Delaware Street in Independence. Do you know that there was not one clothes closet in any of the bedrooms when we moved in here? The White House was built when everyone used wardrobes. We did have a small one built for Margaret."

"How is she?" Letty asked politely.

"Enjoying what she calls her 'vacation,' " Bess Truman replied in her no-nonsense manner. "She has her Bachelor of Arts now, and she'll be ready soon to start a musical career. It's what she's wanted for such a long time. Just what direction that will take remains to be seen." She paused. "It's very difficult to be the daughter of a President, Letty, even under the best of conditions, but to choose to go into such a difficult field where the competition is so great—well, I only wish that she had chosen a career that was less involved with the public."

"I'm certain there'll be those who'll say that she has used her influence to open doors. We had the same problem about Clement when he first started out in music. Friends said we had pushed him, which wasn't true at all. Then, when he started his first Cherokee Jazz Band, a lot of his own people felt that he was exploiting *them*—when he was only trying to help the cause by giving talented musicians with Indian blood a chance."

Bess Truman smiled in a friendly way. She was not so austere now. "I've always felt that my husband, who plays the piano, was a little envious of professional musicians, although I doubt if he'd have been happy playing in an orchestra."

"No, I agree with you, usually politics and music don't mix."

In the lounge, Harry Truman had chosen a wingback chair opposite the sofa where Bosley was sitting. "We're going to be in a terrible mess abroad, if we don't do something about it," he continued in his distinctive voice. "England's in the soup financially, France is broke, and the other countries aren't recovering well from the war. Rebuilding is costing billions. We can't let people starve. You remember what the Depression was like?"

"I surely do, Mr. President. Anyone who lived in the Midwest, as you and I did during those times, will never forget the poverty, despite President Roosevelt's New Deal programs."

"Well," Harry Truman countered, "we're going to have a depression in Europe that'll make that one look like small potatoes if we don't stop it. And once it starts over there, it'll be over here in no time at all, just like it was last time." He paused. "I'm going to Congress to try to do something about it, but right now I'd like to prepare the way. As I said before, President Hoover has accepted honorary chairmanship of the Famine Emergency Committee. I'd like for you to throw your weight behind him."

Bosley swallowed hard. "Frankly, Mr. President, I don't know what I could do."

"You run one of the biggest oil companies in the United States, and you've also got influence abroad," Harry Truman retorted. "What we need is executive ability. Until I can get support for a major plan from the Hill, we must show those countries over there that we haven't forgotten them. President Hoover has had wide experience with relief work, but a lot of people are shocked that I asked a former Republican President, who hasn't been heard of since his administration, to head the committee. I've had a lot of flak, dammit, and I'll get more, but there's not a man anywhere who's more fitted. But he needs a lot of help. If you and other Democrats are appointed to serve with him, we'll have a program that we can be proud of."

Bosley squared his jaw. "It'll take a lot of time, Mr. President, a lot of time."

"I know that." It was a statement. "But I also know that if you want a job done, always pick the busiest man around—not some ne'er-do-well with lots of extra time on his hands, who'll outplay you on the golf course and give a lot of rhetoric, but won't deliver."

In her sitting room down the hall, Bess Truman glanced at her watch. "I think we'd better go rescue your husband, Letty." She gave a conspiratorial smile, which lit up her very blue eyes. "We've been in the White House over a year now, and I still can't get used to the heavy schedules."

She opened the door of the sitting room, and they went into the central hall. "Every hour of every day is taken up with something—even Sundays. That's why the President called this morning—he had two hours of free time." She paused outside the lounge and took Letty's hand. "I hope we meet again soon, Letty," she continued warmly. "We are very private people, as I know that you and your husband are, but we'll arrange time to be together now and then." She opened the door to the lounge as Harry Truman was saying, "Hell, Bosley, if I knew I was doing you a favor, I would have asked for a lot more!"

In the limousine on the way back to the house on Connecticut Avenue, Letty looked at Bosley. "What did the President mean when he said he was doing you a favor?"

Bosley took a deep breath. "He was joking, of course. The upshot is, you know how long I've wanted to retire from the company, Letty. If the Japs hadn't bombed Pearl Harbor, I'd have handed in my resignation then. I've been on the verge of clearing out my desk a dozen times since. Now that we've bought out Desmond, and the company is expanding, it's time to bow out. This new appointment, to work with Hoover, will pave the way. That's what I told the President, and that's why he laughingly said that he was doing me a favor."

"You've made a good decision. By the way, I kept wondering why Harry Truman kept referring to Hoover as President?"

"I suppose," Bosley replied reflectively, "he realized that once you're a President, you're always a President. Anyone who has survived that office—and few have—deserves all the respect in the world."

Later that afternoon, Dr. Platt telephoned from Angel. "Bosley, you'll never in the world guess who called me last night. The President of the United States, that's who! He wanted to know the state of your health."

Bosley chuckled. "And what did you say?"

"When I could get my voice together and realized that it wasn't some joker, that it really was Harry Truman calling, I told him that as far as my records show, you're as fit as a fiddle."

"Then you think I've got a few more years left?" Bosley queried.

"More than a few, Bosley, more than a few." The doctor paused. "He also wanted to know about Letty. I gave her a clean bill, too. So don't be surprised if you hear from him, Bos."

"I already have." Bosley laughed. "Letty and I saw the President and Mrs. Truman this morning."

"My God!" the doctor exclaimed. "He certainly doesn't lose any time, does he?"

"Nope," Bosley replied. "That's one of the reasons I like him. He knows what he wants and then goes after it. He's a cautious man, that's why he called you. If I had one foot in the grave, I wouldn't have received the appointment."

"What appointment?"

Bosley laughed. "You'll have to read about that in the papers, Doctor."

"Then I take it it'll be a while before you'll be coming back to Angel?"

"I'm afraid," Bosley said slowly, "that it'll be a long, long time."

Bosley and Letty were having breakfast on the terrace of the Connecticut Avenue house, entertained by a feisty robin that had become their friend. The bird fluttered about the table, twittering anxiously, waiting for crumbs of toast, which Bosley occasionally threw on the flag-stones. He was thus engaged when Jessie, the elderly maid from the agency, brought in several magazines, which she placed by the coffee service. "Your grandson made *Life*," she said airily. "He's a handsome lad."

"Oh?" Letty remarked casually. The fact that the servants read the newspapers and periodicals before either Bosley or she did was disconcerting, but she did not know quite how to handle the situation. She disliked to complain about such a small matter because Jessie and her husband, Tim, who acted as butler and also helped in the kitchen, most usually knew their place, and they were wonderful to guests.

"Page three," Jessie announced flatly, pouring more coffee.

"Thank you," Bosley said, and waited until she had gone back into the house before he threw Letty a questioning look and opened the paper. There was a three-column wire photo of Luke Three and a beautiful girl getting into a taxi. The caption read: HERON OIL HEIR GOES NIGHTCLUBBING IN SOHO. Bosley flushed and showed the picture to Letty.

Then he read aloud: *"Luke Heron III, sightseeing in London, attended The Four Seasons dance pavilion in Soho, in the company of Ardith Huxley-Drummond, who recently made her social debut. The heir to the Heron Oil millions, 20, is headquartered in Tulsa, Oklahoma. His step-grandfather, Bosley Trenton, was recently named to the Famine Emergency Committee by President Truman."* He threw down the paper. "I think that's disgraceful. Publicity of this sort gives the company a bad name."

"Oh, I think that's rather sweet, Bos," Letty replied smoothly. "Luke Three taking out the Huxley-Drummond girl. After all, the family was wonderful to George and me when we were over there. Now Luke Three's paying back some of that hospitality."

"Well," he replied grudgingly, "that's not so bad. It's bringing my name into it that I don't approve of. The impression given is that while our committee is trying to feed the starving people of Europe, Luke Three's over there living it up, nightclubbing and all. I tell you, it's bad publicity. Gives the wrong impression of the way we live, for one thing, and it makes Luke Three sound like a playboy."

"As usual, you're making a mountain out of a mole-hill, Bos! Don't forget, we've had our pictures in the papers and in magazines."

"Yes, there have been articles in the *Petroleum World* and *Life* magazine, and you were once photographed on a horse for *Town and Country*."

"And don't forget that long article in *Fortune*."

"But that was *business*. This makes Luke Three appear like he's in café society." He got up. "I'm going to call Luke."

"Oh, don't do that, Bos," Letty pleaded. "We don't want to get the boy in trouble. It's not his fault that his picture's in the paper." She paused. "Besides, he's very photogenic, don't you think?"

He glared at her. "You mean you approve?"

"The world is changing, dear, and we've got to face it," Letty answered with conviction. "Luke Three's young and attractive. As long as he stays single, he's going to be thought of as quite a catch. There's bound to be talk and gossip. It's not as if he's involved with a movie star. Ardith Huxley-Drummond is the daughter of a knight." She smiled. "He could do worse!" She paused and held out her hand. "Bos, we've escaped a lot of talk because we were older and never did anything controversial. After all, I have been married three times, and George was a celebrity of sorts, involved as he was with Indian affairs; only in those days the newspapers didn't make anything out of it. When he passed on and I married you, there could have been quite a bit made of it, because you'd been a friend of the family for many years. Thank God we were living quietly in Oklahoma. Now that everything's international, there's bound to be pictures and stories. People today, particularly since the war, hunger for items like this."

He took her hand. "Well, maybe I'm old-fashioned, but with him over there on foreign shores, gallivanting around ..."

"Look at Clement's publicity!"

"That's a different thing altogether, Letty; he's a *Story* and *famous.* The Trenton and the Heron names don't come up all the time. We're conservative. Clement established his own name *before* the Heron Oil Company really got started. It's a different kettle of fish altogether." He frowned. "A *playboy*, a glamour boy—our Luke Three? Preposterous! I knew it was a mistake for him to go off with Robert Desmond." He held the cup to his lips and grimaced. "Can't a man get a cup of hot coffee in his own home?"

At midmorning the telephone rang, and Letty picked it up in the pantry. "Yes?" A smile spread over her face. "Oh, Patricia Anne, I'm so glad you called. Yes, I saw the paper. It's disgusting, isn't it? What?" She listened intently, and then sighed. "I don't know what gets into these Heron boys, Patricia Anne. It must be something in the blood. Lars should understand; he's studying such things as behavior patterns, isn't he?" She paused. "He's not? Well, anyway, Mitchell went off for years in Europe and no one knew where he was, and then Luke Three simply doesn't want to come home. His dad is thinking of just firing him—temporarily, I guess—until he gets this thing out of his system."

"Do you think it's a girl?" Patricia Anne asked.

"I can't think of anything else a Heron man would go into a spin about!"

"Grandma!"

"Well, it's true, my dear. Personally, I think they should leave him alone, he's a good boy, a little naive maybe, but ..." She paused. "Can you and Lars come for dinner on Friday? Good. What? Oh, no, it won't be social, just us."

Patricia Anne hung up the telephone and turned to Lars. They were sitting in the library of their small house in Chevy Chase, Maryland, taking a coffee break from the data that they had been compiling since seven o'clock that morning. "What it all boils down to," she said, rubbing the back of her neck and pursing her rather generous lips, "is that Luke Three is torn between being a Heron and being himself. He has all that responsibility hanging over him, and his father isn't all that interested, frankly." She looked up at him and smiled. "Oh, I'm glad I found you, Lars. Otherwise I'd have ended up an old maid, taking innumerable courses at Phillips University!"

"I doubt that, my sweet," he replied, running a hand through his blond hair and squaring his jaw. "Now, let's continue. In our experiments yesterday, when I took as much of the powdered mushroom as would fit on the head of a pin, how long was it before I began to feel the effects and speak about what was happening to me?"

She checked the chart on the clipboard on her lap. "One minute and thirty-five seconds. Your first reaction had to do with Captain, who was caged. Your words were: 'Pat, let the bird out; he wants to fly.' When I did so, you said, 'He's happy now.'"

"Ah yes, I remember. Why I zeroed in on Captain, I don't know. I was lying on the couch and I suddenly felt a *oneness* with him. It was if we were communicating. Now, logically, that's tommyrot, but then I saw every feather in minute detail—and remember, I was across the room! I felt his rage at being cooped up." He paused. "What else?"

Patricia Anne cleared her throat. "Then you said, 'Close the window, the breeze hurts me.' When I did so, you said, 'That's much better, thank you.'"

"The wind seemed alien to me. I was aware that it belonged outside, not in the room, and I think that's what bothered me. It wasn't that the wind actually was painful. It was as if it hurt me *emotionally*."

"That doesn't make sense, Lars."

"Well, it does, dear, in a certain context. You see," he explained patiently, "when I inherited Dr. Sam's files and all his material on these mind-altering drugs, he noted several times that our usual thought patterns are changed. He didn't know why, but he suspected that it had something to do with altering our point of view—from inward to outward. On the two occasions that he utilized this mushroom, at the death of George Story and his own demise, he said something to the effect that the drug made pain bearable. It separated the actual pain from the body—or so it seemed—so that it wasn't all-encompassing. It became, in a way, like Captain, who I thought wanted to be released from his cage, or shutting out the wind from the room." He leaned forward. "You see, Pat, I was thinking about other matters than myself. I became less important as an individual."

"Do you suppose, then, that's what he meant when he indicated that if the drug was administered to a person suffering from split personality, schizophrenia, he would be able to *observe himself?*

Lars nodded. "I believe so. "Now, in today's experiment I will take as much powdered mushroom as can be piled on *two* pinheads. Theoretically, that should produce twice the effects of yesterday."

After he had consumed the drug with a teaspoon of water, Lars lay back on the couch, and Patricia Anne noted the time: ten forty-five. One minute later, he stirred. "There's a butterfly on the windowsill. My God, Pat, he's huge. You mustn't let him in!"

Patricia Anne stared at her husband. His blue eyes were staring at the window, and his hands were clutched at his sides, his body stiff, his toes curled upward through his dark socks. She wanted to comfort him, yet it was her job to observe and make notes. She kept her voice very low and unconcerned. "Oh, I don't think it's anything to worry about. He's quite harmless."

"Fool!" he shouted. "He'll break the window!"

She wanted to take him in her arms and comfort him,

yet dared not, hoping the phase would pass quickly. "I'll shoo him away, dear," she said soothingly.

"No! Don't go near the window!" he exclaimed. He had brought his arms up to his head, as if warding off an expected blow. "What's that?" he asked.

"What do you mean?" she inquired in a gentle voice. Her own heart was beating very fast and she was afraid; yet she must not show her concern, because it would affect the experiment, and Lars had told her that she must never become personally involved in the other person's commitment. "What is it, dear?"

"Oh, my God, my God." He began to sob, but there were no tears, only a dry, wrenching sound that was, in itself, terrifying. "The couch, it's so hard, it's hurting my back and my legs. It's so painful. I can feel my skin bruising. I can feel my thighs swelling. Help me, I must get up, I must stand, help me!" He had stopped sobbing now, and his face was drained of color.

Patricia Anne and Lars had never discussed touching the other person who was having an experience. Yet he had *asked* for help. She noted the time on her pad, then took his arm. "Now, just get up very slowly, dear," she said quietly, humoring him.

He placed his feet on the floor, then, with her assistance, as if he were a very old, arthritic man, he rose but bent over at once. "Oh, the pain is worse. The pressure ... on the soles ... of my feet ... unbearable ... the pain ..."

"Let me help you walk," she said, trying to think of something that would distract him.

"Walk? You fool," he spat out savagely, "how can I walk when the pain is shooting up through my legs?" He began to breathe easier, and in a moment he straightened up, and from the expression on his face she knew that the experience was over. His forehead was wet with perspiration. He looked at her with wonder. "My God, Pat, my God, none of Dr. Sam's notes indicated anything like what I've been through. He only wrote about good experiences, never bad!" He sat down. "Now, let's analyze this thing that happened to me."

"Was the pain real?" she asked, squinting her eyes at him.

"Oh, yes! I felt as if gravity had been reversed and that the weight of the whole house was on my body and my feet. I thought the couch was going to crush me."

"And the butterfly?"

"Its wings seemed to be made of heavy stained glass, strong enough to break the window into smithereens." He shuddered. "It was all very peculiar—and very real." He ran his hands through his hair. "Now why were the other experiments so good and this one so bad? We've got to think this out." He seemed to be speaking more to clarify his own mind than to provide information for her. "I took the same amount of water as yesterday. The amount of the drug was still almost infinitesimal. Dr. Sam took three capsules for his journey, so the amount ..." He looked with wide eyes at Patricia Anne. "Do you suppose that could be it? The *capsules*? Perhaps the drug must reach the stomach ... and not become mixed with any of the enzymes of the mouth or throat. *What if the substance itself is an enzyme*?"

"But why didn't you have the same result yesterday, Lars?"

"It might have been a fluke; the amount was so small that the sip of water may have washed all of it down at once. Obviously, today some of it stayed in my mouth."

"What does it taste like?"

He shook his head. "There is *no* taste, and apparently it dissolves almost at once." Excitement built in his voice. "Oh, Pat, after all this time, after all of these studies, I feel that we're getting somewhere at last!"

When the limousine taking Luke Three, Robert Desmond, and Eric Huxley-Drummond headed into the

English countryside to the field office, the engine sputtered suddenly, as if on cue.

"I hope we're not out of petrol," Sir Eric said. "The
driver filled the tank this morning before we picked you
up." he laughed. "Only it's not Heron no-knock gasoline!"

The motor coughed again. "It's the carburetor," Luke
Three said with conviction, "and from the sound of it,
we'd better find a service station soon."

The driver spoke through the tube. "I think it'll start
behaving properly," he said, "once we get back on the
highway and can maintain speed. It's acted up like this
before, but it usually quiets down."

The pinging noise continued, and Luke Three shook
his head. "It's not going to quiet down this time." He
spoke into the tube, "Driver, would you pull over to the
side of the road, please?"

"What are you doing?" Sir Eric asked.

"We don't want to burn up the engine," Luke Three
replied, frowning. When the limousine glided to a stop
under a tree, he got out, had a short conference with
the driver, shook his head, then went to the front of the
car.

"Why, Luke Three is opening the bonnet!" Sir Eric
exclaimed.

Robert Desmond smiled. "He knows what he's doing."

"I say," Sir Eric expostulated, "how extraordinary!"

"Not really," Robert Desmond replied dryly, proud of
the boy. "He's worked in a Heron Oil station for about
three years and is very familiar with engines." He got out
of the back seat and sauntered up to Luke Three, who
was under the hood. "What do you think?"

"This is my first experience with a Rolls"—Luke Three
laughed—"but I see what the trouble is. Driver, would
you let the engine idle for a few moments?"

The driver started the motor, which sputtered once
and then clipped along smoothly.

Luke Three snapped the hood down and wiped his

hands on his handkerchief. "That should take care of it—if we're lucky."

They got back into the car, the driver pulled out on the road, and Sir Eric shook his head. "It sounds better than it did before," he said appreciatively. "What did you do?"

"Shook some grit out of a filter, that's all." Luke Three was playing it cool.

"Let me shake your hand, young man, for a job well done."

"Thank you, Sir Eric," Luke Three replied. Then he looked down at his hands. "What do you know, Bob? It's just like home; I have grease under my nails!"

Luke Three sat at the head of a long table in the private dining room in the rear of the Wilhelm Restaurant in Rotterdam and stifled a yawn. The fish course had just been served, and he was already bored. He looked down from the expanse of damask, china, crystal, and multicolored flower centerpieces, at the six men and their wives, to Robert Desmond who was holding forth at the end of the table. He was engaged in a lively conversation with an oilman, Hans Brinker. *Hans Brinker!* Where were his silver skates? Luke had almost laughed in the man's face when they were introduced, recalling the famous story, familiar to every schoolchild. But Brinker was a multimillionaire, willing to put money into drilling in the North Sea and was being courted by Robert Desmond as assiduously as if he were a virgin debutante whose father owned stock in the Chase Manhattan Bank.

"Vat ere you laughing aboot?" Mrs. Hendrickson, the wife of the regional manager, who was seated on his left, was saying.

Her accent added a note of hilarity, but Luke Three kept his face straight. "Nothing in particular," he answered soberly. She threw him an amused look and took a sip of the champagne. She was already a bit tipsy, as were most of the other guests, who were not accustomed to Dom Perignon served with meals. There was no one at the table, excepting himself, under forty. Hollanders were a gracious people, yet none of the men he had individually met this last week had offered to introduce him to girls his own age. None of them apparently had single daughters whom they were willing to introduce to him. The photograph of Ardith Huxley-Drummond and himself had been widely published in the European press, and it was apparently known that she fucked all of the field men.

The hours crept by, and finally the dessert was served, something made with apples and raisins and a sweet lemony sauce, but the coffee was excellent.

Luke Three stood beside Robert Desmond at the door of the private dining room and dutifully shook hands with the men and their wives. When they were alone, he confided, "I'm very tired." His shoulders slumped. "I'm going to bed. Will you take care of the bill?"

Robert Desmond threw him a quick look. "Of course."

"When is our first appointment tomorrow morning?"

"Ten. You can sleep late, if you like."

"Thank you. Good night."

"Good night."

Luke Three brightened visibly as he left the restaurant. He had had enough champagne to feel marvelous. He nodded to the doorman, who whistled down a taxicab. Luke pressed a bill into his hand. "Where can I find a girl?" he asked, feeling rather like an old roué.

The doorman's eyes twinkled. "The Club Mystic is very nice."

When Luke Three gave the name of the place, the driver gave him a quick look. "You are American?" he asked in perfect English.

"I am from Oklahoma."

The driver nodded. "I spent five years in Chicago before the war. Are you meeting a group at the Mystic?"

"No. But the doorman said it's a nice place."

"It *is*, for couples. Single men must sit at the bar, and you can't get a good look at the floorshow. Most guys like the Hague, which is located a little farther away in another district. It stays open until all hours, and a couple put on a good show after twelve."

"It sounds like what we'd call a honky-tonk at home."

The driver laughed. "It is, but order is kept. There won't be a raid."

"Is English spoken?"

"Enough."

"Take me there."

The Hague was located in the basement of an old hotel that sported bright magenta neon. There was a decadence about the place that appealed to Luke Three's present mood. The sound of an accordion and a piano could be heard faintly as he came down the stairs. The bar was full, but there were a few empty tables. Several languages were being spoken, but he heard no English.

He wedged himself into a position at the bar and ordered whiskey and bottled water. To his right, a man with a cap pulled down in the middle of his forehead was carrying on a conversation with a redheaded woman in a low-cut green gown. To his left, a young couple, speaking French, were looking around the place with wide eyes; obviously tourists.

With his second whiskey, Luke Three found that the place was taking on an air of familiarity, and the music being played on the squeak-box added to the foreign mood of a city steeped in romance. He was becoming mellow, and his head whirled from the champagne he had consumed earlier and the whiskey he was sipping now. He had reached that plateau where he felt in complete command. He had been watching a young blond girl with hair down her back, who had been sitting at a table with a dark Spaniard. When the man left abruptly, Luke Three eased up from his seat and sauntered over to the table. "Good evening," he said, smiling.

She appraised him coolly before inviting him to join her. "May I buy you a drink?" he said slowly and distinctly.

"Calvados."

Without asking, the waiter brought a whiskey and another glass for Luke Three and placed a small bottle of apple brandy on the table. He did not return change when Luke Three gave him a bill.

"Vat iss name?" the girl asked plaintively.

"Luke. And you?"

"Hedvig." She sipped the brandy slowly, looking at him intently, and when there was a sudden fanfare from the accordion and the lights were lowered, she turned to the dance floor. A pink spotlight was thrown into the middle of a small clearing surrounded by tables. A black form was hunched on the floor and as a recording of a violin solo blared over the sound system, the figure rose slowly, the black cape opened like a tent, then fell dramatically to the floor, disclosing a muscular young man in a small loincloth, and his partner, a beautiful dark-haired girl dressed in only a G-string. Luke found himself blushing in the dark. The girl's large bare breasts moved independently of each other as she swayed to the music.

Then, as the violin hushed, the couple assumed various poses that Luke Three recognized as erotic attitudes displayed on Green vases in the British Museum. He was fascinated at the artistry displayed. The couple moved in exact time to the music, freezing in a suggestive pose now and then. Legs and arms were raised and lowered, or placed flat against their bodies. The woman was now nude, and when the man turned, he dropped his loincloth. The poses grew more stimulating, and the audience, enraptured at the sight of the two exotic dancers, leaned forward expectantly. The man grasped the breasts of his partner, and she placed her hands on his buttocks, and they swayed from side to side and backward and forward. In the darkness, shot only with the weak pink spotlight, it took a few moments for the audience to realize what was taking place.

Luke Three had never seen such a demonstration before. The couple slipped into an intimate embrace. The violin segued into a frantic pizzicato movement. Now all pretense of dancing was abandoned as the couple moved wantonly, their bodies heavily beaded with perspiration. At that moment, Luke Three felt a searching hand on his thigh, and a soft voice inquired, "Shall ve go?"

The couple on the floor were obviously in the throes of complete surrender. Luke Three drew in his breath and got up from the table, his head whirling. Hedvig steadied his arm in the darkness and led him to a stairway at the back of the bar. As they reached the landing, he turned back to the crowd. From his high position, he saw that the dancers had slipped to the floor, and several other couples were making their way toward the stairs.

"Come," Hedvig said, "it iss over." And surely enough, as she opened the door, the lights flashed on, and as they came into the deserted lobby of the hotel, applause could be heard behind them. He saw that she had brought along the bottle of Calvados.

A few moments after they emerged from the open second-story lift, they were in her tiny room. The pink bedside light threw a rosy hue over the white sheets on the bed and the embroidered scarf on the bureau. There was no other furniture in the room. Luke lay down on the bed, his head whirling. He sighed when he felt his clothing being removed piece by piece. She expertly moved him this way and that, working his arms out of his coat, slipping his necktie over his head. As she performed her duty, she caressed him slowly, her fingers tantalizing his chest, and when she loosened his belt and unzipped his trousers, she patted him gently.

She dropped her dress to the floor; she wore nothing underneath, and her body gleamed in the pinkish haze reflected by the lampshade. His eyes cleared as she poured two small glasses of Calvados and handed him one, which he drank down at once; the liquor burned his throat deliciously. She placed her hands under the elastic of his jockey shorts and brought them down slowly over his thighs, knees, ankles, and feet, running her fingers lightly up and down his legs.

"Ah," she said appreciatively. "Big! Clean! Vat age?"

"Twenty."

"I twenty-five." Even in the pink light, she looked older, he thought, yet her body was young and her small breasts were firm and rosy-tipped. He lay as still as a toy while she caressed him. They were facing each other now on their sides, and as she kissed him, the smell of the apple brandy was everywhere, in mouths, nostrils, ears.

He liked the musty taste of the brandy combined with the warmth of her mouth. She moved next to him, and he felt a sudden partial blaze of heat, which increased as she worked very slowly, kissing him all the while. It took a very long time until he felt an encompassing flame and she pressed up against him.

"It is time to begin now," she whispered. Did she believe him to be inexperienced? He felt so relaxed that he did not know if it was because the brandy had released all inhibition or if it was because she was so casual about what she was doing. He began to move within the restriction of her body, striving to make the delicate, wavering sensations last, yet he could not restrain himself and arched his back and it was over. He shuddered pleasurably. "I'm . . . sorry," he stammered. "I know that you did not . . ."

"Not important," she answered softly. "Rest."

He dozed in her arms and then slept. He was awakened by the tinny sound of an alarm clock. She shook his shoulder, and when he looked up, he saw that she was dressed. "Four," she said softly and bent down and kissed his forehead. "Time."

He arose groggily and put on his clothes. He was exhausted. She opened the door. "Good night," she said.

"Good night, Hedvig."

She smiled. "Big. Young. Clean," she whispered and closed the door. He shook away the cobwebs in his head and when he came out into the street, smelling the dank, heavy air, he knew that it was going to rain. Rotterdam at that time of morning had the same atmosphere as Angel just before a storm.

The taxicab let him out at the side entrance of the hotel, and he went up to the Heron suite via the service elevator. He did not want to be seen in his rumpled condition. He let himself silently into his bedroom, undressed quickly, and was already in bed before he thought about bathing. No, he decided, he would wait until morning. Her scent, mixed with the smell of the Calvados, wafted up from his body. In a way, it was as if he had never left Hedvig.

9

Berlin Corridor

Mitchell Heron's journey to Berlin required a change of planes in London and Frankfurt, but the ticket on the Austrian airline was a round trip so that he could go on to Paris.

A high fog enclosed Berlin's Tempelhof Airport, so Mitchell could see nothing of the city. He was disappointed, because his first glimpse of Berlin was a huge cemetery over which the plane flew before touching down. Apparently there was only one landing strip; the others appeared to be in various stages of repair. Several large bomb craters were still being filled by American trucks carrying macadam. A half-dozen military transport planes were being unloaded at a nearby hangar.

The drab airport structure had been strafed with artillery shells and its walls peppered with machine-gun fire. Had this evidence of the war been left to impress visitors, or had the commanders more immediate priorities than the repair of a once grand facility? He wondered idly how many times Hitler and his henchmen had flown in at this very spot where he was deplaning?

In the Palace of Justice, that famous prison in Nuremberg, were incarcerated the remainder of the *Bonzen*, the Nazi bigwigs: 1) Reichsmarschall Hermann

Göring, Hitler's successor; 2) Joachim von Ribbentrop, Foreign Minister; 3) Wilhelm Frick, Minister of the Interior; 4) Hans Frank, Governor General of Poland; 5) Field Marshal Wilhelm Keitel; 6) General Alfred Jodl—twenty-four in all. Also Rudolf Hess, Hitler's deputy before his notorious escape to Great Britain. Paul Josef Goebbels, founder of the Gestapo, and Heinrich Himmler, who had been in charge of the concentration camps, were dead. Hundreds of others would be tried, and it was Mitchell's mission to free Steinmetz so he could also testify. It was a big responsibility, and for a moment he was fearful of his ability to function as Herr Professor Schneider.

The lobby was filled with the military personnel of many nations: America, Great Britain, France, and Russia—besides a smattering of other uniforms not so easily identified. Conversations in several foreign languages rose into a harangue; flights were being announced over an old public-address system that had obviously been damaged and never repaired—also a constant reminder of the war? There was a general air of confusion that was disconcerting to Mitchell, who could not show his discomfort and apprehension. He adopted a vaguely superior air as he made his way through the crowd, his buttocks pressed together, scrotum tight.

"Herr Doktor Schneider?" a voice called behind him.

He turned slowly, a supercilious look on his face. "*Ja?*"

The voice belonged to a blond, white-uniformed nurse. "I'm Hilda Schumann," she said in a soft Viennese accent without smiling. "If you will give me your stubs, I'll fetch your luggage. I have a car waiting outside."

He presented the stub. "Thank you," he said civilly. "I have only a briefcase."

"You may wait in the car, it's more comfortable," she replied gravely. "The blue Citroën at the curb."

He nodded curtly and walked primly through the open,

badly scarred doors. He sniffed the heavy air. The fog had lifted; the night was clear. Because there were only a few streetlights, the heavens seemed very dark and the stars were huge and bright. There was a disconcerting stillness, marred only occasionally by the sound of aircraft arriving or departing. He placed a brown cigarette in a bone-and-silver holder and bit down hard, but not hard enough to disengage his front teeth caps. He lighted the fag with a small prewar German lighter and watched the traffic flow with supposedly bored unconcern. Actually his heart was racing. Where was that woman? Why was she taking so long? Had she seen through his disguise and was at this very moment telephoning friends who would soon abduct him?

There were a half-dozen civilian automobiles parked at curbside, a few lorries, one old taxicab, whose driver was arguing with a potential passenger about the price of the fare into Marienkirche, and a great number of jeeps with spit-and-polished young soldiers waiting patiently for the brass. Mitchell climbed into the Citroën, and a few moments later the nurse brought out the briefcase. There were perspiration stains under the arms of her white uniform, and it was not that warm. This trip was obviously a trial for her. "I'm sorry for the delay, Herr Doktor, a problem at customs," she replied brusquely, sliding into the front seat beside him, and starting the motor.

To pass the time, since he did not want to engage in small talk, he opened his briefcase, pretending to look over some papers, actually checking to see if the contents had been tampered with, but they were in order. He took no notice of where they were going, although he would have very much liked to look about the city. His look-alike made frequent trips to Berlin, so he would not be curious. As they sped through the empty streets, he had only an impression of immense devastation. He yawned behind his polished fingernails. He wanted very much to ask where the ruined Brandenburg Gate was located in East Berlin, but he dared not.

At last Hilda Schumann inexpertly parked the Citroën in front of the hospital, only part of which was still left standing. Mitchell picked up his briefcase, nodded curtly to his driver.

He stopped at the desk on the first floor and threw down his card, tapping his fingers impatiently on the counter. The middle-aged nurse glanced at the card and flushed so warmly that her glasses steamed over. She stammered, "The administrator ... will see you ... immediately, Herr Doktor." She reminded him faintly of Belle Trune, except she had brown hair instead of red, and a long whisker on her chin. He came back to the present with a snap of his head. "Well?"

The change-of-life nurse looked puzzled and then realized that he did not know how to proceed. "I'll have one of the RN's take you up," she said and pressed a buzzer. A young woman appeared. She was quite pretty, with ash-blond hair and wide blue eyes. "Good morning, Herr Doktor," she said, obviously impressed with his reputation. She preceded him down the hall and into the elevator.

"One thing that I dislike," Mitchell proclaimed in a bored voice, "are menopausal nurses forced to greet the public!"

The RN said nothing at all, but her mouth twitched in agreement. He smiled to himself at hospital politics. They stepped out of the elevator; she guided him into a small reception area and opened the door to a small, sparsely furnished office. There was a large stain on the wall in back of the desk, where a picture had once hung. Who had been so honored? Mitchell wondered. The little man with the mustache who had placed a pistol in his mouth and blown out his brains in the bunker across town?

"My name is Helmut Danker." Mitchell shook hands

with a fortyish man in a brown business suit with black
hair and bushy eyebrows. "Sit down, please, Herr Doktor
Thank you for making this trip just to examine one old
Jew."

Mitchell nodded coldly, tapped his nails on his briefcase

Mr. Danker put on his spectacles and picked up a file
"Our observations indicate that the patient has been
deteriorating rapidly. Here is the report."

Mitchell ran his finger down the page to the prognosis
"The lung has cleared up, then? Good." He turned the
page and read two paragraphs slowly so that he could
assimilate the information. "Apparently he has exhibited
signs of paranoia from the first arrest"—he glanced down
at the paper—"on May twenty-third, nineteen-forty-five,
when he was taken to a camp in the Valdai Hills."

"Yes," Danker sighed, "along with one hundred seventy-
nine thousand, nine hundred and ninety-nine others!"

"So many? It was a black day."

"Admiral von Friedburg committed suicide to protest
the arrests."

"I knew him only slightly." Mitchell arched his back
and assumed a more upright position on the chair. "I
wonder," he continued wryly, "how many of the other
one hundred seventy-nine thousand, nine hundred and
ninety-nine also exhibited signs of paranoia?"

Danker smiled thinly. "Steinmetz believed he was to
be taken into the courtyard and shot if it was discovered
that he was a deputy assistant to Herr Kaindl, Commandant of Sachsenhausen. He seemed to improve
then and was almost cheerful, but he contracted pneumonia and was sent here. He became violent three
weeks ago and had to be subdued."

"Why prolong this?" Mitchell asked, looking at his
watch. "I must leave shortly." He turned the diamond
ring around and around on his finger. "May I examine
the patient, Herr Danker?"

The administrator accompanied him to a rickety elevator that moved slowly and with great hesitation. On the fourth floor, an iron gate that separated the elevator from the ward beyond was thrown open by a burly guard. When the vacant, echoing *click* of the gate rang out behind him, Mitchell felt a cold stab of fear run down his spine. Did they know that he was not the real Herr Professor? Had he been enticed into this security facility only to be thrown into a cell?

His panic subsided. He was being absurd. They were now walking rapidly through the ward, but he did not look at the bed patients, afraid of what he would see; he did not enjoy suffering. Danker stopped before a cell, one of the several at the rear of the ward, and nodded to his guard. "I'll leave you now, Herr Doktor," Danker said, his mouth in a hard, thin line. "Please stop by my office before you leave."

"Certainly," Mitchell replied coldly, swallowed quickly, and went into the cell. A barefoot rolled-up form, clothed in a shapeless gray gown, was huddled in a corner of the room, gray head on a pillow. The small cot was still made up with an army blanket.

Mitchell sat down on a folding chair provided by the guard. "Leave the door unlocked," he barked as the guard left. Somehow he could not endure being locked in a cell; his poise and equilibrium would ebb away. "Now, Herr Steinmetz," he said not unkindly, "how are we today?"

The old man did not change positions, his body remained folded up in the fetal position, but he moved his gray head and opened his large brown eyes slightly. "You are from Berlin," he mumbled. "I can tell by your accent. Did you know Der Führer well?"

"I attended to him once or twice when he was younger."

"He's on the floor above," Steinmetz said confidentially, unfolding his arms and legs. "We exchange messages sometimes. I hold no bitterness toward the man. I fooled him for many years. They all thought I was Heinz

Dorpmüller, you know, because I changed my name in nineteen thirty-three. *Sieg Heil!* They did not find me out until the very end." He looked quickly about him and then glanced at Mitchell slyly, his eyes wide, his mouth slack. "They did not know that I was the Jew Steinmetz." His feet and arms began to twitch. "I do not have a big nose. I do not have big ears. I have forgotten my Yiddish." He threw back his head defiantly. "I am a German and I will remain a German." He reached into the pocket of his gown and removed a scrap of paper, which he thrust at Mitchell. "This was Der Führer's message last night," he said convincingly, "It's in code and reads: 'Do you have any tobacco?' "

The man's performance was so real that Mitchell found himself looking at the paper, half expecting to see the words spelled out, but instead there was only a series of digits, which just might be, he concluded, a telephone number. He placed the paper in his pocket. "Tell me, Herr Steinmetz, how do you communicate with Der Führer?"

The man looked around swiftly and his expression changed; his eyes narrowed and glittered, and his lips drew back over yellow teeth. He almost caught Mitchell unaware as he whispered loudly, "There is a mouse that runs along the battlements outside the window." He threw back his head and laughed gleefully, and Mitchell saw that the back of his mouth gleamed with gold fillings. He suddenly looked exactly like a monkey as he delivered his line, the *pièce de résistance*: "For a piece of cheese, he will deliver anything!"

Mitchell lowered his head to conceal a smile, then glanced up soberly, and asked in a conspiratorial tone, "Do you attach the messages around his neck?"

Steinmetz looked at him incredulously. "*Nein!* He carries them elegantly between his teeth!" He paused, then went on defensively, "If you don't believe me, look at the marks on the paper!"

Mitchell removed the message from his pocket; sure enough, there were slight indentations along the edge. Was this also some kind of code that the old man thought he might miss? He nodded and replaced the paper. "Tell me, Herr Steinmetz"—he spoke to him as if he were a child—"what day is this?"

"Sunday."

"The date?"

"May twenty-third, nineteen-forty-five."

"Thank you." He paused knowing that the old man was frozen in time. "Are you in touch with other political leaders in this building—other than Der Führer?"

"*Nein.* All of them are dead except the Reichschancellor. He alone survived—just as he always said that he would."

Mitchell stood up. "Good day, Herr Steinmetz," he said formally, and upon leaving, nodded to the guard to close the cell door. The man looked heavenward and made little circles at his temple with his forefinger. "There are no mice in this building," he whispered confidentially. He broke into a nervous laugh. "But there is a *rat* or two!" The guard thought his remark a huge joke and went off chuckling to himself.

Downstairs, Mitchell knocked once at Danker's door and was admitted. "Are you aware that Der Führer is on the floor above the old Jew and that they send messages back and forth via a mouse? I have been brought from Vienna for this?" He grimaced, opened his briefcase, and pulled out a legal pad of paper, from which he tore a long, formal-looking sheet.

Danker pushed out his chin. "I used to know him when he was the deputy. Ah, you should have seen him in his uniform. He was always superbly groomed. He was a brilliant administrator." His mouth curled with disgust. "Now look at him! Herr Kaindl should have killed him when he discovered that he was a Jew. He should have killed him for many reasons, not only because of his masquerade, but because he signed all the orders to kill his own kind." He straightened his back, and his body took on a military bearing. "We were at least true to ourselves and to the party. Losing the war was an unfortunate miscalculation." He sighed. "But men like the old Jew—insanity is too good for them, eh?"

Mitchell shrugged his shoulders. "He has no honor." He placed the paper on his briefcase and wrote a few words at the top, then added the professor's signature with a flourish. "Here," he said, "would you have the necessary information typed in the proper spaces?" He looked at his watch again. "I must leave." He shook Danker's hand briefly and went to the door, then, as an afterthought, turned back and said conversationally, "Oh, I would suggest transferring him to the Pandandt Asylum as soon as possible. These cases sometimes turn violent, harm others. They develop surprising strength."

As Hilda Schumann drove him swiftly to the airport, Mitchell studied the ruins. Had the city been the Berlin of old, he would have enjoyed walking near Unter den Linden. So many complete blocks had been bombed out that it was a shock to see one old edifice still standing unmolested.

He nodded coldly to Hilda Schumann and went into the airport. Since an hour and a half remained before his flight to Frankfurt, he thought about the message Steinmetz had given him: was he to call the number before he left Berlin? What would Leary have advised? It would do no harm to call the number; he could always hang up. Later, in the small refreshment room, he had a cup of tea laced with honey, and a Black Forest torte before he made the call.

"Oui?" Pierre Darlan said as clearly as if he were beside Mitchell. "I was waiting for the telephone to ring."

*   *   *

Mitchell Heron and Pierre Darlan met in the side lobby of the Hotel Kempinski on the Kurfürstendamm a half-hour later. The hotel brought back many memories. Mitchell had stayed there briefly in 1936, when the Kurfürstendamm was a glamorous Old World street; now it bore no traces of the elegant district it had once been. But he realized that all would change; grand hotels would rise again, intimate restaurants would open their doors once more, jewelers would hang out their signs, there would be street traffic and neon lights, and lovers would stroll down the wide thoroughfare. Now there was only bombed-out rubble.

Pierre embraced him. "How did it go?"

"As smooth as silk. I played the man as a complete ass."

"Herr Steinmetz?"

"Certified." Mitchell paused. "It is very weird to come all the way over here to pronounce a man insane and then have him give me a contact number!"

"Our nurse slipped it to him this morning because it was imperative that I see you before you left Berlin. It seems that the Herr Professor must make one more appearance before he leaves."

Mitchell held out his hand in protest. "Oh, no, you don't! Who else must I certify? This was the only assignment I agreed upon. You promised me a week in Paris, which I mean to take."

Pierre sighed. "Your early flight to Frankfurt has been canceled for one later this evening." Pierre turned to the wall and examined a bad painting of a purple-and-white plate. "We learned just after you left Washington that the Herr Professor was asked to speak. The receptionist in his office wrote a letter of acceptance."

"Clarify, please."

A frown creased Pierre's forehead. "He is a member of the group that used to meet once a year before the war. Since nineteen-forty, none of these meetings have taken place because of the"—he waved his hand—"the recent conflict. The Herr Professor is to speak to a group of students at eight o'clock this evening at the Free University."

"Oh, my God!" Mitchell exclaimed, horror-stricken. "What are you going to do?"

"Nothing! It is *you* who are going to give the lecture."

When Mitchell regained his voice, he was hoarse with rage. "How in the hell can I do that?"

"Calm down," Pierre soothed, looking around the empty room. "You are what is known as a 'quick study.' A famous psychiatrist, who shall be nameless, was kind enough to prepare, on a moment's notice, a lecture on a subject close to Herr Professor Schneider's heart—if indeed he possesses one. You will go upstairs as soon as the room is ready—there is a great shortage of accommodations—and study those six pages."

"But dammit!" Mitchell said, losing his temper for the second time. "I cannot do that! Have you lost every bit of sense? Have you forgotten all the preparation time for this one little caper, and now you expect me to take on a much larger job at a moment's notice? If I didn't know that you are Pierre Darlan, I would say that someone is impersonating *you!*"

Pierre sat down and crossed his legs. "I have forgotten nothing, *mon cher.* It is not nearly so complicated as you would have it. In the first place, I am going to be with you. I am your assistant, a Herr Mueller, who will drive you to the Free University, and introduce you to the students in my abominable Low German. At the end of your address, I will explain you are fatigued and that time does not permit questions and answers, and we leave on the midnight plane for Frankfurt. From there you can go to Paris, as planned"—he looked at his pocket watch—"with only a ten-hour delay."

"This whole scheme is pure *shit*, and you know it!" Mitchell exclaimed savagely. "Almost as ridiculous as that story about Steinmetz sending notes to Hitler via a mouse. I could hardly keep a straight face. If those Nazis fell for that, they will swallow anything. Tell me who thought that one up—you, or Leary? I mean, think about it, a mouse, Pierre, a *mouse!*"

"The point is, *mon cher*," Pierre replied, smoothing his mustaches, "that many people feign insanity. They act queerly, roll their eyes, twitch, ramble on and on, and make quite a spectacle of themselves. They *enjoy* it too much and give themselves away. But those who are truly disturbed have a *fixed idea* and never make a big spectacle. They may occasionally lose control, fly into a rage, but there is a great difference in behavior patterns. It was decided to have Steinmetz fix on the greatest friend/adversary that he ever had—Der Führer himself. Remember, this man was a Judas. He betrayed his own people. Now he wants to make amends, and he will testify against Herr Kaindl. Himmler, who commanded concentration camps like Sachsenhausen, cannot be put on trial because he bit into a cyanide capsule. But Steinmetz was *there*, and his testimony will provide details, *personal* details. So his fixation has to be unusual, ridiculous, laughable even, but believable."

Mitchell nodded. "He was. He gave every indication of being really paranoid. It was comical—and frightening, too." His face became concerned. "I suppose that he, above all, knew how to portray terror. It was a part of his everyday life for several years. He had seen thousands of his countrymen die."

"That was a part of it surely," Pierre agreed, nodding his head, "but his performance was more basic than that. You could not know that his father was one of the most famous actors in the Yiddish Art Theater! As a boy, he was his father's dresser. So, he knows something about acting and drama." He waved his hand. "I think, probably, that he had never used this background before, but as an old man in prison, full of reparation for his sins, his early life must have come back to him. That was why he was so effective."

Mitchell nodded. "He still haunts me."

"He became a Nazi because he was an opportunist, a careerist, who wanted a good life. I believe he sincerely loved Germany and he only went with the winning party. He had divorced himself early on from his family and Jewish friends, and assumed the name of Dorpmüller. He was Aryan, and that was that. He had no way of knowing that he would eventually rise in the party and become a famous man; and, most important of all, he could not know that he would end up the deputy commander of a concentration camp!"

Pierre paused. "By that time, he was so strategically placed that there was no escape, and it was then, under those conditions, that if he had possessed any substantial character weakness, he would have really gone insane or committed suicide."

Pierre methodically tapped his fingers on the table. "Somehow he kept at his job—if not sickened, then, I would like to think, surely conscience-stricken. Then, during that last three months, when everyone but the Germans knew it was all over, he was found out. Commandant Kaindl at Sachsenhausen had apparently never liked him, and so he was stripped of all honors and made to wear the striped uniform with the yellow insignia of the Jews. He would have been torn to pieces had he been placed with the other inmates, so he was put in a cell, with only bread and water, and in the process lost a hundred and ten pounds. That was when the camp was liberated, and he was transferred to another prison by the Allied commandant."

Pierre got up and went back to the wall and began to examine the fake Picasso again; then he turned to Mitchell, hands folded behind his back. "At this new facility, he made overtures to those in power and indicated that he would testify against the former heads of the concentration camp when the trials open at Nuremberg."

Mitchell shook his head. "I've never understood men who doublecross themselves to get ahead."

"Yet we all make compromises. Steinmetz's compromise was becoming a Nazi. He could not see ahead. I think that first simple treachery led into all the others. At any rate, we are up-to-date on our story. Steinmetz became the most-wanted man on all the still existent Nazi lists. When the head of the prison took a vacation, wheels began to turn and certain pressures were exerted, and he was transferred to a maximum-security prison, where, very frankly, he could be killed. When he developed this pneumonia—they were very cruel to him—he was sent to the hospital where you saw him, which is controlled by neo-Nazis. He could be poisoned, or a stroke could be induced, or the wrong medication administered. That is why we had to get him out before something happened to him. *He must testify at the trials.*"

Mitchell nodded. "That's all well and good, but what I don't understand is why I must appear tonight. Why can't I be taken ill?"

"Because, *mon cher*," Pierre explained patiently, "the hospital has not released Steinmetz yet! He is not scheduled out until tomorrow, and one of the internes will be at your lecture tonight! At this stage of the game, we must not in any way court suspicion. The personality of Herr Doktor is such that he would give a speech on a streetcorner with a temperature of one hundred and four!"

Mitchell was exasperated. "I've never understood why in the hell you and Leary never can come out straight with anything. You beat around the bush until you both drive me crazy. I'll end up like Steinmetz at this rate! It's as if you are incapable of straightline thinking."

Pierre lit a cigarette. "Possibly you are right, but in our work there is always much to hide. A cardinal rule has always been that you never tell any one person very much—the less the better—and you never let an agent know what another agent is doing. That way you protect them both."

"Then how come you have told me everything about this case?"

Pierre blew a cloud of smoke toward the ceiling. "I haven't." He smiled coldly and raised his arm as if to ward off a blow. "But I have told you the *important* points. The rest is of no interest."

"You son-of-a-bitch!"

Pierre laughed. "Sooner or later," he said matter-of-factly, "all my operatives curse me." He paused, "But usually it is *later*!"

Mitchell had calmed down. "I assume that you brought the speech with you. May I see it, please?"

Pierre handed him the small sheaf of papers, and Mitchell smiled laconically. "You've thought of everything, haven't you?" The pages were hand-lettered in large, easy-to-read print, and the paragraphs were well spaced. "Why," he exclaimed, "the technical terms are even phonetically spelled out!"

"We can't have the Herr Professor, who is such a stickler for form, mispronounce even one word," Pierre replied smoothly. "Now let us go up to the room. I shall take a nap while you rehearse."

"I wish to hell," Mitchell said, "that it was the other way around."

The students were waiting quietly in the dusty theater, subdued, Pierre thought, either because of twelve-hour duty or because of the reputation of the man who would be addressing them. He made a brief but flowery introduction. Mitchell walked stiffly toward the podium, which held a yellow light large enough to illuminate the pages, yet small enough to throw an interesting shadow up into his face.

Mitchell looked thin, but more esthetic than emaciated, Pierre thought. He acknowledged the applause, bowed his head slightly, and his silver hair glistened when he held up his hand for silence. He cleared his throat, looked out over the small gathering of students, and gave the first line: "Gentlemen, I am going to speak this evening on crisis—the self-identity crisis."

Backstage, Pierre sat on the lighting technician's stool and listened to Mitchell's delivery. He was thoroughly familiar with the speech, having read it several times on the airplane. Midway through the lecture, it suddenly occurred to Pierre that he was totally absorbed in Mitchell's words. It seemed difficult to realize that the man on the stage was an impostor, a man he had trained for this very job. Mitchell was thoroughly enshrouded in the Herr Professor's persona and, as he spoke, his dry, authoritative voice was both winning and beguiling. Mitchell was obviously enjoying himself. It was a characterization that Pierre would never forget.

It was almost impossible to connect this dapper, erudite, effete man on stage, speaking colloquial German so effortlessly, with the proprietor of the Heron Furniture Company headquartered in Enid, Oklahoma.

At the end of the speech, Pierre found himself standing up and applauding. He was so taken up in Mitchell's aura that it took him a moment to realize that he must appear on stage himself. He walked quickly to the apron and held up his hands. "Unfortunately," he said apologetically, "Herr Doktor Schneider is very fatigued and will be unable to answer questions this evening"

There was an audible collection of "ah-h-h-h"s from the students. Mitchell held up his hand, ignoring Pierre. "I will answer only two brief questions; then I must leave."

Pierre was astounded. Obviously, Mitchell had so taken on the cloak of his nemesis that he was impervious to the danger that lurked in the small theater! It was proper form, Pierre knew, to retire to the wings, but he forced himself to stand on the apron of the stage, not only to remind the students that the evening could not proceed much further, but also to physically draw Mitchell's attention to his own folly.

Mitchell peered into the audience as hands were raised, and indicated a man in the first row, who stood up uncertainly and said, "On behalf of the students, please accept our grateful thanks for your kindness in addressing us." He cleared his throat. "My question has to do with personal identity itself. At what age do you believe the sexual pattern is established?"

"It is my opinion," Mitchell answered quickly, "that self-identity, including sexual orientation, is certainly established by the fifth year."

"So," the man continued, "experimentation in adolescence, then, would have no bearing on the individual's sexual preference later on?"

"I assume," Mitchell replied easily, "that you are referring to mutual masturbation among the same sex? Actually, this practice should have no damaging effect on the psyche. Those who would be affected, of course, would have already chosen, knowingly or unknowingly, their own sexual preference." He paused. "One more question, please?"

Cold perspiration was running down Pierre's rib cage. Talk about dangerous waters! Mitchell was diving into rapids that could catapult him over the falls!

Mitchell pointed to a student in the last row. "Yes?"

"Herr Professor"—the man's voice bore traces of a whispering Viennese accent—"did not Dr. Jung break with Dr. Freud over this very question?"

Mitchell allowed himself a small, dry laugh. "Actually, no. Dr. Jung did not believe that every minor attitude in the child, from babyhood, was triggered by sexual response. Dr. Freud was of the opposite opinion. The babe at the mother's breast was satisfying a sexual urge, according to him, which has nothing to do, in my opinion, with sexual identity or even the identity crisis that I spoke at length about earlier. Now I must say good night."

The students rose simultaneously, giving him a standing ovation, the first that Mitchell had ever experienced. Although his heart was beating very fast, he did not permit himself to acknowledge the tribute, except by a short perfunctory bow.

He also acknowledged Pierre, who was standing in the same position on the wide apron of the stage. The lights came up in the theater, and Pierre unceremoniously left the stage, accosting Mitchell, who was calmly sipping a glass of water in the wings. "You fool!" he whispered, "You arrogant fool. This could have been the end of us!"

"Nonsense." Mitchell arched his back, drew his buttocks together, and replied in studied tones of the Herr Professor Schneider, "I was having fun."

"Which is the most dangerous of all! *Having fun!* An *amateur!* You've overplayed your hand!"

"Nonsense," Mitchell whispered in his own voice. "I had sense enough to stay up a couple of nights in Washington, after you and Leary had gone to bed, doing homework. Oh-oh—here come the students. Let's get the hell out of here." He waved soberly at the gathering, nodded at the student proctor at the stage door, and preceded Pierre into the alley and the rented 1939 Mercedes.

10

The Leaving

Since he had enrolled in summer classes at the Barrett Conservatory of Music in Angel, William Nestor returned home each weekend.

Friday at 5:00 P.M. he would take the bus from Angel to Perry, change buses for Willawa at Tulsa, and arrive at Louisa Tarbell's back door at midnight. After dallying for an hour or two, he would walk home, and would be up four hours later, performing chores around the farm. Sometimes he plowed fields from sunrise to sunset, when his father was in bed with an attack of pleurisy.

This Friday night, William fell asleep immediately after making love to Louisa, and she could not rouse him. Sitting on the edge of the bed, she held his hand. His face, softly illuminated by the beaded lampshade on the nightstand, sagged with fatigue, and there were dark circles under his eyes.

Finally at four o'clock, he awakened with a start and, eyes wide, clasped her to him. He was shaking all over. "Hey," he breathed with relief, seeing that he was safe in bed, "I just had a dream. You and I were in this room, and Poppa rushed in and found us sleeping together and he had a pitchfork in his hand." He shivered. "I can still feel it in my back. What time is it, Lou?"

"Four."

"Oh, if I could only stay here with you all night, just *once*." He looked at her longingly. "But I guess it'll never happen."

She turned away. "No, I suppose not."

He got up and dressed quickly. "I've got to get home. It'll be daylight in another hour." He paused, right foot in his jockey shorts, and grimaced. "I've got to finish the back twenty this morning," he said, voice quavering, "and I've a paper due on Monday." He placed his left foot in the shorts and brought the material up snugly around his middle, adjusted his iron bar, which was now soft rubber, and reached for his shirt. His pale midsection and legs contrasted with the deep tan of his face, arms, and torso, from the outdoor work. She reveled, as she always did, in the sight of his young, muscular body that she had seen grow from early adolescence to manhood.

"William," she said persuasively, "you can't go on keeping this insane schedule. Your folks shouldn't expect it."

He grinned wanly. "Oh, it's not only that," he said, "but otherwise, how would I get to see you?"

"I'm not important just now," she replied gently, "but school is. Clement Story's giving you an opportunity that few young men could expect. You can't fail in your studies just because of your family." Her voice was filled with emotion, and her thin face was strained.

He pulled on his jacket, "But Poppa's counting on me to help him bring in the harvest." He sat down on the side of the bed and touched her wispy brown hair with his hand. "Dean Phelps has invited several well-known musicians and conductors to give seminars. Even Mr. Story has said that he'll come for a two-day class, and he's going to bring Sonny Mitchell, his arranger, to hold a question-and-answer session." He counted on his fingers. "There's going to be Isaac Stern, Leonard Bern-

stein, Carmen Dragon, André Kostelanetz, and Lily Pons
and others whom I can't recall at the moment. It's going
to be the biggest shindig ever held at the conservatory.
can't afford to miss it." He lowered his voice. "I know
that we were planning lots of good times this summer
but—"

"You must speak to your parents this weekend. You
simply can't continue to jeopardize your career."

"My career." He smiled grimly. "That term sounds so
strange to me, Lou. For years I went to school, played
the organ in church, and planned to take over Poppa's
job on the farm ... but now, suddenly I have a career
I'm not used to it yet."

"There's going to be no sharecropping in your future
William," Louisa replied fervently. "You're going to be
come famous, very famous." She set her jaw. She glanced
at her watch. "It's four-fifteen. You *must* go!"

He kissed her full on the lips. "I want to stay here with
you," he said simply, placing his hands over her breasts
which were covered with the flimsy cotton nightgown.

She placed her palms over the backs of his hands
and shook her head gently. "No, my love. That would
be easy, but you've got responsibilities." She kissed him
on the cheek. "Now, go, it'll be light soon. You can't be
seen leaving my house. Go through the cornfield."

He got up reluctantly and grinned, looking very appealing, very boyish. "It would be silly to be found out
now."

"Yes," she replied quietly, "especially since we're so
near the end of this road."

After he had gone, she lay down on the coverlet and
ran her hands over the empty body that had been filled
with him a few hours before, and she prayed, "Oh, dear
God, I can't give him up, I just can't!" She began to cry,
then her emotions quieted. The logical schoolteacher's
mind took over, and her thought patterns changed
They had been with each other for five years; some

marriages did not last that long. There had never been a cross word between them, and their lovemaking had grown more intense and satisfying as time passed. Her body was still comparatively firm and yielding, and her hold over him had been complete. No young girl could have given him what she had offered freely, and she knew that she had satisfied him physically, emotionally, and intellectually.

It was logical that his future would be filled with girls his own age or younger, and she could or would not compete with them. When he left the Barrett Conservatory of Music, she had long ago decided he would also leave her physically as well as psychologically. The umbilical cord had to be severed.

Louisa Tarbell drowsed happily after William left, then finally arose at her usual time of seven o'clock. Her upper arms, breasts, and stomach, she saw, were red. Had she broken out with some kind of summer rash? She examined her skin more closely. Why, she thought with alarm, the marks had been made by William's hands! Now she remembered that his palms seemed to scrape her skin during the lovemaking. At that particular moment she had been so lost in bliss that it had never occurred to her that his hands, roaming over her thin body, were leaving marks. She was troubled all day, and when William came by that evening on his way to take the bus to Tulsa, she turned up his palms and looked at the tough white calluses. She kissed his fingers but said nothing.

The next morning she backed the little blue roadster out of her garage, made a stop at the Willawa First National Bank, then headed down the section road to the Nestor farmhouse.

Arma Nestor, barefoot and wearing a large straw hat, was busy in the potato patch. Her slim form, clothed only in a thin cotton dress, was bent over a row of potatoes. One hand carried a tin can filled with coal oil, and the other was busy among the plants. Hearing the motor car, she looked up, shading her eyes with her hand against the sun. "Mornin'," she said grudgingly, her face petulant.

"Good morning, Mrs. Nestor," Louisa said civilly. "I came over to talk to your husband."

The woman jerked her head in the direction of the house. "He's in bed. The pleurisy has him ag'in. If you want to see him, you'll have to go inside."

"Will you come with me?" Louisa asked gently.

Mrs. Nestor gave a long sigh and nodded. "My can's full of potato bugs anyway," she answered, and with a weary air of resignation preceded Louisa to the shack.

Louisa noted that the tattered screen door was half off its hinges and flies were buzzing into the living room, drawn, she discovered, by a plate of half-burned eggs on the dining-room table.

"Finney?" Mrs. Nestor called.

"Yeah?"

"Miss Tarbell is here."

There was a grunt, which Mrs. Nestor interpreted as permission to enter the bedroom.

Finney Nestor, wearing gray, perspiration-soiled long underwear, was propped up in bed. He nodded in an attempt at cordiality. "I'm down with it ag'in," he complained. "It hit my arm pretty bad. What can I do fer ye? It's about Billy-boy, I s'pose?"

Louisa Tarbell took a deep breath. Oh, how she disliked the man! She nodded, then went on with a rush. "It's about his working so hard here at the farm." She paused, and, seeing the man's mouth open, ready to protest, she went on quickly. "William's hands are very precious. If something should happen to them, his career would be nipped in the bud."

Nestor frowned, and his mouth turned down—an old expression of defeat. "Billy-boy is strong. Nothin' ain't gonna happen to those hands of his'n."

"Yes, that's true, because he won't be working in the fields." She gathered up her courage, looked him straight in the eye, and lied, "Clement Story has authorized me to pay you the sum of a hundred and fifty dollars a month for a hired hand."

Nester worked his mouth. "*What?* He's givin' me that money to replace my Billy-boy?" His face broke into a smile. "Why, I can git me the best . . ." He broke off, his eyes suddenly suspicious. He glanced at her curiously. "He's doin' this out of the goodness of his heart?"

Louisa swallowed quickly. "You might say"—she smiled suddenly—"he's doing it for the Lord." And she said a quick prayer of forgiveness for the untruth, but she had to get through to this man.

Finney Nestor nodded and sucked his brown teeth. "I calculate he's doin' it for himself, too, not altogether for Jesus. Anyways, tell him that we're much obliged, although I still don't see what a little work can do to hurt Billy-boy's music talent."

"Finn," his wife scolded from the doorway, "let it go. Mr. Story isn't trying to replace Billy-boy with the hired hand, only his *work.*" She looked helplessly at Louisa and the two women shared a moment of understanding, and Louisa thought: *This woman surely had dreams once. She must have looked forward to a better sort of life when she married this big, complaining man. When William was born, she must have hoped their life would change.* But there was defeat in her eyes, and a terrible weariness to her sloping shoulders. Still, she was William's mother, and she had to be proud that the famous Clement Story had given her boy a scholarship.

Louisa sensed it was time to go and looked directly into Finney Nestor's eyes again. "I've been authorized to give you the cash today, the fifteenth. I'll be back in a month." She opened her purse and counted out five twenty-dollar bills and one fifty slowly into his outstretched palm. She could see the greed in his eyes.

* * *

Herbert Hoover rose to his feet and shook Bosley's hand, and his face lighted up with pleasure. "Our paths cross again," he said.

"Yes, Mr. President, we seem to encounter each other about every ten years," Bosley replied warmly. "I believe the last time was in nineteen-thirty-eight or 'thirty-nine at a fund-raiser here in Manhattan."

The meeting was taking place in the Hoover suite at the Waldorf Astoria Hotel in New York City. "Please excuse the disarray," Hoover was saying, indicating a pile of statistical reports on the sofa, "but I have so much reading to do." He brought his fingers together in a characteristic gesture that Bosley remembered. "It's strange being called into harness after being away for so many years, but it's rewarding to be back in the starting gate again."

"They could not have picked a better man for the job," Bosley said slowly.

Hoover's face was grave. "Thank you." He shifted his body around in the chair, and Bosley noticed that he had gained weight. "The reason that I want you on the committee," he said, looking Bosley in the eye, "is because you are an expert on Midwest economy."

"But what has that to do with feeding Europe, Mr. President?"

Hoover frowned. "That, of course, is the current problem, and I'll want you on that committee also, of course. But we are now putting together a federal commission to research ways and means of eliminating unnecessary government expenditure in this country. Formidable bureaucracy has built up over the years, and consequently twenty people are doing the work of two. When I was in the Oval Office, I tried to clean out various departments and do away with endless repetition of tasks, and I only partially succeeded. Each administration builds up more paperwork that is filed and never read; projects are okayed without proper research. I'm afraid it's still the old 'pork barrel' concept. But President Truman recognizes the need to put a new plan into operation as soon as possible. He's very thrifty about his personal expenses, and he's appalled at the government waste. Millions of dollars are going down the drain." He paused. "There are entire packing crates of material that must be read and evaluated."

Bosley nodded. "I'm conservative too, and there seems to be graft and corruption everywhere I turn."

"Being an outsider, with no political point of view, is a very important asset," Hoover replied. "You have nothing to lose or gain by being a part of the commission; no constituents to satisfy, no superiors to bow to in times of pressure, that's why you're doubly valuable, Bosley."

"Thank you, Mr. President," Bosley replied sincerely. "Now, what can I do immediately that will help lighten your load of work?"

"I'll send over material for you to peruse. President Truman mentioned that you are staying in the Connecticut Avenue house in Washington."

"Yes, we're making our headquarters there now. We go back to Angel for holidays, and that's about it. Now that I'm acting only as a consultant to Heron, I can give the commission my full attention."

Herbert Hoover rose and extended his hand. "Thank you for coming to see me, Bosley," he said. "We'll be in touch very shortly."

Once in the street, Bosley looked at his watch. He had an extra half-hour before meeting Luke at the permanent Heron suite at the Sherry Netherlands. The weather was bracing, and although there was a touch of moisture in the air, he decided to walk and dismissed the driver. Letty was always telling him that he did not get enough exercise, and then too, he would have a few moments to think about the next appointment. He looked forward to meeting their Saudi Arabian friend Muhammad Abn, whom he and Luke had visited in Jeddah in 1938, and who had visited the farm in Angel in 1945. Since that time, every few months an invitation to come to Saudi Arabia had arrived—a routine query, because no one could visit that country without a personal summons. It was understood that Luke and he would make the journey when they could take time away from Heron business.

There was a brief knock on the door, and when Luke answered, a tall form loomed on the threshold. Muhammad Abn, wearing a British-cut blue serge suit and gray homburg, nodded politely without smiling.

Luke nodded formally. "*is-salaam 'alaykum*," he said.

"*wa-'alaykum is-salaam*," Muhammad Abn replied.

"*massa' il-khayr.*"

"*massa' in-nuwr.*" Muhammad Abn's face was a mask.

"It is good to see you again," Luke replied warmly. "How *are* you?"

"Fine, praise be to Allah!"

One more formality remained. "I trust," Luke said with dignity, "that King 'Abd-al-'Aziz ibn-'Abd-al-Rahman al-Faisal ibn-Sa'ud is in excellent health?"

"Yes, indeed, Luke."

Luke held out his hand. "Please come in and sit," he said with a wide smile, the traditional meeting ritual concluded.

Muhammad Abn shook hands, and his shoulders relaxed. "It is such a great pleasure seeing you again, my friend," he said in his soft Cambridge accent. He took a chair opposite the sofa where Luke had a number of papers spread out. "I find New York very tiring," he continued, "and the General Assembly of the United Nations, with all of the simultaneous translations and the headsets and the tribal dresses and pomp and circumstance, is wearying. How much better it would be if all business could be conducted in English!"

Luke smiled. "But the air of excitement must be contagious."

Muhammad Abn stroked his black goatee and smoothed his mustache, his eyes very dark and brooding. "Yes, of course, but events proceed at the pace of an anteater—and you must remember everything in the kingdom of Saudi Arabia moves slowly, but at Lake Success the harangues seem interminable."

He chuckled. "I was fortunate to be educated in England, so I can take my place in the international world, but some of the delegates have not had that advantage. Then, too, I am often asked very stupid questions. There was a certain persistent congresswoman who obviously had never been to the Middle East. Finally, when I could no longer endure the line of questioning, I told her that to be able to place the Arab world in proper perspective, she must remember that in her terms we had changed very little in the last two thousand years. If she ever visited our country—which would be almost impossible, since she was a woman—she would discover a culture essentially biblical." He smiled and nodded his head. "Even that statement did not penetrate her closed mind, and when she brought up the differences between Christianity and Islam, I could do nothing but walk away."

Luke pursed his lips and frowned. "These things must be very frustrating."

Muhammad Abn sighed deeply. "They are, but we all must study and learn the beauties—and the disadvantages—of other cultures, or we are forever lost. The United Nations will hopefully bridge that gap eventually. But there are some matters that are of great concern to me. You understand, Luke, that I embrace progress, but progress over a long period of time. What concerns me now is that the kingdom is on the brink of great conflict.

I do not mean militarily, of course, but our great period of isolation is coming to a close."

He went on quietly, his voice filled with sadness. "The drilling of each well brings so-called 'civilization' nearer. Our peoples will not have time to adjust, I fear. Time was when three-fourths of our population was migratory. What will happen to the Bedouins who will be attracted by the riches of the city? More airports will mean an even greater influx of people, not only Muslims who make the honored pilgrimage to the Holy City of Mecca, but the hundreds of thousands of foreign people whom the oil companies will eventually bring in to oversee their equipment. There will come a time, in the very near future—two or three years, perhaps—when there will be huge foreign compounds near every large city, especially the encampments on the Arabian Sea. I see more and more concessions being given to oil companies."

Luke nodded. "But you must also think of the money."

"Ah, yes, the money," Muhammad Abn replied reflectively. "That, of course, is the root, perhaps in this case, that separates good and evil. What will we do with these millions?"

"Schools, universities, the modernization of towns?"

"Yes, that will certainly come about. But what we must do, I think, is to be certain to educate the younger generation to take over industrial positions, instead of permitting others to administrate our prime resource, which, of course, is petroleum. This is why, in our concession agreements, no matter whether they are given out for thirty, fifty, or a hundred years—at the end of the time span, the facilities built by foreigners must revert to us."

Muhammad nodded his head gravely. "When that time comes, we must be ready to assume the responsibility and possess the technology. This expertise will be crucial in our development as an important nation. That is why I believe that King 'Abd-al-'Aziz ibn-'Abd-al-Rahman al-Faisal ibn-Sa'ud will very shortly appoint a council of ministers, a legislative body, to look after such things as foreign and domestic policies, finance, education, and other matters, both executive and administrative. As it now stands, the monarchy is steeped in the past, and one man, no matter how brilliant, can only do so much work. We must evolve from a tribal and regional society."

He lowered his voice, and his manner became hesitant. "I hesitate to speak of it, but King 'Abd-al-'Aziz, although he looks much younger in person, is almost seventy and somewhat fragile." He pulled at his goatee. "I am being very candid with you, Luke, because when you visit the kingdom, I want you to be able to understand the current situation there. I do not mean to press you, but since our last meeting, when do you think you will be able to accept an invitation?"

There was the sound of a key being turned in a lock, and Luke arose. "I will give you an answer very shortly, when my stepfather, Bosley Trenton, comes through that door."

William Nestor stayed in the music room after class that Friday afternoon to play the portable organ purely for pleasure.

Looking down at the small keyboard, he wished that he was back in church, playing the old triple keyboard that he knew so well. As wheezy as that old contraption was, it still produced a superior sound. As his hands ran over the keys, he felt a certain power, missing from the old days. He picked up some sheet music at random and glanced at the notes. What had been missing before, of course, was the ability to see a page and read what was noted there. Now he had been taught to understand intellectually what he was reading, and this total experience was a surprise every time he sat down at the organ.

He began the first few bars of the old folk tune

"Comin' Round the Mountain," and then, out of habit, looked up at the ceiling and began to improvise, in the same way that he had done so often in the loft in the church at Willawa.

Suddenly he began to doodle, working on a phrase of "Comin' Round the Mountain," then pulled out the F stop and brought in the *clippity, clip, clop* of horses' hooves, and hummed *da da, da, da da da, da.* He thought of the college kids whose families were farmers and whose forebears were the settlers who punched cattle and roped steers. A line came to him: *College frats in sheepskin chaps.* He grinned, doodled some more, and fit the line into the *da, da, da, da, da, da.* It melded together perfectly. He pictured one of the boys at the conservatory in a cowboy outfit, and sang: *"Shootin' irons stuck down in holsters, brown 'n' fuzzy from the dew . . ."*

He laughed out loud and worked out the phrase musically. The beat was full-blown and filled with irony, made even more satiric because of three-quarter waltz time. He chortled again, and the second phrase came to him, and then the third. He was exhilarated; it was as if he was tuned into some outside force that was feeding him the lyrics along with the music.

Excitedly he drew a music staff and transcribed notes on the page. His hand couldn't move quickly enough. Once in awhile he would stop and work out a difficult phrase on the organ, then stop and realize that he was writing for the piano. When the room became so dark that he could no longer see the page in front of him, he switched on the lamp beside the nearby desk and immediately returned to the page.

He went over the refrain once more, then, wet with perspiration, switched off the light. He was too tired to play the piece from beginning to end. As he closed the door to the music room and crept upstairs to the dormitory and to bed, he had never felt more exhausted in his eighteen and a half years of life. But, under the muscle fatigue, he felt an exultation that was very much akin to that satisfying aftermath that he always experienced after making love to Louisa—only this time his bar of iron remained soft and yielding. It was as if nothing remained in his body to expel.

William was awake before the sun illuminated the long line of empty beds in the dormitory. He lay stretched out, glad that everyone had taken the weekend off; while the students were enjoying the company of their families, he would exult in a rare bit of privacy. He got out of bed, bathed, shaved, and dressed, slowing down his movements, afraid to go back to the music room and look at what he had written. Vagrant notes, swirling around in his brain, made no sense at all. He looked at his watch. It was ten minutes to seven. Since the cafeteria would be closed, he pulled on a sweatshirt and walked the mile and a half from the Barrett Conservatoy of Music to the brand-new building that housed the Red Bird Café. Trucks were already lined up outside. He opened the door and edged down on a seat at the counter.

Belle Trune, at the grill, waved a spatula at him. "Morning," she said, nodding her red head, which was several shades darker than usual. "Biscuits and gravy, William?"

He nodded, then glanced down the counter at the truckers—rough men with callused hands. He looked down at his delicate fingers, then turned his palms upward. His hands were as callused as theirs.

Belle set a steaming plate in front of him, poured a cup of coffee from the old-fashioned copper urn, and placed her hands on her generous hips. "You been doing manual labor?" she asked, looking at his palms. "Those aren't the paws of a music major."

William ate slowly, savoring the rich cream gravy and

the flavor of the hot, flaky biscuits; then he paid the check and took the long way back by the Chenovicks' farm to the conservatory—anything to delay confronting the music stacked on top of the organ.

Finally he could bear the suspense no longer and ran into the music room, sat down at the keyboard, glanced at the first page, and began to play. A chill ran up and down his spine; what he had written in that first flush of inspiration was good, darned good! When he finished, he sat enjoying the mood that he had created. The lyrics were funny, he felt, and the waltz tempo added a wry counterpoint. It was unlike anything he'd ever heard before. He placed the sheet music in his portfolio. He would never show "The Cowboy Waltz" to anyone.

"Before we arrange another trip abroad, bub," Robert Desmond was saying, "you must enroll in a quick French course at Berlitz."

Luke Three grinned. "I can hardly speak English as it is!"

"French is the language of diplomats, the most elegant in the world." Desmond smiled one of his rare smiles, and he looked rather boyish. "I learned classical French from a governess."

"The one that taught you a lot of other things that have also come in handy?"

"Ah . . . yes."

Luke Three leered at him suggestively, because the talents of the governess had been many and varied, and had apparently included some instructions the nature of which Robert Desmond kept rather vague.

In this thirteenth week of their tour of the Heron offices, they were house guests of a Belgian countess, Jolene Fertig, who was occupying an old hunting lodge outside Antwerp. The compound, which was surrounded on all sides by industry, once had been quite remote, before the war. "You must excuse the noise from the bicycle factory next door," their hostess, who was in her middle thirties, said cheerfully, running a nervous hand through her long mane of hair the color of blackstrap molasses.

Her fingers were decorated with several huge topaz rings, and the smoky color matched her eyes, which were light brown. She wore a long white evening dress with a badly soiled hem and a neckline that showed her bosom. "I would have preferred to keep the acreage, but my foreign oil leases were not producing, and I had to sell a portion to keep body and soul together. During the war I was forced to mortgage the rest of it; then I could not keep up the payments."

She threw back her lovely head and laughed, as if she had given the punch line to a very good joke. She pursed her red lips and raised her thin eyebrows, and Luke Three thought she was very attractive indeed. "I even married a count, who I thought had a fortune." She opened her eyes innocently. "But he had been cleaned out by the Germans and had even less than I! He died, leaving me with numerous gambling debts." She smiled, which was out of context with the serious matter she was discussing. "I shall live the rest of my life in single blessedness." Rapaciously, her eyes gleamed. "And with the help of you gentlemen, perhaps in luxury as well." At that moment there was a hissing sound from the kitchen, and she rose quickly. "Excuse me, I believe our dinner has boiled over!" She ran from the room, holding her long white skirt over tarnished silver lamé sandals.

"What a strange and exciting lady," Luke Three remarked. "I think she's the first ... aristocrat I've ever met. She's like a movie star in an old war movie."

"Yes, you do expect Peter Lorre to light her cigarette," Robert Desmond replied quietly, smoothing his impeccably tailored blue blazer. "I wouldn't have accepted her invitation if I'd known she was in such a bad way financially, without a car or servants."

"Are you a snob?"

"I didn't mean it *that* way, bub. She's actually *cooking* for us."

"But she seems so unconcerned about everything, as if nothing bothers her."

"That's because she thinks life is 'preordained.'" He mouthed the word lovingly.

"What's that?"

Robert Desmond drew in his breath at the boy's naiveté, and patiently explained, "She believes that a person has no control over life, that some kind of a force has everything worked out before birth."

"But that's a crock! We're responsible for our own lives!"

"That's her philosophy. She may be right, however, about becoming rich again, if we can make a deal for her oil leases. When her father's wells were spudded, Cable Tool Equipment could only drill down a couple of thousand feet. With our new rotary motors and the wildcat bit, we'll be able to go deeper. Those old wells may produce more oil than ever. I'm told the petroleum sands are still there."

Jolene Fertig returned, wiping her fingers with their long, gleaming nails on a tattered lace handkerchief. "The rare beef has now been turned into a pot roast," she said gaily, "and the little new potatoes that I wanted to serve whole with a bit of parsley are going to be mashed because they overcooked. But I promise an excellent dessert."

She sat down by Luke Three on the horsehair sofa and looked expectantly into his face. "I'm so pleased that you have decided to follow in your father's footsteps instead of taking up some other business. I have a son who is now nineteen, who has no interest in anything except having a good time. He hates the smell of petroleum, was expelled from the Sorbonne, impregnated two women to whom he had not even been properly introduced, became intoxicated one night and was arrested for driving on the wrong side of the street, so I cut him off, disinherited him." Jolene Fertig had recited this litany in a cheerful, pleasant voice as if she had been discussing the weather.

"I was married at fifteen to a man twice my age because the family fortune was, even then, dissolving rapidly, only I didn't know it. I could own half of Monte Carlo for the hundreds of thousands of francs my family has spent at the tables. I've been surrounded all of my life with gamblers, yet I wouldn't wager a sou! At any rate, gentlemen, dinner is served."

She led them into the dining room, dimly lighted by an enormous crystal chandelier whose hundreds of prisms were encrusted with grime. The tablecloth of fine damask was spotted and unclean, and when she disappeared into the kitchen, Luke Three followed Robert Desmond's example and wiped the corroded sterling silver flatware with his napkin.

Their hostess reappeared a moment later with a large Meissen platter piled with bits of stringy meat, a few whole, brown carrots, and a mound of yellow-looking potatoes. "I thought I had some pâté for the first course, but it had gone bad." She smiled sweetly and placed the platter grandly in the middle of the table. Robert Desmond rose and politely seated her at the head of the long table.

"Please sit, gentlemen," she said graciously, waving her topaz-weighted hands as if the meal were a gargantuan repast. "Oh, I've forgotten the wine." She fled from the room and returned with a half-empty bottle of red wine. "It's been corked, but it's wet!"

Luke Three tried to find something charitable to say as he studied the dried-out beef. Finally he smiled at his hostess. "You serve just the way we do at home," he said, "family-style."

"Please take as much as you like, because there is quite a bit left in the kitchen. I only cook twice a week. There are so many interesting things to do with food that's already prepared."

Luke Three took a bite of the meat, and the more he chewed, the larger the mass of connective tissue became. At last he was able to swallow a portion of it, and when she was not looking he deposited the remainder in his napkin. The unseasoned carrots were at least tender, and the mashed potatoes, mostly composed of hard bits, could be masticated, but the meat was impossible.

After they had somehow managed to consume the stringy portions, their hostess cried gleefully, "Oh, I forgot the sauce! Well, no matter, it will make the basis for a ragout tomorrow." She stacked the empty plates on top of the platter of meat and vegetables and disappeared into the kitchen.

Luke Three made a face and pointed to his stomach, but Robert Desmond waved his finger at him. "Mind your manners, bub!" he whispered just before Jolene Fertig returned with three small dishes.

"I wanted to prepare an English dessert, and I thought a trifle might be nice, but fresh fruit is not available. Instead we're having another famous English provincial dish, Spotted Dick."

Luke Three looked at her incredulously, not certain that he had heard her correctly. The dessert, which turned out to be rather good—at least it was sweetened properly—appeared to be a bland version of raisin-custard pudding.

Their hostess served demitasses in the tiny, dusty mahogany-paneled library, which was presided over by a blackened ram's head above the fireplace and a small insect-infested quail in a dome glass on the mantel.

After offering second cups of the thick coffee, which her guests politely refused, Jolene Fertig sat down at the huge Bechstein in the corner, which was badly in need of tuning, and played Debussy. Then she sighed and began to play a song that Luke Three recognized. She sang in a throaty contralto:

> *Vor die Kaserne,*
> *Vor dem grossen Tor,*
> *Stand eine Lanterne,*
> *Und steht Sie noch davor,*
> *So woll'n wir uns da wiederseh'n*
> *Bei der Lanterne woll'n wir steh'n*
> *Wie einst, Lili Marlene . . .*

She swiveled on the piano stool. "That song haunts me. My father sang it between the two wars." She looked up apologetically. "Forgive me. I only know the German words, I do not have a good English translation. It's sadder in its original form, I think, but it's not so good in French." She got up brusquely, but her voice was filled with gaiety. "I suppose if there is another war, soldiers will still sing it as they go off to battle." She tossed her long auburn hair and laughed. "If we could choose our destinies, would we make a bigger mess of our lives?"

Robert Desmond got up from the big chair. "I'm very tired."

"Yes," Luke Three countered, "it's been a long day."

Jolene Fertig roused from her reverie. "It has been that. I don't miss servants, really, only when such things as luggage must be transported upstairs, and I can't cook partridges. I always forget how long they have to hang. Either I take them down too soon, and they are tough, or I leave them up too long and they are too ripe."

She brightened. "Perhaps, if it is decreed, I will one day have servants again; otherwise I'll continue to do for myself. I won't escort you upstairs; each door is numbered." She turned to Robert Desmond. "You have Number Two, and Luke has Number Three—a good touch, I thought! I'll stay down a bit and wash the dishes. We'll have country ham tomorrow for breakfast, if it's not too dried out."

"Which reminds me," Robert Desmond put in quickly, "we must leave very early."

"But I thought you would stay tomorrow night as well?"

"I wish we could," he replied graciously, his stomach beginning to turn, "but we must go on to Paris. And we only have coffee in the morning, nothing else." He caught Luke Three's grateful expression.

"I'm disappointed," she replied animatedly. "Well, we will make up for it on your next visit." She held out her hand. "Good night." They wished her good night and carried their heavy suitcases upstairs.

Luke Three examined the tiny bedroom, which had obviously been swept out, because there was a thick coat of dust under the bed. The sheets were ivory-colored with age, and the pillowcases smelled of musty lavender. He was surprised to find a featherbed, but when he undressed and stretched out, all he could feel were huge lumps where the down had clumped together. Since his feet hung over the end of the bed, he drew himself into a ball and went to sleep.

He was awakened by a movement on the featherbed, and as he rubbed the sleep out of his eyes he saw that Jolene Fertig, quite nude, was lying on the counterpane. "Good morning," she said brightly, as if she were performing an exotic ritual. She was a vision of pink lips and blood-red finger- and toenails. She was the first woman that he had ever met who did not shave under her arms.

"Good—morning," he managed to reply, still shocked that she was lying beside him.

She kissed him on the mouth, her plump breasts

pressing against his chest. Luke Three, still not believing what was happening, certain that it was a dream and she an apparition, was surprised at the thrill of her warm mouth.

Her hand darted under the sheet. "Well"—she smiled—"what have we here?" His heart began to race as she threw back the quilt. *"Magnifique!"* she cried, examining him more closely than he had ever been examined before. He looked at her in wonderment. She seemed so matter-of-fact. It was as if they were children and she was entranced by the very difference between the male and the female anatomy.

Now that his heartbeats were returning to normal, Luke Three found that he was not embarrassed. "I should think," she was saying in that marvelous good-natured way, "that if you ever decide to get out of the oil business"—she handled him expertly—"you could make a terrific living with just—*this.*"

She stood up on the bed. Luke Three, who had never experienced such a wanton movement before, was fascinated at the sight of her pendulous breasts and long, smooth legs that seemed to reach to the ceiling. Then, looking down from above, she knelt quickly, a leg on either side of him, and enveloped him completely. Before he could cry out in pleasure, she bent her head to his and kissed him again. Her tongue stayed in his mouth as she moved her body. At once, far too soon, he felt his climax approaching, and he tried to make a sound. She stopped moving immediately. When she felt him subside, she began the fabulous movements again. He hugged her close so that he could feel her breasts beneath his chin. He would burst at any moment, he thought. But again she stopped undulating.

He lay there, then, in a state, it seemed, of suspended animation, with her moving and then pausing, moving and then pausing. He had never been involved in anything quite so exquisite; he was hanging on a tightly wound thread between pleasure and pain. After what seemed like hours, with her in complete charge of his body, he murmured, "Please ... now!"

She continued kissing him, but ignored his pleas, until all of his senses were gathered together in that most vulnerable area of his body.

"Please," he begged.

"Not yet," she answered joyously. "Relax, my sweet."

How could she possibly expect him to relax, imprisoned as he was? She swayed again, from side to side, and he took advantage while he could for a second and thrust himself up, hoping to achieve the wanted depths of feeling, but she stopped as still as a frozen nymph. When she began again, he once more caught her off guard and pushed upward and was almost overcome with a mighty inward upheaval.

"Naughty boy!" she exclaimed and, in revenge, clamped down on him more tightly than ever. Then, with him still shuddering, panting, perspiring, moaning, and uttering little cries, she began a set of wholly different manipulations. Weakly he lay on the featherbed, his skin damp, every pore attuned to her gyrations.

Again, after what seemed like hours, he began to gather his strength, and this time she did not stop but continued on, even more feverishly, even more frantically. Giant waves of pleasure emanated from his solar plexus, engulfing him with exultation, as his heart beat so ferociously he thought he would faint. "My God," he whispered weakly. "My God."

She looked down fondly at his flushed face. "God"— she laughed softly—"had nothing to do with it!" She exclaimed happily. "Was it good, my lover?"

"I've never felt anything so satisfying in my life."

"Well, of course, you're very young!"

He paused, suddenly shy. "How was ... it ... for you?"

She glanced at him with her yellow-brown eyes. "It

was happening for me—all the time." She removed herself adroitly from his embrace and lay down beside him, her flesh covered with dew. She grasped him again in that most tender of places. "You will make many women happy with this," she said, her eyes still filled with appreciation and awe. "As I said before, with *this* you could become the playboy of the Western World." She paused and laughed shyly. "Or the Eastern World. Of these matters, I know a bit about!"

11

End of the Road

Plaisance-du-Gers had changed almost not at all since Mitchell, as Michel Bayard, had stomped up and down its rough streets in his wooden shoes.

Heavy, huge-wheeled carts still carried produce to market, and what postwar money had trickled into the community was not reflected in the clothing of the citizens, nor in the obvious poverty everywhere. But, as poor as the town appeared, licking its wounds after the Occupation, France looked fabulously rich indeed compared to the Germany he had just exited.

Mitchell had joined a group of tourists in Lyon, who were visiting farming communities to the southwest, because he wanted to see the countryside not only in concert with others, but also from the anonymity of a large bus. He was fearful of being lonely and needed company on this journey to recapture his wartime experiences. He had been tempted to rent a car and driver and work out the identical itinerary he had taken before, but discarded the plan because, inside, he knew that he could not visit the old familiar place as a "rich American." And he truly enjoyed the companionship of the motley group of sightseers as the big blue bus careened around the back roads. He left the tour at Plaisance-du-Gers to forage for himself.

He stayed at a small hotel with an intimate courtyard that had once played host to German officers, and he selected a hot, fragrant croissant at the bakery that he had patronized before when the proprietor shamefacedly sold white bread heavily laced with the rye flour required by the government. Now the showcases were laden with all varieties of breads, salted and sweet, along with pastries that looked so light that they could have floated heavenward out of the shop, if not protected by the glass case.

He rented a bicycle for the day and wheeled down the country road to the site of the farmhouse which Paul and Madeleine had torched to warn him that the place was no longer "safe." Nothing remained of the house but a rubble of old stones, many of which had apparently been carted away to repair other buildings in the neighborhood, or perhaps shore up stone fences to keep in the dairy cows. Weeds were everywhere, and Mitchell sighed to think that in three short years the area had once again become wild.

He pedaled on down the dusty road to the Château Latte, which had been permanently turned into a hospital, and waved at several nuns taking water from a well. He thought of the lovely Lise, the brilliant metallurgist who had worked with Fermi. Pierre Darlan had told him she had checked the formula that he had brought from Washington. Perhaps she had made some minor calculation that might have speeded up the development of the atomic bomb. He would never know, just as he would never know if his entire mission in Berlin had been successful. He was one character, performing one scene in a movie which he was destined never to see. The thought did not particularly bother him; it was important only that he had won the part in the first place.

Later he strolled by the clockmaker's shop, and although the building now housed a cobbler, in his mind's eye he saw old Georges bending over his jeweler's bench, attended by the boy Etienne. They were all dead, Lise, Paul, Madeleine, Georges, and Etienne; murdered by the Nazis because of their involvement with him, the man who had dropped out of the sky one dark night.

He wished that he could feel pity for them, but he could not; only a strange detachment bothered him. Why had he no sentimental feelings about anything? He had always been that way; that trait differentiated him from the rest of the Heron and Story families, who had emotions which would be divulged at the drop of a pecan. A strange curiosity had brought him back to Plaisance-du-Gers. He wanted desperately to feel the sweet pull of nostalgia, but could not.

After a nap in the afternoon and a simple *dîner du jour* at a little provincial restaurant that had been closed when he was in the area before, he went into The Golden Apple, which, he saw with satisfaction, was still operated by the old couple. The set-up was exactly as he remembered—including the smell of spilled wine and stale beer.

He selected the same seat at the bar that he used to occupy and removed his hat. The proprietress sauntered up to him as if he were a regular habitué, and for a moment he thought she recognized him, but when she greeted him formally with "Good evening, monsieur," he knew that she did not. She always addressed her customers with the familiar *tu*. He ordered a glass of wine and was pleased to discover it was no longer watered. The vineyards of France were producing a superior vintage; there was no need now to stretch out the seasonal product.

The bartendress served him politely and exchanged comments on the weather. Since the place was not crowded so soon after dinner, Mitchell leaned across the bar. "Three years ago, Madame," he said gently, "I was visiting friends here for a time; perhaps you knew them, Paul and Madeleine? I went by their farm this afternoon, but nothing is left."

Her voice quavered. "Yes, I knew them well. They were taken one night and were not seen again. The Germans said a transmitter was found secreted in the oven. The house was burned. It was also said that they had hidden a parachutist." She paused. "So many were murdered because of harboring the sky men. We never knew what they did, those men that we sent home via the underground." She glanced over the bar, her eye checking to see if drinks were needed. "Sometimes it seems as if that happened yesterday, then at other times it appears that it never happened at all, that it just came out of our imaginations."

"Yes," Mitchell agreed, "those were strange days. . . ." He toyed with the idea of revealing his identity to her but decided the information would have no purpose. He felt no loyalty about his mission at this late date, because he could not be connected with what happened later, but it might involve other explanations that he did not wish to elaborate upon. "Madame," he continued, leaning forward, "look at my face. I was hoping that you would recognize me. Of course I looked a bit different then. I wore a mustache and my hair was dark."

She studied his face carefully and shook her head. "So many come here now and want to be remembered. You must not have come here often, because I have a very good memory. If I do not recall names, at least I remember faces."

Mitchell colored. "I only came here a few times," he replied lamely, "but the reason that I was hoping that you'd remember me was because there was a young man—about twenty-five or so—who frequented this place. His name was Jean, and I could see that you thought that we were related; there was a resemblance between us."

She continued to look at him, but shook her head. "Why didn't you speak with him then?"

Mitchell looked down at his hands. "I could not, madame, it was inconvenient."

"You are a nice-looking man,"—she smiled—"but you do not remind me of anyone." She frowned. "This is important to you?"

"It is," he replied quietly. "I have come a very long way."

She laughed suddenly. "From the soulful expression on your face, I suspect, monsieur, that you have come back to recapture a romance. Did this Jean have a sister?"

He shook his head. "*Non,* madame, *non.* That man whom I spoke about, I believe, was a regular customer." His voice grew urgent. "You do not remember a young man named Jean?"

She gestured helplessly. "I know several Jeans, of course, it is a common enough name, but no one that resembles you." She looked at his empty glass. "Would you like more wine?"

"Please."

When she had filled the glass to the brim, he continued, "Would your husband, perhaps, remember?"

"Him?" She indicated the man in the rear, who was talking earnestly with a customer. *"Him?"* She repeated. "No. He never notices anything. We had an arrogant Nazi lieutenant who used to come in here every night and ask to see identity cards. There was cruelty in his eyes, and he would arrest village people with legitimate identification just to harass them. A year or so ago, I looked up one evening and saw this same man talking to my husband. He was dressed in civilian clothes, and his blond hair was longer, and he had taken to wearing glasses, but it was unmistakably the same person. My husband had not even recognized him, and they were joking and laughing. I told the Nazi that he was not welcome in this place, and my husband objected. Only later, he remembered."

She grimaced. "I would have left him years ago, but the war came along and we owned this place and he had shrapnel in his legs from the First War, so he could not serve again, and he did help the mountain boys during the Occupation. Now I'm too old to go anywhere else, or do anything else." She smiled sadly. "Or find anyone else." She wiped the bar slowly with a damp towel. "Do you want another glass?"

Mitchell shook his head, laid a few francs on the bar for a gratuity, and put on his hat. He went to the door and turned to wave good-bye to the proprietress.

He had just closed the door and had taken two steps down the street when he heard a cry. "Monsieur, monsieur, come back, come back!" She was standing in the doorway, and as he turned, she looked up into his face, which was illuminated by the streetlamp. "It is the hat!" she exclaimed breathlessly. "You should always wear a hat; one notices your eyes then." She nodded. "Yes, that young man did look like you."

"Did?" Mitchell echoed weakly. *"Did?"*

"I put him in the past," she explained, "because I have not seen him in years. Jean Baptiste Faubert turned out to be a collaborator." She spat into the street, and her eyes narrowed. "Perhaps you were in it with him!"

Mitchell replied impatiently, "How could I be, madame?

I only saw him once. Would I come looking for him if I knew his story?"

Her face softened. "I suppose not. It's just that the Nazi soldier sticks in my mind. I have to remember not to be doubtful anymore. It was suspicion that ruined this country. When you have trusted no one for so long—close friends, even—it is very difficult to go back to the way you were." She glanced up at him with narrowed eyes. "I suppose, then, that Jean Baptiste is a long-lost relative?" He nodded. "I hope you find him, even if he is in jail. It seems to be important to you. So many were killed, as you know." She sighed. "You seem to have been out of France for a long time. There is something foreign about you."

Mitchell nodded uncomfortably and tipped his hat. "I was one of the men who came out of the sky."

There was an old French proverb, Mitchell knew, that said "all roads eventually lead to Paris," which he found was true. He had first inquired at Lyon about documents that dealt with collaborationists, and had been told that the only records in existence were filed away in the French capital. The civil servant who imparted the information was almost a duplicate of Pierre Darlan, even to his shiny blue serge suit and spectacles. Only his mustaches were not as magnificent as those of his look-alike.

Mitchell spent three days examining the files of various agencies. Long alphabetical lists of names, followed by cryptic comments: *"garrotted in an alley 9-8-44"; "sentenced to two years in prison, 10-4-45"; or in the case of women, "head shaved publicly, 7-8-44, not further detained because of lack of hard evidence"; or "beaten badly, 8-6-44, taken to hospital, released 8-7-44."* And, although there were hundreds of Jeans and a dozen or so Jean Baptistes, there was no Jean Baptiste Faubert.

After spending the morning at the archives and finding nothing, Mitchell was depressed. It was strange to be in a black mood; he had always prided himself that, while he was not a normally optimistic person, neither was he pessimistic: he usually traveled a serene pathway between the two.

He ate a badly prepared luncheon in a small sidewalk café that he fondly remembered from World War I, when he and Françoise had stayed in her flat all day making love, only coming out after dark to have dinner. Being AWOL, he knew the military police patrolled the streets all day. A wave of guilt came over him. He had forgotten that she had paid all the bills after his supply of money ran out during that first week. How she had laughed as she stuffed his pockets with the almost worthless postwar francs. During their second week together she had taken two modeling jobs—one for a painter and one for a sculptor—because they needed money so badly. The past was gradually returning, and he was not happy with the memory.

He sat on the terrace of the café and opened a newspaper, *Le Monde*, one of the small independent, elite dailies. He would have preferred a *presse d'information* newspaper, written for mass appeal, but there were no free editions available. He scanned each page, and then his eyes were riveted by a small paragraph that spoke of a soon-to-be-published book by Gertrude Stein, entitled *Brewsie and Willie*, which dealt with her experiences with soldiers during the war.

He thought kindly of the large friendly woman and her dark-haired companion, Alice B. Toklas, who had befriended him, providing a "safe house" for one night in Culoz as he was fleeing France for Switzerland after his mission in Plaisance-du-Gers and Tarbes.

Now, apparently, she was back in Paris. He closed his eyes. If he recalled that evening in detail, perhaps he could remember the address transmitted in conversation. Nothing came back, but he was sure it was the name of a woman, a holy woman! He smiled suddenly, Christ ... *Christine!* Gertrude Stein lived in the rue Christine! He concentrated once more, but the number eluded him. It was very possible, he decided at last, that she had not given the exact street address. She had lived in France for so many years that she must have established some sort of contacts with Parisian official-dom. Perhaps she would help him once more.

He stood on the corner, waiting for an empty taxi to pass. Finally a hack stopped; he could tell from the smell of the engine that it had been converted from gasoline to wood alcohol. He climbed in and said very slowly in French, "There is a literary lady whom I must find. She lives in the rue Christine. Her name is Gertrude Stein."

The driver, cap pulled down over his forehead, turned around and examined his passenger very carefully. "I know where it is located. It is near the Faubourg St. Germain." The man looked like a gangster from one of those old shoot-'em-up movies of the thirties, Mitchell thought, especially when he wet a dangling homemade cigarette from his thin lips. "You must have been a GI," the man went on, showing yellow teeth. He pronounced GI as "Gee."

"No, not in the last war, the one before. Why do you ask?"

"I have taken many *Gees* to that apartment. They all come to pay her homage."

Although Mitchell had not been in Paris for many years, he knew that the driver was taking a circuitous route that would bring four times the fare to which he was entitled. But as long as he arrived at his destination, he would pay a king's ransom.

At last the driver turned onto the rue des Grands, made another turn on the rue Dauphine, and stopped in the rue Christine, pulling up before a bookbinder's. He jerked his head upward. "Second floor, number five."

Mitchell presented him with a large tip over the scandalous fare he demanded and bade him a successful afternoon. He climbed the stairs and when he reached number V his heart was beating rapidly. He knocked twice in rapid succession, and the door was opened a sliver. He could see a pair of dark eyes peering at him. *"Oui?"* a thin voice asked.

He decided to continue his impersonation of his cover Frenchman. "My name is Michel Bayard," he replied in his impeccable, unaccented French. "I was your guest for one night, three years ago in Culoz."

The door swung open. Alice B. Toklas, dressed as he had remembered her, in black, her mouth in a wide grin that somehow emphasized her dark mustache, nodded. "Ah, of course. You brought the fresh perch! Gertrude is out for a walk with Basket, but she will return shortly. I'll fix you some tea, if you like." She motioned him into the foyer, where there were Japanese prints displayed on the walls. As he came down the hall, he noticed several strange-looking unframed monotone paintings, arranged with other more striking works. He paused in front of a green and pink canvas. "Interesting," he remarked, wishing he knew more about art.

She looked at his face and nodded. "Picasso's early cubist period."

"I appreciate, but ..."

She nodded her dark head and her eyes sparkled, and he noted that, without Gertrude near, her personality was very engaging; she was no longer a figure in the background. "He was here just yesterday, for lunch— Picasso." She indicated the drawing room. "Go in, I'll bring tea."

The large room was crowded with furniture, most of it very old cherrywood, covered with horsehair, piled with down cushions, Mitchell noticed, and there was exquisite woodwork that would have impressed his father, who was in awe of craftsmen with a genius for carving. Every table displayed a variety of objects, bibelots of wood and glass; on the walls, paintings fought for prominence. Among the many framed canvases, one in particular caught his eye. It was a small painting of yellow-green apples that was so simple, and yet so artfully rendered that it recalled the apples from the trees that bordered the pecan orchard on the Heron farm.

There was a furious barking outside, and a moment later a heavy step was heard in the foyer. "Gertrude," Alice said quickly, "we have a visitor. Remember the young man who visited us at Culoz one night?"

"Of course," was the reply. Gertrude Stein strode into the drawing room, hands outstretched. The imposing paintings on the walls were now overwhadowed by the presence of the big woman with an open, friendly smile. She took both his hands in hers. "I was wondering," she said in French with her flat American accent, "if we would ever see each other again, because the war was very bad then and with the roadblocks we did not know whether you could escape or not, or perhaps you would be sent to a Nazi concentration camp."

The white poodle jumped on Mitchell's lap, and his hostess placed her hands on her large hips and laughed. "How is it that he knows you and yet, sometimes, does not know me?"

Basket nuzzled down by Mitchell's left arm.

"You look well"—Gertrude glanced at Mitchell's beautifully tailored suit—"and prosperous." She glanced at Alice. "Is there tea?"

"Of course." Alice disappeared, fluttering like a little bird, and Gertrude turned back to him, nodding her close-cropped gray head. Her generous body, covered with rough brown tweed, took on the air of some heroic sculpture. Mitchell was awed by her.

"Do sit down," she said. Occupying a couch, she turned and looked him directly in the eyes. "I am glad you have come to visit," she said. "It seems that I have entertained hundreds of GI's since the Liberation. Some of them have come just to see me, some have brought stories and poems for me to read, some have carted in food and bottles of champagne, but all of them have had a purpose, and I always ask where they are from because I love the sound of American states spoken with American accents. I have often thought about that morning that Alice prepared a packet of food for you to take on your journey. She was very sly."

Mitchell nodded and laughed. "Yes, and when I got to the bottom of the packet and found the popcorn, I knew that *Rebecca* had given me away."

Gertrude laughed uneasily. "We thought it highly unlikely that a Frenchman would be reading Daphne du Maurier in English," she replied, "and we speculated what your true nationality was. But I had the strangest feeling that you weren't British at all, and we included the popcorn just in case you were American."

"You're right, I am American," Mitchell replied in English.

Gertrude laughed out loud. "I was right." She was triumphant, switching to her native tongue.

Alice B. Toklas came in with the tray, which she placed on a small table.

"He is American," Gertrude said.

"Then the mystery is solved at last!"

"Yes," Mitchell admitted, taking a sip of the strong, delicious tea brewed to perfection. "I had fooled Frenchmen into thinking I was a native, but you were both a challenge. I was under great physical and mental strain at that time. I had been parachuted into the Plaisance-du-Gers countryside to complete a mission. It was over by the time that I spent the night in your house, and I was sure that I would get back home safely. As it turned out, a plane was waiting near Lake Geneva."

"Where are you from?" Gertrude asked.

"Oklahoma."

A smile spread over her face. "Of all my GI visitors, only one or two have been from Ok-la-homa." She pronounced the word lovingly. "I like the sound of it, although I have never been there. What does your father do?"

"He was a cabinetmaker," Mitchell replied, "and I am carrying on his work." He paused. "I mean, I have a chain of custom furniture stores. I'm not a craftsman myself, although I balanced gunstocks in a factory in Tarbes for a while when I was under cover."

Gertrude nodded her large, impressive head. "And why have you come back? To see Paris as it used to be? It hasn't recovered yet from the war, and it will be a long time before it does. Of course, the people are trying to take up where they left off, the shopkeepers are keeping shop again, and we are eating better because there is meat and butter again and fine white flour for pastry, and we get shipments of fruit, and there is a trickle of visitors, but it will be a long while before Paris is ready for tourists again."

Mitchell set his empty cup on the table and politely refused a second. "I don't want to bore you with a long story, but I am searching ... for a man who I think might be related." He tried to chose words that would reflect his true feelings, but hesitated.

"Start from the beginning," Gertrude said quietly. "It is always best to start at the beginning." And Mitchell found himself blurting out the account of his ill-fated affair with Françoise.

Gertrude shook her head. "Some of the collaborationists, of course, were shot by the *maquis,* the mountain boys, who played Robin Hood by chasing away the shopkeepers who had befriended the Boches and who turned over their stores of goods to the people whose homes had been burned by the Germans. Some of the collaborationists were sent to Paris for trial, and this Jean Baptiste Faubert might have been one of them." She paused and fingered the simple brooch at her throat, her mind far away; then she looked up with a penetrating stare. "What happens, Mitchell, if you find him and he has a legitimate father and is no kin of yours?"

Mitchell shrugged his shoulders. "At least I won't be haunted by it anymore. It keeps gnawing away at me. I keep seeing his face down the bar."

Gertrude nodded sympathetically. "Very well. I will make inquiries by telephone. Can you come back late this afternoon? I will either have information or I won't have information." She arose and had difficulty straightening up for a moment. "I'm having a bit of a digestive trouble," she said apologetically. "I think it was the strange food that we ate during the war. We never had enough fresh fruit, and it's so useful for digestion."

"Thank you for the tea," Mitchell said to Alice B. Toklas, and he turned to Gertrude Stein and took her hand. "And thank you for your kindness."

"It was nothing," she replied, inconspicuously holding her side. "Come back at four."

After he left, Gertrude shook her head. "Still they keep coming, these boys, and they all want something, but this man is different. I remember now that there was a Heron petit-point footstool in my father's house in Oakland." She sighed gently, "I will call the mayor of Plaisance-du-Gers. I met him once in Belley. Let's hope that the connection goes through quickly."

When Mitchell knocked on the door of V rue Christine promptly at four, he was greeted cordially by Gertrude. "I have been telephoning ever since you left," she said, "and I do have some results. The present mayor of Plaisance-du-Gers is not the one I met, but he asked a deputy who was there during the Occupation, and it seems that Jean Baptiste Faubert was not a collaborationist after all. . . ."

"Thank God!" Mitchell exclaimed.

"He was, as it turns out, a *maquis*. It was very dangerous, as you know, for the boys to come down from the mountains, and so the rumor started somehow that he was working with the Germans. Apparently he did nothing to disillusion the villagers, because then they would leave him alone and he could gather what information was necessary to carry back to his compatriots. So, just before the Americans came, when the few German soldiers left in the area were being very nice and polite to everyone, because they knew they were finished as a nation, Jean Baptiste Faubert returned to the village in broad daylight, with a patriot's band on his sleeve, leading the mountain boys into the village."

Mitchell was puzzled. "But I wonder why the proprietors of the café did not recognize him?"

Gertrude moved her large shoulders impatiently. "They might not have seen him—who knows? He was apparently only in for a day or so, and then he went away and no one has seen him since, and that is all the news I have for you, Mitchell Heron. The deputy thought that he might have gone up into Normandy as many of the mountain boys were needed there, but that is only speculation."

There was a knock on the door, which Alice answered. She returned a moment later. "It's two GI's," she said quietly.

Gertrude shook her head. "Tell them to come back tomorrow at teatime." She turned to Mitchell. "All this company is getting to be rather a trial, and I am always home unless I'm out for a walk, and even then I'm often stopped. American soldiers now are different from those of the other war. Then they were quiet and didn't have much to say, but now they seem to know everything and can converse on any subject. I am like that myself, so they talk a great deal and I like to hear about home, but I've been so weary the last few months and I go to bed early, and of course I always sleep late. I don't like to get up in the morning. I never did. Do you?"

Mitchell smiled. "I've been getting up early all my life. Even when I lived here in France in the nineteen-twenties and 'thirties. I was up early, getting my wares together. I sold glass figurines, and I wasn't very successful. It took me a long time to settle down. I was about forty when I went home to Angel, Oklahoma, and worked my mother's farm."

Gertrude nodded. "That was the point of my earlier statement. You were in the First War, and there were a great many soldiers like you who stayed over here and drifted around from one area to another, but the men in this war were Depression babies, and I think that had a lot to do with the way that they talk and act."

Mitchell nodded. "I remember reading somewhere that you coined the phrase 'The Lost Generation'—*une generation perdue*—that Hemingway used in *The Sun Also Rises*, about World War I people."

"That has become a famous quote," Gertrude admitted, "and Ernest says that I said it, and I may have said it, because I had so much to say at that time about those who were old enough to go to war in nineteen-seventeen, but, funnily enough, I don't remember saying it, but even if I didn't, it fits that generation well." She stood up, and he could see she was very fatigued. She grasped his hands firmly. "Good luck, Mitchell Heron," she said quietly. "At least you will return to the United States knowing that Jean Baptiste Faubert was a patriot."

He nodded. "I have two more days in Paris to find him. Wish me luck."

"I will." She drew in her breath gently, and she was very serious. "I wish I could say that I will remember you in my prayers, but I don't pray."

"Neither do I," he replied softly, then added, "but I will always remember your kindness to me."

She smiled, and then Alice came into the room with a book, which she handed to him. "Gertrude and I thought you might like to have this," she said.

He was outside in the hallway before he looked at their gift. It was the same copy of *Rebecca* that he had been reading that night that he had spent with them at Culoz. A strange wave of apprehension overcame him as he saw that a bookmark had been placed at the very page where he had stopped reading.

12

The Bridge of Doubt

Madame Renaud, the tall, thin, birdlike woman with gray hair braided on top of her head, looked wearily up from her desk in the crowded cellar of the old building in the rue Depew.

"Are you yet another of Gertie's boys?" she asked, not unkindly, in English, her speech patterns placing her as a native of Normandy. "Whom are you looking for? A child you used to give chocolate to after the Liberation?" She was patronizing and looked at him out of the corners of her eyes. "Could it be a girl?"

Mitchell regarded her with compassion and dismissed her vague insinuations. Her job could not be easy: going over endless lists, listening to hundreds of inquiries about people, many of whom were long dead, taken away in the middle of the night, never to be heard from again. She dealt, he could see from her vacant eyes, mainly with death, and she dared not offer hope. "Who is it, please?" she asked, her fingers already caressing the card file on her desk.

"His name is Jean Baptiste Faubert," he replied in French. "He worked for a time in Plaisance-du-Gers. He was there in the fall of nineteen-forty-three. I know nothing else about him, except that it was rumored he was arrested as a collaborationist."

She set her jaw. "Then I cannot help you," she announced coldly. "The Germans destroyed almost all the records, and the ones that still exist use only cover names. What was he called?"

"I cannot say. But you misunderstand, Madame Renaud. He was not a traitor, he was a mountain boy."

"Why did you not say so in the first place?" she asked irritably. "We deal in facts, not rumors! Where was he born?"

Mitchell shook his head. "Possibly here in Paris. I think it might have been in November or December, nineteen-nineteen."

"Is there no other information, monsieur?"

"I'm afraid not, and I have such a short time before I must leave the country."

"How important is it to you to find this man?"

Mitchell thought that she was asking for money, but when he took out his wallet she waved her hands at him. *"Non, non!"* she cried. "You misunderstand! What I am saying is, if it is a casual inquiry about someone that you met briefly—if you are merely curious about his whereabouts—give up the search, please. It is worth looking through innumerable records to reunite a family, find a lost mother or father, or attempt to locate a child in a displaced persons camp, but to endure fighting the hardships of bureaucracy just to find a casual friend.... You understand, do you not?"

Mitchell nodded and leaned over her desk. "It is very important, madame. The lost boy, I believe, is my son."

Mitchell was exhausted. Many records were in French, some in German, but most of them were not typewritten, and after several hours of reading names, with accompanying data scribbled by hundreds of hands, the pages swam before him. It seemed that his eyes would fall out of their sockets. Yet even with the distraction of deciphering handwritten lines that covered every page of the yellowed entry books, he felt very much obliged to the archivist who had allowed him this privilege.

The department was understaffed, and Madame Renaud could not assign a clerk to go over the data to look for the name of some obscure man, when there was no basic information. It was unlikely that Jean Baptiste had been interned in a displaced persons camp, unless he had suffered from battle fatigue or had become mentally confused. Mitchell realized that he could well be lying in a cemetery in a family plot, could be buried along the road or on some hilltop where he had been slain by enemy bullets, or he might even have returned to civilian life. At this moment, he could be going about whatever trade he had picked up before the war. The possibilities were limitless. He might be occupying a flat down the street! The only thing that Mitchell knew for certain was that Jean Baptiste had been true to his country. Gertrude Stein had found that out for him, bless her good American heart!

At the end of the second day of his research, Mitchell went downstairs to the Office of War Information to see Madame Renaud. "Have you uncovered anything for me?"

She seemed even more weary than before. *"Non,"* she answered, "nothing." She paused, and the circles under her eyes seemed darker than before. "What will you do, monsieur, if you find this man? Can you take the time to make his acquaintance properly? What if you discover he is not your son?"

"I don't know," Mitchell replied simply.

She nodded sadly. "What about the hornet's nest that you will have stirred up? What of him? What of this Jean Baptiste?"

"I don't know what you mean, madame."

"Every day I come in contact with people who are looking for other people; many, of course, are family members looking for lost relatives; others, I suspect, have motives that they do not wish to divulge. For instance, a man who owes a large sum of money disappears, and his creditor comes here, seeking his whereabouts. A woman whose husband has conveniently slipped out of sight demands his address. A man comes looking for his wife, who has run away with someone else." She paused and smiled sadly. "It is difficult enough for us to locate a legitimate missing person, but those who *want* to vanish. . . .

"Shall I give you advice?" She looked at him sharply. "You have no concrete evidence that this man is your son, except a chance resemblance and the fact that, agewise, the possibility is within the realm of chance. It seems to me that it would be easier to locate this Françoise. She must have relatives; there must be a trace of her somewhere. There are birth and baptismal records, marriage licenses, death certificates. You will certainly be able to discover if Jean Baptiste is your son if you locate this woman. I believe you are taking the wrong channels." She sighed. "At any rate, however you pursue it, it is going to take a very long time. How many more days do you have, monsieur, before you must return to the United States?"

"I leave tomorrow," he answered lamely, and suddenly the futility of his journey to Paris overwhelmed him, and his shoulders slumped.

"Is there a possibility that you can sometime later return to France, monsieur?" she asked more kindly.

"Yes," he answered, "but I have the feeling that somehow time is drawing to a close, that the longer I wait, the farther he slips away."

She nodded. "Everyone who comes here has those same feelings. Do return when you have more time." She looked down at her ledgers again. He was dismissed.

Mitchell went out into the street. A low fog was rolling in, snarling traffic, already heavy at the end of the day. Now, looking back from the evening sounds of Paris, he was not even sure that the man in the bar had resembled him all that closely. Was it possible that, being so far from home, so removed from the Oklahomans, and under such mental pressure portraying Michel Bayard, he had only imagined that Jean Baptiste had the Heron look? Lonely and afraid, yearning to see a familiar face, had he psychologically grasped at a straw and thought the man possessed features that he did not?

Pierre Darlan was waiting for Mitchell at the airport, pacing up and down because the plane from London was an hour and a half late. He pumped Mitchell's hand. "Did you vacation well in Paris?"

Mitchell was tempted to tell him about his investigation in Plaisance-du-Gers and Paris, but decided against it; there were some areas of his personal life that he wanted to keep private. After all, they knew almost everything about him already. "Yes," he lied with a grin. "It was—fun." He paused. "What's on the agenda?"

"Nothing very much, except Felicia will return your hair to its natural color, and I promise a good dinner." Pierre looked at him critically. "You did not put on more weight, I see."

Mitchell shook his head. "There is not too much food in France yet—certainly nothing gourmet."

When they reached the house in Georgetown, Felicia grasped his hand warmly and led him into the kitchen. "Sit here on the stool," she said. "I've got everything ready." She examined his scalp critically and laughed. "It's a good thing you didn't stay longer"—she ran her hands through his white hair—"because dark roots are showing."

Pierre nodded. "We once lost a young operative in Munich just before the war. He had coal-black hair and bright blue eyes, and he was a husky sort of a fellow. We turned him into a picture of Hitler Youth with ammonia and peroxide. With the yellow hair, he could have fooled Herr Himmler himself. The young man was to take the train into Germany, do his job—which would last about five minutes—change clothing, and catch another train out of Germany."

Pierre pulled at his mustaches. "Unfortunately, he was struck down in the street by a caravan and suffered a severe brain concession. He lapsed into a coma in the hospital, and when he came out of it two weeks later, his roots were black, which blew his cover. Also, he had mumbled some English words. He was taken from the hospital to a prison for interrogation, and convicted of espionage, although he had had no time to complete his mission and therefore was quite innocent! We got him out eventually, but he was so demoralized that we could not use him again." He raised his heavy brows. "So we have been very careful about disguises since then. It's better not to use them, especially this hair-dyeing business."

Mitchell laughed ruefully. "You always regale me with stories about agents who've run into trouble. Why don't you ever tell me about successful missions?"

Pierre smiled weakly. "There are too many of those to

even enumerate. Besides, I never remember the successful ventures, only those that have turned sour!"

Felicia's hands, encased in rubber gloves, worked a brown lather into Mitchell's hair until his scalp was stinging.

"How women can go through this time after time is beyond me!" he exclaimed. A moment later his head felt cool and the tingling sensation ceased.

Felicia dried his hair with a furry towel until it was bone dry. "I don't think people will notice," she remarked casually, "but of course I couldn't put the gray back in your hair. It's all brown now—all over."

"Thanks!" Mitchell replied testily. "What do I do now when it all grows out?"

"My advice is to go to a barber in a strange town and get a short crew cut—it's quite the style now, since so many servicemen have been discharged. You can always let it grow out, or you might find that you like the style and decide to keep it."

"Oh, God!" he said with a mock concern. "What I do for my country."

"Speaking about your country," Pierre remarked, hoping to distract him, "thank you for bringing me a very important message!"

"But I brought no information to you!"

"But yes, Herr Professor, you did. Remember the strange indentations on the slip of paper with the telephone number that Steinmetz gave you?"

"Yes."

"Turned over, the indentations became bumps—Braille. Steinmetz's sister was blind. He had learned how to communicate with her when he was a boy!"

"Well, I'll be damned." Mitchell addressed Pierre. "By the way, I forgot to ask you the most important question of all—were you able to get him out of the asylum?"

There was a long pause. "Oh, yes," Pierre replied

quietly. "He is safe now, in hiding. He is free to testify at Nuremberg, only ..."

"Yes?"

"He was drugged before he left the hospital. Sometime between the time that he was taken from his cell and deposited in the asylum"—Pierre's voice took on a note of indescribable sadness—"sometime in that interim, the neo-Nazis cut out his tongue."

The quiet streets of Enid looked very peaceful to Mitchell after his travels abroad.

He was relieved to be answering the telephone, taking orders, and making trips to his other stores in Guthrie and Oklahoma City, instead of always being on guard, impersonating the Herr Professor Schneider. The farmers in overalls picked up supplies at feed stores; housewives in light summer cotton dresses shopped in Kress's; barefoot children played catchball in the streets; large families picnicked in Spring Lake Park; everywhere Mitchell looked, there was peaceful, unhurried prairie charm. It was like going back in time. Berlin, Plaisance-du-Gers, and Paris seemed remote. As the days passed, he began to wonder if he had really ever been away from Enid.

Glancing through the Monday morning paper on July 29, 1946, his second cup of coffee in front of him and the smell of bacon frying in the pan, he saw a small item on the obituary page that caused a sudden attack of vertigo: GERTRUDE STEIN DIES IN PARIS. The accompanying paragraph swam before his eyes. "Cardiac arrest ... American Hospital at Neuilly-sur-Seine ... July 27 ... lived in France since 1902...."

From far away he heard Mrs. Briggs say, "What's the matter, Mr. Heron? Are you all right?"

His vision cleared, but he was still feeling shaky. "Yes, I'm okay. It's just that I don't feel like having breakfast this morning." He got up slowly and took a walk around the small estate, his mind in a whirl. He felt lost. He ambled vacantly back into the house and picked up the telephone. After a long pause, he reached the Trenton residence in Angel. "Aunt Letty?" He made his voice sound casual. "Are you going to be home this morning? I'd like to come over for a cup of coffee."

Letty laughed. "Hasn't Mrs. Briggs learned how to work the coffeepot yet?" She had given him a new glass vacuum coffeemaker for his birthday.

"Oh, yes," he replied, "but I just want to see you."

The thirteen-mile drive seemed like thirteen hundred miles, and when at last he drove up before the Heron clapboard his armpits were damp with perspiration. He slipped into the house the back way, the same route he had always taken as a small child, and found Letty seated at the kitchen table, a mug of coffee in her hand. He kissed her on the cheek.

"Well," she said, looking up in surprise, "what was that for?" Family members did not often show outward affection.

"Just for being my favorite aunt," he replied.

"I'm your *only* aunt," she quipped, grinned, and poured him a cup of coffee. "Sit down. Let me heat you a cinnamon roll."

"No, thank you. I'm not hungry." He sat down and sipped the dark fragrant brew, his eyes troubled.

"Come on, Mitch, no one's here but me. You can talk. What's bothering you?"

Suddenly he wanted to tell her about Herr Professor Schneider, Jean Baptiste Faubert, and his short experience with Bernard Baruch's cold war. She would be tolerant, but she would not believe him; she would think the story was one of his fancies. "I just lost a friend," he said at last, "and I don't want to be alone this morning."

She looked at this man whom she had known all his life, and it occurred to her that she did not know him at all. He was the strange one in the family, and although he was now a successful businessman, he still had itchy feet. She would not be surprised if he never returned from one of those vacations that he sometimes took, when he was away for months on end. "Can you talk about it?" she asked quietly.

"You see, Aunt Letty, I only met this person twice, but she ..." He had not meant to say "she," but now that he had spoken about Gertrude, he went on slowly. "She befriended me both times. I owe her a debt of gratitude. Now she's dead, and I can't ever let her know what an inspiration she was."

"So many people don't get around to thanking others until it's too late." Letty took his hand. "I'm going to tell you something, Mitchell, that I've never told anyone before. When George Story died, I had so many letters from people he had befriended that it took several weeks to answer all the mail. Some were pure Cherokee people, others were mixed-blood, but there were also lawyers with whom he had worked on cases, and a few clients, and just plain folks who'd revered him, I guess. Among all the correspondence was a letter from a woman. I'll never forget her name. It was Clarissa Morton. She wrote about a meeting that she'd had with him and how he had affected her life. It was a tender, beautiful letter, and the more I went over it, the clearer the meaning became."

"There were no details, nothing—yet I knew that they had had a ..." she drew in her breath and looked out the window "a ... romance. Her intense feeling for him was between every line. And it hurt terribly, knowing that I had shared him with her—if it was only one time. It took a long while, but I finally answered in a very polite way. I told her that the mail I received from people had helped me over my grief, and I thanked her for sharing her thoughts with me." She paused. "You see, Mitch, it finally occurred to me that if George had a relationship with Clarissa Morton, it didn't have anything to do with me—with us. If, somehow, he gave her comfort and she was able to turn her life around, that was what was important. The same thing goes with your friend."

"There wasn't any . . . romance, Aunt Letty."

"It doesn't matter whether there was or wasn't," she continued, her voice very low. "You must have shown that you were grateful."

"No," he replied, "I didn't. I probably said 'thank you,' I can't remember, I was so upset at the time. I thought that I would write her, but I didn't—and now she's dead."

"You were brought up well. You've always been polite. I can't believe that you didn't show your true feelings some way. You mustn't feel guilty, Mitch."

"But I do. She helped others who never gave her the time of day afterward." He thought of all the "Gees" who had beaten a path to Number V, rue Christine. "Now I'm just as bad as all the others. I ran away without letting her know."

"Is there anyone that you can write to?"

"Yes, she had a friend."

"Then write to that friend. It will make you feel better."

"I will." He drained the coffee cup. "Where's Uncle Bos?"

"Working in the orchard. It's restful after Washington worries."

"Do you suppose he'd like some help?"

"He'd be very grateful. He's slowed down, and he complains that it takes him forever to do a job. He gets more impatient, it seems, with age. There's an extra pair of overalls on the back porch."

"Thank you, Aunt Letty."

After he had joined Bosley, Letty poured herself another cup of coffee from the pot that was always on the back of the stove. She knew it had been years since Mitchell had worked with his hands. When he offered to help with the pruning, Bos would understand that in a way Mitchell Heron had come home.

That night, Mitchell wrote a letter to Alice B. Toklas. So much had happened to him in the last few months, and it seemed a long time since he had been in Paris, but time had escalated. In short, simple English sentences, he thanked Gertrude and her for befriending a man they scarcely knew. He wrote that they had saved his life once in Culoz and perhaps his sanity the second time in Paris, because he had decided to give up his search for Jean Baptiste Faubert.

Pierre Darlan took a small piece of dental floss from his pocket and started to clean his teeth. H.R. Leary drew in his breath and looked away. They had finished dinner and were still occupying a private booth in the rear of Harvey's Restaurant; otherwise Leary would have spoken to the Frenchman about his obvious lack of etiquette.

"So what is the latest news about Steinmetz?" Pierre asked. "Or do I have to check the record myself?"

"You are getting salty in your old age, Pierre," Leary replied. "Steinmetz will testify by writing in chalk on a large blackboard; his words will be translated by an interpreter. His appearance before the International Military Tribunal should be remarkable. What we must prove now, in connection with his own appearance, is the fact that he was mutilated by the neo-Nazis in order to make his appearance before the tribunal more difficult. Those bastards!"

"Doctors, I am quite sure, will testify that the wounds in his mouth are fresh. And, of course, three psychiatrists must swear that he is indeed sane." Pierre wound up the dental floss on a tiny spool. "And our nurse will say that he was all right when he was transported from the hospital ... but you cannot do what I know you are thinking." He paused and placed the spool in his pocket. "You cannot bring Herr Professor Schneider to the trial to corroborate her statement that when he certified

Steinmetz the old man spoke at length and, therefore, very much had a tongue. That you cannot do, because Mitchell Heron could never pull it off, and the lawyers of the opposition would make—what is your Thanksgiving term?—mincemeat out of him on the stand."

Leary passed a hand over his weary face. "There is complication upon complication! We cannot, morally, use an impostor—Mitchell Heron—as a witness, yet the real Herr Professor would never appear on our behalf, even if he was on our side, because, of course, he had nothing to do with the Steinmetz certification! There are so many points to prove. The tribunal will understand *why* we had to spirit him away from the enemy in order to protect his life, but we must find out where and by whom this terrible operation was carried out—somewhere en route to the asylum. Damn it to hell, why did we get into this business in the first place? My father had a drugstore and begged me to go to pharmacy school. Why, oh, why didn't I listen to him?"

Pierre smoothed his mustaches knowingly and added, "After the atomic bombings, I thought we would have a moment's peace. Yet it has been worse. Cloak-and-dagger has changed so that no one is safe anymore. Everyone lies now all the time, instead of just occasionally! Doublecross agents thrive until no one knows who works for whom! Then this Nuremberg business comes up, and all those war criminals must be punished, yet . . ."

"What do you mean, *yet?*" Leary snapped.

Pierre pursed his lips. "One thing is very obscure, my friend. One fly is in the ointment. We are going to convict war criminals, surely, yet there is one inescapable fact. We must find them guilty of *violating laws that were not in existence at the time the acts were committed.*"

Leary turned away in disgust. "Morally," he said, giving Pierre a hard look, "the Nazi leaders were wrong and are wrong. The tribunal has already ruled that 'crimes against peace,' the planning and waging of aggressive war, are illegal. But this is the first time that war has been legally defined in the courts! Wars have always been wrong, since before the days of the Bible, but no nation has actually said so legally. Now that has been done for clarification. That is part one; part two is, of course, to prove that there's been untold violation of law or customs of war, including the killing of hostages and the savage ill treatment of prisoners of war. Part three is the so-called 'Crimes against Humanity,' murder, enslavement, deportation and other inhuman acts, such as that perpetrated on Steinmetz, and which he perpetrated against his own race while deputy of Sachsenhausen. Our side must prove, Pierre, that the neo-Nazi influence is still rife in Germany, and even with the war over, they operate clandestinely in a very superior way. This element is still very strong and powerful. Nazism is not dead."

Pierre let out his breath all at once with a little hissing sound. "Yes, yes, yes, but proving all of this is not our job, H.R.! We are small men in a small business. Let some of the others dig into this field. I have no taste for it."

"Neither do I!" Leary exclaimed.

"We did our part by freeing Steinmetz from prison," the Frenchman continued wearily. "It is not our fault if the backup team, working in Berlin itself, failed to offer adequate protection for the man on that fifteen-mile trip from the hospital to the asylum. The ambulance attendant and driver should have been *theirs*. They failed, H.R., they failed. And it is not our fault that they failed!"

H.R. Leary reached for the check. "Let's go," he said. "We can stay here all night arguing about these issues, but the fact remains that, whoever does it, positive proof must be offered to the tribunal that Steinmetz was mutilated by the neo-Nazis, who have since gone underground; otherwise the German lawyers will argue for months that the Jews cut out his tongue! The ambulance drivers have disappeared—killed, probably, who knows? This is an international incident, Pierre; we aren't dealing with simple ruses or espionage pacts executed between two governments—the 'I will swap my Agent X for your Agent Y' nonsense, which happens all the time. We are dealing with world-shaking events, and somehow we must not fall back."

Pierre placed a five-dollar tip on the table and followed Leary out of the restaurant. "I do not like any of this, H.R. I think I will get out of it while I have my own sanity. I am going to hand in my resignation." He was suddenly very angry. "And to hell with all of you!"

13

The Eye of the Sparrow

Robert Desmond had awakened with an upset stomach and a fever.

The house doctor at the George V Hotel in Paris had diagnosed it as a mild type of influenza that would probably last forty-eight hours. He prescribed several pills the size of horse tablets, to be taken every two hours, and a light diet.

Jorge hovered around the bed, which made Desmond angry. "For God's sake, go press some pants or something," he shouted. "If I need you, I'll call. I can't stand to be stared at, I'm not going to die, and as for you, Luke

Three, you must attend the reception at the American Embassy by yourself." He took a sip of water, then continued weakly, straightening his pale blue silk pajama top, "When you are introduced, do not fail to repeat the name carefully, so you'll attach the right name to the right face later on. Also, remember which lady is introduced as *madame*—a married woman—and *mademoiselle*—a single woman—so if the name escapes you in conversation, at least you won't insult them. All men are *monsieur.*"

"I wish I had a flair for languages."

"How do you know that you don't? That depends entirely on your teacher. There will be a long reception line; shake hands lightly. There's a very good reason that the ladies wear those elbow-length gloves—it's to hide the bruises!" He grinned weakly. "Don't have too much champagne, and stay away from the hors d'oeuvre table. There will be such items as caviar, which you won't like, and little hot dishes with sauces that will taste very strange. Stay exactly one hour—no more, no less—and don't forget to say good-bye to the ambassador and his wife. Spend at least two or three minutes with him, and if he asks you what you think of President Truman, say: 'He's all right in my book. He just appointed Perle Mesta as Ambassador to Luxembourg. She's from Oklahoma, you know!' Can you remember that? It'll get a laugh. Now get dressed before I give you more advice which you won't heed."

"I'm sorry you can't go," Luke Three said. "I'd sure feel better if you were along."

"Well, it's high time that you handled one of these affairs yourself, bub. You'll make thousands of these appearances before you'll be ready to retire!"

"Right now I wish I was pumping gas back in Angel." Luke Three got up from the bedside chair. "It's a hell of a lot easier than putting on a soup-and-fish and smiling at a lot of foreigners that I don't care a tinker's damn about."

"These 'foreigners,' as you call them," Robert Desmond said as furiously as his condition would allow, "are your customers! Some of these people at the reception own huge blocks of Heron British or Heron Dutch, so get off your damned high horse!"

"Yes, sir," Luke Three replied quietly. This was the first time that Robert Desmond had truly been angry with him.

"And as you go out, ask Jorge to come in. I have to go to the bathroom."

"Yes, sir," Luke Three replied and then, when he summoned Jorge, he cautioned, "He's really got his bowels in an uproar!"

Jorge managed a small, tight smile. "Yes, Mr. Luke," he said softly. "I would say in more ways than one—if you know what I mean."

The exterior of the American Embassy was festooned with the flags of all nations, and when the door of the limousine was opened for Luke Three there were a number of distinguished men and women lined up on the steps, all expensively attired and wearing decorations. He swore that the Austrian count was wearing an army sharpshooter's medal tucked in among the crosses and beribboned brass.

After a glass of champagne, when Luke Three was conversing with the British ambassador, a fresh-faced girl with bright red hair, dressed in dark green, approached. The ambassador smiled and kissed her on the cheek. "I'd like you to meet one of your countrywomen. Linda Roman, this is Luke Heron the Third."

She giggled and shook his hand. "You mean," she said mischievously, "that there are *two* before you?"

"Yeah, but everyone calls me Luke Three. It's not so stuffy."

The ambassador excused himself. "I must say good-bye to the Italian consul. Please extend my felicitations to your grandfather."

"Thank you, sir, I will," Luke Three replied in his Sunday voice.

"Get him!" Linda said as soon as he was out of earshot. "He's one of the most boring men alive, next to the Italian consul, of course!"

Luke Three regarded her with appreciation. "You're the first person I've met over here who seems to have some life. I'm glad you came today."

She grimaced. "I *had* to. Daddy's chairman of the board of Roman Textiles. This is a command performance, but I'm going to disappear ungracefully soon. I've been nice to all the old hens. You know, Lukie, some of these Limey roosters who've been, oh, so proper, why, they've been looking down my dress." She regarded him with amusement. "Have you been propositioned yet?"

"Beg pardon?"

"You know, have any of the old dames asked you to go to bed?" She gave him a look. "Why, you're turning red!" she exclaimed. "I've finally run into a man who still blushes. I thought your species were all extinct."

"Would you like some champagne?" Luke Three asked, changing the subject.

"I've left my glass somewhere. That would be nice, if you can find a waiter in this miserable crowd. However, I'd rather talk to you. If you leave me, I'll surely be pigeonholed by some old codger with a dirty mind." She giggled and hailed a passing waiter with a tray of glasses. "You have two customers, my good man."

The waiter looked down his nose at her as she swooped up two glasses of champagne. "Here, Lukie, this is vintage stuff. It'll clear your sinuses and Lord knows what else!"

Luke took the glass awkwardly by its stem and sipped. "It is a lot better than cider," he conceded.

"*Anything* is better than cider!" She gave him a frank, evaluating glance. "What are you doing later?" She saw his blank look, and qualified, "I mean for dinner, after the reception."

"I was going back to the George Cinq."

"Oh, my God, Lukie, that's not any fun at all! Look," she continued confidentially, "we're having some people on board the *Saratoga*—that's our boat—which is moored off the Left Bank. You're invited."

He was confused. "What time?"

"As soon as we can duck out of this place."

"Like this?" He indicated his tuxedo.

"Of course. Over here we just dress every which way when we relax. Some will probably be in swimming suits. It'll all be very relaxing."

"I don't know, Linda . . ." He was dubious.

She took his arm. "How long has it been since you've had a good cheeseburger and french fries?"

He grinned slowly. "Not since I left Oklahoma!"

She ran her hand through her short, red curls. "My God, Oklahoma!" she exclaimed. "I should have known. You're one of the *oil* Herons?"

"Afraid so," he replied with a wink. "But, I'm still invited, aren't I?"

"Of course. I won't hold that against you," she said gaily, downing the last of the champagne. "But I warn you right now that our family uses Texaco."

He was having fun. "Then I won't hold *that* against *you!*"

"Let's get out of here, Lukie, but not before we have another glass of champagne." They made their way through the crowd to the buffet table at the side of the huge room, and she took a small canapé. "Ugh! Fish paste! Oh, that's vile!" She made a face and placed the partially consumed cracker back on the plate. A waiter replaced their empty glasses.

"Put on a gray face," she said under her breath, "and we'll pay our respects to our host and hostess. I'd introduce you to Mommy and Daddy, but you'll meet them later. See the tall man with a red nose? Well, that's him. The woman in blue with the white corsage is my mother. Today is their thirty-seventh anniversary. I hope they don't get high too soon. After all, it's an occasion."

"I'm supposed to say hello to the American ambassador before I leave," he said. "Have you seen him?"

"Do you want to get into a discussion of the price of Heron oil?"

"No."

"Then avoid him. Come on, let's do our duty."

Very decorously, with the dignity befitting the occasion, she took his arm and they approached the ambassador who shook hands with Luke Three. "Give my regards to your grandfather and I am sorry that Mr. Desmond is indisposed. I would suggest a guide to show you 'the city of light,' but you are in excellent hands with Mademoiselle Roman."

"Thank you, Ambassador," Luke Three replied and gave him a small salute, the same farewell he always bestowed upon customers at the Heron station in Angel.

Luke Three and Linda Roman paused on the steps outside the embassy. "My car's parked around the corner," she said, "if you don't mind walking. It's easier than getting one of these frog attendants to bring it around."

"We have a slight problem," Luke Three replied. "I have a car and driver."

"There are several solutions," she answered, frowning furiously with mock seriousness. She held up her fingers and counted. "One, let him drive my car, you drive the limo, and I'll be your passenger. Two, I drive my car and you follow with the driver as passenger. Three, you drive my car, I drive the limo, and we leave the driver here. Four ..." They both burst out laughing.

"You're *mad*, you know that," he whispered in her ear.

"Of course. It runs in the family." She took his hand. Her eyes were very green. "Why don't you dismiss the driver and come with me? I'll see that you get back to your hotel later."

Her car was a cream-colored Rolls-Royce, and when she started the engine and backed into the opposite street before heading down a narrow passageway, Luke Three patted the dashboard. "You really should switch to Heron. We have a new knock-free gas that would make this baby purr like a kitten. Now it sounds like a Mack truck."

She threw him a sidelong glance. "How do you know so much about engines?"

"I'm in the business, remember?"

"Sure, but I thought you were just a figurehead or something."

"I'm a mechanic at heart."

"Really?" She shook her head, and her short hair tumbled over her forehead. "Sounds boring as hell. Anyway, how long are you going to be in Paris?"

"We leave at the end of the week. I'll be glad to get home. We've been over here almost three months. I'm hungry for home cooking."

"You know, Lukie, you're an interesting man. Different from the gang I pal around with. You're unspoiled. I like you."

"I like you, too, Linda, but please keep your eyes on the road."

"You're safe with me. I have a wonderful guardian angel." She paused at an intersection. "It's not far now." She peered at a street sign. "I love Paris, but the traffic is absolutely chaotic and the lighting is awful. I think I'm supposed to go to the right here. If I turn to the left, we'll end up in the Louvre. Have you seen the Venus de Milo?"

"No."

"Well, she's rather good-looking for a broken-up old dame. Ah, I made the right decision." She sped down the street. "You wouldn't recognize this place in the daytime, bookstalls and easels everywhere and the *strangest* people." She pulled into a side street and parked next to several small cars on a tiny wharf. "Here we are, kiddo," she said, "and it looks like the gang has assembled." A small yacht was moored on the shimmering river, its deck strung with lights. There were spirals of smoke wafting up from the deck, and the odor of burning charcoal. Jazz music filtered out over the water.

"Oh, God, that smells good." Luke sniffed appreciatively. "If I close my eyes, it seems that I'm outside the smokehouse on the farm."

She threw him an amused look. "Don't you mean *ranch*?"

He laughed. "No, Linda, we don't have ranches in Oklahoma, only farms."

"And I suppose you don't have 'ro-day-os' either?"

"Nope. Only rodeos, and they are just for show nowadays."

"It must be a strange world that you live in, Lukie."

He shook his head and indicated the yacht. "No, Linda, it's you who live in a strange world."

"Then welcome to it!" She giggled and scrambled up the gangplank. When she reached the deck, she turned with her hands outstretched to him. The wind blew her short red curls around her head and outlined her bosom under the green chiffon dress. Luke Three realized that she possessed something more than mere beauty; she had energy, vitality, enthusiasm, and something that Robert Desmond would have classified as "animal magnetism." But what was most impressive to him was the fact that she obviously did not care what anyone thought of her. He had never known anyone who behaved exactly as they pleased.

"Come on, cowpoke!" she called out as he sauntered up the gangplank. She began to laugh. "You're wearing boots!"

"What's the matter with that?" he asked. "They match my tux—they're black."

"Can you dance in those clodhoppers?"

"Of course." The combo was playing a samba, and she began to sway her hips with the music. "Let's dance."

He grasped her hand. "Let's have a drink instead."

A small bar had been set up near the first cabin, presided over by a tall Negro. "Clyde, this is Luke Heron III."

The black man showed all of his teeth. "Champagne, sir?"

"Two."

When the music stopped in the salon, Linda raised her hands. "Hey, quiet down, everyone. If there's anyone on board who doesn't use Heron gasoline, now's your time to escape, because I want you to meet my new cowpoke, Lukie Heron, from Oklahoma."

Luke Three flushed with embarrassment and, to his surprise, was greeted with a round of applause. He felt more out of place because he was the only man in a tuxedo; the others were wearing elegant casual clothing, slacks, shirts, and sweaters. The women wore skirts and blouses or sequined sweaters.

The combo began a fox trot. "I feel like a dummy in a store window," he said to Linda.

"Oh, don't be silly. I'm in an evening dress, and I'm not going to change. Let's dance, but first down your champagne!"

He emptied the glass and took her in his arms, guiding her away from the other dancers to a quiet part of the deck that was not illuminated with the tiny sparkling lights. "Hey," she exclaimed, "you're a good dancer! Just remember that my shoes are open-toed."

"Haven't mashed a foot yet!" he shot back, and she laughed. They danced the next number, which was a two-step, and finished with a rhumba.

"You're a joy!" she exclaimed. "Most men over here are lousy dancers. They either hold you too close and breathe in your ear, or improvise steps badly. I didn't realize that Okies dance so well."

Suddenly he was piqued. "I suppose," he said tersely, "that you expect all of us to 'do-si-do' in a barn!"

She giggled. "Don't be so thin-skinned, Lukie."

"And you can stop calling me by that silly name. I'm Luke Three."

She danced up close, and he could feel her breasts and her thighs and her stomach press up against him. She reached up quickly and kissed him on the mouth. "Settle down, cowboy," she said, "don't be so damn serious." She disappeared, returning a moment later with two glasses of champagne. "Here," she said, "cool off. I don't mean to be nasty. This is just my way. Oh, dear God! Mommy and Daddy have arrived."

Luke Three followed her gaze. Her father was holding up her mother, who shook off his arm, turned her florid face to the group, and shouted, "Stop the music. All of you parasites go home!" There was a sudden, shocked silence.

"She's just joking," Linda said loudly. "Please go on with the party." The music started again, Mrs. Roman slumped against her husband's shoulder, and they were swallowed up by the dancers. "Excuse me," Linda whispered in Luke's ear. "I better go help her."

Luke Three decided to have another glass of champagne, and since everyone was ignoring him, he refilled his own glass at the bar, then went to the barbecue grill and addressed Clyde, who was now wearing a tall chef's hat. "A cheeseburger, please, well done, with all the trimmings."

The man smiled. "Yes, sir."

"You don't seem to be doing much business," Luke Three remarked, pointing to the patties on the edge of the grill.

"It's too early, Mr. Heron," Clyde replied with a twinkle. "This crowd likes to drink first. In about an hour they'll be lining up for chow. There's a blond duchess from the Balkans who can eat everyone under the table. She has three millions more than the Romans!" He handed Luke Three a plate. "I took the liberty of serving you some french fries. The baked beans are Southern style, not quite like Okie pinto beans, but they're good just the same."

"Thank you. Where are you from?" Luke Three took a bite of the cheeseburger and grinned with approval.

"Savannah, but I never go back. I stayed over here after the war, married a French girl who's now a maid here on the *Saratoga*. It's an easy life, and the pay is excellent. I like it over here. Those race riots they're having at home are ridiculous, and me with a white war bride...." He laughed, flashing his white teeth again, then bent over and looked up dully, rolling his eyes and whining, "No, suh, massa, I ain't nevah goin' back down South. Why, those nigrahs would likely tar and featha me. By the way, suh, what's a nice fella like you doing among this rich, po' white trash?"

Luke Three grinned. "As soon as I finish this burger, I'm taking off." He paused, indicating the group. "Does this go on all the time?"

"Every night in summer. In winter, they move into the salon."

"Don't you get sick of it?"

Clyde flashed his teeth again. "It could be worse. I have a credential. I could be teaching school some-where, wearing my heart on my sleeve, trying to drum some education into my people's children. Half would drop out after the seventh grade, and after trying so hard for so many years, I would get to the point where I wouldn't care anymore." He shook his head. "It's better here. All I have to do is be pleasant. I like the surroundings. In fact, Mr. Heron, the people are nicer when they're smashed than some back home who are sober all the time. I like the sea. All in all, it isn't a bad life." He paused. "I've been talking too much." He straightened his back and bent over the grill. "Anything else I can get for you, sir? Those beans are mighty good, suh, mighty good."

Luke Three winked and held out his hand. "It was a pleasure meeting you."

They shook hands quickly and unobtrusively.

"Sir?"

"Yes?"

"I like your family products. Your oil is much better than Mobil's."

Luke laughed. "Thank you."

Under his breath, Clyde said, "Here she comes."

Luke Three was not surprised when he felt Linda pressing up against his thigh. "We've just put Mother to bed, and the gang is getting ready to eat," she whispered, "Shall we do it?"

"Do what?" he asked.

"Shhh," she said *sotto voce.* "You know." She pressed her thighs against his buttocks.

He was not really certain that he understood her movement. "I'd like another champagne."

"You mean," she said in a little-girl voice, "you have to be drunk to go to bed with me?"

He was confused. "I meant ..." He couldn't finish the sentence because he truthfully did not know what he meant. He guided her into a cabinway out of Clyde's line of vision to tell her that he must go back to the hotel. But the moment that they were protected by the archway in semidarkness, she kissed him full on the mouth, inserting her tongue between his lips.

A wave of euphoria caught him off guard, and he took her in his arms. She opened a tiny stateroom and drew him to the bunk. They caressed each other through their evening clothes. His head whirled as he fumbled with the zipper on the back of her dress.

"You're wrinkling my Valentina," she murmured and started to remove her clothing. He took off his coat and she unsnapped his cummerbund, then, lying down on the bunk, watched him remove his trousers. He finally stood up shyly in his shorts.

"I'm enjoying this." Linda smiled knowingly. "I always undress for men; it's nice when the shoe is on the other foot. I'm tired of parading around in my undies! Come on, Lukie, you look ready for the playpen. Take off your shorts."

He turned away from her and slid the white material down around his ankles, then quickly joined her on the bed. She kissed his neck and chest, then swiftly came up to his mouth. "Do you always go to bed with your boots on?"

"Oh, my Lord!" he exclaimed. "I've had so much to drink . . ."

"Don't blame it on the booze, Lukie, it's quite all right with me."

Red with embarrassment, he removed his boots and socks, then climbed back on the bed and into her arms. She hugged him tightly. "Do you do it often, Lukie?"

"Well . . . not as often as I'd like to. How about you?"

"I only started last year, and I just can't get enough. Make it good for me, Lukie?"

In a way, he felt as if he were back in Mr. Ayres' dancing class, counting by the numbers. He was not terribly excited, but his head was spinning, and although they had not even begun to make love, he felt very much like placing his head on her shoulder and going

to sleep, but of course he could not, because he was
expected to perform.

"Nothing's happening, Lukie," she whispered in his
ear, and she began to help him in a way that he had
never been helped before. Peculiarly, then, she moved
away from his embrace and fished around on the nightstand as if searching for a cigarette. He thought it was a
strange time to smoke. She flipped the cigarette lighter
until it flamed high, then held it over his waist.

"What are you doing?" he cried in alarm.

"I just wanted to see it," she said. "Oh, Lukie, it's so
beautiful!" She snapped off the lighter.

There was a pause while he gathered his thoughts for
a reply. "Thank you, Linda." He was embarrassed. "You're
. . . beautiful too."

She giggled. "Come on, let's have *fun* with it!" She
snuggled into his arms again.

He found that he was having the same sort of difficulty with Linda as he had had with Ardith, but this time
they both worked quietly, if enthusiastically, and, panting
and perspiring, at last accomplished their goal. "Ah," he
breathed.

"Ah," she echoed his sentiment, and they began to
move together as if they had always been joined. As the
waves of euphoria increased, he thought that he had
never experienced anything quite so exquisite. When it
happened, they lay quietly in each other's arms.

"Oh, it was so good, Lukie, so *good.*"

The base viol gave a low rumble. "Oh-oh," Linda said
with a giggle. "It's Skin Time."

"Beg pardon?"

"Skin Time." She laughed, throwing back the covers.
"Hurry up and get dressed. We don't want to miss the
fun. Everyone can drink as much as they like, only we
don't allow anyone to get falling-down drunk. That's a
no-no."

A few moments later they made their way through the

crowd that had grouped around the tiny bandstand in the salon. The beautiful blond duchess, who had exhibited a great deal of poise and dignity, was reeling, the long fringe on her dress swaying in erratic time to the plucked strings of the viol. Linda's father unpried her fingers from the champagne glass that she clutched in her right hand, and removed the cigarette from her left. Ned and Derek, the hefty stewards, who obviously had performed the ritual many times, held up her body as if she were as light as a matchstick. Their timing was perfect. It was as if they were onstage, executing an exotic kind of dance. Ned held her feet, removed her high-heeled shoes, adroitly ran his hand up her leg, and pulled off her right stocking in one sweeping movement, then repeated the gesture with her left leg. Without pausing a beat, Derek held her head, zipped down her dress from the back, deftly disengaged the sleeves and bodice, and, in the silence that followed, dexterously flipped off the dress. They held her over their heads and the viol's strings in a fast piccata reverberated over the salon.

The duchess wore a lace half-slip and a generously padded brassiere. The crowd jeered and applauded. The atmosphere filled with tension, changed subtly. The place was filled with evil. The stewards held her high over their heads and paraded to the side of the *Saratoga* and nonchalantly threw her overboard.

Stationed at the edge of the wharf Clyde stood, dressed in a swimsuit in the event that the duchess did not surface immediately. He carried a huge wool blanket in his arms. The woman came up sputtering and reached for his outstretched hand. He threw the blanket around her shoulders, and she huddled in his arms, slowly and painfully regaining her breath. Her perfectly dressed hair now lay plastered on her cheeks and neck. The crowd made a path as he helped her up the gangplank and on board the *Saratoga*. Humiliated but pristinely sober, she cowered down into the blanket as she was led into a rear cabin.

The big event of the evening over, the combo began a boogie beat and there was again the sound of tinkling glasses, laughter, small talk, and the din of feet being pushed around the dance floor.

"My God!" Luke Three exclaimed. "I've certainly never seen anything like that before. I can see why you call it Skin Time."

"You see, cowboy, what happens to people who can't hold their liquor," Linda replied lightly.

"Does it happen often?" He was incredulous.

"More often than you'd believe."

"But aren't you ever sued or anything?"

She gave him a long look. "Now, really, Lukie. It's a boat rule. If a guest feels tiddly, there's always an empty cabin available in which to take a nappy."

Luke Three shook his head at the antics of this strange group of people into which he had so innocently stumbled. He wished that Jerrard Jones had been present to watch the spectacle. His tongue would still be lodged out of his open mouth. Luke smiled to himself. As terrible as performance had been socially, it was fun, he decided, to see the impeccable Balkan duchess lose her dignity, and he would never have pegged those magnificent breasts as artificial.

Sometime toward morning Luke Three and Linda broke apart at last and slept and were not conscious of the movement of the boat, which steadily moved out into the middle of the Seine.

Luke Three awakened at seven o'clock with a parched mouth. He stumbled to the bathroom and drank three glasses of water before his thirst was quenched; then he was conscious of the ship's movement and ran to the porthole. All he could see in the pinkish dawn was a grassy bank and gently rolling hills. Feeling momentarily nauseated, he opened a porthole and took deep breaths of musky, cool air.

He searched his mind, trying to remember the day's itinerary. Robert Desmond had canceled a meeting with a French supplier because of his illness. What else remained on the agenda? Luke couldn't think. He was feeling very dizzy indeed. He zigzagged back to the bed and turned on the nightstand light. "Linda," he whispered, and shook her shoulder. "Linda?"

She roused and ran her hand through her short curls. "Lukie?"

He grinned. "Who did you expect?" He joined her between the sheets.

She snuggled down into his arms. "Oh, what a night to remember!" She looked up into his face and then shamelessly placed her hand under the cover.

"Stop that!" He laughed. "It tickles."

"It's supposed to, cowboy," she drawled.

"Let's be serious for a minute."

"I *am*."

"I'm in a hell of a predicament," he confided. "We're somewhere on the river, and I have to be back at the George Cinq. How am I going to get there?"

She grinned. "We'll be back this afternoon. We always come up to Mantes-Gassicourt on Thursdays to pick up provisions. You can use our ship-to-shore radio if you like."

"But it's embarrassing, with your folks on board."

"No problem at all," she replied patiently. "We'll just mess up a bed in the stateroom across the cabinway. We're accustomed to having guests—either those planned or unplanned." She giggled. "We never know who's stayed with us until breakfast."

He ran his fingers lightly over her breasts. "Linda, what sort of work do you do? Do you always live here on the boat? Is your father retired?"

"Just a moment, cowboy," she said lightly. "I really

don't feel like answering questions. I'd much rather do it again." Her hand was busy under the sheet.

"I'm not feeling very sexy," he replied.

"Well, we'll remedy that...." She brought her body over his and began nibbling at his ear and neck.

"Don't leave any hickeys," he cautioned.

"I won't, if you won't." Then she was kissing him and he was returning her kisses, and their body heat was increasing. They went through the same rituals as the night before, when a pattern of lovemaking had been established. Afterward they drowsed, then the ship's bell awakened them fully.

Linda propped her head on her elbow and ran her fingers over his chest. "I'm a sort of color coordinator."

"What?" he replied sleepily.

"You wanted to know about my work. We have an office on the *Saratoga*. I select colors and design fabrics." She laughed. "Daddy and I *do* work during the day. We live here about six months of the year, the other part in Southampton—the one on Long Island, not England. Daddy is semi-retired, and the mills are in Portland, Maine. We also have a cabin in the White Mountains. Later on, I want to design clothes. Now what about you?"

"This is my first trip abroad. I'm visiting the Heron field offices with a vice president of the company. I was in Okinawa during the war, and I like you very much."

The ship's bell rang out again, and Linda stirred. "We *must* get up. Dress and sneak over to Number Three, while I see what's going on for breakfast. Come to the salon in about fifteen minutes."

"In my tux?"

She giggled. "What else? You probably won't be the only one!"

Robert Desmond was awakened by the telephone. "Yes?" He said, finding that he was still nauseated.

"What? Repeat that, please, this connection is lousy. Luke Three? *Where?* The Romans? Never heard of them." He paused, listening intently, then replied weakly, "The day is free as far as that's concerned, but ..." He was really feeling quite dizzy. "I don't know how you get in these predicaments, Luke Three. Well, all right, but you've got to be back by six o'clock, because you'll have to make an appearance at the dinner party that the Director of Information is giving for the Volkswagen people. What? I'm still sick. All right, see you tonight." He hung up the telephone and shouted for Jorge and placed his head back on the pillow. He was barely thirteen years older than the boy, yet at the moment he felt old enough to be his grandfather. At the same age he had been in charge of the Desmond trucking division, and was putting in a twelve-hour day routing vehicles all over the southwestern part of the United States. But Luke and he were a generation apart, and their backgrounds were entirely different. His head began to clear somewhat, and the room no longer swam before his eyes.

"Good morning, sir," Jorge said, raising the blinds and looking out over the gray rooftops. "It's a gray day, looks like rain." He coughed discreetly behind his dark hand. "Mr. Luke's bed has not been slept in, sir."

"Yes, I know. He just called from the *Saratoga*. He's up the Seine, but he'll be back this evening."

"A boat trip after the reception at the embassy?" Jorge remarked smoothly. "I don't believe he took a change of clothing."

"I expect not. It appears he met some people named Roman at the party, and he was invited at the last minute."

"Ah, yes."

"And what is that supposed to mean?" Robert Desmond exclaimed hotly. His head had begun to ache again.

"The Romans have rather fast reputations."

Robert Desmond was on the point of losing his temper. "And what is that supposed to mean?"

"They're in the columns frequently. The girl, Linda, is a madcap."

"Madcap?" Robert Desmond frowned. "There are times when you are really exasperating, Jorge. If you have something to say, don't beat around the bush, say it!"

"She's been engaged three times this last year, once to an East Indian."

"With a lot of money, I suppose?"

"Not one rupee. The Romans are loaded, though; sheets, pillowcases, blankets, towels. You've slept on them, sir."

"Which I assume Luke Three is still doing!" Robert Desmond snapped; then he sighed. "Is Linda pretty, Jorge?"

"She's the outdoorsy type."

"Sometimes they're the best." Robert Desmond mused. "I suppose Luke Three is entitled."

"What, sir?"

"Oh, nothing. By the way, I'm beginning to feel nauseous again. I better take my medicine."

"You *are*."

"What?"

"Nothing, sir," Jorge replied as he went into the bathroom to find the tablets. So Luke Three had spent the night on board the famous *Saratoga*! Jorge was beginning to admire the young master, who was obviously a man of quality.

14

The Shattered Dream

The Saratoga *salon, thought Luke Three, looked like a movie set, all light and shadow.*

The paneling had been painted the same shade of dazzling yellow as the exterior of the boat, he noticed in the bright sunlight. Shadows had masked the effect the night before. The bar was upholstered in white leather, the flooring was polished oak, and there were green plants everywhere. At a corner table, a man in a tuxedo with a rumpled shirt, minus a tie, and a woman in a magenta evening dress were drinking Bloody Marys, and as Luke Three escorted Linda to the buffet, they raised their glasses in a mock toast.

"Hi, Flo. Hi, Henry!" Linda called. "Meet Lukie."

They waved drunkenly, and the salon took on an air of unreality. It was obvious they had been in that same location all night.

"I'm *so* thirsty," Luke whispered.

"Well, don't drink any more water or you'll be smashed. Champagne does that to you." She pursed her very red lips together. She wore no other makeup, he noted, and in the daytime she looked very tanned and wholesome. Her eyes were clear and blue-green—the color, he thought, of grass growing around rocks back home in the pasture.

"I hope I didn't drink too much?" he asked seriously.

"A bit, maybe." She lowered her voice, "But wasn't *it* fun?"

"Yes," he whispered back, pressing her waist with his hand. "I've never done it so much at one time."

"You're young yet." She giggled. "Now, help yourself to the sideboard." She recited, "There's beef hash, but it has onion in it ... creamed chipped beef, ham, Canadian bacon, little pig sausages, scrambled eggs, toast, and sweet rolls. The menu never varies. Want to build your own eggs Benedict? That's hollandaise in the little chafing dish over there."

They had just filled their plates and sat down when there was a stir in the cabinway. "Here's Mommy and Daddy," Linda said. "I've forgotten—did you meet them last night?"

"No, they were ... ah, under the weather."

"Might as well get it over with." She took his hand, and they stood near the double doors that led out on deck. The woman called Flo and the man called Henry arose unsteadily; they too were heralding royalty. Clyde escorted his employers into the room and winked at Luke Three. Ignoring everyone, they rushed immediately to the sideboard.

Linda stood back a moment, made a decision, and propelled Luke Three to her parents. "Luke Heron, I'd like you to meet my mother, Victoria Roman."

The woman turned. She was plump and dressed in a sunsuit a size too small for her large body. Her florid face was devoid of makeup, except for long eyelashes that Luke Three was certain were not her own. Two tiny eyes peeked out of ridges of flesh. "Hel-lo!" she said, raising her eyebrows. She had difficulty focusing her eyes. "Didn't I meet you at the embassy?"

"I don't think so," he said uncertainly.

"Well, did you or didn't you? I got potted, absolutely potted on champagne. I hadn't had luncheon yesterday nor, as it turned out, dinner last night, so I'm famished, absolutely famished." She turned to the sideboard and then looked back over her shoulder. "Nice to have met you."

Linda pressed her father's arm. "Daddy?"

The man appeared to see her for the first time. "Hi, sweetheart," he said, unsmiling, and pushed his seaman's cap back on his forehead, then kissed her on the cheek. He must have been handsome once, Luke Three thought, but his face was ravished now.

"Luke Heron, this is my father, Alphonso Roman."

"Hi," Mr. Roman said with no enthusiasm whatsoever, sticking out his left hand because he held his breakfast plate in the right. They shook hands awkwardly. "Children," he said, "please return to your table. Your food will get cold. Maybe we can have a game of shuffleboard—or something—later, when the fog clears."

"Yes, sir," Luke Three replied politely. He almost added that what fog there was must be in Mr. Roman's head. The weather was spectacularly clear.

After breakfast, when the sun was already a hot, blazing disk overhead, Luke Three and Linda, in swimsuits, lay on deck chairs in the sun. "I feel naked," he said, looking down at the tiny patch of flowered material. "I've never worn so little in my life."

She giggled. "It's called a flap. We picked up a couple of dozen in all sizes in Nice. I think they're very flattering. What's the matter, don't you like to show *it*?"

He turned over on his stomach. "You people live a lot differently over here than we do at home."

"Punching cows?" She laughed.

"I wish you wouldn't make fun of me," he said quietly.

"Oh, Lukie, I'm not making fun! We just don't believe in conventions, and neither will you when you get to feel more comfortable around us. We have a good time and we don't take a lot of things very seriously. If we did, we'd hole up in Portland and worry about all the starving children in the world." She faced him earnestly. "You see, Lukie dear, there are many things you can't do anything about, so why concern yourself? I'm real. You're real. We exist, and we'll be around a long time if we look after ourselves."

"That sounds pretty selfish."

"It is, baby. Let the Pope pray for all the hungry. He has clout, I don't." She lifted her brows. "We Romans live for today."

"But your mother and father, they don't seem to care about—well, about what you do."

She raised herself up on one elbow and regarded him humorously. "I'm twenty-two, Lukie, and my parents treat me like a guest on the *Saratoga*, but when we work in the office, it's all business. They realize that I have my rights. I respect *their* rights, too, and if I have a boyfriend who spends time on the boat, I don't flaunt him. He has his stateroom and I have mine. I'm not smooching with him all over the deck, and we don't make eyes at each other over dinner. He's my guest. Our family has its own code. There are house rules. There are parties and we have fun, and sometimes people—like Flo and Henry, who've been going together for an eternity—stay over, but there are no orgies in the salon, and people don't make love on the deck. If someone creates a disturbance, our two stewards, Ned and Derek, or Clyde, bundle them off in a hurry." She paused, and, with the sun backlighting her short curls, she was very beautiful—not exactly angelic, Luke Three thought, but beautiful.

"There's something important that I want to talk about. At the end of the week we're off to the Greek isles. They're so peaceful. The air is like crystal. We'll be visiting about ten or fifteen places, starting with Corfu, then Cephalonia and down beyond the Tainaron Peninsula to Cythera. Crete, of course, and then up through the Aegean Sea to Milos, which is my favorite, and then probably all the way up to Samothrace. We're going to be gone for several months." When he hesitated, she took his hand. "I like you so much, and I *love* doing it with you. Please say that you'll come with us, Lukie."

He looked at her in surprise. "I'd like nothing better, but I can't. I have an important job."

"Oh, I know that," she replied quickly. "I didn't mean that you had to stay with us the entire trip. You could leave whenever you like. We'll sail into Piraeus, which is the big port of Athens, and you can catch a plane there." She paused. "How long has it been since you've had a real holiday?"

He considered her question quietly. "The thing is, Linda, we Herons don't have formal vacations. Dad always says that when we travel that's our . . . holiday."

"Didn't you have any time off after you got back from the South Pacific?"

"No, I went back to work. I'd have liked to have seen a few things that I heard guys talk about when I got out of the service, but there wasn't much money."

She threw back her head and laughed until her short curls danced. "You must be kidding, Lukie. Don't you have an allowance?"

"No."

"What did you do for spending money?"

He felt very uneasy. "I had my pay at the station, and if I needed something big, like clothes, I just borrowed from my grandfather."

"Borrowed? Did you pay it back?"

"Of course."

"Well, you told me that you were now an executive for Heron. You must get a decent salary."

He frowned. "I get a hundred dollars a week."

She looked at him incredulously. "You know that you're getting screwed, don't you?"

"What?"

"Oh, Lukie, they're taking advantage of you! Certainly you have something to contribute to the company. I only design fabrics for Roman Textiles part time, and I make thirty thousand dollars a year."

Luke Three whistled through his teeth. "My God, Linda, that's a fortune!"

"Of course it is, but I'm an only child. Part of that money is for my work, of course, but most of it is my allowance. How many are there in your family?"

"Two. I have a younger brother, Murdock, four years old, who was a change-of-life baby." He paused self-consciously, then defended, "But you must remember that you people live a lot differently than we do. We're a very conservative family."

"So it appears! But you travel in ambassadorial circles."

"Some of the time. The trip, though, is tax deductible."

"Of course it's tax deductible!" she exclaimed. "So is the *Saratoga*! Someone's been giving you a snow job, Lukie." She waited for her words to register; then, when she saw him frowning again, she continued, "When are you scheduled to go back to the States?"

"As soon as the VP gets over the flu."

"Come with us to Greece, and when you want to leave, we'll take you to Athens, where you can get a flight home." She pressed his hand. "And we'll have an opportunity to see the scenery, which is really spectacular, and we'll do it lots, too."

He thought of the way that he enjoyed her body; certainly she was wonderful in bed, a woman who enjoyed sex for the joy of sex. She was like a man in that regard, he felt. "Okay," he said. "I've just decided to go on vacation. Your folks won't object?"

She giggled. "No, you'll be very welcome." She pressed his hand again and was suddenly very desirable. "You're my first boyfriend in a long time," she said. "Also, it doesn't hurt that you're a Heron."

* * *

After the provisions had been brought on board, the *Saratoga* headed back to the slip off the Left Bank, and Luke Three, in borrowed shirt and slacks, went into a telephone box and rang the George V hotel. When Jorge came on the line, he asked, "How's the old boy?"

"The 'old boy' "—Jorge coughed delicately—"is slightly better. I'll put him on."

"Yes?" Robert Desmond's weak voice came over the wire.

"Bob, the Romans have invited me on a cruise to the Greek islands, and I've accepted."

"What?"

"It's only for a couple of weeks. You know, I've never had a real vacation, and I know there isn't anything pressing at the office. You know I just came along for the ride."

"The hell you did," was the angry reply. "You don't know what I went through with your dad to get him to agree to this trip. He didn't want you to go; I really put on the pressure. If you stay over here, it'll look like it was a planned collusion." His gravelly voice lost a portion of its Oxford poise. "Get your ass over here. I'll send a car for you."

"No, I won't!" Luke Three blurted. "I've worked like hell with no time off. Sometimes I'd open at eight in the morning and close at six and have a couple of cars to work on at night. People would call me on Sunday to open up for some part, or someone would need gas. I didn't get any overtime, just a lousy hundred bucks a week. I'm going to take a vacation."

There was a long pause at the other end of the wire. Robert Desmond's voice was strained. "Listen to me. These Romans have terrible reputations. The old man's a drunk, and the old woman is not far behind, and that girl will go to bed with anyone. It's time you knew—"

"Bob, I'm having *fun.*"

"All right, Luke Three, let me put it this way. Come

home as scheduled, do what work there is to do around the office for a couple of weeks, and then come back for a legitimate vacation. Let's be sensible about this. I don't want to be held responsible ..."

"How can you be? Jesus Christ, Bob, I'm not a kid! I know what I want to do and what I don't. It would be silly to go back home and then come right back again."

"We've got to be businesslike, Luke Three."

"Why? Was it businesslike treating me like a god-damned mechanic without proper pay?"

"I don't understand your attitude, Luke Three. When you went to the embassy yesterday ..."

"I didn't have my eyes open. I do now."

"Call your dad, then."

"Why?"

"Because you can't go off on a wild goose chase without ..."

Luke Three was shaking. "Just watch me! Have Jorge pack my clothes. I'm at the Humboldt private slip on the Left Bank." He slammed down the receiver so hard that it hurt his hand.

The transatlantic call took two hours to put through. Finally Robert Desmond heard Luke's voice, accompanied by piercing static on the line, come through faintly. "The trip has been going wonderfully well," he said, balancing the telephone on the pillow, "except I'm bedded down with a Parisian bug."

"Bedded down with *whom*?" Luke asked, amid a new series of crackling noises.

Robert Desmond chuckled. "A bug! I have the flu."

"What about the Fertig leases?"

"The countess signed the papers. I'll give a full report the minute I return."

"How's Luke Three?"

"He's mainly why I'm calling. You know, the boy hasn't had a decent vacation since he got back from

Okinawa, and he's worked hard at the station. He's been invited to tour the Greek islands with the Romans— he's the textile king." Robert swallowed and went on persuasively, "I'll give him the go-ahead—of course, with your approval, Luke."

There was a long pause, filled with fresh crackling sounds, and Robert Desmond thought for a moment that the call had been interrupted; then Luke's voice wavered over the line. "I assume that he wants to go?"

"Very badly. He'd have called you himself, but he's on their boat now."

"Hell, he's a good kid. Tell him to enjoy himself. The Greek islands, huh?" Luke chuckled. "I've always wanted to go there myself."

There was a new group of people that night aboard the *Saratoga*, a few of what Clyde referred to as "boat trash," but the guests were mainly Parisians whom the Romans had known from past seasons. Among them was a very dignified foreign ambassador with a magnificent head of silver hair, to whom Luke Three was hurriedly introduced, but his very long name and the name of his country had been mumbled. From the man's coloring, Luke knew that he must hail from somewhere in the Middle East.

After dinner, while the combo played softly in the background, Victoria Roman stood up and hit her wineglass with a knife for attention. "We're going to have a game. It's called 'the Greek isles.' Have any of you visited there?"

The ambassador, his wife, and two other couples out of the forty guests raised their hands, and Victoria continued, "I'm sorry, but because of necessity you and all we Romans are excluded from the game, but please do pick up a demijohn of champagne at the bar when you go home this evening as some measure of compensation." She paused. "Everyone choose a partner, but no man and wife can be on the same team. Ned and Derek will pass among you, handing out tablets and pencils. Each team must decide upon twelve words that describe the Greek islands." She paused. "Your Excellency"—she nodded to the ambassador—"would you kindly be the judge?"

Luke Three was one of the last to find a partner, who turned out to be a man of about his own age, Jean Paul Dupree, who spoke very little English. Together they came up with the following words: *moody, greasy, fog, shoreline, craggy, ocean, purple, foreign, Athens, expensive, mutton, beautiful.*

Ned and Derek, who always reminded Luke of professional wrestlers but were actually polite and reserved men, gathered the slips of paper in a large silver tureen, which they presented to the ambassador.

Then more champagne was served and as the combo switched over to jazz, Luke Three sought out Linda, who was sitting with her parents.

"Do you think you'll win?" she asked impishly.

He shook his head. "No. Jean Paul thought up most of the words, and I don't think they're really very good."

Victoria took a deep breath. "With the amount of champagne the ambassador has been lapping up all evening, it will be a miracle if he still remembers English!" She hit her wineglass with a knife again, and the music promptly stopped.

"I have made my selection," the ambassador announced, standing up. "The winning ballot is signed 'Felicia and Gerald.' " A murmur arose from the group, and there was a swift round of polite applause.

Linda whispered to Luke Three, "She's the wife of a restaurant owner, and he's the husband of an actress. A most unlikely pairing."

The ambassador held up his hands for silence, and his wife held her back erect, a bored half-smile on her face. It was obvious that she did not approve of her husband engaging in parlor games.

"These are the winning words, and, I might add, they are very good indeed, for people who have not visited the islands: *sunlit, whitewashed, retsina, hospitable, archaeological, Homer, heritage, simplicity* . . ."

The ambassador's voice faltered; he shook his head slightly and cleared his throat. Taking a sip of the champagne, he seemed to regain his composure. "I'm sorry," he said slowly and distinctly, "I seem to have a frog in my throat."

Linda giggled in Luke Three's ear. "That's a *faux pas* if I ever heard one! And with so many French people here, too!" He pressed her hand for an answer.

The ambassador was continuing. "*. . . boats . . . trad-ition* . . ." Again he was having difficulty pronouncing his words, and he took another sip of champagne.

"He's drunk!" Alphonso exclaimed under his breath, and Luke Three gasped at the import of his words. Surely, he thought, Skin Time wouldn't apply to this distinguished guest!

The ambassador placed his hands flat on the table to support his weight. He was very flushed. He swallowed and went on valiantly, "*. . . seafood . . .*" He swallowed again, and as he fell forward into his dessert plate rasped out, "*ser . . . en-ity.*"

There was a shocked silence as Ned and Derek came silently through the crowd. The ambassador's wife rose and began to protest loudly in some foreign tongue that no one could understand. The stewards ignored her cries, picked up the ambassador as if he were a rag doll, and carried him to the dance floor. Ned positioned himself at his head, and Derek at his feet.

The violinist raised his bow and began to play "A Pretty Girl Is Like a Melody" to the hushed group. First to be removed were the ambassador's shoes, one at a time, in rhythm to the music. Everyone sat fascinated at

what was taking place, not quite sure that the man held
rigidly between Ned and Derek was actually being undressed before their eyes. There were a few nervous
rustlings here and there, and one high-pitched laugh
from the rear of the salon.

Luke Three stared at Ned and Derek, who seemed to
be performing on a stage, having rehearsed their act to
perfection. He had seen break-away clothing in bur-
lesque, attached by unseen wires, where a performer
who had been completely dressed one moment was left
naked the next. But now it was the stewards' expertise
alone that the crowd was watching with such evil fascination. The ambassador's wife was trying vainly to get
through the tables, still screaming incomprehensibly.
Partly, Luke Three thought, to mask her voice, and
partly to accompany the performance, the pianist played
a long run. Ned and Derek held the ambassador stiffly
between them, whilst his clothing was removed piece by
piece. When the trousers were pulled off over his feet in
one continuous dazzling movement, his shirt was pulled
off at the same time. A small whalebone corset was
revealed, laced over his undershirt and shorts.

The ambassador's wife finally reached the pair, and
she began to hit them, in a cold, matchless fury.
Ned and Derek moved away from her and carried the
ambassador calmly out of the salon.

"I can't believe this is happening!" Luke Three
exclaimed.

"He and everyone else know the rules," Alphonso
said. "We won't tolerate people who can't hold their
liquor."

The terrible spell was broken as the crowd surged out
of the double doors of the salon to the deck just in time
to see the ambassador slip under the waves. Clyde, in a
bathing suit, was already in the water and, as soon as
the man sputtered to the surface, towed him expertly to
the wharf. Ned and Derek were waiting with warm blan-

kets. The ambassador, white hair askew from a quick toweling, was helped up the gangplank, a dazed, uncomprehending expression still on his face. His wife rushed to meet him and held him in her arms, cooing gently. The crowd turned back to the salon, summoned by the smooth sound of the jazz combo. The excitement for the night was over.

Luke laughed nervously. "It all happened so quickly, the drinks must have hit him suddenly."

Linda grimaced. "Lord knows how much he'd had before they arrived, and he was really putting away the bubbly. But it's innocent fun. No one ever gets hurt."

"Well," Luke Three added lamely, "it seems to me that's not a very good way to make friends."

Linda raised her brows and shook out her short curls. "Oh, you'd be surprised at the people who accept invitations again, Lukie."

The orchestra segued into a fox trot, and Luke Three asked her to dance. With her breasts pushed up against him and her breath in his ear, he knew that they would spend what remained of the night making love.

The *Saratoga* had taken a lazy voyage through Korinthiakos Kolpos, the Gulf of Corinth, stopped for supplies at Korinthos, then sailed through the narrow straits into the gulf of Saronikos and dropped anchor at Milos of the same-named island, seventy-five miles north of Crete.

The luncheon crowd of about twelve people had stayed on, playing bridge. Six were members of a prominent Greek family that Alphonso and Victoria had met the day before in Milos, and the others were boat friends who had rendezvoused at the port of Adhamas, south of town.

The next afternoon, late, Luke Three retired to his cabin to read, which he often did when he did not feel like participating in the games or Linda was too bored to go sightseeing. They had already toured the depressing catacombs to the southwest of Adhamas, where the early Christians had fled from the mainland, the partially excavated acropolis of Klima, above Milos, and they had walked through massive ruins at a site near Apollonia, called Phylakopi, which Luke Three could not pronounce. "It's all Greek to me!" he had announced happily after the third try, and Linda had looked heavenward and exclaimed, "I hate puns." But when he had taken her hand and led her into the shadow of a giant moss-covered column and kissed her on the mouth, she had broken away from him. "Oh, Lukie, don't start anything, the tourists will think we're absolutely awful. We're the only Americans here."

He thought it peculiar of her to object to a kiss, even in public, when she was so wanton on the boat. But she was strangely restless these days and could not always be counted on to share his cabin.

"It takes so *long* before it feels good," she had told him once when he had become amorous in the afternoon. "Sometimes I just lose interest, Lukie!" He had to admit to himself that it *did* often take an inordinate amount of time, but the foreplay was so pleasurable to him, he had always assumed that it was also pleasurable for her. But, other times, she was more than willing to spend the entire night making love.

Out of sorts with himself, he finally laid down the book and went out on the deck. A group of boat people his own age had come on board and were dancing to recordings, none of which were his Uncle Clement's. The girls were in sunsuits and the boys in walking shorts; it was extremely hot, and the glare from the whitewashed buildings that faced the wharf reflected the rays of the sun. Luke Three longed for the cool breeze that always blew southward over the Aegean at sunset.

*   *   *

"Dad, this is Luke Three." The voice, originating thousands of miles over the ocean, sounded as if it were coming from another world, wavering and distant.

"Where are you?"

"In Athens for the day." There was such a long pause that Luke thought the line had been disconnected. "Hello? Hello?" he shouted.

"I can hear you all right, Dad. What I'm calling about is . . . I want to stay over here longer."

"But you can't, Luke Three, you've already been gone for months! We need you."

"But Dad, I've never been anywhere so beautiful. It's another world, and there's so much to see."

"Look." Luke was becoming angry. "You're a young man and can visit the Greek isles on your vacation every year from now until you're ninety, but you can't postpone coming home. As long as you're in Athens, get on the plane."

"Dad, I don't want to fight with you, but I've made up my mind. I want to stay at least another month."

"You can't! Here you are over there, spending money right and left, and we need you here. Bob's reorganizing the company, and we've got to fit you in right now. After all, Luke Three, it was your idea to place Jerrard Jones in charge of the mechanics' school. I need you here to help coordinate—"

"Dad, I'm happy about Jerrard, and I do want to help, but I've got certain things to work out, things I should have thought about when I was in the service, and didn't. I've got to have more time to myself. The *Saratoga* is a wonderful place to mull things over."

"I'll bet! From the reports I've heard, there's nothing but drinking and carousing. I don't know why you got involved with those people in the first place."

"You don't understand at all, Dad. The Romans are party people, but the yacht is big and there's lots to do besides."

"You're not making a very good case for yourself. You're a spoiled, foolish kid, and I never realized before that you were so irresponsible."

"I'm not irresponsible, Dad. I just need a vacation."

"Christ, you were over there for three months with Robert Desmond. You've seen half of Europe."

"But that was *work*. I was under pressure and on display all the time."

"What kind of a vocabulary are you picking up? What is this 'pressure' and 'display' crap? You're in the oil business, that's your life and breath." Luke drew in his breath angrily. "What's she like, Luke Three?"

"Who?"

"Goddammit, who do you think? Linda Roman. Obviously she's the reason that you want to stay. She must be awfully good in bed."

Luke Three was embarrassed, and his voice was suddenly an octave lower. "She's a nice girl, very different from the other girls I've met."

"Are you in love with her?"

"I don't know." Luke Three's voice grew hard. "Were you in love with Stella?"

"You have no right to throw that up to me," Luke shouted, "If you were here, I'd knock your block off!" He was furious. How dare the kid bring up the girl that he had so often visited at The Widows?

"We're not getting anywhere with this conversation, Dad. I want to take another month."

His temples throbbing, Luke held the receiver in his hand a moment, regaining his equilibrium. "Luke Three," he said flatly in a voice so strained with emotion that he could hardly be heard, "as of this moment you are on an extended leave of absence that may be permanent." He threw the receiver into its cradle. Then he sat down slowly on the divan, thankful that Jeanette had gone shopping and he was not forced to face her. Tears gathered in the corners of his eyes. That damned silly kid! Then a thought came to him, wending out of his unconscious. Was he angry because he envied Luke Three? Did he begrudge him the good times on the *Saratoga*? Did he envy him the company of a beautiful girl? He tried to picture what they would look like stretched out on a bed together.

He shook his head and got up quickly and lighted a cigarette. Was he jealous of his son because he was having an open affair with a woman on foreign seas, when he himself had been married to the same woman for twenty-five years? Did he really feel competitive with the boy? Did he envy him because of what he had between his legs? Had there always been a sort of competition between them? Why had he never paid very much attention to him?

Luke's mind was whirling with strange ideas that he had never faced before, but could he face them now? He went to the sideboard and poured himself a glass of whiskey, and his hands shook as he downed the drink. It occurred to him that he had never really loved his son, and with that realization in mind, he poured another drink and lighted a cigarette. Then another thought wound its way from deep down inside. A chill ran down his spine. Was it also possible that Luke Three did not love him?

15

The Net Tightens

Bosley had just met with the European Recovery Program's administrator, Paul G. Hoffman, and his head was full of figures.

It was like going back to college, re-training his memory to absorb statistics that would have even bored him as a younger man. Now, he was feeling his age; he slept later in the morning, went to bed earlier at night, and no longer felt guilty about taking an afternoon nap when he could manage it in Washington. He was feeling his age, and yet there was so much work yet to be done ...

The chauffeur helped Bosley into the limousine and, when he had placed the heavy briefcase on the front seat, handed Bosley a newspaper. "Thought you might like to see this, sir," he said. "Mr. Luke Three is on the society page, lead column."

"Thank you, Ernie," Bosley replied, and leaned back for the short drive to the Connecticut Avenue house. It was quite possible, he mused, that a person could become a recluse, cut off from newspapers, radio and audio-video, and never hear anything from the servants about what was transpiring on the Hill, but it was impossible to remain ignorant of social doings.

Hired help, it seemed nowadays, lived in the reflected

glory of their betters, especially those society swells who had shaken the dust of the United States from their well-shod feet and had taken up residence abroad. He opened the paper to page four and "International Gossip," a column written by Deborah Wassell, a local radio hostess. His face blushed a mottled purple as he read:

Luke Heron III, estranged heir to the petrol fortune (he's been excommunicated after a spree in Paris grabbed headlines) is basking in the Greek isles on the *Saratoga*, the luxurious yellow yacht of textile magnate Alphonso Roman and his entourage. The Fabulous Foursome, Agile Alphonso, wife Vivacious Victoria, daughter Luscious Linda, and Lucky Lukie, picnicked on Skorpios Sunday on Beluga caviar, Dom Perignon, Westphalian ham and fried chicken. "Just Okie-French food," quipped the Oklahoman in high good spirits. It was only later, escorting Luscious Linda through some ruinous ruins, that Lucky Lukie turned noxiously nasty and smashed a cameraman's lens. Will a marriage be announced from the yellow yacht? Will the Fabulous Foursome run out of champagne? Will the new bikinis arrive in time for the next swimming party? Tune in tomorrow. . . .

Bosley angrily tore out the page and rolled it into a ball, which he threw into the front seat. "Dispose of that garbage," he told the driver.

"Yes, sir," Ernie replied smugly.

"And, furthermore . . ."

"Yes, sir?"

"Oh, never mind. . . ." He was going to tell him not to call such trashy items to his attention, but Letty always read the newspapers, and it was best that he was kept informed. Women always took what they read more seriously than men, and he would have to think about some words to string together that would comfort her. Luke Three had always been the apple of her eye.

He shook his head sadly. What was happening to the younger generation? How could a boy like Luke Three go off on such a tangent? Was there a taint in the Heron blood? Mitchell had been unstable for most of his life. It was only in his thirties that he had come to his senses and given up his gypsy ways. Was Luke Three now exhibiting those same characteristics? Perhaps, Bosley told himself, Luke Three was only sowing what the older generation called "wild oats." It was possible, of course, that his sex drive was prodigious. Of course if he, Bosley, at the same age had been wealthy and was attracted to a beautiful young girl living on a yacht who had invited him on a romantic trip to the Greek isles ... would he have accepted? He did not know the answer.

Luke Three came into the salon, waved to the Romans, who were having breakfast, and mixed himself a Bloody Mary from the sideboard. The tomato juice and vodka refreshed his throat, irritated from too much smoking. He dished scrambled eggs and a fat brown kipper onto a plate, along with some vanilla scones, before joining his host and hostess.

"Never thought I'd like fish for breakfast, but I really like kippers."

Alphonso took a sip of coffee. His face was very red, and he was obviously recovering from a hangover. "Where's Linda?"

Luke Three almost replied that she was sleeping. Instead, he said casually, "Haven't seen her this morning." If they wanted to keep up the pretense, he would certainly go along. "We got in rather late last night. We were at a nightclub where there was belly dancing. It was fun."

Mrs. Roman smiled wanly and pushed a stray lock of very blond hair back from her forehead. "I know the place. Rather an odd crowd, though."

"Not really," Luke replied after he had taken a bite of the fish. "At least after midnight the bazooka musicians played swing. The sound is a little strange, but the beat was right in there." He laughed. "Before I came to Greece, I always thought that a bazooka was a missile that the Allies used to launch against tanks!"

Alphonso grinned. "The wailing sound is about the same."

"Don't be nasty, Daddy," Linda called from the door. "Morning, Mommy. Oh, it's a beautiful day. The sky is clear as a crystal." She went on breathlessly, "How's my cowpoke this morning?"

"Fine. How's my roly-poly?" he shot back with a twinkle.

"I resent that. I'm trying to lose weight, really I am. I only need to lose five pounds." She went to the side-board and poured a cup of coffee and took one piece of dry toast. "I'm starting to watch my food intake this morning." She had just washed her hair, and it stood out around her face like a red halo. She looked so healthy that Luke Three stared at her in admiration.

She joined them at the table. "Daddy, why don't you break the news to Lukie?"

Alphonso nodded. "All right. I thought you might like to do it. Well, young man"—he thrust his leonine head forward—"we've decided to rent a villa on Skorpios, and we thought that if you could get a sabbatical, you'd like to stay with us. The place was once owned by an oil man who lost all of his money during the war—a count—I think his name was Fertig."

"It's surely a small world!" Luke exclaimed. "I met his wife, Jolene, when I was in Rotterdam with Robert Desmond. We're taking up some of her oil leases. She's a very strange lady." He was surprised that he could talk about her so casually, but now he found that he could often discuss controversial subjects without giving himself away by turning red or stammering.

"What happened to the count?" Victoria asked.

"He kicked off. Jolene wasn't too specific about how."

He smiled inside and wanted to say that she probably fucked him to death, but of course he could not. He went on breathlessly, "I hope the villa is cleaner than her house in Rotterdam. It was filthy." He paused. "I guess I shouldn't have brought that up, because she's broke, can't even afford a cleaning woman. But that will change when Heron redrills those wells." He turned to Alphonso. "We're using some new techniques. We've used salt water injection in hundreds of oil wells that haven't been producing, because it tears loose some of the hardened crude. But now we're experimenting with liquid steam, which melts some of the hydrocarbons, which are then more easily pumped to the surface. We're going to try this system with the Fertig wells."

"Luke, do you think you can get more time?"

He frowned. "I don't know. I didn't realize I was so exhausted. Here on the *Saratoga*, I feel so relaxed. I don't like to think of going back to Tulsa, it's really a world away—in more ways than one."

"Then why ask permission?" Linda said quietly. "Just tell them that you're going to stay longer."

"Now, Linda baby," Alphonso admonished. "Sometimes a man can't do what he wants to do, and if Luke must leave, he must leave." He looked at Luke affectionately. "But if you do find a way, we'd like very much to have you as our guest. You know, Luke, you're damned good company for Linda."

Luke Three drained the coffee cup. "Thank you, sir."

"And no one has called me 'sir,' except servants, for years. I like that. You've been brought up well."

"We Okies may have a lot wrong with us," Luke Three joked, pleased that he could call himself an Okie and not feel guilty about it, "but most of my generation were brought up to say 'sir' and 'ma'am.' " Then he added, "Most kids now say 'hey, you' or simply don't reply at all."

Alphonso replied, "When I was young—and I'm a

generation older than you—we always said what was on our minds." He glanced up. "It was only later that we learned to lie, when we went out into the business world, where the truth is always stranger than fiction." He looked at Luke earnestly. "Luke, you're so open and aboveboard. Don't change, no matter what they do to you."

Victoria got up quickly. "How about some bridge? I always play better when I'm hung over. A penny a point?"

Luke grinned. "I already owe you forty-two dollars!"

"Who knows"—she laughed—"this may be your lucky day." She sat down at a table by the porthole and started to shuffle a deck of cards expertly. "Come on, Luke, it's me and you against the rest of the world."

That afternoon Luke Three went into the cable office and quickly wrote out the message that he had so carefully thought out that morning:

LURE OF GREEK ISLES IS TOO MUCH FOR THIS OKIE. I'M ON INDEFINITE SABBATICAL.
                                          LUKE III

He was very careful not to include an address where he could be reached.

Furiously Luke thrust the cablegram at Jeanette, who glanced at the message and asked plaintively, "More coffee, dear?" Her face did not change expression.

"God damn!" he cried. "Don't you have anything to say?"

"No, except the Romans must be very generous people to put him up for so long."

Luke's face was mottled red. "I don't know what's wrong with you! I've half a mind to fire him!"

Jeanette took a sip of coffee and a bite of a breakfast

roll. Her voice was steely. "Luke, you've never given a tinker's damn for that boy! He's worked like a common laborer in that station in Angel. It took a stranger to the family, Robert Desmond, to make an effort to do something about his abilities. All the other executives, except you and Bosley, take a month now and then and go fishing or hole up somewhere away from the telephone. Don't begrudge this holiday."

"But ... this Linda Roman! How can you be so casual, so unfeeling?"

"I am *not* casual and I am *not* unfeeling. Luke Three belongs to another generation. There's a great difference in values. If, after a bit, he doesn't see the light, then put on the pressure. Remember, he didn't take any time to rehabilitate himself after his duty with the Marines."

"I didn't take any time when I came back from service!" Luke shouted.

"World War One was a million years ago, Luke! If he's inherited the Heron glands, which I assume he has, you can't expect him not to have these little affairs."

"Affairs?" Luke spat the word out angrily. "What you mean is, he's sleeping around."

She looked at him coolly. "You were not a virgin, Luke," she went on patiently, "when you married me."

"That was quite another matter."

"What difference does it make where one gets experience?"

"And what do you mean by that?"

"I mean," she said evenly, looking him straight in the eye, "it's common knowledge that Bosley took you to The Widows on your thirteenth birthday and that you continued to patronize the place for some years after that. If Luke Three is finally getting around to sowing his wild oats, at least he has selected a girl who's obviously been around and know what's she's doing. She's no Stella!"

He pounded the table with his fist. "How dare you throw that up to me! That was years before I met you!"

"Of course, dear," she replied calmly, toweling up his spilled coffee. "I'm just putting things in perspective for you. Also, if I hadn't held on to my virginity until we were married, I don't think you'd have asked me to be your sweet little bride."

His red face drained of color. "What ... makes ... you say that?"

"I've often thought about it. It may have worked both ways." She folded up the stained napkin and calmly poured him another cup of coffee. "Because if we'd had an affair, I don't believe that I would have married you."

"What?"

She looked at him blandly and continued in a maddeningly calm tone of voice. "After I found out that sex was not all that great, I might have waited until someone really smashing came along." Her eyes were very dark, her skin taut over high cheekbones. "Don't you think I've known about your infidelities? Jorja Desmond, for one ..."

He cleared his throat, got up from the table, and sighed. "I have a very heavy day," he remarked vaguely, slipped into his coat, and adjusted his tie. He leaned over dutifully and kissed her cheek. My God, he thought, as he went out the door, how long had she known about Jorja? The affair had been over for years, and of course at the time he had not known she was Robert's sister, or that she was feeding her brother classified Heron statistics while he was planning to take over the company. Thank God he'd been able to buy Desmond Oil, or ...

He was on the porch before he heard Jeanette call cheerfully, "You didn't drink your second cup of coffee, dear."

He turned, opened the screen door, and shouted savagely, "You can go to hell!"

* * *

Luke faced the Heron board of directors and spread out the seven-page agenda before him on the long conference table. "I have been going over plans with each one of you for the last several months, and while it's never prudent to spend money unwisely, I'm going to recommend setting aside some twenty million dollars in reserve funds for the following projects: (1) face lifts for all Heron service stations, excluding those built during the last year, of course; (2) the establishing of a central mechanics' school under the supervision of Jerrard Jones; (3) refresher courses, set up under each regional manager, for all service station franchise employees, which will include proper behavior toward customers, procedures to be followed for filling out of Heron forms, including the end-of-the-day bank deposits and establishing of charge accounts."

He paused and took a deep breath. "When Heron began our credit card system in nineteen-twenty-eight, my stepfather, George Story, personally signed the cards." He grinned and looked over his glasses. "There were four! As of now, we have seven hundred charge customers—not counting, of course, our regular billings to industry. But now, as you gentlemen recommended at our last board meeting, we're expanding a line of credit to the customer, which means establishing a new billing department here in Tulsa. Our surveys indicate that in the next five years credit cards will comprise about twenty-five percent of our business, and by nineteen fifty-eight will grow to fifty-five percent!"

There was a murmur among the men, and Luke nodded. "I know it sounds impossible, but we must keep abreast of the other companies who've already extended credit beyond our capabilities." He frowned. "Texaco, for example, is really shooting ahead. Now I don't watch television, but no one can discredit the success of the Texaco Star Theater. I'm not a fan of slapstick comedy, but Milton Berle is a fabulous success."

Robert Desmond nodded and interjected smoothly, "Does anyone here watch the show?"

Clarence Henderson, the marketing manager, nodded. "I do, I'm a fan of Bobby Clarke. His antics always break me up! It's very clever of the sponsor to cast Willie Field as the 'Merry Texaco Repairman,' because the public identifies with him. It's a shame that we've never gone in for that type of advertising. Radio spots are fine, but to have nationwide exposure . . ."

Luke held up his hand. "Television doesn't have that many viewers yet. In a few years, when more sets become available, we might think of sponsoring a show."

Henderson grinned. "It's too bad your brother is tied up with Aunt Bertha's Oat Flakes; he'd make an excellent spokesman for Heron."

Luke's jaw tightened. "Clement and I never, ever, mix business." He paused and then consulted his agenda. "Getting back to the Texaco push, Bob Desmond has suggested changing advertising agencies, and I'm in agreement. We should explore the possibilities for a complete new Heron image. I like the way Sinclair Oil emphasizes its dinosaur."

Metcalf, who was in charge of trucking, raised his hand. "We could make more use of the Blue Heron."

Luke nodded in agreement. "Years ago, when women began to drive, we had a very successful promotion. We gave away brooches and pins shaped like our bird. Patriotic too—red, white, and blue." He paused and looked down at his notes. "I think we should also explore ways to be more helpful to our dealers. When we have our regional managers' meeting in six weeks, some plans should be worked out in detail. Also, Robert Desmond has submitted a plan for restructuring the company, and personally I think it's brilliant. After our luncheon arrives today, Bob will lead a discussion about some of the leases he's picked up, including a new contract with Jolene Fertig." He cleared his throat and went on in a casual voice that was most difficult to produce. "Also, I have given Luke Three another leave of absence."

There was a knock on the door, and the waiter brought in covered plates from the Calico Restaurant. "Today, gentlemen, the menu consists of ham-and-egg sandwiches, baked beans, and apple pie with cheese—and, of course, Bernice's famous coffee."

16

Cause and Effect

Luke Three was suffering from a hangover.

The drinking had started early that morning with Bloody Marys before breakfast, and by the time luncheon was served the gang, most of whom had stayed over the night before, had started to play games, beginning with Ghost, which Luke Three did not care for, but he halfheartedly joined in anyway. Linda was working in the conference room with swatches of material and experimenting with color schemes. She had gone to bed early—and alone—the night before, leaving him to forage for himself. He had spent the night at the bar in the salon, drinking by himself.

The gang consisted mostly of other boat owners who had tied up in the harbor at Athens, and a half-Greek, half-Spanish café owner, Esmeralda, who had brought back several people the night before after she had closed her place. Her colloquial English was so poor that she sat on the sidelines and did not rally until they started charades, at which both she, as it turned out, and Luke Three were adept.

After luncheon almost everyone switched to zombies, a deadly concoction of sloe gin, grenadine, and a variety of liquors, and by three o'clock many of the couples had paired off in various cabins, leaving Luke Three and Alphonso stretched out in deck chairs, protected from the sun by umbrellas. Victoria had not yet made an appearance for the day, which meant that she was either ill with a hangover or was getting her "beauty sleep"—which always meant that she was drinking alone.

Luke Three ambled to the rail and looked out over the busy harbor and thought: *What am I doing here?* He did not care for the current gang; either they were rootless older people with moneyed careers behind them, or tourists who had enough wherewithal to rent luxury boats and cruise through the islands. They all fucked too much, ate too much, danced too much, laughed too much, and were inclined to make asses out of themselves after a cocktail or two, but they took care never to drink too much. Suddenly he yearned for the taste of mashed potatoes and cream gravy and a piece of Angel cake. He was tired of dolmathes, tiropitta, sfougato and moussaka. He yawned and decided to retire to his cabin for a nap.

The sound of the *Saratoga*'s first dinner bell awakened him, which meant he had half an hour to bathe and dress. Although everyone was expected to appear formally in the salon, the men often wore colorful sport shirts with their tuxedos, and the women frequently wore scarves or snoods with their evening dresses.

After a dinner of roast lamb, with a fish course of poached salmon, three different kinds of wine, and the traditional champagne served with dessert, Clyde served mixed drinks. The musicians for the night, a small four-piece rhumba band, already high on ouzo, arrived in a taxi, and while the driver screamed loudly for his drachmas set up their instruments on the sidewalk and, to the delight of the boat owners, wharf rats, and local citizenry, began to play "Begin the Beguine."

Clyde paid the driver, who suddenly turned from a howling demon into music-lover and, pulling his handkerchief from his pocket, began to dance, while the band segued into a classic Greek folk tune.

The motley group began to applaud in time to the music, and Alphonso and Victoria leaned over the rail and cheered. Victoria giggled, and her large hips shook. She was high. "We never did christen the *Saratoga*; let's do it now!"

"Okay," Alphonso replied. Although he had been drinking all day and his face was florid, he was still very much in command. They raised their glasses and motioned to Clyde, who whispered in the saxophonist's ear, and he gave a raspberry on his horn, which attracted everyone's attention. He pointed to Alphonso, who shouted, "American custom. Christen boat."

Victoria cried, "I dub thee *Saratoga*," and threw her champagne glass downward over the bow. The glass plopped uneventfully into the water, and a soulful "Oh-h-h" echoed over the gathering on the pier. "Son-a-bitch!" she muttered under her breath, and Alphonso presented her with his glass. She aimed more carefully this time, and the resounding crash of glass was heard. There was wild applause from below. "Everybody welcome," Alphonso cried. "Champagne!" When he used that tone, it was a command.

The group surged up the gangplank like wharf rats, and Clyde and the stewards ran below for another case of chilled champagne. As the corks popped and the musicians began a series of smooth rhumbas, to which no one danced, there was laughter and a kind of heated atmosphere that had nothing to do with the weather. Luke Three sat down at the bar and was joined by Linda.

"I'm really pooped," she said. "I did about three weeks' work today, and it was all good. Daddy looked in twice, nodded and toasted me with the bubbly, but didn't make any suggestions."

"What kind of a design did you work out?" he asked politely.

"It's a children's motif for matching bedspreads, sheets, cases, and curtains. Mother Goose characters with a modern touch—nothing frilly or old-fashioned." She took a glass of champagne from the steward. "Let's have a look around, Lukie. Any interesting people?"

Luke Three shook his head. "It's early yet. Your father invited all the people on the wharf for champagne. There is one very cute Greek beauty that I'd like to see in the buff, but she's drinking only colas."

Linda ran her hand through her short hair in exasperation. "Really, Lukie, you're beginning to sound like all the others. Don't we do it enough to suit you?"

He looked at her apologetically. "I didn't mean that I'd like to go to bed with her, just see what she looked like without any clothes on."

"Oh, you men are all alike!" She looked over the group and pointed to a slender Greek boy with huge dark eyes and a mop of ringlets about his face. "My God, Lukie, isn't he the most fabulous greaseball you've ever seen?" She sighed. "He's so beautiful and sexy, too!"

"Oh, you women are all alike!" He mimicked her tone of the moment before.

She laughed ruefully. "You're not jealous, are you, Lukie?"

Suddenly he was angry. "No, my *fat* friend, I'm not!" he retorted and, turning away from her, went to the portable bar outside on deck. "Clyde, this champagne is stale, will you put some bourbon in it, please?"

Clyde grinned from ear to ear. "I declah, Massa Luke," he Uncle Tommed expertly, "that ain't no combination for quality white folk. I've been givin' the cheap stuff to this boat trash. Lemme open a bottle of Dom Perignon."

Luke laughed and found that he wasn't angry anymore. Clyde could always lift his spirits. "Did I ever tell you that I think a hell of a lot of you?"

Clyde nodded. "No, Massa Luke, never when you're sobah." He filled his glass.

"Thank you, Clyde. Why don't you quit the Romans and come to work for me?"

Clyde shook his head and dropped his posturing. "Exactly what would my French wife do in Oklahoma? We'd be tarred and feathered." He paused. "Tell me the truth, Mr. Heron, did you have any colored people in Angel?"

Luke was not embarrassed. "No."

"When did you see your first Negro?"

Luke searched his memory. "I was in Enid. I must have been five or six, I guess. I had hold of my mother's hand and I saw a pitch-black man coming toward us, and I stopped and said, 'Oh, Mama, that man must have been burned awful bad!' and she waited until we got across the street and stopped in front of Kress's and explained the difference between races."

"And you want me to go back?" Clyde asked softly.

Luke Three replied, "Why would you want to leave the Romans? I'm sure that you're mentioned in their will."

Clyde drew his shoulders forward again and whined, "The way that those folks is pickled all the time, they ain't gonna need to be 'balmed when they die—which will prob'ly be well aftah me and mah woman, Massa Luke!"

The saxophone wailed. "Excuse me, Clyde, I'm going

to dance again." He downed the glass of champagne
and accepted another.

"Drink it slow, Mr. Heron," Clyde said in his own
voice, and he used a peculiar tone that Luke Three only
remembered later.

The group, led on by Linda, who would not look at
him, had chose up sides for charades. Luke Three
stood on the sidelines and sipped the champagne. He
suddenly lost his vision. His glass crashed to the floor,
and in that split second before the floor hit him in his
face, he suddenly knew the answer to the Skin Time.
Clyde's drink! "No, no," he heard a voice cry out, as if
through a long, hollow tube. "No, no—there has ...
been a mistake ..." But he knew with a terrible certainty that there had been no mistake. Like all the others, he had been selected. He realized then that the
Romans had picked the guests to humiliate. It was the
most terrible game.

A familiar voice came through the ether. "You know
the rules, Lukie. ..."

He felt the stewards' huge, strong hands at his head
and feet, was conscious of a cool breeze hitting his bare
feet.

He shivered as his shirt left his body; then he felt his
belt being unbuckled, the zipper being lowered and his
trousers ... Although he could not speak or lift his little
finger to protest, he knew what was taking place. He had
watched the operation many times. The face of the
foreign ambassador swam out of the smoke-filled salon,
and all of the others that he had seen stripped and
thrown overboard. Their faces haunted him. He felt
himself being lifted above the crowd and he knew that
his body was bathed in the tiny bandstand's pink and
amber lights. He felt cold steel scissors cutting away his
jockey shorts. He tried to open his eyes, but his eyelids
weighed twenty tons.

The saxophonist was ready, he could sense, and when

the last shreds of his shorts dropped away, the horn wailed upward on the scale and there was laughter and wild applause. He felt himself being expertly turned over, and he knew that Ned was at his feet and Derek was at his head and that they were holding him rigidly between them, so that he dangled downward. The applause continued as he was carried to the rail, and his body ached from pinching and mauling. Someone grabbed his testicles and squeezed hard just before he was thrown over the rail. He recognized the touch. That bitch!

His eyes snapped open immediately as soon as the icy water engulfed him. He surfaced, cold sober, and he swam swiftly to the wharf, where Clyde waited with a warm blanket.

"Why . . . did you do . . . it?" He shook Clyde away, and the blanket fell to the dock flooring.

"It's the game that all the rich yacht people play sooner or later, Mr. Heron." Clyde grinned. "I must say that you've lasted longer than most. Here, you're freezing. Take this blanket."

"Go to hell!" Luke shouted. His body was suddenly warm as he knew what he must do. He threw back his shoulders and stepped on the wharf, naked. There was dead silence as he walked up the gangplank to his cabin below the poopdeck. Furiously he dressed, combed his hair, then tossed his clothing into a suitcase. The crowd parted for him as he left the *Saratoga*.

His last impression was of Linda Roman dancing cheek to cheek with the beautiful Greek boy.

Luke Three stood in the phone box near Piccadilly Circus and let the telephone ring.

"The Huxley-Drummond residence." He recognized the butler's voice.

"Is Sir Eric home? This is Luke Heron Three calling." He tried to be as formal as possible.

"No, Mr. Heron, he's at the club, but he should return

for dinner. Shall I have him return your call? You are putting up at the Savoy?"

Luke Three smiled to himself. The little hotel down the street specialized in middle-class tourists. He was paying the equivalent of four dollars a day, and, as it was, he had only a hundred dollars left in his wallet. "No, actually it's best if I call him back," he said impersonally. "Thank you."

He went to a cinema that afternoon and did not recognize any of the players in a farce that he did not understand, then picked up a double order of fish and chips wrapped in the traditional newspaper, and went back to the hotel to enjoy the feast.

He sat by the window and looked over the roofs of several shops as a thin drizzle became torrential. He dreaded the thought of going home. The idea of showing up at the office every day at nine o'clock and staying in an airless room until five o'clock was sickening. He took a long nap, then called Sir Eric again. Hearing the man's cheerful, ebullient voice restored his confidence, and they made an appointment to have luncheon the following day in the Savoy Grill.

Luke Three arose early the next morning and spent two hours at the British Museum. He had not realized how poor the war had left the British people when he had visited London before in the company of Robert Desmond. The austerity program had left its mark; the populace was ill fed and ill clothed. He heard constant complaints that the purchasing power of the pound sterling was considerably lower than in 1939. Yet there was an air of excitement that poverty could not quell. London was an anonymous city, kept alive by the courage of its people.

Sir Eric pumped his hand, his face wreathed in a toothy smile. "Good to see you again. By the way, that's a magnificent tan that you have. For a moment, I thought you were East Indian!" he exclaimed. "I suppose you are on your way back to the States? I heard you were on sabbatical."

Luke Three shook his head. "Not exactly. That's what I wanted to talk about."

The waiter hovered nearby, and they ordered vegetable soup, and Sir Eric recommended chicken-salad sandwiches. "The best in London," he confided. "Now, what were you saying, young man?" His bushy eyebrows went up and down, and for a moment he looked exactly like the comic in the movie that Luke Three had seen the previous day.

"I don't know how to spring this, Sir Eric, so I'll just come out with it." He took a long breath and blurted, "I want a job. I've decided to stay over here."

Sir Eric looked at him, aghast, as the full import of the statement hit him. "I—I don't know what to say," he sputtered.

Luke Three smiled. "What it comes down to is this: I want to be a mechanic in one of the Heron stations."

Sir Eric smiled indulgently. "Oh, I understand now. Want to pick up some of the British atmosphere first hand, eh? Very clever. Then you'll do a long report." He winked broadly. "I'll help you with that!"

"No, Sir Eric, I'm looking for a job, a *real* job."

"The heir to the Heron petrol empire changing spark plugs?" Sir Eric gave him a quizzical look. "Now, tell me frankly, what's behind all of this nonsense?"

Luke Three pushed his hair back from his forehead and made his voice very calm. "I have some things to sort out in my mind, Sir Eric. Right now I don't know how I can fit into the executive branch of the company— or if I ever will. I want a job that I feel comfortable about just now."

The waiter arrived with steaming bowls of soup, which Luke Three tasted before he continued. "I think my dad's view of the company is at cross purposes with mine right now." He leaned forward. "Confidentially,

Robert Desmond wants to make changes which Dad opposes, and for reasons I really can't understand. If, and when, I go back, I've got to throw support behind one or the other, but I have to *think* ... and I can't think at home." He paused and tasted the soup again. "I've come to the conclusion that I have what the French would call a 'formidable' family. They've smothered me from the time that I was born. I've only been away from them once, and that was when I ran away and joined the Marines. I used another name—Gene Holiday—but when I came back, and all was forgiven, I found myself back in the same old rut.... Do you know, I never thought about protesting, and I liked working at the station in Angel, and there was a girl ..."

Sir Eric finished his soup. His facade had changed and he was regarding Luke Three more respectfully now as he listened to his revelations; gone was the "hail fellow, well met" demeanor. "I understand your viewpoint," he said seriously, "but I really don't know if I can be of service."

"All I want is a job."

Sir Eric nodded. "I'm at a loss, frankly. How can I employ a Heron and get away with it?" His jowls quivered. "I don't know how to put it to you, Luke Three, without appearing like an unfeeling old stick, but Britain is going through a monetary crisis that won't soon be resolved. The field offices are not doing well. Petrol prices ..."

The food had arrived, and Luke Three bit into the chicken-salad sandwich with relish. "This *is* good! Almost as good as ..." He paused. "I was going to say Grandma's, but it's really better." He chewed thoughtfully. "I don't want to get you in dutch," he said at last, "and if you turn me down, I'll understand. But somewhere in this country is a service station—whether it's Heron-owned or not—that needs a good mechanic. I know that I can get work somewhere. I would like to be with the company, but if not ..."

Sir Eric pushed the sandwich plate away. "Do you mind if I smoke?" And when Luke Three shook his head, he lighted a cigar and then went on slowly, "I assume that you have money put aside to carry you over?"

Luke Three smiled uncertainly. "I would live on my salary."

"Do you know what that means? Mechanics make a pittance. You would only have enough for a rat-infested flat or perhaps a dingy room in a small hotel. As a member of the working class, living over here would be entirely different than what you're accustomed to in the States."

"I know that," Luke Three replied honestly, "but we've always lived simply at home. We never put on the dog." He smiled at Sir Eric's startled look. "That's a country expression. It means 'showing off.' I'd be content."

Sir Eric blew the smoke out in a perfect ring. "What if it goes like this." He spoke slowly, choosing his words carefully. "British Heron employs a mechanic, say in the Eastbourne or Chelsea division, by the name of ... Gene Holiday? Personally, I have nothing to do with this employment. In fact, I have never met this man, nor, for that matter, will I ever." He paused and studied Luke Three's face. "What I will do—and the only thing I will do—is give you a list of stations that need attendants ... and, at the moment, with jobs as scarce as they are ... there may be no openings. I don't know, I'll have to look into it. You'll have to furnish your own transportation and lodging until there is an opening. There can be no connection between us." He snubbed out the cigar in a crystal tray. "If something should happen that you have difficulty with the manager of the station, or there are other problems, you cannot come to me. Is that clear?"

"Yes, sir. I know you won't be sorry. I'll do a good job."

"I hope that I'm not making a mistake, Luke Three. If it should ever come out that I helped you ... I don't want bad blood between us."

"I'll be on my own, Sir Eric."

"Do you need cash?"

"I'll get along, I promise you."

"Very well. Shall we go?"

The place had quieted down from luncheon, and Luke Three looked about the room. It would probably be the last time that he would be patronizing a first-class restaurant. A mechanic's salary would not include chicken-salad sandwiches at the Savoy Hotel.

Sir Eric shook his hand. "It was nice meeting you, Mr. Holiday," he said cordially. "By the way, don't forget to give me your address."

Louisa Tarbell stared at her checkbook. She had added and subtracted the figures three times and still could not believe that only nine hundred dollars remained in the bank.

She had kept the backyard victory garden that she had started during the war, and still canned vegetables and fruits in season, so her grocery bills were very low. Only when William came to visit, once a month, did she prepare more elaborate food and allow herself the luxury of baking a cake or pie. But no matter how parsimoniously she lived, there would still not be enough money to make regular payments to Finney Nestor until William graduated.

She put on her cloth coat and walked to the grocery store for milk, and on the way back dropped into the five-and-dime store and asked Lydia Merrick, who was pregnant and suffered from dyspepsia, if she could clerk in the store while Lydia had the baby.

Lydia, who weighed two hundred pounds and had an

effervescent personality, put her hands on her hips and laughed. "My heavens, no, Miz Tarbell, if this kid is like the rest of 'em—it's going to be a boy, I can tell from the way he kicks—he'll come along in the evenin' and I'll work right up to about noon. Then I'll take a week off and come right back to work with him in a basket in the back. He's due the middle of August, when most everyone takes a vacation, so it'll work out just fine." She peered at her. "Why do you want to work anyway during the summer months?"

Louisa picked up a spool of white thread and fished in her purse for change. "I'm just bored," she said lightly. "Do you know anyone else who might need someone?"

Lydia thought for a moment. "Not offhand. How about doing some tutoring?"

"The children who need it can't afford lessons," Louisa replied sadly. "If you hear of anything, please let me know."

"I will."

But the days passed, and there were no offers of summer employment. She devised a plan. When William came dutifully through the cornfield and scratched at her door on Saturday night, even before kissing her, he blurted out, "Mama said she heard that you were going to put the house up for rent." There was panic in his voice.

She kissed him on the mouth quickly and summoned a bantering tone of voice. "But you know, William, this house is too big."

"I don't think so," he replied. "It only has two bedrooms."

"But it's old. Some cheap apartments are being built over in the new addition. I've always wanted a modern kitchen and a tile bath; then, also, if I want to travel, I don't have to worry about having the grass cut or if anyone is going to break in."

"Does this mean you're going to go away this summer?" he asked quietly.

"No, but I may go to Europe next year. I'll be free of a house that takes a great deal of upkeep." She was sounding so persuasive that she almost convinced herself. "I'm really looking forward to a maintenance-free place. But it may take a year to rent."

"How much are you asking?"

"I think I can get a hundred a month. It's been free and clear for years, and the taxes aren't much."

"That's a lot of money," he said soberly.

"Yes," she said, "it is." Of course she could not tell him that by the time she paid off his father, she would still be in the hole. She changed the subject. "How is school?"

His face lighted up like a neon sign. "It's easy for me. Some of the students are doing badly, but when the instructors lecture, I *know* what they're talking about even before they get the words out. Everything is so clear to me. What's so fascinating—and you know how much I love history—is that musical notation has changed so much, but I can look at a fifteenth-century manuscript with diamond-headed notes, which are just as familiar to me as the round-headed notes that we use now. It seems as if I've studied all this before, and I'm just taking a refresher course. It's the weirdest thing, Lou.

"Also, I'm learning to copy old orchestrations in the evening. It's a thankless, tedious job, but it's good discipline, too. Once in a while I'm copying, not really concentrating, and I see some musical ornamentation that's not effective, doesn't seem to reflect the composer's mood, and it occurs to me at once what kind of a phrase could be used to enhance the general feeling. I experiment a lot because, after all, when I go to work for the band, I'll be doing so much arranging, and I want to feel *free*."

He stopped for a moment and laughed. "I've written a song called 'The Cowboy Waltz,' but it's just a novelty. I don't know whether I should send it to Mr. Story, but I don't want him to feel that this is all I'm capable of. What would you do, Lou?"

"Sing it for me?"

"You know I don't have a good voice, but steady yourself, here are the words!" He sang the lyrics a cappella.

She listened intently, smiling occasionally, and when he finished she nodded her head. "It's good musically, William, and the lyrics are clever. It's got a point of view, but I don't know how this kind of song would fit Clement Story's swing band."

"That was my thinking too. He does sing 'The Old Chisholm Trail,' and this is a kind of narrative song too."

She leaned forward intently. "Why don't you put it aside for a while and find out what the band is recording. Then, if you think Clement Story might like the song, send it to him with a little note that says something about your having just dashed this off and thought it might amuse him. That way, you're not really committing yourself."

The clock struck eight, and he got up and took her hand. "I wish that you lived nearer to Angel," he said. "I get so lonesome." He paused and fought for words. "I don't think I've ever told you, Lou, but you're really an important part of my life. When I'm in the dorm, just before I go to sleep, I often think about us. You've made my life easier. I don't know what would have held me together after my folks got religion, if you hadn't been there to encourage me and make me feel important. Even before they were saved, they never knew what was on my mind. We could never *talk*. It was as if they weren't my parents."

He smiled wanly. "For a long time I thought I was adopted, because I couldn't see any similarity between them and me. I guess I was about eight years old—my mother don't look particularly Cherokee, and I don't think I do either, except for my dark hair—anyway, I went to see old Doc Browder. He patted my head and laughed and said he'd brought me into the world in the back bedroom on the farm, and then he told me something that has stuck with me all these years. He looked kind of strange and said, 'The reason I remember it so well, Billy, was because I never got paid. Your dad was supposed to come up with the thirty-five dollars, but he never did.' I was so embarrassed that I ran out of his office. Someday, when I have a lot of money, I'm going to pay him back—with three percent interest."

Louisa placed her arms around him. "We'd better go to bed," she said quietly, "because you'll want to go back to Angel early in the morning."

17

Round Robin

Fontine Dice checked the buffet table once more.

"I should've baked an Angel cake," she fussed to Maude, the new maid. "Blackberry cobbler is all right, but so many of the girls have dentures now, and one little seed under a plate feels exactly like a pebble as big as a thumbnail. What time is it?"

Maude, who was a large woman in her early forties, put on her glasses and looked at her plump wrist. "Four o'clock."

"I've got two hours, I think I'll still whip up an Angel, just to be on the safe side. I won't have time to stuff it, but a simple icing will do."

"You've so much to do, Mrs. Dice, why don't you let me?"

"Thanks, Maude"—Fontine put her arms through a Mother Hubbard apron to protect her new pink silk dress—"but if you don't mind me saying so, you never beat the egg whites enough. They've got to be so stiff that when you run a knife down through the middle, it'll leave a clean trench. But make the cream gravy. You do that well enough."

Maude placed her hands on her generous hips. "Mrs. Dice, I raised four strapping boys, and they never complained."

"Of course not," Fontine snapped. "As long as you give men meat, potatoes, and gravy, they never complain. Now, use that heavy cream in the ice chest—I mean, refrigerator."

Maude threw her a long look. "Yes, Mrs. Dice." She watched her mistress bustle into the kitchen and shook her head. It seemed the older that people got, the more particular they became.

Fontine separated twenty-two eggs into the electric mixing bowl without getting any of the yolk in the whites and felt very proud of herself indeed. She switched on the mixer, but the blades did not turn; then she adjusted the cord in the socket, then turned on the kitchen light switch, but the bulb remained dark. "Dammit!" she cried and picked up the telephone. "Nellie, is that you? What's wrong with the electricity?"

"I think everyone in town has called," was the tart answer. "It went off about an hour ago, and Jimmy Knowles down at the plant says it's going to be another half-hour at least. Something went wrong with one of the transformers."

Fontine accepted the situation philosophically. "Thank you, Nellie. Don't forget to come over to eat when you get off work." She hung up the telephone. "You were whipping up Angel cakes long before electricity was brought in, Fontine Dice," she said out loud to herself, "and you sure'n hell can whip one up again!"

"What did you say, Mrs. Dice?" Maude asked from the back porch.

"Nothing! Go on about your business." She removed the whisk from the drawer and began to beat the egg whites by hand. She had just added a teaspoon and a half of cream of tartar to the white cloudlike mixture when she felt the first spasm in her chest.

She straightened her back and flexed her hands, and the pain left as quickly as it had come. She picked up the whisk again and began to beat, but stopped in midstroke. Suddenly it seemed that her rib cage was too small for her lungs. She had difficulty getting her breath. Then, as she gasped, the pain came again, and this time it did not go away. She grabbed a kitchen chair for support, finally managing to sit down. "Maude?" She meant to shout, but only a feeble sound came from her throat. The pain had begun to vibrate through her chest now; it was like the waves coming in over the seashore, ebbing through her chest. "Maude," she called weakly, but this time she made herself heard.

The woman came in from the back porch, a large pitcher of cream in her hands. "Yes?"

"Maude ... call the doctor. Something's terrible wrong."

By the time Maude called John Dice at the bank, Fontine was lying flat on her back in the emergency room in a freshly made bed, with a nitroglycerine tablet under her tongue and her arm hooked up to a variety of tubes.

"You can go in to see her in a minute, John," head nurse Emmy Lou Baker said when he came in five minutes later. He nodded numbly.

"Is she bad?"

"I honestly can't say. They're still working over her. Dr. Platt said that the ambulance boys was down there in about two minutes. She was still in the middle of the attack when they brought her in, so no heroic measures were needed."

John Dice wondered what was meant by "heroic measures" but decided not to ask. He paced up and down the corridor, thinking about the days when Poppa Dice and he had come up from Santone for the opening of the Cherokee Strip; then he remembered the way that Fontine had looked when she'd stepped off the train in Enid. She had looked so fragile in the lavender-flowered dress, dark shawl, and straw hat, no more than a thin rail, pale and undernourished, but oh, how wonderful she was in bed! Of course he was a hot young buck then too, and they had really made the bedsprings rattle. He smiled softly. No, there were no bedsprings to rattle in those days, only hard planks. It had been three or four years before they'd been able to order a proper bedspring from Sears and Roebuck in Chicago and a bedstead from Edward Heron. My God, he thought, looking back, he had forgotten to pay for that work, he just knew it, and Edward had never reminded him.

It was no good remembering about the old days, if all he could recall were mistakes! Of course, he reasoned, both he and Fontine had been illiterate then; that was years before Sam had taught them their ABC's and Rochelle Patterson had taken them through first to eighth grades.

Oh, what would happen to him if he lost Fontine? What had brought on that attack? She always worked too hard, even with the succession of maids and house-keepers that they'd employed since they'd first struck oil. She was probably cooking for the ... party. He went quickly to the reception desk. "May I use your phone, Dottie Mae?"

"Of course." She handed the instrument to him. "Nellie, is that you?" he asked.

"Yes," came the hushed voice, heavy with sympathy. "I know why you're calling, John. I've already notified all the girls not to come to the buffet, and furthermore, I told them not to bother you at the hospital. If there's one time a body don't need a lot of chirping hens around, it's when someone's taken bad." She paused. "I've got to go now, my switchboard's lighting up like the Fourth of July."

"Thank you, Nellie," he said emotionally into a dead receiver.

Dr. Platt came out of Fontine's room. "John," he said, taking his shoulder, "you can go in now, but you can just stay a minute. I've given her something to make her sleep, and she must be kept very quiet. I don't think that her heart has suffered much damage, but I have called in a specialist from Enid. I would have had the ambulance take her over to Doctor's Hospital, but there wasn't time. She can't be moved yet."

"She's not going to die, is she, Doc?"

"She's got every chance of recovering, John. She's in excellent health for a woman her age."

John nodded numbly and went into the darkened room. Fontine's platinum curls were spread over a thin rubber pad on the bottom sheet. She was lying flat on the bed, and it was a shock to see that she was only a large mound under the sheet. He had been thinking of her as that frail little thing who had stepped down off the train in 1894.

He took her hand, but she did not open her eyes. "Jaundice?"

"Yep, it's me, Fourteen."

"The girls . . ."

"The party's all been taken care of. Don't you worry your pretty head about anything. You can trust Doctor Platt, and you have me."

"Charlotte . . ."

"Why call her all the way from Washington? You're fine, honey." He patted her hand. Then he saw that she had begun to snore, and he tiptoed out of the room.

Letty and Bosley were waiting in the corridor. "I know we can't see her," Letty said, rising, "but we had to come anyway."

"Is there anything that we can do?" Bosley asked.

John's brow furrowed. "I don't know if it's proper to ask, but Fourteen's been calling for Charlotte, and Lord knows where your company plane is right now."

Bosley snapped his fingers. "We're in luck. It is in a hangar at Newark, New Jersey, and that's just a hop, skip, and a jump to National Airport in Washington. Luke's in Tulsa, and Robert Desmond's in New York; Luke Three's somewhere in Greece, I think. I'll notify Currier and Ives to pick up Charlotte." He paused. "Why don't you call her from here?"

"Charlotte Dice's wire," an impersonal female voice answered on the second ring.

"This is Charlotte's father. Do you have a number where she can be reached?"

"Just a moment please, Senator," the girl answered. In Washington, he reflected, if one was once a senator, one was always a senator. She came back on the line. "She didn't leave a number, but I expect her to call in at any time. Is there a message?"

"Yes. Tell her her mother has been taken ill. If the line

should be busy here at Angel, have her call Luke at Heron headquarters in Tulsa."

"I'll give her the message, Senator," the girl replied and hung up; then she paused, telephone plug in hand. Where was that woman likely to be at this hour? It was seven o'clock. It was possible that she was playing hostess at the USO. She called, but Miss Charlotte Dice was not there. She thought for a moment. Somewhere, there was Dominick Lake's number. She flipped through her card file and dialed. Mr. Dominick Lake informed her coldly that not only was Miss Dice not there at the moment, but he did not expect to see her any time in the foreseeable future! The operator's face burned. Obviously the affair was over. She tried Perle Mesta's secretary, but Mrs. Mesta was out of town, and she did not know where Miss Dice could possibly be, but perhaps if she didn't hear from her by tomorrow . . .

The operator knew that sometimes Charlotte Dice had dinner at Napoleon's, but she also ate at Harvey's and thirty other Washington and Georgetown restaurants, and had been known to go as far as Alexandria, Virginia, or Chevy Chase, Maryland. Obviously she could not call every restaurant in town. "Oh, please, Miss Dice," she said out loud, "call in soon and don't be tipsy!"

Charlotte headed her new bright red Ford coupe down Pennsylvania Avenue. It seemed that she had driven around for hours, yet it was only eight o'clock. This was the last day of the month, and usually the bus stop in front of the mint, where the rickety old bus paused to pick up soldiers bound for Fort Belvoir, was crowded with men in and out of uniform. After payday, the boys piled into taxicabs and shared the fare back to the base, but usually her luck was very good just before Uncle Sam's eagle flew.

Alas, the bus must have just preceded her, because

the corner was empty and ghostly. At the next stoplight she glanced in the rearview mirror at her face. Her makeup was good, if somewhat heavy, but for having just celebrated her forty-eighth birthday she looked quite presentable, and she knew the low V-necked, rose-colored dress showed off her perfect small rounded breasts to advantage; it had been designed by Oleg Cassini for just that purpose.

Charlotte pulled around the corner and headed for the last bus stop. She was in luck; two soldiers were standing in front of the bench, smoking cigarettes. She slowed down at the curb. The tall one was rather attractive, blond, with a generous mouth; the other was shorter, darker, and Italian-looking. She paused, rolled down the window, and leaned over the seat.

"Hello," she said with a wide smile, focusing her gaze upon the tall soldier. He nodded politely and ambled over to the car; he looked about sixteen, but she knew that he must be at least two years older, and possibly more.

"What can I do for you, ma'am?" he asked with a heavy Southern accent, which she classified as Alabaman.

"I was wondering," she said quietly, without a trace of coquetry, "if you would like to have dinner with me?"

"Sorry, ma'am, I gotta git back, guard duty."

She swallowed. His gaze was so open, his expression so sincere that she was not embarrassed. Yet she was tired from driving, and the evening was slipping away. She controlled her face so as not to show inward anxiety. "Then," she replied, "perhaps your friend would take your place."

The boy gazed at her for a long moment, a perplexed expression on his face; then the import of her invitation hit him, and his jaw hardened. "Sure, lady," he drawled, "I'll see what I can do."

He had a short conversation with the other soldier and came back to the car. "How much?" he asked, his face a mask. Gone was the open, friendly look of a moment before.

She felt her face flame, and her brain echoed: *howmuchhowmuchhowmuchhow?* She felt as if she had been struck, physically maimed. Her heart beat rapidly, and she could feel the blood pounding in her temples. She put the car in gear, sped down the street, and almost collided with a taxicab at the corner. She pulled over into a parking lot, turned off the motor, and placed her head against the steering wheel. She could hear the boy say again, "How much?" How much what? How much love? How much money? How much time spent in bed earning that money, and for what?

She had, of course, paid before—not exactly per orgasm, but she had paid nonetheless ... in clothing, theater and sports tickets, restaurant and bar tabs, besides an occasional fifty-dollar bill idly tossed across the coffee table for "cigarette money." But none of the others had blatantly asked, *How much?*

She glanced up at her reflection again in the rearview mirror, and in the darkened lot, with only a rear light for illumination, she saw what she was: an overly made-up, fat-faced woman. She might as well face it: with the war over, few golden boys were waiting to be drafted, seeking one last good time before basic training and overseas duty.

These young men at the bus stop were obviously more experienced, and, although badly in need of a love affair, were not about to climb in to a car with an older woman without adequate recompense.

Charlotte took a deep breath and said to herself, not without humor, "Miss Dice, if you're going to cruise bus stops, then you must be prepared to offer decent porterage." She would not haggle. She would offer—what? Was five dollars enough for the Italian's lovemaking, which was certain to be breathless and over much too quickly? Was it an insult to whatever masculine image he had attained at his young age? He would certainly never miss that spasm, because there were so many thousands of spasms to follow. Someone had said that each man was capable of ten thousand over a lifetime. What was *one* worth?

She pressed her foot on the starter and wheeled out of the parking lot and drove swiftly around the block. Luck was holding. The bus had not scooped up the young men during her moment of truth. She stopped the car, and the dark young man climbed into the front seat, smiling a very wide, confident smile, showing all of his perfectly white teeth. "Hi," he said softly. "I knew that you'd be back."

He was so attractive that her reserve melted at once, and she swallowed a sarcastic comeback. Instead she said, "Since it's the last of the month and everyone's so broke, I imagine a ten-spot would be awfully welcome." When he nodded, she added, "What time do you go on duty?"

"Not until eight in the morning," he replied.

"Belvoir?"

"Yes."

"I'll be happy to drive you back," she said.

The doorman opened the car door and said good evening, and Charlotte told him not to have the car put away, that she would be going out later.

The young man, whose name was Nick, followed her silently into the foyer and down the hall to the elevator, and when they reached her floor she presented him with her key. He looked at her blankly for a moment, grinned boyishly, and placed the key in the lock and opened the door, then awkwardly handed the key back.

"It's been so warm," she said softly as they came into the hall, "why don't you take a nice cool shower, and I'll fix a drink. What would you like?"

He paused, obviously searching his mind for a reply. "A Manhattan," he said at last.

"I don't think I have any vermouth, Nicky."

"Oh, that's okay," he replied with a little shrug. "Just make it without, then."

She sighed gently, stemming her impatience. "And I don't think I have any cherries, either."

He obviously didn't know what to say. "Okay, then a beer's fine."

She laughed. "I'm turning out to be a hell of a hostess. I don't think there's any beer in the fridge, either. Look"—she touched his shoulder—"go take your shower, and I'll surprise you with something I think you'll like. I'll also turn off the telephone so we won't be disturbed."

He brightened, smiling through a frown, his eyes dark and shining. Suddenly she could see what he would look like at thirty, when his face had developed angular planes and his jaw had softened. He would not ever be one of the golden boys, but he could pass for a dark Italian god.

"Hurry," she coaxed, giving him a little shove toward the bathroom. She switched off the phone, went into the kitchen, and poured generous glasses of bourbon over ice, added a small portion of ginger ale, a touch of bitters, and crushed a mint leaf which she rubbed over the edge of the glasses, then crowned the top with a little twist of lemon peel.

She heard the shower running, and placed the drinks on the bedside table, turned on the soft pink light, and hurriedly undressed. She was aware that her body looked more seductive under the sheets. He came in from the bathroom, still toweling his middle, and she looked with dismay at his wet footprints on the beige carpet.

"Hi," he said, dropping the towel, which he proceeded to step up and down on rhythmically. "This is the way my dad used to stomp grapes in the old country." She watched his pendulous manhood swing back and forth as he repeated the ritual. She opened the bedcovering. "Come on in," she said, "the water's fine."

He crawled in gently beside her and took her awkwardly in his arms. She pressed her breasts up to meet his chest, and he sighed. He had probably made love to high school girls in the back seat of a car, she thought, or on a blanket at the side of the road, but as he ran his hands experimentally over her body she knew that this was the first time he had stretched out beside a nude woman in a bed.

He can truly enjoy this experience, she reflected, because he is not required to fight pullover sweaters, brassiere straps, unwieldy panties, or a tight garter belt. She was there, all perfumed and ready, and it was obvious he didn't know how to proceed gracefully. She kissed him lightly on the cheek, to remind him that she had a mouth, and he closed his eyes and began to kiss her softly. Her other young men had been immediately passionate, but Nicky seemed in no hurry to get on with it.

With his tongue in her mouth, he maneuvered himself until he was looking down into her face. "My God, lady," he exclaimed, "you're soft!" Charlotte smiled and opened herself to him in such an adroit manner that before he knew what had happened he was enclosed. She moved slightly, subtly urging him on, and, like all young men, he took her lead, and with that, coupled with his natural biological urges, he began to move quite effortlessly. She moved her fingers across the length of his back, and he shivered. How marvelously muscled he was! His shoulders were wide and tapered down to a small waist. His buttocks were lean and hard. She began to move her inward muscles, and he sighed at her expertise. Sex caught between double features in a drive-in movie or on lover's lane with a virgin or near virgin, with the possibility of flashlights interrupting the performance, was more of a release than actual pleasure, she imagined. She was enjoying him, and she meant that he should enjoy her as well.

This was what she loved most of all, this feeling that she was being possessed; this was what she had missed most as a young girl. If she had known the act of love / could be this sustaining, she would have gone to bed with the Heron and Story boys as well as other young men in Angel!

Her mother had drilled the principle into her that a girl kept herself for her husband. But when she was twenty-one, even with her inheritance, there had been no one to whom she was remotely attracted. She had moved to Washington immediately after college, but her sex life had not begun even then. She had never fallen in love, but that feeling of *wanting* to be loved, to be desired, to be possessed, lingered on and on. At twenty-five, she had gone to a party in Southampton one summer night, was introduced to the son of the hostess, a twenty-year-old collegiate named Daniel, who had filled her with champagne and taken her up to his bedroom, where he had expertly given her a number of orgasms which she still fondly remembered. The affair had lasted for a year and a half. He stopped by her apartment regularly twice a week on his way to Columbia University. She later discovered his weekends were dedicated to making a New Jersey girl as happy as he had made her twice weekly.

Alas, Daniel had moved away, and it was no surprise to Charlotte when he was snapped up by a debutante at her coming-out party. She moved him promptly to Majorca, out of everyone's grasp. Daniel was the first of a long succession of young lovers.

Nicky breathed warmly on her neck, and she knew that he was approaching what Napoleon's biographers had referred to as "his Waterloo." If she wanted to finish with him, she decided that she'd better forget the past and take care of the present.

It was over very quickly for him, as she knew it would be, but she also knew that he would stay firm, and while he was recovering strength, with eyes closed contentedly, she began to move expertly, correctly gauging his capacity. Soon they were launched upon another experience. She brought him to his second orgasm sweetly, savoring the moment. "Ah," he breathed, "you're so soft."

She thought that he might be a bit more original; certainly there were other attributes to which he could draw attention. Then she felt him subside, and she surreptitiously looked at her wristwatch. It was twelve-thirty. "Ah ..." she sought to remember his name and succeeded "... ah, Nicky, I think we'd better get dressed. You should get some sleep in your own cot before duty tomorrow. I'll take you back to Belvoir."

Later, as they drove through the dark, empty streets of Washington, then headed toward Arlington Cemetery, to Alexandria, Virginia, and beyond, he told her about his life in the Napa Valley of California, and about his family, who worked for a large wine-grower. At last, when they reached the post, he told her to take the road that led by Service Club Number Two, in the rear of which his barracks was located. She kissed him lightly on the cheek. "Good night, Nicky."

"Can I see you again?" he asked.

She smiled and dug into her purse, extracting a calling card. "Telephone me when you can," she said, thrusting the card into his hand and closing her purse at the same time. There was a pause as if he was waiting for something, and she looked about the front seat to see if he had brought anything with him, then remembered that he did not even have a ditty bag with him. She kissed him. "Good night again." Still he did not open the car door.

He finally glared at her. "Ah—ah," he stammered, "wasn't I worth the ten bucks?"

She blushed and quickly reached into her purse and removed two five-dollar bills. Since their initial encounter, she had truly forgotten about their financial arrangement. He pocketed the money, said a hurried good night, gave her a half-salute, and bounded up the starkly lighted pathway. She looked after him until she could no longer hear his footfalls, then turned the car around and headed back toward Washington. This was the first time that she had made a clearcut business deal with a young man, but it probably would not be the last.

When she reached her apartment, she placed the telephone back in the cradle, and she had taken only two steps when it rang. "Yes?"

"Oh, thank heavens you finally came home." The telephone operator's voice was concerned. Charlotte listened in shocked silence to the message, then called home.

Maude answered. "Oh, Miss Dice, I'm so glad they reached you!" she said sleepily. "Your mother's condition has improved, and your father is at the hospital. In the morning you're to call Luke Heron. The company plane will fly you right here."

"What was it?"

"Oh, a heart attack."

"Thank you, Maude." Charlotte hung up, sat down in an easy chair, and nervously lighted a cigarette. She had avoided going home for fifteen years. There would be two trials ahead; one was visiting her mother, and the other was seeing the town of Angel. She did not know which ordeal she disliked most.

At eight o'clock the next morning, Charlotte called Tulsa and recognized the twang of Luke's voice. "I hope I didn't awaken you," she apologized.

"I'm up at the crack of dawn. I was waiting for your call. I'm sorry to hear about your mother."

"She was better last night."

"Thank the Lord," Luke replied. "By the way, the *Blue*

Heron is on runway nine at National. You can leave any time that's convenient."

"I don't want to put you out, Luke," Charlotte said. "I can easily take a commercial airline."

"There'd be too many stopovers and changes of planes, and you'd be exhausted by the time you reach Angel, Char."

She stiffened. She had known Luke Heron all her life, and he had never called her Char before. Was it because her mother was so ill that he was trying to be familiar, trying to establish an old family relationship that had deteriorated over the years? She disliked being under obligation to anyone, especially the Herons, who were a peculiar family. She could see the middle-aged Luke sitting at the breakfast table in Tulsa, playing the Grand Seigneur. Jeanette was probably seated across from him in hair curlers, reading the Tulsa *World* and motioning to her husband to pass her love to "Char."

"By the way, Jeanette says to give you her love," Luke said.

Charlotte blanched. "And give her mine too, of course," she replied as warmly as she could. They had always disliked each other.

"Currier and Ives must file a flight plan. When would you like to leave?"

"Ten o'clock would be fine," she replied.

"I'll notify them," he answered. "Don't forget, runway nine. Good-bye, Char."

"Good-bye, Luke." She hung up and immediately started to pack. She selected two suits, several blouses, a dark dress, and simple accessories appropriate for Angel. There would be no need for an evening gown, a diamond necklace, a feathered cocktail hat, a sable scarf, or, she reflected wryly, a whirling syringe.

18

The Poppies of the Field

Fontine opened her eyes and turned her head.

The nurse at bedside was so engrossed in a new Agatha Christie mystery that she did not realize her patient had awakened. At the price of private nurses these days, Fontine thought, she should be more alert. She coughed, none too discreetly. "What time is it?"

"Eight in the morning, Miz Dice." The nurse answered in a nasal voice, guiltily hiding the book, and, assuming a professional air, took her pulse. "Mr. John has the next room. Shall I call him?"

"Not yet! Will you get me a mirror, please?" When the glass had been thrust into her hands, Fontine looked at her reflection. "I look simply awful," she said more to herself than to the nurse, "and my hair looks like a rat's nest!" She raised her voice. "Would you call Miss Birdie Landrop at home? Ask her to bring a comb and some waveset over here on her way to the beauty shop." She peered at the nurse again. "Aren't you one of the Baker girls?"

"Yes. I'm Emmy Lou. My sister Dottie Mae works here too, but she's only a receptionist, not an RN."

Fontine shook her head. "I never could keep track of all you girls. How's your mother?"

"Still running the store."

"Good for her. You know, Emmy Lou, I remember the day your parents hung out that shingle, and that must have been eighteen-ninety-four. The first thing that I bought, I think, was a spool of lavender thread."

After Birdie had coaxed Fontine's platinum curls into some semblance of order, she shook her head. "We really should change your hairstyle one of these days," she said.

"Why? I've been wearing it this way for about thirty years. When Jaundice was a senator and we lived in Washington part of the year, all the Senate wives thought it was fabulous. It was widely copied."

Birdie, who was a realist, doubted that statement, but she held her tongue. Fontine, whatever her faults, was a good tipper, and good tippers were hard come by in postwar Angel.

After Emmy Lou had assisted her with breakfast, which was not easy, considering that she had to remain flat on her back, Fontine asked for her husband. John Dice paused in the doorway, suddenly withdrawn and shy. "How's my honey?" he asked in a little boy's voice.

She laughed. "Don't keep standing there, Jaundice, come on in and give me a big kiss."

He brushed his lips to her cheek. "My, you look pretty," he said, and she remembered that before they had learned to read, write, and pronounce words properly, he had always said, "purdy." She laughed.

"What's so funny, Fourteen?"

"Oh, nothin'," she replied, "nothin' at all."

"How're you feeling?"

"Better. Only I don't like to lie flat on my back. You know I always have two pillows, the softer the better." She touched the back of his hand. "Do you remember that first winter we spent in the dugout? We had warm comforters that Mama had quilted in Santone, but our pillow cases were stuffed with straw." She grinned. "But even one of those straw pillows would feel good right now." She glanced at him slyly and had opened her mouth to speak, when her face contorted and she doubled up with pain.

John Dice stood by helplessly as Emmy Lou ran out into the hall and immediately brought back a doctor and another nurse, who worked frantically over her. A few moments later, the doctor looked up. "It was a bad seizure. I've given her a hypo. She'll sleep now."

She was still in a semicomatose condition when Charlotte arrived at seven o'clock that evening. She kissed her father, who was still sitting beside the bed. Fontine opened her eyes, looked at her daughter blankly for a moment, then a look of recognition fluttered across her face.

"Charlotte?" Her voice was very faint, and there was a tiny smile around the corners of her mouth. "I was looking for a little girl, somehow. I guess I'd forgotten you've grown up. Sit down beside me and hold my hand." Charlotte obeyed, just as she had always obeyed her mother as a child. John Dice went out into the corridor.

"I wanted you to come back so I could tell you a thing or two," Fontine went on, her voice somewhat stronger than it had been before. "First, I've been harping all these years about you not marrying and giving us any grandchildren." She squeezed her hand. "But I want you to know that it don't matter a tinker's damn. Never was cut out to be a grandma, anyways, nor Jaundice a grandpa neither." She had slipped back into her old Santone ways of speech. "Anyways, I guess some are jest not bent toward marryin'. And if that's the way you've been feelin', why, baby, that's all that's important."

Tears gathered in Charlotte's eyes, but she did not want to draw her mother's attention by brushing them away. She did not believe in breaking down. "Thank you, Mama," she said. She had not called her Mama in years, and she felt Fontine's hand tighten again.

"The second thing that I want to pass on to you is that you gotta face the fact that you're no spring chicken and them young men that hang around you in Washington are just after your money, but I'm not tellin' you anything you don't rightly know already. Now where was I? Oh, yes." She paused, gathering her thoughts. "Another thing, baby, if you find a suitable man your own age, you want to be *sure* you're going to be happy. Maybe's you and he could live together *first*, then if it works out, you could get married...."

Charlotte knew what that suggestion had cost her mother, who was as strict and formal about proper behavior as were any of the oldtimers in Angel. "Thank you, Mama," she said brokenly.

"Now"—Fontine's voice had lost some of its vibrancy—"go out there and tell that worthless Dottie Mae Baker to get you a hot cup of coffee! I'm gonna rest a mite."

"All right, Mama," Charlotte said. Before she left, she kissed her mother's cheek; then she went out into the corridor and held back her tears until her father went into her mother's room, when she placed her head against the doorjamb and cried as if her heart would break.

John took Charlotte's place beside Fontine. "Everyone's waiting out there to see you, Fourteen," he said softly, "Letty and Bosley and the Bakers, and Belle Trune and Bella and Torgo."

She looked at him with such love in her eyes that he thought he would have to look away to keep from weeping. "Oh, Jaundice, I do care for all of 'em, and bless 'em for comin' and all," she said faintly, "but the only one that I really want to be with me now—is *you*." She paused, gathering her strength. "And as far as me passin' out when I was makin' that Angel cake"—she chuckled, deep in her throat and went on with great

effort, her pale forehead beaded with cold perspiration—
"why, if I ever get to actin' up like that ag'in, you got my
full permission ... to slap me silly ..." Her voice
trailed away and she was quiet.

Fontine, hair arranged about her face like a yellow
halo, looked exactly as if she had gone to sleep. John
Dice knew that there was no need to call the doctor. He
took her warm hand and knelt by the side of the bed
and whispered over and over and over, "Oh, my honey,
oh, my honey ..."

The dry, arid prairie wind that sometimes races out of
the northwest in autumn came up the morning of
Fontine's funeral, and Letty, dressed in black with matching hat, went out on the porch of the clapboard and sat
in the swing. Fontine had been her dearest friend for
fifty-four years. They had always laughed and joked and
made fun of each other, and even during those years
when the families were not speaking because the Herons and the Storys and the Trentons had switched to
the Democratic ticket, she and Fontine had occasionally
met in secret to exchange confidences.

Letty needed time to be alone; here she could grieve,
but not at the church. She had never cried in public
before, and she would not cry now.

Hattie called from the living room, "Mrs. Trenton, it's
Mrs. Chenovick on the phone."

"Very well." She got up slowly and went into the
house. "Hello, Bella."

"Oh, Letty," Bella said in a strange husky voice, "I feel
so bad ..."

"I know," Letty broke in gently, "so do I."

"I mean that way too, of course," Bella replied tearful-
ly, "but what really hurts me, is that John Dice asked
me to play the organ for the funeral, and I had to say
no. I played for Little Betsy and Poppa Dice and George
Story and even for Sam Born-Before-Sunrise. It seems

I've just played for everybody, but my fingers just won't obey me anymore, and I'll be switched if I'll get up there before the whole town and make a fool of myself, hitting all those wrong notes on that new organ. It's got stops I've never even heard of!"

"Oh, Bella, I'm sure he understands."

"I don't know, Letty, he's so broken up. He doesn't realize, I think, that we're all about the same age. He knows Torgo can't play the violin because of his arthritis, and when I said I couldn't play either, he shouted, 'Hellfire woman, I can't bury my honey without you playing.' "

Bella began to weep. "And it just hurt me so bad. I told him to call William Nestor over at the Barrett. He's a whiz. John just doesn't know how close Fontine and I were all these years. I'd give anything if my fingers . . ."

"That's all right, Bella." Letty paused to regain her own composure. "He understands, I'm sure, deep down inside."

"You do everything so beautifully, Letty, make him know how I feel."

"I will, Bella, I will," she replied gently. "Now, go dry your eyes, it'll be time to go soon." She hung up and straightened her back.

The church was not well attended, which surprised Letty; if all the old settlers were present, the younger generation was not. Many of Fontine's old girlfriends had gone on to their reward and, she supposed, one or two had stayed home because of illness, and certainly it was difficult for those who had moved far away to come back to Oklahoma.

Of her own family, Luke was busy getting approval on a government contract in Tulsa; Jeanette had the flu; Sarah was accompanying Clement on a tour of one-night stands; Patricia Anne and Lars Hanson had not been all that close to the Dices and couldn't be expected to drop everything and come home—particularly since they had made the long trek back from Washington, D.C., for Christmas. Luke Three was still away, living his own life somewhere. Mitchell was seated in the third row, and Bosley and she represented the Herons, the Storys, and the Trentons. It was still a very poor turnout for the "banker's wife"—who some of the second generation called Fontine. But flower tributes were extremely elaborate, huge wreaths, baskets, and one cross composed of white roses.

William Nestor was certainly an accomplished musician, and admittedly the new organ, for which the congregation was still paying, was a magnificent instrument. He played "In the Garden" and "Nearer, My God, to Thee," which were Fontine's favorite hymns, then some very solemn, very tender unfamiliar pieces; but Letty recognized sections of Vivaldi and Brahms. Then, majestically, in the measured style of Mendelssohn, he played "And Her Golden Hair Was Hanging Down Her Back." The flesh on the back of Letty's neck froze. Bella had played the old popular tune at Poppa Dice's funeral, which had shocked all of the old settlers. She supposed that none of the third generation even knew the old tune. God bless William for finding the sheet music. Bella Chenovick, especially since her sight was fading, had made a wise choice in allowing the youngster the courtesy of playing the complicated instrument.

The service was very simple. Two hymns that Fontine had specially liked were sung by the choir; most notably absent was Janie Strand, who had sung at funerals as far back as anyone remembered. She had a voice, Letty recalled, that Fontine had said was a combination of a "screeching opera singer and Ella Fitzgerald singing alto." Letty smiled. She would miss Fontine's irreverent sense of humor.

John and Charlotte Dice sat alone in the first row. There were still a few relatives in Texas, but that part of the family had broken with the Dices when they had come north to Indian Territory to make the Cherokee Strip Run. Letty could hear Fontine say, "They were all afraid that when we disposed of everythin' in Santone, which wasn't much, and followed the Old Chisholm Trail up here, that we'd go bust and come back and sponge off them." Fontine was always so angry when she related the oft-told tale that her curls danced around her head like wire springs.

"Words were hot and heavy, I can tell you. Then we got rich and opened the bank, and Jaundice became a senator and everything, the family could hardly welcome us back. We never heard from them—except when one of the third generation got in trouble and needed a handout. I wouldn't have sent them one tax mill, but Jaundice, with his big heart, helped them out now and then. I've never seen any of them kids, and I don't expect they'd even come up here to attend our funerals, knowing full well we wouldn't leave them anything!" And, Letty acknowledged, Fontine had been right—no one had come up from San Antonio.

Reverend Miller, the new minister, who frankly didn't know any of the townspeople well, read a few verses from the Song of Solomon, which Letty thought was a nice touch. He spoke briefly about Fontine's involvement in local social clubs and the part she had played in politics in Washington, and how she'd rallied support for the Angel library, and then suddenly the service was over and everyone was filing by Fontine's coffin at the rear of the church.

Fontine, posed sedately in the flower-banked casket, which was covered with a blanket of pink orchids, looked exactly as if she were sleeping. Letty thought she looked rather like Aunt Pittypat in *Gone with the Wind*, a sentiment which Fontine would probably not have appreciated, she reflected, but it was true nonetheless.

Bosley took her arm, and they joined the other mourners on the lawn outside the church. Soon the pallbearers—all young men, Letty noticed, including Jerrard Jones, who had closed the Heron station on Bosley's orders, carried the casket down the steps. Bosley and other elderly members of the community had been listed as "honorary pallbearers" on the printed church memorial. Last of all, John Dice and Charlotte came down the steps. She was holding his arm tightly as he walked with strong, purposeful steps. Charlotte wore dark glasses, which seemed a foreign touch.

As was the custom in Angel, everyone followed John and Charlotte to the Dice plot, located on the other side of God's Acre—which over the years had become God's Acres, because the original land that Letty had given to the town for a cemetery had long since been utilized. Gradually, when it was needed, over the years, the owners of the surrounding land had deeded acreage to the church. The new mausoleum had been donated by the Chenovicks, who everyone knew were Catholics and had to be buried at Perry on hallowed ground.

The congregation gathered in rows around the grave, which had been covered with false grass, and listened to the new minister exclaim unctuously, "Ashes to ashes, dust to dust ..." as he sprinkled a spoonful of red Oklahoma sandstone dust over the coffin.

There were no tears; eyes were wet, Letty was certain, but not one sob excaped one throat. Townspeople did not "put on a show" in Angel, and Fontine would have been mortified if there was a display of emotion. The crowd began to disperse, one by one, and wordlessly a few of the old settlers took John's arm or shook his hand, showing their love for him. When everyone had gone, Letty and Bosley came up to John and Charlotte. They stood looking at each other for a long moment while the bronze casket gleamed in the afternoon sun as it was slowly lowered into the grave.

An hour later, Maude was presiding over the buffet table at the Dice mansion. It was first thought to have the food served in the church basement, as usual, but John had told Cissie Baker, who was in charge of the Ladies Aid, "Fontine would be demoralized to think her good china and silverware wasn't used. That old crockery at the church is chipped and cracked, and the tablecloths are all stained. You know, Cissie, Fontine always set a good table."

It was strange, Letty thought, that John now referred to his wife as Fontine, when as far back as she could remember he had always called her Fourteen. Already, then, he was making an important transition. He was investing Fontine with a new aura: in death, she was becoming a figure of his past. He was allowing her to become the woman that he had never permitted her to be when she was alive. Thus he was assuaging his grief. He remained remote but cordial, gracious, and dry-eyed throughout the long afternoon, the perfect host, slightly distant, as if he had thoroughly rehearsed his role.

Charlotte's dark glasses still struck the only peculiar note at the gathering. She kept busy by helping Maude replenish the buffet table, wash and dry dishes, and make dozens of pots of coffee, refusing the other church ladies' offers of assistance. Reserved and polite, she was willingly, if rather awkwardly, carrying out her duties as hostess.

Looking over the buffet table, Letty recognized famous dishes. There was Belle Trune's ham hocks and lima bean casserole; Rochelle Patterson's German potato salad; Mamie Baker's baked beans; Cissie Baker's California fruit salad; Patty Stevens' Sally Lunn rolls, and, of course, Bella Chenovick's peach pie, along with dozens of other food items. Maude had stuffed the Angel cake that Fontine had been mixing when she had her first heart attack. "She'd want it that way," John had told Maude. Letty herself had contributed the traditional sour-cream raisin pie—which everyone called Funeral Pie because it was never made except when someone died, when, as

Fontine used to say, "everyone needs a little extra bit of iron in their system to help along their grief."

Toward evening, when the crowd was thinning out and farmer families were saying good-bye preparatory to going home to perform the evening chores, Letty drew Charlotte aside. "You've been just wonderful," she said.

Charlotte took off her dark glasses for the first time. "Thank you, but I think this is all quite uncivilized, Letty. In Washington, the family has a short graveside service. Custom has mostly done away with displays like this. A memorial gathering is held a week or two after the person is laid away, and that's that." She shook her head. "The funeral this morning was bad enough, but everyone coming over here and eating is just pre-posterous."

Letty held her breath for a moment and controlled her resentment. "Charlotte, Angel is not Washington by a long shot. Your mother would have been scandalized if this had been held in the basement of the church, as usual, because she loved this house. She would want to have all the traditional food everyone brought today. She had baked an Angel cake for the family of those who'd died ever since I can remember." She went on more gently, "And she would have heartily approved of this afternoon."

Charlotte turned away without replying, and then Letty knew why she had worn dark glasses: it was not to hide her grief, but to mask her anger.

Bosley encountered Mitchell on the front porch. "Hop-ing we could have a little chat," he said. "Frankly, I need some advice."

Mitchell laughed. "Now that's a real switch, Bos. Want some advice on your love life?"

Bosley chuckled. "Unfortunately that's not a problem anymore! Now, seriously, Luke and I have been thinking about a promotional stunt for Heron that we think might go over well. Frankly, our company publicity has been lagging lately; we haven't done very much that's spectacular for a long time. Robert Desmond got the idea when he saw some kids flying a tiny toy blimp. Apparently they'd drawn a cartoon of Mickey Mouse on it, and as it flew overhead the blimp caught the sun in the right way, and it looked full-sized. He thought that it would be effective to have a real blimp constructed, with the Heron flying bird logo painted on its sides." He warmed to his subject. "You see, Mitch, we'd fly the damn thing at the opening of every new Heron station, and at conventions and sales meetings. What do you think?"

Mitch shrugged his shoulders. "It's certainly original. Sounds like a good idea to me."

"No, that's not what I meant. You know a lot about drawing, and you know a lot of fabricators who manufacture a lot of stuff for your company. Do you think you could design and execute a project like this?"

Mitch frowned, and suddenly his resemblance to his cousin Luke was heightened. "I'll have to look into it, Bos, but I don't see why not."

"Good. You've never benefited very much from the Heron name," Bosley said with conviction, "but this is one project that would make you some money, I think. And then, too, it would throw some prestige Enid's way if you can find a local company that could do it."

Mitch nodded. "I'll check into it, Bos," he replied, and a week later he called the Tulsa office and talked to Luke. "I've found a facility that can manufacture the Heron blimp for you." They spent the next hour talking about prices, and a deal was struck.

John Dice hunched down in his swivel chair at the bank, his feet, encased in cowboy boots, propped up on the desk. He paused in the dictation of a letter, lighted a cigar while he gathered his thoughts, then continued in a clear voice: ". . . therefore, Luke, I have decided to retire as president and chief executive officer of the Dice Bank, effective at the beginning April first, nineteen-forty-eight. My first vice president, Don Addams, whom I have taken into my confidence during the last three-year period, and who has been my right hand, will make a notable successor." He paused and looked at his secretary. "Better change 'notable' to 'worthy'—no, I don't like that either, makes me sound too all-fired important—better make it 'suitable.'" He removed his feet from the desk and stood up and stretched his arms to the ceiling. "Now I'm going to lunch over at the Red Bird."

It was fifteen minutes to twelve, and the truckers had not yet lined up at the counter of the café. Belle Trune adjusted her hairnet over her dyed red hair and smiled when she saw John Dice opening the screen door. "Sit down here at the end of the counter," she said, pouring a cup of coffee for him from the large copper urn. "What'll it be?"

"What's the Blue Plate Special? Lima beans and ham?"

She grinned. "No, that's Thursdays. Today is Swiss steak and mashed potatoes."

"Sounds *alaripin*!" he exclaimed. "Fontine brought the family recipe for Swiss steak up from Santone, but, I think it was in nineteen-thirty-eight or 'thirty-nine, a housekeeper came to work for us who'd once worked in a French restaurant. She brought some red wine and, without telling Fontine, put some in the Swiss dish, and I swear, that gravy was the best stuff we ever put in our mouths. When she told us what she'd done, Fontine laughed, looked up at me with those big twinkling eyes of hers, and said, "We're living high on the hog, Jaundice, eating Texas-French!"

Belle laughed heartily. "I can just hear her say that, John."

"Yep, she was a corker." The silence grew deep. When he pushed his plate back on the counter, Belle studied his haggard face. "How about a piece of lemon meringue pie? It's just out of the oven."

"No," he said flatly, "I'm not hungry anymore." He got up abruptly and went out into the street, forgetting to pay the bill. His shoulders slumped, and his steps zigzagged down the sidewalk. Belle shook her head, knowing that his eyes were so full of tears that he could not see where he was going. Fontine had been dead less than six months, and he wore his grief in every movement of his body. She mourned with him. A light had gone out of all their lives with the passing of Fontine Dice.

After John Dice cleaned out his desk and removed the personal correspondence from the bank filing cabinets, he drove home in his black Cadillac and did not stir out of the house for two weeks. Then he put the car up on blocks in the garage, saddled up his part-Arabian horse, Morgan, and rode out to inspect the farm. The upper pasture had lain fallow for years, and the lower forty, which had been prime wheat acreage in the thirties, had not been planted since the war, when Tom Baker, who had sharecropped the land, went into the service and got killed on Guadalcanal.

John Dice rode back to the barn, hitched the old plow that hadn't been used in twenty-five years, to Spotty, the workhorse, and proceeded to start the first furrow on the lower forty. He stopped at the end of the row, looked back at his work, and shook his head. "Spotty," he said out loud, "we're out of practice. That furrow back there looks like it has been gouged in the earth by a hired hand drunk on corn whiskey. You and me better get into shape!"

When Maude picked up groceries at the grocery store that afternoon and the clerk asked her how the "boss" was doing, she remarked that the "boss" was plowing with a horse, and the word was passed on to Cissie Baker, when she came in for a loaf of bread, and Cissie told her husband, Thomas, when he got home from work. The next day, everyone in Angel knew that John Dice, with enough money to buy out the John Deere Equipment Company, including their entire line of tractors, was using a hand plow.

When Letty informed Bosley about the matter, he nodded. "Doesn't anyone realize what he's doing?"

"Well, Bos, remember Poppa Dice got childish in his old age. John had just come into all that money, and the old man was convinced they were still broke. He ended up hanging himself in the barn."

"Yes, yes, but that was entirely different, Letty, young Doc Schaeffer said the old man had a series of little strokes and all he could remember were the days when they'd just come up from San Antonio. But nothing's wrong with John Dice. He's working out his grief."

"You're right, I suppose, but he's too old to slave out there in the hot sun. He's been indoors too long."

"He's no fool," Bosley replied.

"Do you think we should invite him for dinner?"

"No formal invitation. He'll be over one of these days, when he feels like talking."

But John Dice stayed on the farm. Dressed in overalls and wearing a big straw hat, it took him two and one-half weeks to plow the back forty acres, but the rows were completely symmetrical, and Maude, trudging up from the house with a mason fruit jar full of iced lemonade, admired his progress. "It sure is pretty," she announced, and his face lighted up as if she had given him the greatest compliment in the world.

When he plowed the last row at sundown, he sighed gently, patted Spotty on the rump, and rubbed his callused hands together. He looked up into the sky. "Well, Fontine," he said gently, "we did it."

John Dice had become a recluse; by June, 1948, it had been two months since he had left the bank. Townspeople had finally stopped calling. He had been polite on the telephone, evasive but polite, and the few businessmen who had dropped by for advice, trudging up to the acreage where he was plowing, had found him to be uncommunicative.

He would stop for a few moments, his heavy work shoes stuck down in the moist red loam, and shake his head. "I wouldn't know about that, don't keep my nose in the bank anymore. Why don't you go in and see Don Addams? He's a good man. I trained him properly." And sometimes he would bend down and pick up a long earthworm and hold it up to the sun. "You can see right through him," he'd say. Or he would disengage a pink piece of quartz or an Indian head from the soil, rub the dirt from the surface, and remark, "I wonder if there's any value in this thing?"

Once, when Jerrard Jones ambled up to the hill to inquire about a loan he had taken the year before, John Dice had shaken his head and asked, "Want to see something unusual?" And he had removed a split-down-the-middle human skull from a basket of treasures. "It's Indian, I betcha. That looks like a tomahawk cleft to me. Probably Cherokee or Osage, or maybe a tribesman just traveling through in the Territory days." He went on with some ancient local history, but he would not discuss the loan.

The weather became balmy, the peach trees in the Chenovicks' orchard were in full bloom, and the tender young yellow-green grass sprouted out of the red soil along the graveled section roads that crisscrossed the community and looked like a game of tic-tac-toe from the air.

Farmers bought seed wheat, and since the crops had been good the year before, there was new farm equipment in every barnyard, bought on time payments at the John Deere showroom in Angel.

John Dice had laboriously removed the rust from the

seeder, a task completed during the winter months, hitched up Spotty, and planted the wheat in new furrows that obliterated the rows he had plowed the year before. "That's soil conservation," he told Maude proudly. "This way, the spring rains won't wash the crop away."

The first of June, 1949, John Dice moved up to the upper land again, and that was where Maude found him when she brought up the iced lemonade at ten in the morning. Lifeless, he was slumped over the plow. He had apparently been stricken in the middle of a furrow, because there was evidence that Spotty had proceeded to the end of the row, dragging him behind. When the horse could go no farther, his bridle had been caught in the barbed-wire fence.

John Dice had not died immediately, she knew, because his right hand was stretched out. He had written one word with his finger in the soft moist loam. The word haunted her. He had written: *Fontine.*

Word about John Dice's death spread through the community very quickly. When Don Addams called Bosley in Washington, he sat down quietly and listened intently. "Of course," he said evenly, "we'll come back. Have you called Charlotte?" And when Addams replied that he had just spoken to her, Bosley was relieved. "Now that she knows, I'll call her in a few minutes."

He hung up, put on his sweater, and went out to the back of the estate. He trimmed a rosebush whose suckers were endangering the growth, and added mulch to a flowerbed, then, when he was under control, he went back into the house and told Letty about John Dice's passing.

She broke into tears, and he took her in his arms and they clung together. "It was a heart attack," he said. "He was up on the hill plowing."

"It had to be his heart," she said when she could trust her voice. "The coroner will find that it is broken to smithereens."

*   *   *

Reverend Miller scooped a bit of red earth from the mound beside the grave and intoned, "Ashes to ashes, dust to dust ..." And at that sacred moment Mitchell Heron looked up to find Charlotte Dice looking at him intently. It surprised him that she was wearing white, not black. Their eyes met, and he nodded his head slightly.

The minister selected a single yellow rose from a huge spray and presented it to Charlotte with a little ceremony. Dry-eyed, she took the flower, whispered to him for a moment, and then was suddenly surrounded by townspeople whom she had not seen since her mother's funeral. She had difficulty recalling the names of those she knew.

Belle Trune was crying softly into her handkerchief, which surprised Mitchell, because he had not known that she had been fond of John Dice. He turned away from the group and was about to approach Letty, when he felt a presence beside him. Charlotte murmured under her breath, "Would you come back to the house with me, Mitch?"

He took her hand. "Of course. I'm so sorry. John Dice was—"

She squeezed his hand and gently interrupted. "Thank you, Mitch, but I really don't feel anything at all. I will, probably, later, that's why I need company now." She sighed. "The real ordeal is ahead, you know, when everyone comes over with food and I have to stand there like a Washington hostess in a reception line." She grimaced. "It was difficult enough when Mother died, with Dad at my side. He showed his true strength of character then." She looked up at Mitchell earnestly. "He was a strong man, wasn't he?"

Mitchell nodded. "My dad knew exactly how strong; so did Aunt Letty and Uncle Bos." He paused, "Do you want me to drive you back in my car?"

"Would you, please?" She gave a little dry laugh. "I

came with Letty and Bos. I was hoping that they'd drive the pink Caddie—which would almost make my trip home to Angel worthwhile." She raised her eyebrows expressively. "But of course they gave the pink Caddie to Luke Three. What's become of him? I've heard rumors ..."

Mitchell shook his head. "He's had a fight with his Dad, and no one's heard from him in well over a year— that is officially. Unofficially—and you must keep this under your hat, Charlotte—he's working in a filling station outside of London. A Heron station."

"What?"

Mitchell smiled ruefully. "No one understands his position except me. It may take him a bit of time, but he'll come around." He took her elbow and glanced back at the crowd. "Can you face them now?"

She shook her head. "Give me little longer, I'm gathering my courage. I suppose sooner or later I've got to play the grieving little girl." She gave him a quick look. "That sounds strange, I know, but I'm numb inside, completely numb. I'd get drunk if I could." She sighed. "I guess that's not funny, Mitch."

She looked around at the knots of people talking to each other, and gave her little dry laugh again. "They're all here ... some of these people only get together at weddings or funerals or on Memorial Day ... it's a treat for them. I suppose it gives an excuse for gossip." She shook her head. "I'm strange today, not myself at all. That little girl inside wants to run over to that place in the ground over there and look down in the hole and cry for my daddy, but the big girl outside wouldn't approve."   •

She looked up at him solemnly. "You and I, we never did fit the pattern, did we, Mitch? You were always off somewhere, and I was away too, 'on my own,' as Mama used to say. Oh, God, she would have given anything in the world to be a grandmother!" She blanched. "I almost accommodated her once, but I was thirty-eight and he was twenty-seven. I think we spent two weeks together."

Her rather hard face took on a gentle expression. "He was a pilot in the RAF. It was shortly before the war, and he was ferrying planes from Canada to England. Well, I didn't have the little flier after all. A doctor in Georgetown took care of that."

She looked him in the eye. "Mother was so desperate for a grandchild that I'm sure she would have waited out my accouchement with me somewhere, but I didn't want to spoil my figure." She smiled. "My figure? Who is kidding who? I've never had what could be called a figure. Remember, I've always been fat. 'Fat little Charlotte Dice,' the kids used to taunt, pointing their fingers at me. Remember when you boys used to gather under the swings at the playground to watch my big bottom encased in those white bloomers as I swung back and forth? Belle Trune and me, both with floursack asses."

Mitchell colored. "I never . . ."

"Oh, come on, Mitch, it was practically a local pastime! I can't speak for Belle, but I rather enjoyed it." She glanced around the little groups, which were breaking up. "We'd better leave. As hostess of this mess, I've got to get home before everyone else." She looked around at the graves and continued softly, "I feel so lost, Mitch. There's room for me here too, at the Dice plot, but I don't belong here. It's too ostentatious with those rose-pink monuments from Italy that Mama had flown over. I think they're vulgar. But my family, in a way, were vulgar, too, with all that money and not knowing what to do with it."

She turned away, sighed, gained control of herself, and turned back. "In Washington, cemeteries are bare, no headstones, just little bronze plaques in the earth. All that can be seen for miles and miles are acres and acres of green grass and little squares shining in the sun. I think it's rather nice not to make over the dead. It's not like here, with all these hideous monuments. The rich people have big ones, and the poor people have small ones. Have you noticed that there is no in-between?"

"That's the way it's always been, Charlotte," Mitchell replied, "but the Dice stones are very small in comparison to the Chenovicks'."

"Well, after all, Mitch, they're Bohunks!"

"Charlotte, you're not prejudiced!"

She shook her head. "No, not really. It's just my mood, I guess. But isn't it like Bella and Torgo to have their stone erected with their names and birth dates already engraved, just waiting for the dates when they finally kick off?"

"It's perfectly logical," he replied gently. "There's no one to take care of that for them."

"I think it's hysterical." Her mouth formed a tight smile. "What happens if the stonemason dies before they do, and the new mason can't match the letters already engraved on their stone?"

"I hadn't thought about that, Charlotte."

"I warned you, I'm in a peculiar mood."

"So am I."

"Who's going to get the Chenovicks' money?"

"The library."

"It'll be endowed in perpetuity, then." Charlotte laughed dryly. "But what really should be preserved—no pun intended—is that little fruit stand. That's the real monument. I suppose one day Bella will have a cardiac arrest as she hobbles down to the stand to sell her peach preserves, and Torgo will find her, and he'll have a heart attack too, and they'll die in each other's arms."

"Charlotte!"

"I know, I'm being impossible. I warned you." She took his arm. "One thing about me and you, Mitch, is we've always understood each other. Out of the whole crowd who graduated from Angel high school, we had sense enough to move away."

He nodded. "Yes," he replied sadly, "and just look at us. We're middle-aged, Charlotte. What do we have to show for all of our experiences? We're both still single. I've got three productive furniture stores, and you have an apartment in Washington and a job at the Department of Justice."

"And nothing else, eh?" Her voice turned brittle again. "What you're really saying is that we're not very useful."

"Are you going to keep your job?"

"Of course. Otherwise I'd end up in a mental institution. I'll go on just as before. This time, during my month's vacation—that's what senority gets you—I'll be able to take a first class trip around the world."

"And meet eligible men, too?"

"Of course." She smiled to herself. It was unlikely that she would meet a dreamboat on such a journey. She was able to protect her flanks, and it would be far wiser not to trust in fate. To be certain of expert technical displays in the bedroom, she would take a young man with her. Then the only slip-ups that could take place were the prescribed ones—in the dark.

Bosley parked the black Lincoln in front of the Needham Building. Although it was ten o'clock in the morning, the streets of Enid were almost deserted. A few townspeople—women in thin summer dresses and men in open shirts—were going about Monday morning business as usual.

Charlotte got out of the back of the car and was struck with the bucolic scene. Now that she was back in Oklahoma, after so many years in Washington, the contrast between the peaceful villagelike atmosphere of Enid and the hubbub of life in the nation's capital seemed almost other-worldly. An air of peaceful existence came over her.

Bosley helped Letty out of the front seat. She wore a blue-and-white dotted-swiss dress that made her look middle-aged. She did not look like a grandmother. Seeing them together, Charlotte felt a pang of regret; obviously they were happy and enjoying their old age. To what had she to look forward? A string of memories of the various young bodies who had shared her bed—and, yes, her board—over the last twenty-five years? She sighed gently at the irony of her situation.

Upstairs in the Joshua Mueller counselor-of-law suite, a tall, thin birdlike woman, who was impersonating a receptionist none too well, greeted them nervously. "Mr. Mueller will see you in a moment," she intoned nasally and busied herself among a stack of important-looking papers, now and then stealing a glance at Charlotte, who tried to look composed and unconcerned.

A moment later the door opened and one of the most handsome men that Charlotte had ever seen came into the room. He must be about twenty-five, she thought. He shook hands with Bosley and nodded to Letty, then turned to Charlotte and looked directly into her eyes. "Miss Dice, I'm Joshua Mueller."

Charlotte thought that there was an unmistakable foreign look about him that she associated with ... whom? Then she was a little girl again, looking up at George Story, who had the same dark skin and regular features. Joshua Mueller's mother, she was certain, was of Indian extraction, possibly Cherokee. As he escorted them into his office, she wondered why she was not attracted to him. He was a beautiful specimen of manhood, but she had not mentally undressed him as she did the young men who always made her blush with anticipation. Yet she liked him immediately, and furthermore trusted him, but for some unfathomable reason she would not want to go to bed with him.

The room was opulently furnished: law books in glassed oak bookcases; dark green walls, relieved by a few good prints of hunting scenes, dogs, and geese; light green plush carpeting that reminded her of the meadow in back of the house in Angel; and a large stuffed fish on the side wall with glassy eyes that she imagined were gazing at her soulfully.

Joshua Mueller indicated that his guests should sit down, then opened a portfolio. He cleared his throat and succeeded in looking rather pompous. Charlotte almost burst out laughing. He was so handsome that he would have seemed more at home holding Betty Grable in his arms than trying to muster the dignity the occasion demanded. Why had her father chosen this young lawyer, who obviously had not passed his bar exam too long ago, to represent the Dice interests when he could have conscripted one of the famous old-line law firms, whose partners specialized in oil and mineral rights? Was it because he was terribly brilliant or terribly Indian?

He stood before them, leaning slightly on his desk, and cleared his throat again. "We are gathered here today for the reading of the will," he said unctuously, and Charlotte sighed inwardly. It was like a scene from a horror movie, she thought. For a moment she was transported back to her father's funeral, when the minister had said, "Dearly beloved, we are here today to pay homage ..." In Washington the epithet, "dearly beloved" was reserved for the opening line at weddings.

The lawyer was well into the opening paragraph, past the "being of sound mind and body" part, when Charlotte's attention came back to the purpose of the visit. She was having difficulty concentrating on his words as he went into the various small bequests that included most of the household help still living, whom her mother had employed over the years.

A trust fund, which she knew about, had been set up for the Angel library's Dice Wing, and another trust fund, which she had not known about, was to be formed to establish a chair at the Barrett Conservatory of Music for the study of Middle European musicology. She had not known that her father had been interested in either Middle Europe or music. He had seldom danced even at the soirées that Bella and Torgo Chenovick had held all those years ago, and only once, she remembered, he had grabbed Bella's tambourine from her hand and shook it vigorously, and not in very good time, to Torgo's violin. And that occasion, she suspected, had been prompted more by the spiked punch than by hidden musical talent. Was the Barrett Conservatory of Music now going to offer courses in the proper utilization of the tambourine? She caught herself up sharply before she giggled. What was wrong with her? Her mind skipped wildly, conjuring up comic images from the past as if they were drawn by a clever newspaper cartoonist.

Joshua Mueller, having dispensed with the minor bequests, paused a moment and looked up over the legal-sized papers in his hand. He cleared his throat again, and Charlotte realized this little habit served as a prop, while older lawyers might use gold-rimmed glasses or pince-nez.

"Now," he was saying quietly, "we come to the part that interests us the most. I should give a preamble to what I'm about to read." He looked into Charlotte's eyes. "Your father, Miss Dice, came into this office six weeks ago and announced that he wanted to change his will. He said that he had a premonition."

Joshua Mueller looked down at the paper and, without looking up, read: "All the rest, remainder and residue of my estate I leave to my beloved daughter, Miss Charlotte Fontine Dice ..." he paused, and a flush spread over his face "... upon the provision that she establish permanent residence on the Dice homestead near Angel, Oklahoma, for the period of ten years. Should she fail to accede to this request, the estate, in toto, and the entire Dice holdings shall be placed in a separate trust for the maintenance of the Angel library, and Miss Charlotte Fontine Dice shall be given a certified check for the sum of one dollar."

The ride back to Angel was so silent that a tiny squeak in the motor, which no one had noticed on the drive over to Enid, reverberated through the car, sounding very much like the call of a magpie. Charlotte sat stone-faced in the back seat, idly watching the flat landscape pass before her glazed eyes. Those two had gotten even with her, after all, for living in Washington, for not marrying, for denying them grandchildren. They had succeeded in placing her in a kind of purgatory. In ten years she would be fifty-eight years old, and the best years of her life would be behind her. How dare they do that to her! How dare they dictate her life beyond the grave?

The moment Bosley let Charlotte out of the car, Letty sighed with relief. "I've never spent such a terrible half-hour in all my life. She didn't say a word but, oh, the air was blue with hate!"

"Can't say I blame her," Bosley replied gently, "You know what life here on the farm entails after all the glamour of Washington. . . ."

"Yes, but I'm always *happy* to be coming home!"

"Me too. But that's us. You must remember Charlotte doesn't feel anything for the land; she didn't have to claim it like the settlers did. Remember, even as a little girl she was odd."

"Well, so was Fontine, but we loved her just the same. Oh, I don't know, Bos, if families should interfere with their young. I always tried to raise mine independently, as individuals. I don't know what got into John Dice when he changed that will, but we'll never know. Do you suppose Charlotte will stay?"

Bosley turned the steering wheel, and the car sped

into the garage smoothly. "What else? She can't have saved much money supporting all those young boys."

"Bosley!"

"Well, it's true. She'll either have to stay here in Angel and be a very rich lady or return to Washington as poor as a church mouse."

Luke Three lay on the bed in his furnished flat over a small apothecary shop and read a popular novel in French, with a dictionary on his stomach. Topical French was easier for him now that he had picked up the idioms, but he had yet to crack one of the classics. His teacher, Monsieur Lafayette, had complimented him on his lack of an American accent. Thinking of cousin Mitchell, Luke had grinned. Whatever was wrong with the Heron bloodline, it did not include an ignorant attitude toward foreign languages, as he had feared when he had started studying French. He was an excellent student, or so said the excellent Lafayette.

He loved his work, and he was slowly becoming acclimated to the British philosophy of living. But while his single male friends popped in and out of bed with the greatest of ease, he had not had a serious affair with a girl since he had left Linda Roman on the *Saratoga* two years before. He had quickly discovered that Gene Holiday did not have the sexual allure of Luke Heron the Third. He had met several young ladies, it was true; had worked on the car of a delectable young girl the day before, but he was a *méchanique*, she the customer. There was always a veil—sometimes very thick indeed— between the women who came into the petrol station and him. American males were not highly regarded since the GI's had gone back to the States, leaving strings of broken hearts behind.

So in his bed at night he fantasized, conjuring up the females of his past experiences, and created a kind of lost magic.

19

The Changelings

Louisa Tarbell removed the FOR RENT *sign on her front porch very carefully because her eyes were full of tears.*

She put on her old cloth coat and walked the two blocks to the bank and deposited the check for two hundred dollars, first and last month's rent; then she walked another two blocks to the new Shangri-La Apartments and rented the cheapest flat, a tiny one-bedroom horror that featured a stall shower but no bathtub, a tiny kitchenette, and a wall heater that smelled like burned chicken feathers when lighted. She wrote out a check for forty-five dollars for the first month's rent. She had the same eerie feeling of impending doom that she had experienced twice before in her life; once when she had laid her mother away in 1939, and again when her father suffered his fatal heart attack the day after Pearl Harbor.

She began to pack immediately, and two weeks later, when the teenage boys next door borrowed a truck to move her into the apartment, she gave instructions that all of the old, heavy pieces of furniture should be placed in the garage and stacked floor to ceiling.

In the apartment, she supervised the arrangement of sofa, chairs, dining set, and bedroom suite, then sat down at her sewing machine to make new curtains for the place.

When the curtains had been hung, several days later, she stood back and looked at her handiwork. The tiny rooms looked warmer now, and suddenly she felt a marvelous sense of elation, which was also mixed with fear. She was starting what was in essence a new life; she had finally cut the umbilical cord that had bound her so tightly to the past.

The Saturday before the new school term started, William had written that he would be home on the five-thirty bus. Louisa parked her car in front of the drugstore where the Greyhound paused on its way to Tulsa.

When he climbed into the front seat, he flushed with pleasure. "Hi," he said, his eyes lighting up with that special look that meant he had to restrain himself from taking her in his arms on Main Street. That penetrating look removed any doubts she might have had about selling the house. No sacrifice was too great for this wonderful boy.

She drove out the section road to the remote Durham place that had been burned years ago and parked the car in a grove of Hedgeapple trees. William took her in his arms, holding her tightly. "I miss scratching on your door," he said quietly.

"It was a sound I always looked forward to, because it meant that you were going to make love to me." Her throat constricted, and she hugged him tight; then she removed a blanket from the back seat of the car and led him to the back of the old barn. Without removing all of their clothing, he made tender and passionate love to her.

The long, glowing sunset had brushed the landscape with gold as she headed the car in the direction of the Nestor farm. Their bodies satiated, there was no conversation. Being together was enough. When she let him out at the mailbox, she handed him an envelope. "Mr. Story's check arrived today," she lied. "Here is the money for your father."

Reluctantly William took the envelope. "It sure makes me mad that Poppa takes his money every month. I wonder if Mr. Story knows that he didn't take on a hired hand?"

Louisa placed her hand lightly over his mouth. "Hush, don't you know it's really a bribe? You only have one semester left, William; then you'll be on your own."

"Does that mean that I won't have to see my parents ever again unless I want to?"

"If that is your decision."

He leaned over to give her a kiss, but she drew back. "Please, William, someone might be looking. We must be more careful than ever, now that I've moved." She patted his thigh. "You're a grown man now, and we don't want to give any reason for people to talk." She went on very gently, "When you were still a schoolboy here in Willawa, I was simply your teacher. Now that you've been away for almost two years, you're a young man of quality. Write me when you can, and if I don't see you before, I'll be at your graduation!"

" 'Bye," he said, and he looked at her with such love that a sob caught in her throat. She watched him stride down the pathway to the old shack, and her pride turned to grief. How could she ever give him up? She turned the car around in the driveway and took the section road back to Willawa, trying without success to steady her shaking hands. Finally, when she could no longer steer straight, she parked by the side of the road. Sobs overtook her, and she placed her head on the back of the seat and wept.

The green hordes had come in the late afternoon, a menacing black plague out of the northwest blue sky, and by the time Mitchell had pulled up his new Chrysler in front of the Dice mansion, the earth seemed to be moving, jumping, and undulating under a groundcover of huge grasshoppers.

He glanced back at the road, where his tire tracks were quite visible; then, as he watched, they were gradually obliterated. He shuddered and rang the doorbell, and when Maude answered she said, "It's really terrible, isn't it? I've lived in Garfield County all my life, and I've never seen it this bad. The radio says they're moving on, and I just hope they keep going! Come in, Mr. Heron, Miss Charlotte—"

"I'm right here behind you, Maude." She went on in a joking voice, "Please remember not to call me *Miss* Charlotte!"

Maude adjusted her apron. "I'm sorry, only it's difficult to call my betters by their first name."

"For one thing, Maude, I am *not* your 'better.' We have a working arrangement. You are a *professional* housekeeper."

"Yes ... Charlotte," Maude replied, "but still ..." She went into the kitchen, still muttering.

Charlotte laughed. "Do come in, Mitch. Maude and I go through that routine at least once a day!"

Mitchell took her hand and kissed her on the cheek. "Thank you for inviting me for dinner. How's it going?"

"I'm becoming adjusted, thank you."

"That's a very pretty dress."

She smoothed the long purple crepe skirt over her generous hips and adjusted the large diamond brooch at her neck. "Thank you. I wanted to dress for dinner. No one here does, of course, but you're more cosmopolitan. Sometimes I want to get 'spiffied up,' as Mother would have said. I even curled my eyelashes for you! Come in and have a cocktail before dinner."

Mitchell smiled softly. "I bet that you have the only liquor cabinet in Angel."

"Well, at least the only one that's *full.*"

They sipped whiskey and soda and then ate a slightly rare rack of lamb, parsleyed potatoes, and banana cream pie, then retired to the living room for coffee and a brandy.

"How is it really going, Charlotte?" Mitchell asked, taking a sip of the liquor and waiting for its fiery path down his throat.

"Better than I thought," she replied quietly. "The townspeople have been very encouraging, and I try to be outgoing too. The Ladies Aid came for lunch last week. Since I do have a Steinway, I'm having the Music Society—the same one that your mother formed many years ago—next Wednesday afternoon. William Nestor, who's going to Barrett, is going to play. As you may know, he's Clement's protégé."

"No," Mitchell replied, "I didn't. I don't keep up with the family news the way I should. Sometimes the thirteen miles from here to Enid equals fifty thousand kilometers."

"Strange you should say 'kilometers' instead of miles, Mitch."

"I did?" It was the first slip that he had made in a very long time. He went on quickly. "Even after all of these years, I sometimes say something very un-Angel-like. I did spend almost twenty years in France, you know." He looked at her across the coffee table. She was very carefully made up, he saw, and Fontine's pink lampshades threw a glow over her face. He decided that she was a handsome woman. "What would you say has been your greatest problem in slowing down your life here in Angel?"

She took a cigarette from a silver box and lighted it from a match before he could reach for his lighter. "Sorry," she said, "I'm so used to doing for myself." She paused and answered his question. "I think it's the attitude of the people. I have to censor myself mentally before I speak. I must keep telling myself that these people have lived here all of their lives, they haven't been exposed to very much, and consequently they're inclined to be narrow-minded. In Washington, one learns to read meanings behind innocent-sounding conversation." She took a puff of the cigarette smoke, which she expelled immediately, gave a dry laugh, and went on, "Mitch, whatever people say here, they *mean*. As Ethel Barrymore used to say to end her curtain calls, 'That's it, there isn't anymore!' "

"I can't be anything but aboveboard." He could not say that the assignments that occasionally took him away from the United States made coming home easier; that the trips gave him the excitement and the sense of peril of the old days on the road, and provided the one true spice of his life; that because he lived a lie over there, he could not live a lie here. "By the terms of your Dad's will, must you stay here all of the time?"

She snubbed out the cigarette in a tiny crystal dish. "I've got to get some decent-sized ashtrays," she remarked. "These things are no damned good." She leaned back on the sofa. "My lawyer said that I must live eight months of the year here to qualify Angel as my principal place of residence, so that means I can spend a couple of months or so in my pied-à-terre in Washington, and then take a trip abroad. I get a very handsome allowance— enough to keep this house from going to rack and ruin and to keep the lawyers happy and to buy a new car every year, that sort of thing, but the big money—the millions—will not be handed over to me until nineteen-fifty-nine. That's it in a nutshell."

"Don't you miss your independence, Charlotte?"

"Oh, God, yes! Most of all, I regret not being able to make one move without everyone knowing about it. That's the biggest restriction. The first six weeks that I was in this house, after Dad died, I thought I'd wear the carpet out between the window and the bed, and then I had a talk with myself." She gave a wry grin. "And, strangely, Mitch, and I don't know if you'll understand this, but I'm getting used to the slower pace, and I find it kind of comforting."

"I know what you mean," he replied, thinking of his assignment in Germany and his quest for Jean Baptiste Faubert in France, and how he welcomed walking the streets of Enid after his return. "Yes, there's a lot to be said for this rural kind of existence." He looked at her quizzically. "Is—or was—there a man in your life, Charlotte?"

She laughed dryly. "You would ask that, wouldn't you? Just like a Heron."

He became confused. "I'm sorry."

"Oh, that's all right. I was only kidding. I'll be frank with you, Mitch. There never has been an important man in my life, except one, and I didn't know that at the time. You remember I went with Clement when we went to high school; then he took up with someone else. I mooned around, I suppose, as Mama would say." She closed her eyes a moment, then smoothed her dress. "I went on to Washington after graduation from William and Mary. I never realized that I still cared for Clement until his plane was shot down. When he was declared missing . . . well, it hit me like a ton of bricks. I cried out my grief, and when he was found alive in the nursing home in England, I rejoiced, but the man that I had loved was dead." She took up another cigarette and patiently waited until Mitchell found his lighter; then she puffed energetically a moment. "What about you? You've never married?"

He shook his head. "No." He was tempted to tell her about Françoise, but decided not to. "Oh, there are women now and then when I can't stand being alone anymore. But, as I get older, the women who are attracted to me—widows and housewives who want a little extra excitement—well, that isn't for me." He looked her straight in the eye. "I've never found a woman who interested me both intellectually and sexually at the same time, and that's the magic combination, as far as I'm concerned."

"Didn't you ever want children?"

He laughed suddenly. "No! I have never had the slightest paternal instinct. And you?"

She joined in his amusement. "I'm not cut out to be a mother, either. I suppose I cut my nose off to spite my face, because had I given Mother and Dad a grandchild, I wouldn't be in this predicament now. I'd have my fortune."

The telephone rang, and she answered it, leaning against the refectory table. Although she had lost weight, she knew the hostess gown was flattering to her full figure. "Why, yes, if you like," she said easily. "You may come over now." She hung up and glanced at Mitchell. "That was William Nestor, who I was talking about earlier. He wants to practice for the program next Wednesday. I thought it might be nice to have some music. If he was a beginner, I'd have told him to come some other time."

"What's he like?"

"You'll see for yourself. A rather sweet boy, Cherokee. I think his mother is a full-blood. Anyway, he's very bright. Taught himself to play the organ. Now he's quite good on the piano."

They were having their second brandy when the doorbell rang and Maude answered, coming in a moment later with the boy in tow.

"You don't need to announce me," he said, then grinned. "Hi, Miss Dice."

"Hello, William. I'd like you to meet Mitchell Heron, Clement's cousin."

William held out his hand. "Gee, it's a pleasure, sir. Soon I'll know the whole family. Luke brought Mr. Story over to Willawa to audition me."

Mitchell grinned. "I've heard very good things about you, William."

"Thank you, sir." He turned to Charlotte. "I didn't mean to barge in, Miss Dice, if I had known you had company ..."

"It's quite all right, William," Charlotte replied warmly. "I've known Mitch since we were tots. And, besides, I thought it would be nice to have some after-dinner music."

"I'm pretty rusty," he replied, sitting down at the piano.

Mitchell turned politely to the Steinway, willing to indulge the boy, and was pleasantly surprised at the dexterity with which he performed the warmup. His hands ran up and down the keyboard with such speed that his fingers could barely be seen. He dominated the instrument as if it were part of his body. Mitchell drew in his breath, because it was almost an act of tacit masturbation on a grand scale.

The boy, after a short, meaningful pause, began "The Wedding at Trouldhagen," which he played flawlessly. The room rang with the thunder of the piece; then he segued into the gentle "Afternoon of a Faun," followed by several showy Chopin études, and finished with a delicate, breathtaking "Ave Maria."

Charlotte was very moved. "That was beautiful," she said and applauded lightly, and Mitchell joined in quietly. "Clem always says," he interjected, "that a musician should never end with anything religious, because the public doesn't know whether to applaud or not!"

William nodded in agreement. "I won't end with a hymn on Wednesday, I assure you! But tonight I just played whatever popped into my head." He paused, and his eyes twinkled. "If you'll bear with me, I'll play the first piece that I wrote when I came to Angel. I'm not a singer, but I'll recite the lyrics as I go along. You've got to picture a kind of reedy, twangy voice." He started the introduction. "Oh, I forgot to tell you, it's called 'The Cowboy Waltz.' It's got a million verses, but I'll only 'talk-sing' a few. If you don't like it, interrupt at any point and I'll slip into some Debussy." He played the introduction again, and then recited in rhythmic verse:

> Middle-aged curs in Silver Spurs,
> Ties folded 'round
> Scrawny Adam's apples found
> On dusty drovers on the trail ...

Mitchell laughed out loud, and as William continued singing the various verses, he found himself applauding now and then over a particularly telling lyric, and when William finished with:

> ... Sipping malts, discussin' faults,
> And doin'—the Cowboy, yes doin' the
> Cowboy, yes, doin' the ... COWBOY WALTZ!

Mitchell was on his feet, applauding. "That's great, William."

Charlotte was flushed with pride. "The song is more than clever, it's very sophisticated. So incongruous, set to waltz time! Whatever gave you the idea?"

"Dunno, Miss Dice; it was *there*, just like I reached out and grabbed it."

Charlotte grew nostalgic. "We had a great Cherokee friend, Sam Born-Before-Sunrise, who's no longer with us. When he was promoting his autobiography in Washington, we had a long talk, and somehow the subject of spiritual matters came up in the conversation. He said something to the effect that there was a sort of giant storehouse of knowledge that was available to all of us, if we just knew how to tap it. He seemed to believe that artistic people often made use of this 'bank,' and when anyone was in a creative frame of mind, the fog between our world and the next disappeared and all of this 'force'—that was the word he used—was there for the taking."

William nodded solemnly. "Maybe that's just Indian

lore, but I understand what he means. Even in Willawa, when I was just doodling—improvising—on the organ, it seemed that I was stealing musical ideas from somewhere. When I wrote 'The Cowboy Waltz,' the notes and the words came so quickly that I had difficulty writing them down." He turned to Mitchell. "Have you ever had an experience where you felt 'out of yourself'?"

Mitchell considered the question for a long moment. He thought of Michel Bayard, his French counterpart, and Herr Professor Schneider, his German alter ego. How had he drummed up from inside the knowledge of how to portray these men? He just *knew*; it was there, inside. "No," he said, "I've never had an experience like that, have you, Charlotte?"

She shook her head sadly. "Of course, I'm not in the least creative, but I know certain phenomena exist. I feel Mama in this house every day, for instance. She's here in every room. Now, Dad I don't feel at all. It was Sam's theory that after death—which he called 'transition'—some spirits stay here on earth for a time, and others have to go through a kind of orientation process. I guess Mother had time to adjust, because she knew she was dying. Maybe her transition was easier." Her voice was very low, barely above a whisper. "But Dad went quickly, without any preparation." She turned to Mitchell. "If Sam's beliefs were right on target, maybe Dad's spirit doesn't know how to get back yet from the transition area."

William shrugged his thin shoulders. "It's all very strange. The hair on the back of my head is standing up right now. But if what Sam said is true, that there is a storehouse of ideas out there somewhere in the blue, I'm going to try to find the key. If I found it once, maybe I can find it again."

"You've got to send the song to Clem; he'll get a kick out of it. Don't you think so, Mitch?" Charlotte asked.

"Why not?"

"Maybe he'll use it in a movie," she quipped.

William threw her a long look. "It's not his type of song—professionally."

She adjusted her neckline, which the heavy diamond brooch was pulling down. "Oh, I don't know."

"He'll appreciate what you did with the subject matter," Mitch said, "although he's not a fan of hillbilly music."

"It's not hillbilly," William announced.

Mitchell smiled uncomfortably. "That's what we used to call songs like that, and I'm not being derogatory."

"Would you like a piece of apple pie?" Charlotte wanted to change the subject, and she suspected he was hungry. Most boys his age had prodigious appetites for food as well as sex. She was well acquainted with both.

He grinned. "I sure would. The dormitory chow is pretty awful."

She appreciated his boyish looks and attitude. He was rather attractive in his way. "Tell me, how can it be *pretty* and *awful* at the same time?"

"I'm taking musicology at Barrett," he replied quickly, "not grammar and syntax, but I see what you mean." His face colored.

"Oh, don't take any notice of me," she said, getting up, "but I've been away from regional expressions for so long that they stick out like a sore thumb."

"Sore thumb?" Mitchell expostulated. "That doesn't sound like 'Washington talk' to me!"

Charlotte laughed again. *"Touché!"* She was having fun. "These old-timey expressions keep creeping into our speech, don't they? What are some others?"

Mitchell drew his brows together. "What about 'Great balls of fire!', 'Well, I swan!', or 'I'll knock you forty ways from Sunday!'"

William came in quickly, "'Two shakes of a lamb's tail!' and 'I haven't seen you in a coon's age!'"

"Or," Mitchell suggested, "'When I get through with you, you'll be flatter than a pancake!'"

"Mama used to say, 'She's as slow as blackstrap molasses!'" Charlotte exclaimed.

"And Mrs. Briggs, my housekeeper," Mitchell countered, "is always going on about 'It'll be a long day in December before the tiger changes its stripes.'"

The trio continued remembering old sayings until Charlotte looked at William and exclaimed. "My God, I've forgotten your apple pie! Excuse me. Would you like some homemade vanilla ice cream? It's my mother's recipe."

"Yes, please."

"And you, Mitch?"

He shook his head. "No, thank you, but if you don't mind, I'll take a piece with me. I really 'hanker' for apple pie for breakfast."

They all laughed; then Mitchell got up slowly. "It'll be bedtime before I get back to Enid." He held out his hand to William. "It's been a pleasure meeting you, young man. Don't forget to send Clem the song."

"I'm afraid it's not good enough," William replied seriously.

"*I* think it is!" Mitchell replied, and kissed Charlotte, who had just come in from the kitchen with the pie wrapped in cellophane, on the cheek. "Good night."

"Good night, Mitch."

She walked with him to the door and turned on the light over the ornate porte cochère that her mother thought was so elegant. "It's bigger than the one at the White House," she had always told guests. Charlotte waved good-bye, then went into the kitchen. As she wiped a Spode cake plate with a cloth, she saw her reflection framed by the flowered border edged in gold. Her face was lined, even though she had taken a long time before Mitchell arrived completing her makeup. The delectable William was waiting in the living room.

He was not as handsome as her Washington golden boys, but he was young.

Before she placed the wedge of pie on the plate, she looked at her face mirrored in the plate again. Although she had lost weight, her face was still plump. Should she make a move?

She had still not made up her mind whether to proceed or not as she served him, and, watching him eat with a little-boy concentration, a look of pure delight on his face, she found that he really did not attract her. His face was too angular, his body too thin and underdeveloped, his hair too plastered with brilliantine, his mouth too slack, his ... Then it occurred to her that she was making excuses why she should not seduce him. She found this revelation disturbing. If she had been introduced to him by a friend in Washington, or he had worked at the State Department, or she had encountered him at a bus stop in uniform, she would not have hesitated at making the first move. She had had several affairs on vacation in the islands. Over there she might have even been willing to pay him to go to bed with her. But, tonight ...

"Thank you, Charlotte," William said, arising. "The pie was delicious."

"Just like your mother used to make?" she asked with a twinkle.

"Afraid not." He did not want to tell her that his mother had not baked since she had been 'saved' and the family had given up sugar for the Lord. "I've got to go now."

"Please come and play the piano any time you like," Charlotte said graciously. "This old house gets very lonely."

"Thank you, I will," he replied. "Good night."

"Good night." She stood on the porch and watched his thin figure disappear in the darkness in the direction of The Widows pond. She was not sleepy, she decided, going back into the living room. She picked up the pie plate and, as she went into the kitchen, saw that the floor was badly streaked. Maude had forgotten to rinse out the mop. She sighed and resignedly filled a pail with warm water, removed a cloth from under the sink, got down on her hands and knees and removed the thin layer of scum on the linoleum floor.

William stood for a moment in the darkness, looking back at the mansion silhouetted by the moon. He felt sorry for Charlotte Dice. She was a nice lady, but there was something desperate about her wandering about like she was caged in the big house. She was a terribly lonely person, he decided, as he turned back to the dormitory, almost as lonely as he was without Louisa Tarbell.

Clement finished a playdate at the Orpheum Theater in Wichita which had been highly successful; his only competition in town had been Ina Ray Hutton, who was completing an engagement at the Blue Moon Nightclub. He had visited her backstage one night after the evening gig, and she had returned the courtesy after a matinee. They had known each other for a long time. She was blond and beautiful, wore striking off-the-shoulder gowns that showed off her svelte figure, and no one could take their eyes off her when she fronted her all-girl orchestra. They spoke about how difficult it was for the big bands in the aftermath of the free-wheeling war years, and she told him that he was fortunate to still have Aunt Bertha's Oat Flakes as a radio sponsor, make an occasional film, appear regularly at hotels, perform in concert, and cut recordings. "You've got a marvelous career, Clem," she said sincerely, "but I don't think you realize exactly how lucky you are."

On the way back to Kansas City, Clement thought about what Ina Ray Hutton had said, and he had to agree with her. Perhaps he did take his career for granted, and he resolved to do something about it in a positive way.

When he arrived at Fairfax Airport, Sarah was waiting, as always, and he surprised her by lifting her off her feet, swinging her around, and giving her a rather wet kiss.

"My heavens, Hotshot!" she exclaimed, catching her breath. "What was that all about?"

He grinned. "Just to let you know that you're appreciated, Squaw!"

At home, they discovered a fat parcel on the front porch. "What do you suppose it could be?" Sarah said. "It looks like a CARE package."

He opened the package and read the note:

Nov. 8, 1949

Dear Mr. Story:
    Please find some of your mother's special oatmeal hermit cookies, which you can enjoy in case you don't like the enclosed.

Best regards,
Wm.

He studied the lead sheets and frowned. This was a cowboy tune, a waltz, but a very different sort of waltz than he had ever heard before. He noticed the combination of instruments that the boy had used in the orchestrations and marveled at the subtle interplay. He had known that William Nestor was talented, and his sixth sense had told him the boy was a natural arranger, but for him to work out the whole composition for the entire band without so much as a by-your-leave meant that he was either a genius or a fool, or maybe both! The boy had guts.

Clement turned the lead sheets over again and mouthed the words. The lyrics were strange and humorous, delightfully unexpected words in beguiling rhyme. Suddenly, in his ear, he heard that wailing horn backed by the strings, and he laughed out loud. To hell with Tracy's foggy throat; he would perform the number himself! It would do very nicely on the flip side of "All I Want Is You," a steamy, sultry ballad that would appeal to romantic olders. "The Cowboy Waltz" would be strictly for his fans—those kids who lined up for tickets at his one-night stands.

"Sarah," Clement called. "Come in here, I want you to hear something."

She came in from the bedroom, dressed in a flannel nightgown that came up to her throat. "Yes?" she asked in an insinuating voice.

"You minx!" He laughed. "I'll take care of you in a moment, but *first* I want you to hear something that's very extraordinary. Little Billy Nestor has written a number that'll set you on your ear!" He thought of his fans again. Would they expect this song from his Cherokee Swing Band? Well, he reflected, if they accepted "The Old Chisholm Trail" . . .

And, thinking of those fans, he tried to judge their reaction to this new song mentally, but could not, so he went back to the piano and played and sang:

> *College frats in sheepskin chaps,*
>   *Shootin' irons stuck down,*
> *In holsters, brown 'n'*
>   *Fuzzy from the dew.*
>
> *Teenage cats in Stetson hats,*
>   *Gum in their jaw,*
> *'nstead of a chaw*
>   *Of leafy dried and green.*
>
> *Three-piece suits in roun'-tip boots,*
>   *Ridin' a caboose,*
> *But no lazy cahoose*
>   *With a mind of his own.*

He paused to laugh, and then went on with the chorus:

> *Teenage cats in sheepskin chaps,*
>   *College frats in Stetson hats,*
> *Three-piece suits in roun'-tip boots,*

All sippin' malts, discussin' faults,
And doin' the cowboy, doin' the cowboy,
Yes, doin' the COWBOY WALTZ....

Clement felt an electrical shock go through his body, and he was not close to any electrical equipment. After all his years in the world of music, he knew a hit when he heard it, and if "The Cowboy Waltz" did not make it, then musicians like himself should retire, and he had no intention of throwing in the sponge.

20

The Big Event

The commencement of the class of '50 was held on campus at the Barrett Conservatory of Music, specifically the front lawn of the old Victorian house.

A hundred and seventy-five attendees sat on wooden folding chairs, which had been placed neatly in rows under the old shade trees that had guarded the driveway since the days when carriages had been lined up, when the place was known as The Widows.

Letty, seated in the front row, was feeling quite nostalgic until she remembered that neither she nor any of the other ladies would have been caught dead anywhere on the property in the old days, let alone the front lawn! She tugged at Bosley's arm and whispered, "Do you realize exactly where we are?"

He gave her a blank stare, then smiled suddenly, reading her thoughts. "It's not as though we expect to see Leona Barrett running down the front steps, dear."

Letty raised her brows. "No, although I'm certain that she's here spiritually, and probably Sam Born-Before-Sunrise too, seeing that one of his own kind is graduating today. Oh, if this old place had ears, the stories it could tell!"

"Oh, I don't know, Letty. You and I go back too far. This place has been a conservatory of music for over forty years. It was only—well—a house of pleasure for thirteen, so I'm certain all those old memories are lost in time somewhere." He grinned, looking almost boyish. "And probably a good thing, too!"

She smiled crookedly. "I suppose you're right. The students today, I'm sure, couldn't care less about the things that went on here."

He nodded. "Yes," he put in gently, "or what's been going on since—or even now. Barrett has always been coeducational."

"Yes, Leona took care of that!" Letty managed to get in before Dean Phelps walked to the microphone. She suppressed a giggle because the sound of his squeaking shoes reverberated under the old elm trees and added to the informality of the formal occasion.

Owl-eyed Dean Phelps, not known for his brevity of speech, began a long harangue that incorporated such diversified elements as (1) the surplus of male students, courtesy of the GI Bill of Rights; (2) the possibility of building a chapel next to the dormitory; (3) fencing the "lake"—which he did not add had once been known as The Widows pond—because some of the students had been caught swimming there late at night.

All of these subjects Letty thought inappropriate for a commencement address. But at last he got down to the business of the speech itself, which she thought sounded faintly reminiscent of Thoreau, and the dispensing of sheepskins. As each student's name was announced, there were little flurries of applause from well-wishers, friends, and family members; trembling hands were shaken and diplomas clasped in sweating palms. Another wave of excitement acknowledged the student's return to his peers in the roped-off section to the left of the platform.

When William Nestor's name was called, Letty and Bosley applauded politely and were shocked to discover that only two other persons also applauded; one was a plain-looking lady in a flowered dress, and the other was Charlotte Dice.

"I wonder if that lady in the print is his mother?" Letty whispered to Bosley. "She doesn't look Cherokee at all!"

"Maybe it's his father who's Indian," Bosley rejoined.

At last, when a short, bespectacled girl by the name of Marie Zimmerman had been duly awarded her diploma, Dean Phelps bade the crowd good afternoon, and the throng broke up into little groups.

"Let's go say hello to Charlotte. We haven't seen her since she returned from three weeks in Europe. It looks like she's gained twenty pounds."

Charlotte waved and came forward with outstretched hands. "So good to see both of you!" she exclaimed. "I haven't even unpacked, but I couldn't miss William's graduation."

"How was the Continent?" Bosley asked.

She looked skyward and shrugged her rather heavy shoulders. "London foggy, Paris rainy, and Amsterdam stifling! I came back a week early. Europe hasn't nearly recovered from the war, and I was a fool to think it would be the same. Everyone is starving. Even parts of London are still a mess after all this time. Personally, I don't think Paris will ever recover."

Bosley nodded. "We've approved of millions of dollars for relief, but it's going to take more than money.

It's going to take love and care and understanding. Punishing war criminals is fine, but we've got to be certain that a political situation never again arises where the climate will produce another Hitler or Tojo."

"It's going to take years before the populace of the world returns to normal, Bos. Everyone's so suspicious and wary, and of course they think we're millionaires and consequently we're expected to hand out fortunes in tips. . . ." She glanced over the crowd. "Who's that mousy woman with William?"

Letty replied, "She's probably his mother, although she looks much too young."

Charlotte shook her head. "No, his family wouldn't be here. They don't approve of his musicianship. Apparently they're religious fanatics, from what he's said."

William waved, and they joined him. He looked tall and incredibly handsome in his maroon cap and gown. His eyes were shining as he held up his rolled-up diploma. "Here it is!" He cried jubilantly. "Never thought I'd get it."

"Nonsense," his companion said, reaching out to steady herself on his arm. The turf was uneven. "The dean just told me that you're his most brilliant student in years."

"I doubt that," William replied, then paused. "I'd like all of you to meet Miss Louisa Tarbell, my teacher from Willawa. This is Mr. and Mrs. Bosley Trenton and Miss Charlotte Dice."

They shook hands, and William sighed contentedly. "Miss Tarbell 'discovered' me," he said proudly. "I guess that's the term. She was responsible for putting me in touch with Mr. Story."

"Oh?" Charlotte Dice interjected. "That's interesting indeed." And, when she saw the woman flush, knew at once that her polite comment could be taken two ways, although she had not intended a double meaning. Had

Louisa Tarbell taken William under her protective wing in more ways than one?

Charlotte glanced at Letty and Bosley, who were continuing small talk with Dean Phelps, who was obviously courting scholarships, and she knew that they didn't suspect an ulterior motive in the schoolteacher's interest in her protégé. She smiled to herself and suddenly felt a kinship with Louisa Tarbell. They had something other than their spinsterhood in common.

"Tell me," Charlotte said smoothly, looking Louisa in the eye, "when did you discover William possessed such talent?"

Louisa Tarbell coolly returned her gaze and replied introspectively, "Oh, I don't know. I suppose since he began to play the organ in church, and I realized that he had no formal training."

William smiled widely; his face was suffused with pleasure. "I was fourteen," he announced, "when Miss Tarbell invited me to listen to her classical record collection. Do you know she's the only person in Willawa who has the Rachmaninoff piano concerto? I finally wore out the records from playing. Then came Brahms and Beethoven, and my favorite, Shostakovich."

Fourteen, Charlotte thought ... *practically a child!* She glanced surreptitiously at William and Louisa. Could it be that she was mistaken? Perhaps this woman was a dedicated breed with a sharp eye for talent. But she did not appear to possess a sharp, inquiring mind. "What grade do you teach?" she asked conversationally.

"Seventh."

Why, the woman, Charlotte thought with some surprise, was not even a high school teacher, so her salary was necessarily low. From the look of her clothing, no matter how conservative her views, she could not have an outside income. Her shoes, although obviously newly polished, were in a deplorable condition, and furthermore she had a run in her stocking.

She sighed inwardly. Oh, if she only had a current young man upon whom she could shower affection! There had only been two in Europe; one in Antwerp, who was circumcised but practically impotent, and one in The Hague who was not, but who was too tipsy to make love.

Louisa Tarbell carefully studied Charlotte's face and thought with a pang: *She knows!* What had given them away? She was always vigilant about treating William in an offhand way when they were in public, and he always gave the impression that she was a teacher whom he, naturally, respected a great deal. Their attitudes were so perfectly executed that it was unthinkable that anyone in his right mind could possibly think that they were having an affair. She courted the impression of seeming to be rather vague—an absentminded spinster whose juices had dried up long ago, possibly around the time she had reached her majority.

It was only when she was in bed in the dark, with William laboring so sweetly over her, that she became the full, compleat, passionate woman, with undulating torso, heaving breasts, and a throaty voice that kept urging him on and on until they were both satisfied. In tender moments he'd grin and call her "the Flame of Willawa." She giggled inwardly.

After a night of lovemaking, she always adjusted her attitude over the seven-o'clock news while she had Post Toasties. She discarded the Flame of Willawa image and became Louisa Tarbell, Spinster, First Class. She glanced up at Charlotte Dice. "I beg your pardon, what were you saying?"

"What was your major in college?"

Louisa almost replied that she had received her degree in physical education, which was exactly the sort of reply that this nosy woman deserved, but instead, she said lightly, "Philosophy." She also wanted to add that she kept the diploma rolled up among the books on

sexology in her hope chest, as a reminder of the futility
of earning a degree for which she would never have any
use. And, truthfully, the books with pen-and-ink drawings of various couplings had proven far more valuable
in the long run.

"Where did *you* go to college?" she asked brightly,
hoping that Charlotte Dice had not received a higher
education.

"William and Mary, but I received a B.A. in ancient
history, of all subjects, which hardly prepared me for a
job in the State Department!"

"Oh, I don't know," Louisa replied smoothly. "The
way our government has been progressing since the
crash of 'twenty-nine, I should think that some of those
lessons that you memorized so diligently to obtain your
degree would have come in handy. Personally, I can't
see much difference between the Dark Ages and modern civilization."

Why, the bitch! Charlotte thought. Now she *knew* that
this pithy lady was indeed having an affair with William,
because she was counterattacking with no reason. Should
she square off at her? But, with Letty and Bosley present, she had to remain a lady, so she countered with,
"Apparently we both made unfortunate choices of
majors."

"Are you here in Angel on vacation, Miss Dice?"

"No, Miss Tarbell," Charlotte replied civilly, "I've given
up my position in Washington." And she almost winced
when she continued, "I've come home—to live," and
she almost added: *For ten years—a decade—forced
into living in a town that I hate, so I can inherit the
fortune that should have been mine whether I decided
to live in Kamchatka, the Isle of Man (a pleasant thought),
or midtown Washington.* "Do you still live in Willawa?"
she asked politely, knowing the answer.

Louisa Tarbell pursed her thin lips. "Yes. It's a miracle
that the town survived the Depression. Most of the farm-

ers still sharecrop, and many are Indians who were cheated out of their land allotments in one way or another."

Charlotte nodded. "It happened more often than we whites like to admit. Clement's father, George Story, was a tribal lawyer. I remember my parents talking about the fights that went on for years between the Indians and the government—and are probably still going on, for all we know. It's one of the disgraces."

"Yes." Louisa sighed gently. "We live with it every day in Willawa. Mixed-blood, third-generation Cherokees are poorer than they've any right to be. . . . Many, including William's parents, can't read or write. Born into terrible poverty, they'll die the same way. And to think that their forebears were cultivated people who went to the seminary in Tahlequah, spoke both beautiful English and Cherokee. But when the government broke up their concept of tribal rule, closed the seminaries, abolished their newspapers, and tried every way in kingdom come to assimilate them into the mainstream of American life, it broke their spirits."

Despite their personality clash, Charlotte was warming to this woman. "Yes, it's much like missionaries in China, 'saving heathens.' They take away their gods for our God, and then sail merrily home to America, leaving the poor Chinese with no gods at all!" She paused thoughtfully. "There are terrible acts in this world committed in the name of righteousness."

Louisa nodded grimly. "Yes, Miss Dice, that's why I was bound and determined to see William escape from a destiny that was preordained, before he was born. He *had* to be given his chance. If he fails in his chosen profession, then at least he's been provided with a boost over the wall."

Charlotte scrutinized Louisa's face and suddenly felt close to her. She had misjudged this woman. "But, what about *you*, Miss Tarbell?" she asked gently.

Louisa opened her eyes wide. "Me?"

"You've given William his boost over the wall, and what now?"

Louisa gestured helplessly. "Why, he'll go to work for Clement Story—that's part of the agreement—and he'll have his chance."

"But what will *you* do?"

"I'll go on teaching, of course, what else?" she replied quickly. "Now that times are better, I'll probably try to get a better-paying job, possibly as a grade-school principal."

William had come up behind them and chided gently, "What are you two ladies so engrossed about?"

Louisa turned with a Gioconda-like smile. "Wouldn't you like to know?"

"If you must know, we were exchanging recipes, William," Charlotte put in with a laugh.

He looked from one woman to the other. Neither certainly appeared to be very domestic, and he doubted that Charlotte Dice was any more inventive. He thrust out a yellow envelope. "Here. Read this. I'm going to frame it."

Louisa opened the envelope and read:

JUNE 3, 1950

CONGRATS TO A GRAD STOP IN SHOW BIZ PARLANCE STOP BIG
DEAL COMING UP STOP I RECORD COWBOY WALTZ PERSONALLY
TOMORROW STOP ORCHESTRATION AND LYRIC FABULOUS
CLEMENT STORY

She showed the telegram to Charlotte Dice, who hugged William. "I think that's wonderful," she said. "I've known Clem since we were kids, and I value his opinion very highly."

"Thank you," William replied, eyes shining in his boyishly open face. "Oh, there's Dean Phelps. I've got to show him this." He snatched the telegram out of Charlotte's hand and cantered across the lawn like a young stallion.

Louisa Tarbell laughed. "He's at that age when he's grown-up one moment and childlike the next." A soft light came into her eyes, which Charlotte did not miss.

"Miss Tarbell ..." she said, lowering her voice. She spoke very earnestly, and Louisa nodded her head again and again.

Fifteen feet away, Belle Trune stood talking to Bella Chenovick. "I would give my eyeteeth to know what those two old maids are talking about," Belle said. "Look, they have their heads together, just like a couple of old setting hens."

Bella nodded, although she did not quite follow the logic. Old maids were one thing, but setting hens, who were obviously no longer chaste, were another. "Tell me," she said, taking Belle's arm and changing the subject at the same time, "when you prepare your famous ham and lima bean dish, which do you boil first, the ham or the beans?"

Belle Trune beamed. It was indeed a pleasure to give her recipe to Bella Chenovick, who was one of the best cooks in northwest Oklahoma. "Well," she said, lowering her voice so that no one else could hear, "naturally, you boil the ham first ..."

Clement Story gave the orchestrations for "The Cowboy Waltz" to Tracy. "These are fantastic. This number will be the perfect novelty that we need just now."

Tracy hummed as he read the notes, a smile spreading slowly over his face. He came to the ending fanfare. "Whatever gave him the idea of using a schmaltz trumpet backed by delicate strings? It's a great gimmick."

Clement nodded. "And to think Luke practically had to drag us out to Willawa to hear that boy!"

"It was one lucky day."

"Yeah," Clement replied thoughtfully. "It's funny, Tracy, no one is more pedantic than Luke, Lord knows, yet he had a feeling that I guess could be called psychic. It was probably the only time in his life that he went out on a limb."

Tracy stuck out his lower lip. "Even for being half-brothers, you're not very much alike, and that's for sure."

"True"—Clement laughed—"but he wasn't born in a cloudburst like I was. Sam Born-Before-Sunrise always said that babies born during thunderstorms were bound to have musical ability." He went on humorously, "No one ever believed what Sam had predicted except Mama, but I can tell you one thing, Tracy, according to my father no one in his family could carry a tune. On the Indian side, he used to laugh and say that they couldn't even 'carry a chant'—and that was demoralizing!" His face sobered. "William Nestor said that no one in his family—Indian or white—had one iota of musical ability, either. Maybe it *does* have something to do with the Great Spirit, after all! Do ya suppose?"

"Search me, boss," Tracy replied, "but, speaking of the Great Spirit, the local bootlegger is due any time. I hope the bourbon isn't watered. I'm tired of paying for hundred-proof and ending up with sixty!"

The recording session had gone well, Clement thought, as he lounged down into the canvas director's chair and sipped a cup of coffee. He nodded to the engineer to play back the recording, and listened to his own voice bleat out William's lyrics. He hated to hear himself sing, because he could always hear the words coming out of his brain as if he were Frank Sinatra. But he could not fault the music itself. "Play it again," he asked the engineer, and this time he listened more closely to his voice. He got up and paced the floor, lit a cigarette, and paced some more.

He called Sarah in Kansas City. "Hey, Squaw," he said in a mock confidential tone, "wanta hear something wild? Hold on, and I'll have the engineer play it again."

He held out the receiver at arm's length in front of a speaker.

By the time that the lone trombone began its snake dance during the bridge, he had to sit down because of the jittery feeling in his legs. When the number ended, he hugged the receiver to his neck and lit another cigarette. "What do you think, honey?"

"Clem." Sarah's voice was strange, guarded, with a tone that he had never heard her use before. "What *is* going on? Was the whole band stoned? What kind of an exercise was that supposed to be?"

It was as if she had physically struck him. "Explain your meaning," he said quietly.

"You made me feel uncomfortable."

"How?"

She paused. "Honey, I know you didn't mean to do it, but your drawl—the nasal twang was overdone. The lyrics are satiric; you don't need to howl."

She was skimming over the truth, he knew. "Okay, honey, it was your opinion that I wanted, and I got it. It's a joke." He paused. "I'll be home at the end of the week, if the company plane is free; otherwise, it'll be the day after, if I catch a commercial aircraft. Love you."

He hung up. Sarah had never steered him wrong. She was Middle America. She'd always been right before. From jazz to swing, she had always been his most enthusiastic supporter. "It's what everyone wants," she had told him earnestly. "It's time to change. Jazz is old-fashioned now that Prohibition is over, and with the Depression people want to rely on their old relationships. No one has any money to entertain or booze around. They want to relax in the arms of their wives and husbands, and be uplifted by each other. Your swing music will bring them together." Sarah had made sense then, Clement reflected, and she made sense now. His version of "The Cowboy Waltz" would remain as a master wax cut, tucked away in no-man's land—

the drawer of empty dreams that all recording companies maintain—and there would never be a duplicate.

Clement called Tracy into his office when he came back from lunch. "I've had a change of heart about 'The Cowboy Waltz.' It stinks."

"Hold on, boss, have you gone crazy or something? It's great!"

"Yes, as a song—a number—I agree, but I don't like what I did with it. I've been thinking all morning. I don't like William's arrangement."

"It's brilliant!" Tracy interrupted. "Something's happened to your sense of value."

"Will you let me finish one goddamn sentence?" His voice rose and then dropped. "What I've been trying to say is, the sound—and my voice, too—is wrong from an orchestral point of view. The timing is bad. It's too hillbilly. I know I'm right about this. What I want to do is try to get the Storyettes together again—just for this recording—and have new arrangements made in swing, a gentle waltz, not blatant like William's concept. The girls will sing it softly, like it would be sung around a campfire at sunset, hauntingly."

"That's pure horseshit, Clem!"

He held up his hands. "Now, stop and think about it. Go into Engineering and have them play it for you again. Listen to it with your eyes closed, and you'll see what I mean."

Without a word, Tracy left and slammed the door hard. He was back in four minutes, his face a mask. "I listened *carefully*," he said slowly. "Honest, boss, your voice is perfect in every way for that song. It's not hillbilly, it's a kind of good-natured 'old boy' Western song, but with a modern twist."

"It's not right for the orchestra's swing image. Will you call the Storyettes, please? I'll call Smitty, he's a good arranger."

Tracy stood up stiffly. "If you go through with this, I'll

hand in my resignation. You've got a hit song, and you're too damn stubborn to know it."

Clement smiled and held out his hand. "Come on, buddy, shake hands. Let's not quarrel, because I've made up my mind."

"Go screw yourself!" Tracy shouted and turned on his heel.

The new orchestrations arrived three days later. Four men had worked around the clock to deliver, and Clement rehearsed the band himself. Claude Thornhill had recommended a pianist just returned from Hollywood, who had played in several studio orchestras. The man was a good general musician, but Clement missed looking over at Tracy and winking while he was conducting.

The Storyettes—Vera from Cleveland, Marcy from Los Angeles, Debbie from New York, and Geraldine from Tampa—had flown to New York the night before, learned the lyrics, and got caught up on gossip before arriving at the studio. As the girls took their places by the microphone, it was like the good old days, Clement thought. The sound reminded him of the late 'thirties, when they had been together for so long. Tears came into his eyes. They cut four records, each perfect, but Clement decided to allow Durwood Shaw, the producer at RBM Records, to make the decision on which one would be released.

Louisa Tarbell awakened abruptly, the way she always did, even at home with the curtains drawn, and luxuriated in the new and revealing warmth of her lover's arms. This was the first time in their relationship that William and she had been able to spend an entire night together. The cheap bed was not the most comfortable haven that she had ever known, but the closeness of his body made up for the lumpy mattress, the musty odor in the bathroom, and the fact that the red neon vacancy sign outside the window cast a pinkish glow through the lace curtains, throwing rather obscene shadows on the opposite wall.

She turned over in bed, and he instinctively moved close, cradling her loosely in his strong young arms. How precious he was, this boy of hers! And how she loved him! Very gently, then, she turned and faced him, opening herself and moving her hips close, partially receiving him. He sighed but did not fully awaken. She clasped him gently, and he sighed once more; then in a half-dream state he pushed himself forward and began gentle thrusting motions.

Although they had been satiated the evening before—going directly to bed after six-o'clock supper—his biological age came to his assistance, and his bar of iron was ready again. He was fully awake now, and he gently slid over her and assumed the dominant position. Looking up into his face, which was half in darkness and half suffused with the red neon glow from outside, she saw how his sharp profile accentuated his Indian heritage. He looked almost savage as his thrusts grew fervid. She lost herself in abandonment. Throughout, he remained in control, bringing her gently to a shattering climax, until he too shuddered and she felt him spew forth. They lay for some moments thus; being a young man, he did not lose his strength, and she clasped him ever more firmly.

His chest rested lightly on her bosom. Supported by his elbows, arms, wrists, and hands, he thought that this was the most rewarding time of all, this aftermath—better even than the engorged feeling that he loved, just before he erupted so voluminously. The lonely feeling that was always with him, except when he was mentally engaged in musical pursuits or making love, was assuaged now.

As they moved on their sides, still coupled, he appreciated once again the marvelous sense of oneness, the feeling of intimacy that could not be achieved in any other way. He was satisfied wholly, and a great feeling of affection and thankfulness washed over him. This wonderful woman took care of his every need. With tensions both at school and at home, he had never had to worry about sexual matters, unlike his male friends at school and church. As pious as they might have been because of their rearing in a religious environment, they nevertheless had felt the need for frequent release, and in fact had spoken of almost nothing else as their teenage bodies matured. He never contributed to these conversations, because of Louisa.

Luckily, his parents had always retired five minutes after the seven-o'clock evening news on the radio, and he had left the house at seven-fifteen, walked the three miles to Louisa's apartment, engaged in that fantastic experience of going to bed with her, and had still been home and in bed by nine-thirty. It had become his way of life, but this experience of spending the entire night with this soft, velvety creature beside him was the ultimate excitement that he had always craved.

To be able to turn to her, even half awake, and begin the motions of love was something that he had often dreamed about. And she was always ready for him, always anxiously contemplating his every movement. But knowing that he had within him the power to make her cry out during lovemaking, knowing that he was giving her the ultimate reward, was the most fulfilling experience of all. He had been in control. He was in control. He would always be in control. Even now, when they had periodically made love all night, he was still tumescent. He changed positions and, guiding her gently on her left side, started to make love to her again, but they were both so satisfied that they soon fell asleep, still entwined, still melded together.

They had breakfast of eggs, bacon, biscuits and gravy, washed down with strong coffee, in a small café near the apartment; then she called a taxi to take her to Ferguson's, the most expensive dress shop in Tulsa.

"Why, missy, you're a perfect size twelve!" the chic, if effusive saleslady exclaimed, sizing her up with a practiced eye before Louisa had said a word. "Where do you teach?" she asked as she flipped through the racks.

Louisa Tarbell flinched. Never again after today, she vowed, would anyone be able to classify her as a schoolteacher. She brought her teeth together and gained control. "Willawa," she answered dutifully, then continued quietly, "I'm going to New York, so I want to be very well turned out."

"New York, eh?" The saleslady brightened, holding out the six dresses on hangers that she had selected. "Try these on, missy, if you like. They're all in the medium-price range. Meanwhile, I'll look in the back room. A few new things arrived yesterday that I haven't gone through."

None of the dresses the saleslady had selected were quite right, Louisa knew. They were summer frocks, fine for what she supposed would be lawn parties, but none possessed the flair that she was seeking. She put on a pink print and pirouetted in front of the full-length pier mirror. In the plush kelly-green-and-white room, she looked very plain indeed. Her brown hair, which she had always thought was an asset, she saw immediately was not; it looked lifeless and dull and made her pale face even more undistinguished. Frankly, she looked forty instead of thirty-four.

The saleslady returned a moment later with four dresses with long skirts; one was pale blue, the same color as Louisa's eyes. "I'm not looking for evening clothes," she said, dismayed because she liked the sweeping neckline of the blue dress and knew the tight bodice would show her small, pointed breasts to advantage. "I don't expect to be going to the theater." After she had spoken, it occurred to her that she didn't know if one dressed formally for the theater or not. There was so much that she did not know about the world outside. New York, she realized, could be another Siberia.

"Oh, these aren't gowns!" the saleslady exclaimed, with what Louisa thought was a note of triumph. "Skirts are longer than ever this year. This blue dress is matchless for daytime."

"How much?" Louisa asked.

"Thirty-nine ninety-five," was the straightforward reply, and when Louisa paused, the saleslady turned, taking the dress with her.

"Bring it back, please, I'll try it on." In the dressing room, she pulled off her sweater and stepped out of her skirt, then slid the soft crepe de chine material over her head. The fabric slipped into place without help, and she turned to the mirror and adjusted the belt. It was the most flattering dress she had ever worn; the fit was so perfect, it could have been designed especially for her. Not since her high school graduation white gown, had she been attired so flatteringly.

"I'll take it," Louisa said to the saleslady. "Now, I'll also need a suit, something in crisp linen, if you have it," she continued purposefully in her best schoolteacher voice, "and I want an afternoon dress, a print, something that I can wear on into the evening, and I want to try on those brown-and-white alligator pumps in the window, and I'll need black heels and a purse, and other accessories also." She paused and drew on her courage. "Could you give me the name of the best beauty salon in Tulsa?"

"My ladies go to Steffen's," the saleslady replied glibly, guessing that her client was in the mood to spend a half-year's salary. "Steffen is rather precious—if you know what I mean—but terribly talented."

Louisa smiled to herself. The woman was not so arch, now that she knew that her customer was not merely a shopper interested in trying on and discarding clothing, who would walk out of the shop without so much as purchasing a handkerchief. "Perhaps," Louisa said, throwing her dignity to the winds, "you could use your influence and get me an appointment for today. You see, I've got to look very special in New York, and I know that I ..." Her eyes were very big, and she went on without a shred of pride left and acceded, "I need help."

The saleslady's attitude changed immediately, and her tone became warm and friendly; she too had once looked mousy and uninteresting. "Steffen will work you in some way, I guarantee." She examined Louisa critically. "Besides a cut, shampoo, and set, you'll also need a manicure, and possibly a pedicure too, if you're going to wear open-toed pumps. Steffen's marvelous with makeup, too. He'll show you some wonderful tricks. Your complexion is excellent, and with an eyebrow and eyelash dye ..." She squeezed Louisa's hand conspiratorially. "I'll make the appointment for you, but there is a condition."

"Yes?"

"You must let me look at you after Steffen's finished."

"It's a deal," Louisa replied, shaking her hand. "Now, while we're at it, I suppose I should have some new underwear."

"Our lingerie department is right over here," the saleslady gushed, "and your new clothes will look much better with a girdle. I've a new one-piece latex model that you'll hardly know you're wearing."

At five-thirty that afternoon, a taxi drew up before the Shangri-La Apartments and a smart woman in a blue dress was helped out of the back seat by the respectful driver. "I'll get your packages, ma'am." He grinned. He was the same cabbie who had taken her to Ferguson's.

"I'm in number ten," she said airily, then walked slowly over the graveled driveway on the new pumps with very high heels. She pushed the door inward and paused on the threshold of her ground-floor apartment.

William was sprawled on the bed, studying a music score, and when he looked up at her, his mouth dropped open. "My God," he said, "you look like a movie star!"

She giggled like a young girl and pirouetted before him, extending her long, false ruby-red fingernails in front of his face. She brought her shoulders back, which pushed out her breasts, raised by the new brassiere. Her brown hair, glinting with an auburn rinse, was swept up on top of her head. In the side part rested a small blue silk rose. Dyed lashes and finely tweezed brows added a sculptured look to her cheekbones. Her mouth, which Steffen had made more generous by the addition of two shades of fire-engine-red lipstick, opened in a wide smile, contrasting with her very white teeth.

"William," she said lightly, basking in his admiration, "please bring in my other new things."

After stacking the boxes on the bureau, he took her in his arms, but she shied away from him. "*Please*, if you hug me, I'll fall apart."

"Well." He laughed, appraising her again. "Take off your clothes, then."

"We've got to be very careful. Steffen says . . ."

"Steffen?"

"He's the beautician." She began to disrobe slowly. "I have to wrap my head in toilet tissue, around and around, before I go to bed. And he showed me how to do this . . . makeup." She indicated her face. "I must get up an hour earlier in the morning until I get the hang of it. He sold me lip brushes and cotton dabs and an eyelash curler and all sorts of things." She looked at him seriously. "It's all very complicated." She hung up the dress and removed her white slip very carefully, revealing a long white girdle that had rolled up around her middle. "The saleslady at Ferguson's said I must never be without this."

He laughed. "Well, if you think that I'm going to work around that thing."

"Oh, silly"—she grinned—"she meant during the daytime!" She came toward him. "I'm not certain how to get it off, so you'll have to help."

"I think," he said thoughtfully, appraising the situation, "that you just roll it down over your hips."

Then she looked at him, "How would you know?"

He could not tell her that Mrs. Lauder, the undertaker's wife, wore one exactly like it, and one warm afternoon years ago, when he had been delivering groceries, he had helped her roll it neatly down over her thighs. Then, because he didn't have to be back at the store for half an hour, she had expertly taken care of his iron bar. "Oh," he said, "one of the guys at school told me all about how it's done." Then he added, "It's rolling it on that's supposed to be the most difficult."

21

Time and Time Again

Patricia pulled at the tiny two-piece bathing suit and turned to Lars.

"I can't wear this in public!" she exclaimed. "I'd feel absolutely naked."

He laughed and indicated his midsection, which bore a small band of blue. "My *underwear* hides more. These Italians believe in showing *everything*."

They sipped the Bardolino wine of the district, on the terrace of their suite at the Hotel Ostrogoth, which overlooked Lake Como, the third largest body of water in the famed Lakes Region of Italy. They had spent two glorious weeks vacationing, before they were expected in Vienna at the famed old congress, where Lars would speak about Sam's death theories.

They had grown quite brown in the sun as they visited all of the tourist attractions. "I feel very Okie," Patricia said, "very unsophisticated." They had been attending a fashion show of the printed silk dresses for which the district was famous, in the grand ballroom of the Grand Hotel Villa Serbelloni. A bespectacled count and his new paramour were on one side, and an Italian movie star, whose name was unpronounceable, and her aged mother were on the other.

"Let's get out of here," Lars whispered. "I feel like I'm intruding, somehow."

"Not before I buy two dresses!" she whispered back. "Grandmother gave me five hundred dollars and said I mustn't come back without some Como silk."

"I didn't realize she was an authority," Lars said dryly.

"Bos and she spent a week here before the war, after one of those London trips. She didn't come back with *anything* and has been kicking herself ever since." Patricia gasped, "Oh, look, isn't that gorgeous!" She pointed to a blue-and-green caftan that shrouded the beautiful Italian model from neck to ankle.

"Yes indeed!" Lars agreed enthusiastically.

She gave him a long look. "I was referring to the *dress.*"

For the finale, the twenty-two models lined up on the carpeted runway as a tall, willowy young man with a pad and pencil came through the crowd, taking orders. He spoke French, Italian, Rumanian, German, and his English was without accent. Lars leaned over and whispered in Patricia's ear, "Obviously, he's multilingual as well as multisexual!" And she was about to reply when the young man came over to them.

He took one look at their clothing and said in English, "Is there something you'd like to take home with you?" He arched an eyebrow.

Patricia nodded. "The blue-and-green caftan and the cerise-and-pink evening gown. We'll only be staying another day. Could you ship it to Washington, D.C.?"

He laughed. "They aren't originals, you know. I have them in all sizes. From your accent, I thought you might be from the Midwest."

Patricia looked at him in amazement. "Actually, I'm from Oklahoma."

He grinned. "I'm from Grand Rapids, Michigan, and I went to the Parsons Institute of Design in Los Angeles."

"But how did you . . ."

He shook his head. "It's a long story. Anyway, I love it here at Lake Como, and the Italians love me for some strange reason." He raised his eyebrows again. "By the way"—he addressed Lars for the first time—"don't bother trying to fish in the lake. You won't get anything. The fish are too well fed and are too lazy to bite." He looked around the room. "Now, if you'll excuse me, I've got to pick up some more orders for my rags."

"My name is Patricia Hanson, and I'm at the Ostrogoth."

"You'll have the garments by this afternoon."

"How much?"

He grinned again, showing his white teeth that reflected the lights from the chandeliers. "I'll give you ten per cent discount. Do you want the amount in lire or dollars?"

"Dollars, please; with the lira so low, the rate of exchange scares me."

"Four hundred dollars."

"Will travelers' checks do?"

He laughed. "Why not? We're both fellow travelers!" He jotted down her dress size, then winked and accosted the

Italian movie star, who, from his delighted expression, must have ordered all of the models.

That afternoon Patricia and Lars made a last tour of the elegant resort area in a rented car. They stopped at the zoo, drove around the three sides of the Piazza Cavour, the main square, and visited the cathedral, where statues of Pliny the Elder and Pliny the Younger guarded the central door. Then they drove through the wine country and photographed the terraced vineyards and hayfields that overlooked the lake. On the way back to the hotel, Lars stopped at the flower market and bought armloads of fragrant flowers that looked like lilies of the valley.

"My heavens, such extravagance!" Patricia exclaimed. "What's the occasion?"

He filled the back seat of the car with flowers. "The occasion is ..." He threw back his head and laughed. "Aw, shucks, lady, I love you."

She was touched. "Silly man." But when he got into the car and started to drive, she cuddled up close to him in the front seat. "Let's go back to the hotel and make love," she whispered.

He looked down at her tenderly. "I'm glad you got the hint," he said. "Why'd you think I bought all those flowers?"

The next day they drove to Milan, saying good-bye to the green mountains and the ivory-colored villas with red-tiled roofs and the parade of boats that were always bobbing over three-pronged Lake Como. The noon plane took them from Milan to Vienna, where they arrived in a thunderstorm. The rain beat down unceasingly, and the small plane was buffeted about with such fury that it appeared the pilots might decide not to land but go on to Zisterdorf, where there was a military airport. But the steward informed the passengers that it was also raining there, and the landing would take place as scheduled.

But the touchdown was smooth, partly due to the pilot's skill and partly due to an absence of wind, although the passengers were dampened on their way from the plane to the lounge, a distance of five hundred feet.

The airport was in the early stages of being rebuilt, and the lobby crowded to the point of overflowing, and passage was made more difficult by sharp-pronged umbrellas, which it appeared, were used as much as weapons as rain guards. At length Lars found an English-speaking driver, who set out for the Hotel Lehar, located near the university, where the congress was to be held.

Hans, for that was the driver's name, was a young fellow whose accent was as soft as a breeze. He pointed to the streets, which had been bombed, and shook his head. "We've not recovered from nineteen-forty-five," he said. "It will take many years to rebuild the old Wien," he went on, taking Franz Josef-Kai, a wide street that followed the Donau Kanal into the downtown area. "We lost so many beautiful buildings—the Opera, the Burg-theater, and so sadly, St. Stephen's cathedral." He went on citing losses from the war, casualties, the hundreds of thousands of persons left homeless by the bombs, without once implying that it was Allied planes that had wrought the havoc. To him, it seemed, the war was just another natural disaster.

He turned down the Scotten Ring, which led into Karl Leugner Ring and finally to Grillparzerstrasse and the hotel. By this time the rain had turned into a torrent, and as soon as Patricia and Lars were in their rooms they bathed and lounged in their bathrobes, determined to have dinner in the suite.

After a magnificent five-course meal, which included thin pieces of *Wienerschnitzel,* over which they squeezed lemon, thick, fragrant coffee was served along with a delicious *Sachertorte.* Lars then picked up the pages of the address he was to give in the morning and went over each point, making pencil marks on certain phrases that he wished to emphasize.

He had expected a lecture hall or theater filled with students and perhaps a few graybeards. But the young doctor, Anton Esterhazy, who came to the hotel to pick him up, gave a polite little bow to Patricia. "You can come along, if you like," he said in soft tones, speaking English like a Londoner. "There will be lots of room in the studio."

"Studio?" Lars asked, opening his blue eyes wide.

Anton, who was much taller than Lars, and rather frail-looking, ran his hand over his jaw and looked down over the top of Lars's head. "Didn't they tell you at Walter Reed?"

"Tell me *what?*" Lars was growing impatient.

"You're going to be giving your paper over closed-circuit television. You see, most of the university was bombed out during the ... ah ... recent conflict. Most of it has been rebuilt. With space at a premium, the number of lecture halls and operating galleries has been cut down. Now many students in classrooms scattered all over the green belts, can watch a speaker or see an operation. It's really the modern way."

Lars tried not to show his disappointment. "If I'd known, Doctor Esterhazy, I'd have practiced my speech a little differently...."

Anton, raised his brows and smiled. "It's really what you'd call a break. Last year, when the television cameras weren't installed yet, our underprofessors gave their papers before only about seventy people, because, of course, the overprofessors had first choice of the halls."

"I'm afraid I'm being dense," Lars replied, keeping his temper down. "I don't understand this over-underprofessor business."

Anton frowned. "I think that some of the explanatory literature must have gone astray. I apologize, because it was my department that was responsible for sending out forms and brochures."

"I received only a subject form that called for a brief abstract of my topic to be given in fifty lines. I mailed this in with my registration money, and that was that. What did I miss?"

Anton nervously lighted a brown cigarette. "The overprofessors are doctors who belong to the Congress Association; the underprofessors, like yourself, are the invitees and are not eligible to become members until after they have presented three papers. Then their name comes up for review, and they're either passed or rejected." He blew a smoke ring. "I assure you, Doctor Hanson, it's a very great honor just to be invited." He paused, then went on hurriedly. "The congress is always interested in new theories, and many of the underprofessors' works are even published."

Lars look at him through narrowed eyes. "You mean there's a possibility that my paper may *not* reach print?"

"Why, yes, it all depends upon the board of governors."

"How many men comprise this august body?"

"Seventy-two, at present."

"And how many will be watching the closed-circuit telecast?"

Anton looked very uncomfortable as he puffed on his brown cigarette. "Some are rather ... elderly ... and may be detained at home by the storm...."

"Can't they *wheel* them in?" Lars could no longer conceal his annoyance.

Anton gave a weak laugh. "I would say quite honestly that perhaps eight or ten may be watching. Surely most of the endocrinologists will certainly ..."

"I didn't come halfway across the world," Lars replied angrily, "to have my paper heard by a few gland men. My subject is far more important than that. What is your specialty?"

Anton tried to make light of the situation. "Actually, I'm a baby-puller!"

"Do you belong to the congress?"

"Yes."

"Then you must be a baby-puller *extraordinaire!*"

Patricia took Lars's arm. "Calm down, dear. You've come to Vienna to give a paper, and we're here, and you've got to make the best of it."

Lars nodded. "I'm sorry, Doctor Esterhazy. Usually I'm not easily upset, but so much has been thrown at me this morning . . ."

"I understand perfectly. Now, shall we go? If we leave now, you'll have a few moments to go over your speech before you go on camera. It's not very nerve-racking. There's only you and the cameraman—he's an interne—and the man in the booth—he's an X-ray tech—so you'll be among friends."

"Sounds cozy!" Lars exclaimed, putting on his coat and helping Patricia on with hers. He was not amused.

"I'm so terribly sorry about all this, but with eight hundred applicants and an undersized staff . . ."

"Oh, that's all right, old man," Lars answered with a wry laugh. "My wife's father is a famous orchestra leader in the States, and one day I asked him what it was like to go out on a stage and perform, and he said something I've never forgotten. He said, 'I just go out there and do it!' Well, that's what I'm going to do this morning. I'm going to go out there and do it!"

Because there were no extra chairs in the studio, Patricia was given a seat in a small room the size of a closet, next to the control room, where a ten-inch television monitor was set up. She heard Lars's name announced over a black screen; then the lights came up and his face appeared. She drew in her breath; he was very photogenic, but he looked about ten pounds heavier than he actually was. "Honey," she said to the face, "if you're going to do this very much, you'll have to lose weight!"

Lars took a deep breath and launched into his subject. "The title of my paper is 'Metabolic Disturbances Induced by Botanically Derived Substances.'"

Looking at the camera's eye, he felt an unusual calmness wash over his body. He was relaxed, perhaps more relaxed than in his own living room, yet his senses were attuned to the project at hand, and his voice took on an uncharacteristic warmth and persuasiveness. He knew then what Clement meant when he said that being on stage was like nothing else in the world. You were in command! "The realm of sensory reception in the human body is very wide and complex, and often contains quite normal delusions. For instance, tactile illusions occur if one foot is lowered into a pail of warm water, and the other into a pail of cold water. If the cold foot is then placed in warm water, the nerve cells perceiving cold are suddenly *inhibited*, but if the warm foot is placed in cold water, the nerve cells perceiving warm are *stimulated*. The result, of course, is that the warm foot feels cold, and the cold foot feels warm. The nerve cells might have been said to be *jammed*.

"Another type of 'jamming' occurs when the receptors in the nose experience a 'fatigue'—as in the case of a perfume chemist, who works with pungent odors and no longer smells the scents with which he works.

"Other intersensory effects can be caused by a rivalry of either visual or auditory stimulus. A person normally masks out all surrounding stimuli when viewing a motion picture, a stage play or a concert, or when engaging in a sexual fantasy.

"Additional illusions, of a pseudohallucogenic nature, can involve persons who perceive demons or spirits at night or mistake shadowy forms of trees for people. Don Quixote thought windmills were enemy knights."

Patricia had begun to relax. Lars seemed perfectly

natural on the tube, and outside of an annoying tic in his left jaw, which she had never noticed before, seemed to have forgotten that he was not lecturing in a formal hall or theater. It suddenly occurred to her, as she began to absorb the ideas in the speech in a new way, that teaching might be facilitated by closed-circuit television. There was no interruption in thought processes. There was a total concentration which might not be possible in the classroom.

"Hypnosis or states of trance," Lars was saying, "have been observed for centuries in the Far East mystics, who are able to gain control of their own dissociative mechanisms to the point where they can leave their bodies and look down from an area and watch themselves. If this state of fixation can be prolonged, there is a general slow-up of the body functions and a state of sleep-wakefulness takes place. '

"This identical state can also be induced from without the body by the ingestion of certain drugs. Under injections of sodium amybarbital, which was used extensively during the war, subjects were forced to recall recent happenings. These are quite similar to other anesthetic drugs utilized for surgical operations. These chemicals impair the sensory input specifically by decreasing the transmission of nerve impulses by raising the resistance of the nervous system to their passage.

"There are other chemicals of a botanical derivation that act identically to those already mentioned. They are; the *ergot* fungus that grows on rye; *tetrahydrocannabinol* from marijuana; *mescaline* from peyote cactus, and *psilocybin* from mushrooms."

Lars paused a moment, for what he thought might be a dramatic switch, and, using a confidential tone, looked straight into the camera. "My researches have been restricted primarily to the *psilocybin* factor, following the preliminary twenty-five-year study made by the distinguished Doctor Sam Korda, a holistic specialist, as an aid to dying."

He turned a sheet of paper, to let the suspense build, then went on calmly. "If the drug is ingested at the time when the patient's body organs are in failure, especially in those cases where morphine or other painkilling drugs can no longer inhibit pain, the patient is able to deal with acute discomfort himself—on a normal experience level. As the drug takes effect, like the Indian mystic, the patient experiences an inner body separation and a feeling of contentment and relaxation. This state can be prolonged by a person who acts as 'guide'—either the physician himself or a loved one, who speaks in low, soothing tones of encouragement and reassurance. As death nears, the patient is able to concentrate on what is happening to him psychologically, rather than on the acute discomfort of a high pain level. . . ."

Patricia was so involved with the speech that she failed to notice how winning Lars had become as he gave his wrap-up "prayer," which was shrouded in technical language far beyond her layman status. The camera now rested on a nervous little man with a white mustache, who had obviously misplaced the first page of his paper. The announcer's voice droned, "This is Doctor Albert Luer, associate professor. . . ." She left the room and encountered Lars coming out of the studio. He was sober-faced, quite pale, and his hands were trembling; all of his on-camera poise had left him. He looked into her face anxiously. "Did the words come out all right? Did I make sense? Was there any of what Clem would call gobbledegook?"

She laughed. "No. Your diction was perfect—not even the sign of an Okie twang." She kissed him on the mouth. "Have you ever considered television as a career?"

"I may end up as a weatherman somewhere in the sticks if this paper doesn't go over," he said wryly.

Anton Esterhazy came out of the studio and pumped

his hand. "Excellent!" he exclaimed politely. "I must say, I enjoyed your topic...."

Lars gave him a long look. "What did you *really* think?"

"What are the side effects?"

"There are none. The person ingesting *psilocybin*, in a correct amount, dies beautifully and peacefully...."

"Well, then," Anton replied airily, "maybe it's all not poppycock, after all...."

Luke Three wiped the windshield of the Mercedes, treating himself to a long look at the neat ankles of his customer, a middle-aged blond lady. The skirts were so long in 1950 that he couldn't see much leg, but the necklines were lower, so he compensated by looking longingly at the generous swell of bosom pushed out deliciously near the steering wheel.

If the day was uninteresting he carried on a conversation with himself in French or switched to German, which he was learning also. But German was more difficult; he had trouble bringing the sounds from the back of his throat.

On Saturdays he dated the daughter of the cobbler down the street, Elizabeth, who was a very proper young lady of twenty, and also a virgin. She was good company, he had to admit, and they enjoyed each other in a kind of simplistic high-school way, but she would only allow him to feel her breasts occasionally, although she loved to kiss. He would go home after a date with Liz, undress in the dark, and lie down on the bed, where he would run his hands over his stomach and below. Then he would think of Jolene Fertig or Hedvig or Ardith Huxley-Drummond, and obtain his fantasy relief. But he never, ever thought of Linda Roman.

Clement Story stood on one foot and then the other outside the Heron suite at the Sherry Netherlands Hotel.

He did not relish the interview that was shortly going to take place. He had told William Nestor to go directly from the airport to the hotel.

For a moment after the door opened, Clement thought that he had knocked on the wrong door. A tall, svelte woman with an upswept brown hairdo stood in the doorway, silhouetted by the sun shining in through the large undraped window that faced Fifth Avenue.

"It's good to see you, again, Mr. Story," the warm voice proclaimed sincerely, and Clement found himself somewhat surprisingly shaking hands with Louisa Tarbell. "Do come in. William is doing his breathing exercises on the terrace."

By the time Louisa Tarbell had guided him across the beige-carpeted room, Clement had regained composure. The few fleeting times that he had thought of her since that first meeting, he had pictured her standing in front of a blackboard in the schoolroom, a look of dedication on her thin face, inspiring her students with her eloquence. It never occurred to him that she would still be championing the talents of his protégé.

William Nestor was seated cross-legged on the terrace, eyes closed, hands held out straight on either side of his body. Louisa Tarbell whispered something softly; he opened his eyes, rose up in a graceful movement that would have been a credit to a dancer, and came forward eagerly, his lips parted in a wide smile that lighted up his open face. "Mr. Story!" he exclaimed happily, as if he had not known the meeting had been previously arranged. As they shook hands he explained, "I was doing my lung exercises. Although there's so much haze across Central Park, I'm not sure that I'm any better for it!" He paused. "It's not like home, is it?"

Clement shook his head. "There's no haze on the prairie, that's for sure. How's Angel—or, more specifically, the Barrett Conservatory?"

William Nestor brushed back a shock of dark hair

from his forehead. "Before I attended classes, I thought that solfeggio was the name of an Egyptian king!"

Clement laughed. "The dean's reports have been extraordinary." He raised his brows. "I'm sorry I couldn't attend your graduation, but I have to accept bookings when they're available. Our business is changing."

"Would you like coffee, Mr. Story?" Louisa asked.

"Not before dinner," Clement answered, "but I think perhaps a drink might be opportune." He decided to allow her to play hostess, a role she was apparently relishing.

"What would you like?"

"A whiskey sour."

While she dialed room service, Clement turned to William Nestor. "First of all, I want to compliment you on the new arrangements for 'Lady Luck.' They're most extraordinary." He ran his tongue over dry lips; with the boy looking at him so eagerly, the encounter was going to be even more difficult than he had imagined. "Tell me, how did it occur to you to give it that unusual beat?"

William Nestor raised his hands up before his face and made a sweeping motion, and a chill went down Clement's spine. It was almost identical to the gesture he had seen his father use so many times, and then too Sam Born-Before-Sunrise had sometimes employed it. Was this old Indian gesture, half remembered, held over from some previous generation of braves; a means of communication that had remained with the men of the tribe even after the Trail of Tears, that long, painful trek from southern climes?

The boy fought for words. "It just came to me—that beat—I got up very early that morning." He spoke so fast, the words tumbling out in quick succession, that Clement was reminded somehow of the staccato sound of a machine gun spewing forth bullets on some forgotten European battleground.

"The arrangement was due," William went on, "and I'd kept putting off the assignment because I hadn't the foggiest notion how it was going to come. Suddenly I sat down, and it was so quiet and peaceful that I looked out the window and I saw the sun was setting over The Widows pond, and that beat sounded in my brain. The entire arrangement came to me like a flash. I picked up the pen, and the notes just tumbled out on the page."

He was so excited that his eyes blazed as he continued breathlessly, "The parts of the orchestra seemed to come out of the corners of the room, and I just couldn't get it down fast enough. I didn't go to classes at all that day, and when I'd finished, it was six o'clock in the evening and pages of manuscript were scattered all over the dormitory, and the guys were traipsing in from supper, joking and laughing. And the funny thing, Mr. Story, was that I wasn't tired at all! I could have gone on and on. If I'd been writing for an eighty-piece orchestra, I'd have had all the parts finished by midnight. I walked up the incline past The Widows pond and sat down under the Heron pecan trees, and it was as if there'd been some kind of breakthrough. I was freer than I'd ever been in my life. I knew that the arrangements were good." He placed his hands in his lap and looked up, his face now devoid of emotion. It was as if he had purged himself of some obsessive behavior pattern and was now drained of excess energy. "They were good, weren't they?"

Clement nodded. "I've been through experiences like that," he replied quietly. "It's quite extraordinary when you're taken over by a creative force." He paused contemplatively. "I once met Eugene O'Neill, and he said that *The Iceman Cometh* almost wrote itself. The entire plot was revealed in a flash and didn't require a great amount of rewriting. Sam Born-Before-Sunrise, used to say that this 'force' was floating out there; it was like a giant electric plug, but one had to be wise enough to form the right connection." He paused. "Apparently you've found it, William."

Louisa Tarbell leaned forward, her face suffused with admiration as she looked first at her student and then at his mentor. "Even years ago, when William first started on the church organ, he seemed to know what he was doing," she exclaimed. "It seemed like he already had some instruction, and yet he hadn't. It was quite peculiar."

Clement nodded. "The same sort of thing hapened to me when I was about five years old—and in church, too, strangely enough. I was fidgeting in my chair at some meeting or other, in the basement, bored out of my mind, I suppose, and then Bella Chenovick—she was the substitute musical director, and a Catholic to boot— hit a wrong chord on the piano. That sound grated on my nerves like a razor blade in a raw wound. I went to the keyboard and hit the right chord. She looked at me in amazement, ended the meeting, and gave me my first piano lesson."

Clement shrugged his shoulders. "How I knew how to locate that chord, I'll never know. But it seemed that the keys *glowed* and I *knew....*" He paused. "I suppose for a moment I'd 'tuned in' to that source of creative energy that Sam had spoken so often about." He laughed self-consciously, then went on humorously, "I wish I'd been able to tune in more often, because learning the piano from Bella was pure hell! I must say I never again saw anything quite so clearly as I did that first time."

There was a pause, and then William Nestor nodded and sighed. "You know, you still haven't said when 'The Cowboy Waltz' will be released."

"We made the recording last week," Clement said simply.

William's eyes lit up. "You did? Well, when will it be released?"

There was a knock on the door, and Louisa bade the waiter enter. She hurriedly signed the bill, then set down

Clement's whiskey sour on the coffee table, handed William a Coca-Cola, and removed a tall glass from the tray. "I've always wondered what a Cuba Libra tasted like," she explained, holding the glass aloft. "Let's have a toast to—well—to 'Lady Luck.'"

As they sipped the drinks, Clement went on in a rush. "I'd like you to meet the band," he said. "Then you must see the sights, the Statue of Liberty, the Empire State Building, Rockefeller Center . . ."

Louisa was a bit flushed from the drink; the taste of the rum stayed in her mouth. "I want to ask you something, Mr. Story. Now that William is going professional, won't he need a manager?"

Clement looked her full in the face. "It depends. Of course, he'll be under contract to me. My lawyer will take care of that."

"Yes, I understand, but won't he need someone to pay his bills and take care of personal items?"

Clement looked at William Nestor. "What do you think?"

"I guess all my talent's in music. I'm not very good at math."

"You'll need someone to keep your checkbook straight, like I do. I can't add two and two."

William flushed. "Remember, I've always lived in a small town. Mama and Poppa have never made enough money to have a bank account. There's a lot of things that I don't think I can do for myself." He glanced at Louisa Tarbell.

"The only teaching position I could find in the middle of the Depression, when I got my degree, was in Willawa," she said suddenly, "and if it hadn't been for William and his talent, I'd have left a long time ago. So I think looking after his private matters for a while will be good for me. Then if I ever decide I want to teach again, I can find another position in a different part of the country, where there's the possibility of a future."

"Then it's decided," Clement replied. "I think this will work out very nicely for all concerned." He finished his drink. "I don't know about both of you, but I'm starved." He glanced at Louisa Tarbell. "Wouldn't you like another Cuba Libra?"

She smiled. "Yes. The first one was delicious."

"Then we'll stop by the bar downstairs; the dining room is next door."

She turned to William Nestor. "You should change. Wear the new pinstripe."

"Okay. What tie?"

"The red and gray, I think. And there's a fresh white shirt hanging in the back of the closet. I pressed it this afternoon."

After he went into his bedroom, Clement turned to Louisa. "I think it's wonderful that you're going to look after his affairs. You're very dedicated."

She smiled coolly. "Don't forget, Mr. Story, it's a big opportunity for me too. All of my reasons aren't altruistic. Do you know what it means to be tucked away in a small, dead town, teaching what is essentially seventh grade?"

"I know very well. There was no place as dead as Angel when I was growing up," he replied.

"But your family had *money*."

"No, not then. That came later, when the oil wells really began to produce, and pipelines had been laid to haul the crude to the refineries. It was tough in those days. In fact, it was years before Heron had a refinery in Angel. By the way, I'll have you reimbursed for your trip. I'd have sent two tickets if I'd known you were coming."

"It's quite all right," she answered quickly. "I've a little sum tucked away. Now, if you'll excuse me, I'll change for dinner."

When she went into her bedroom, Clement looked out over Central Park. He was filled with admiration for the woman. William Nestor, he realized, was a very fortunate human being. He needed someone's full support, and Clement knew from experience that there was nothing so wonderfully formidable as having a dedicated woman at one's side. A wave of affection came over him for Sarah. She had stood beside him from the first, and her strength had always been there for him to tap when his own energy factor was low. William Nestor would also have that same sort of strength available to him.

The boy came into the room, looping his necktie into a four-in-hand. "Here," Clement said, rising, "let me show you how to tie a Windsor. It's the latest thing. Face the mirror. It's easier to demonstrate if I'm behind you." He placed his hands around William's neck and swiftly tied the knot. "There, how's that?"

"Makes my long neck seem shorter, doesn't it, Mr. Story?"

"I think it's about time that you knocked off the 'Mr.' business. Please call me Clem. Okay?"

The door to Louisa Tarbell's bedroom opened, and she entered with the air of a fashion model, her green ankle-length skirt sweeping around her legs.

"You look great," William Nestor said appreciatively.

"Indeed," Clement remarked, noting that the lady was quite pretty. She was too gaunt to be beautiful, but she had a certain distinction. He wondered idly if she was a virgin. She had been cast in the role of a schoolteacher, and, probably from a habit he had picked up as a student, he classified all single female teachers as being chaste. But now, in the hotel room in New York City, with the glamorous new dress, she could pass for a professional career woman of the Madison Avenue breed. She certainly did not look like a virgin schoolteacher from Willawa, Oklahoma.

"If there is a band, will you dance with me, William?"

Clement smiled to himself at her kittenish attitude. "We best be going," he put in, "or the maître d' won't be able to find us a table."

"I doubt that," Louisa put in quickly. "After all, our host is Clement Story!"

"Which means nothing to him, I'm sure," Clement replied with an arched eyebrow. "The Sherry is a marvelous old hotel, but its clientele are mainly from places like Beverly Hills, Paris, and Rome. They cater to a few film people. Mostly the old moneyed families on the Coast stay here."

"Mr. Story—I mean, Clem." William Nestor flushed. "I know I'm beginning to sound like a scratched recording, but please, when will 'The Cowboy Waltz' be released?"

Clement had put off the fateful moment as long as he could. "Soon. The only thing, William, I'm not doing it. The Storyettes are."

William Nestor's expression did not change. "I don't understand. I thought you liked it?"

"I did, and I waxed your version."

"My version?"

Clement paused. "The problem is, William, and I don't know whether you can understand this or not, but it's the *style* that was the problem. You see, if I was looking for a complete new sound for the Clement Story Orchestra as a whole, and was pulling away from a total swing concept, your arrangement would be ideal. But we're not a hillbilly band. So the record company decided that it would be a great idea, and I agreed, to have a new arrangement made with a more modern concept, and by switching the vocal to the Storyettes, it would sound more like the novelty it is. Do you know what I mean?"

William Nestor turned to the window. The lights were coming on in Central Park; entire complements of lamps were switching on here and there, until all the paths were illuminated. "I wrote it for you," he said finally. "I really thought I'd hit on something that expressed the cowboy flavor of the song in musical terms. It was special."

"Which it is, William, it is." Clement's voice rose convincingly. "We were all so enthusiastic musically while we were rehearsing that it was only after the session ended, and we played your version back, that it was apparent that it didn't seem to fit in anywhere. That's why we're going to shelve it, not because it doesn't have merit. I think you'll like the new swing version."

Louisa Tarbell pulled a pale blue silk scarf around her shoulders. "Which means that if it doesn't go over, it'll be trashed and no one will ever hear of it again. *Billboard* magazine says that ..."

Clement was incredulous. "You've been reading *Billboard*?"

"Well," she replied quietly, "If we're going to be in the business, we've got to read the trade papers. I've also taken *Variety*, the first subscriber in Willawa, I assure you! Now, getting back to 'The Cowboy Waltz,' when can we hear it?"

"As soon as we get a few pressings."

Letty looked up at Charlotte over the blackberry cobbler and nodded her head. "You're a good cook; this is delicious."

"Thank you. Mother's recipe. I've been going over her cookbooks. I remember years ago when the first well came in, she hired her first maid. She wrote down all of the recipes that had been in her family for years and presented them to her, like they were the family jewels.

"The maid, Barbara, was shocked out of her mind. And she said something like, 'Miz Dice' "—Charlotte's voice grew high and very Southern—" 'what's lambs' quarta? I didn't know you kept any sheep?' And Mama laughed and replied that lambs' quarter was a wild green that grew by the side of the road."

Charlotte raised her eyebrows. "Well, it turned out all

those family recipes were sharecropper's food. There was lima beans and salt pork—because no one could afford ham—and something called mock apple pie, thrown together when no apples were available, and red-eye gravy. When they didn't have a cow, Mama had made cornbread with chili-pepper-flavored water. Little by little, Barbara introduced new dishes, and it wasn't any time at all till Mama was saying to company, 'I'm so glad that you like my Beef Bourguignon, it's been in the family for generations!' "

Letty nodded and laughed. "Everyone has their favorite Fontine Dice story." A nostalgic smile hovered over her mouth. "Your mother was an original. She was my dearest friend for over fifty years. How I miss my chats with her." She patted her silver coiffure. "She was the only woman I ever met who fit into all strata of society. She could be a member of Angel's Ladies Aid, cooking spaghetti and meatballs in the kitchen in the basement of the church one week, and attend a flossy reception, dressed up like a Christmas tree, the next, and never fall out of step."

Letty looked Charlotte in the eyes. "You know, she never could remember which senators were Democrats and which were Republicans, so she just treated all the wives the same—and they loved her for it! Consequently, she was invited to luncheons in Bethesda and Georgetown by women that wouldn't think of inviting me, because of course, in those days, we were Republican. Remember, it wasn't until Roosevelt's fourth term that we turned Democratic."

Charlotte nodded stiffly. "I felt very badly when Dad wouldn't speak to Bos and you then, but he was a stubborn old man."

"Yes, he was that," Letty conceded. "But we never held that against him. After all, he had been a Republican senator from Oklahoma. He thought that the world was coming down on his head when we defected."

"But you did become friends again, and that was what was important, and he couldn't betray you when it came down to brass tacks. He couldn't bring himself to sell his Heron stock to Robert Desmond, thank heavens."

The antique grandfather clock in the hall chimed one o'clock, and Letty shook her head. "Where does time go, Charlotte? I've got to go home. It's time for my nap." She grinned crookedly, "I'm at that stage of life, if I don't get my forty winks, I'm apt to snap at Bosley over the least little thing and then fall asleep over the supper table!"

They rose and glanced over the huge dining room and the spacious living room beyond with its gilt furniture and pale blue French-style draperies. "Don't you feel strange living alone in this big house, Charlotte? Are you ever afraid?"

"Yes and no," Charlotte replied. "To answer your questions. I've lived alone all my life"—she colored—"for all intents and purposes, so I'm not frightened of noises in the night. I keep my Washington pied-à-terre so I can see my friends when I get really lonely." She frowned. "I'm still puzzled why Mama and Dad wanted me to stay here in Angel. Could the will have been a type of revenge?"

Letty shook her head. "I don't know, Charlotte. We only discussed wills once, and that was years ago, when we all decided to build and endow the library." She went to the door. "Thanks again for a delicious luncheon."

Charlotte laughed. "Thank you. I prepared twice as much as usual. I'm having the same menu for dinner. I hope that Mitchell likes Oriental chicken."

"That man will eat anything he doesn't have to cook himself." Letty laughed, then grew pensive. "I'm so pleased that you've remained friends."

"Well, we grew up together, although that doesn't mean anything," Charlotte replied wryly. "I know people who were close as buttons in childhood who can't stand each other after they grew into adulthood, but Mitch is an interesting man, even though he still gets the wanderlust. At least he's not a stick-in-the-mud ..." And she was about to add, "like Luke," but she caught herself in time. "Thank you for coming, Aunt Letty." She became confused. "I hope you don't mind me calling you aunt. I don't have any relatives now, you know."

Letty, feeling Charlotte's loneliness, took her hand. "I'd be pleased to be called aunt," she said softly. She opened the side door and went down the path through the pasture that separated the Dice land from the Heron holdings, and as she climbed the stile to the back forty, she thought again of Charlotte Dice living alone in that big Federal Restoration mansion on the outskirts of Angel. She wondered what Charlotte's life would become, far away from the glittering social whirl of Washington, D.C.

Mitchell and Charlotte ate at nine o'clock because a sale at the Heron Furniture Store had kept him until seven-thirty. When he had called earlier, explaining that he would be late because a salesman had taken ill, she had laughed. "You're getting reheated Oriental chicken, Mitch, so come as late as you like."

The grandfather clock in the hall struck eleven, and Mitchell roused. "I must go, Charlotte. Tomorrow is a working day, as usual."

"That's one thing I hate, the clocks in this house. Mother had a thing about clocks and mirrors—they're in every room, and they drive me crazy." She rose. "By the way, Mitch, I have something that I want to give you. Do you remember when Dice Number One blew in as a gusher? When the first oil check arrived—I think it was five thousand dollars—Mother threw all of her old furniture in the creek and bought everything new."

Mitchell nodded. "Bird's-eye maple veneer."

"She did keep one item, a solid mahogany footstool

that your dad made, and she told me that it was upholstered with a petit-point cover made by Aunt Letty. I
know that Mother would want you to have it." She went
into the hall closet and brought out the stool. "Here,"
she said. "If you look underneath, you'll find the date it
was finished! April fifteenth, eighteen-ninety-six."

Mitchell rubbed his hands over the rich patina of the
wood and caressed the tiny flowers in the fabric. "I'm
not at all sentimental," he said, brushing his crew cut
with his hands, "but knowing my father made this with
his own hands—well, it gives me goosebumps. It will be
the oldest piece of furniture that I have of his. There's
some older pieces in the Territorial Museum, that used
to be our place, that Sam Born-Before-Sunrise restored
before he died, but this is a good deal older. Thank you.
I think I'll put it in the front showcase window at the
store." He kissed her on the cheek. "Thank you, Charlotte, for a wonderful evening—and I mean it, I'm not
just being polite."

"It's fun getting to know you again, Mitch, after all of
these years. We must do this again soon."

He grinned and looked almost boyish. "The next time,
you must be my guest at my house in Enid. Do you
know where the Garber mansion is? Well, I'm just
down ..."

"... the road a piece?" She finished for him, and
they both laughed at the old regional expression as they
went out onto the porch.

"Charlotte?"

"Yes?"

"I'm glad you're back. *Really* glad."

"Thank you, Mitch." She waved to him as he turned
the car around and headed out the iron front gates,
then she went back into the house and poured another
cup of coffee. The house was quiet. Maude had gone to
bed. Charlotte knew that another sleepless night lay
ahead.

*   *   *

Charlotte headed her convertible toward Angel and slowed down as she passed Phillips University. It was five o'clock in the afternoon, and she had driven to Enid to attend a matinee showing of *All the King's Men* and felt vaguely discontented. The movie had left her with the bitter taste of loneliness in her mouth. The thought of spending the evening alone was suddenly unappealing, and frankly, a bit terrifying as well. She longed to be back in Washington. She stopped at a red traffic light and idly glanced out of the window. A blond college boy, books in hand, stood on the corner, his right thumb raised carelessly upward. They glanced briefly at each other; he grinned and pointed east, she nodded and opened the door of the car. He climbed in beside her, his eyes snapping in friendliness. "Thanks," he said. "I missed my usual ride."

Charlotte put the car in gear and asked cordially, "Did teacher keep you after school?"

He laughed, showing an array of large, even teeth. "Naw, I practice basketball from three-thirty to four-thirty every day, and a civilian who works at the Air Force base picks me up at a quarter to five. I've got to be on the dot because he won't wait." He laughed. "Today I was making baskets and I lost track of time. Say, you don't happen to be going to Covington, do you?"

She shook her head. "No, I live in Angel, but I'll drop you at the 'Y.' You shouldn't have trouble hitching a ride from there." She glanced at him again. He wore ivory-colored corduroys and his blue shirt bulged in the right places; he had a big build. Suddenly she saw him seated across the dining-room table. She slowed the convertible down to forty miles an hour. The trip would last only ten miles, and if he was going to be her dinner companion, she had to point the conversation in the proper direction. "My name is Charlotte Dice," she said simply.

He grinned, and the wind whipped his blond hair about his forehead in a way that was faintly erotic. "My name is David Herring. I bet you're the senator's daughter, aren't you?"

She flushed. "Well, yes."

"I'd heard that you'd come back to live in Garfield County. I think you used to know my mother; her maiden name was Betsy Landon."

Charlotte's mind flew back thirty-five years. She saw a myopic pale slip of a girl standing awkwardly at the head of the class, reading from a book. If Betsy Landon was the ugliest girl in school, she was also the fastest reader. "Yes," she replied slowly, "I remember her well. She had an unusual, husky voice."

"She still does." He picked up quickly. "Dad always said she should have been a radio actress. She sounds a lot like *Young Widder Brown*, you know, the daytime serial."

"Really? My mother used to listen to all the programs," Charlotte volunteered. "In Washington she didn't like to be invited to long luncheons, because she'd miss *The Guiding Light* and *Pepper Young's Family*." She stole a look at the boy again. He must resemble his father, because he was extremely good-looking. "What are you studying?"

"I'm working on my master's," he said seriously. "I'm going to be a biochemist!"

"That's fascinating."

"Most people don't think so. My dad's a farmer. He can't understand why I'm not down at Texas A & M studying agriculture. He wanted me to follow in his footsteps, but when I came back from the South Pacific—I was in the navy—I realized that the farm didn't hold anything for me. That's when I took the GI Bill and started college." He paused.

Charlotte threw him a quick look. "I assumed you were a sophomore."

"Thanks for those kind words." He laughed easily. "I'm twenty-four. Mother says I should be glad that I still look like a kid. I was always having to dig out my ID when I was in service and went into a tavern."

Charlotte had a mental adjustment to make. Obviously, the man beside her was not a schoolboy to be seduced on some back-country road. Should she invite him for dinner? Could she lure him with the enticement of a cabinet full of liquor? She decided to test him. "Are you going to wait to get married until you get your degree?" she asked casually.

"I'm not interested in a family situation right away," he replied soberly. "In fact, I've broken off with a girl from Bison whom I dated for a year and a half. She lives on a farm. She's really a swell gal, but she might not fit in with professors' wives." He looked at Charlotte directly. "I want to teach," he explained.

"You seem to have a good head on your shoulders," Charlotte put in sympathetically, "and that's essential if you want to join academia. So many young men today rush into marriage just for the relationship."

"That's true," he agreed, "yet it's not all that important if you don't want to start a family right away. I want to become established first."

Charlotte smiled to herself. If she worked it right, she had the feeling that he would not only share her dinner, but probably her bed as well. But it had to appear that the idea came from him, because, after all, she did know his mother and she didn't want him to spread it all over Garfield County that Senator Dice's daughter had propositioned him. That was the sort of publicity that she did not need. "Don't you get lonely, David?"

He looked at her curiously. "I've never thought about it, but no, not really." He paused. "Do you?"

She stared at him. The question was unexpected. "Sometimes," she answered slowly. "It's not that I'm particularly lonely, but I do miss companionship. That's what I meant."

He nodded. "I need to be around intelligent people—people who can converse, exchange ideas . . . like we're doing now."

Ah, she thought, the perfect opening! She tried to visualize what his muscular body would look like without clothing. With his service experience, he had probably gone to bed with a variety of women, or at least picked up the rudiments of what it was all about. He would be past the fumbling stage. "I'm rather in the same boat," she added softly. "I grew up in Angel, but having lived in Washington for so long, it's difficult to find someone to talk with on a certain level, especially men, because if you're single, as I am, married men assume that you're fair game. And widowers, at least in my age group, think that you're trying to take the place of their dead wives." She grinned. "There don't seem to be any bachelors over the age of thirty in Angel."

He turned to her. "You know, you're a very interesting woman." He did not appear so boyish now, and his voice was eager. "May I call you Charlotte?"

Her heart skipped a beat. "Of course," she replied warmly. "After all, I've called you David from the moment I knew your name. There's not all that much difference in our ages. Let's not rest on ceremony."

He leaned forward in the seat and adjusted the books on his lap, and she took the opportunity to change her position so that her skirt shifted, exposing more leg. The 'Y' where she was to let him off was not far now. She had the invitation already composed in her mind and had opened her mouth to speak, when he said, "Charlotte, I'd like to know you better. There just aren't any interesting women around. You're so up-to-the-minute. I remember Mother saying that you were very bright, and with all of the family money, you'd probably shake the dust of Angel from your feet, marry a rich man, and live abroad somewhere." He grinned. "But I'm glad you came back."

"Really?"

"Oh, yes." He sighed, and his eyes sparkled. "My mother drove me by the Dice mansion outside Angel one day last spring. I wanted her to drop in and see you, but she wouldn't. I guess she was shy." He drew in his breath. "Mother said that your mother imported a lot of artifacts from Europe and that her dishes were pure gold, and that your father had the best bootlegger and kept a bar stocked full of the best bourbon." He moved the schoolbooks on his knee and stretched out his long legs. "You could put our entire house in your living room. I'd surely like to see that place." He turned toward her. "I've heard that there are three classic cars in the garage—collector's items worth a fortune. I'm interested in antique automobiles. I've heard the hubcaps are sterling silver."

He was humiliating her, insulting her, and the strange part about it was that he did not know that he was being offensive. He was part and parcel of his generation, and suddenly she had had enough. All those strings of bodies over the years seemed to mock her now, and she was very deeply angry.

They were approaching the 'Y' and she slowed down the car. "David, I want to thank you for this afternoon," she said warmly. "It was very illuminating."

He looked at her in surprise. "Covington is such a short distance from Angel, and I thought you'd show me . . ."

She stopped the car quickly and held out her hand. "Good-bye, David. Do give your mother my best."

He shook hands awkwardly. "You're such a nice lady."

"Oh, look!" Charlotte exclaimed. "There's a car coming. If you hurry you may get a ride into Covington."

He raised his long legs over the door of the convertible and climbed out. He was furious. "Mother always said you were a bitch," he spat out. "And you are!" He ran to the crossroads ahead and held out his thumb. The car slowed down, and as David climbed in he held up his middle finger to her. She watched the car speed toward Covington and sighed before placing her car in gear and turning the corner toward Angel.

She knew David would be sitting beside her at this very moment, had she extended the invitation that he had expected. Why had she held back? Somehow, at the last moment, she had seen him stretched out beside her naked, his magnificent shoulders looming up, high as mountains, his big, even teeth enclosed by thin lips drawn back in a smile, and she knew that she couldn't go through that complicated routine again.

That sexual route was so familiar to her. First she must compliment the body—all the young men expected that—then she would be expected to start the machinations of lovemaking, being older and more experienced. She always found that it was easier to make love in the dark, because then she became an object, the soft, rather plump, pliable object of their sexual desires.

Yet she loved to look at the bodies, loved to watch the faces change expressions as they toiled above her; that was a major part of the joy of going to bed with them, and the only joy if they finished before her, which so many did, leaving her in an aroused state of unfulfillment. Most usually they were more careful of her wants if they were getting paid for having sex with her—but then again, not always.

It had occurred to her in that moment of decision, when she had stopped the car, that she could not really endure one more young lad. This David was attractive and he would have certainly warmed her bed, if not her heart, yet she had held back. Perhaps it was because of his mother, her nearly forgotten childhood friend; perhaps it was because he had mentioned her wealth; perhaps it was because she was tired of being used;

perhaps it was because—away from the bright, sophisticated lights of Washington, D.C.—she had taken up some of the puritanical attitudes of Angel. But, whatever the reason, she knew that the era of the golden boys was over.

Bosley rolled out the stratigraphy chart of the Middle East on the conference table at the Heron offices in Tulsa. "This isn't by any means correct," he said, "and Iran is by far more interesting, geologically speaking, than Saudi Arabia. There's been greater underground activity, for instance, in the Central Iranian Plateau and in Turkey. Most of the salt plugs are in Southern Iran, leading down into the lower Arabian Gulf, so offshore drilling is the key to the future. The petroleum industry is really primitive in this area, Luke, compared to what will happen in a few years. There's a major anticline, the Abqaiq, where I believe a major dome of oil is trapped." He looked up uncomfortably. "We're going to be forced to spend many millions in the area for exploration if Muhammad Abn grants us a concession."

"While we're a small company, Bos, compared to Standard Oil and the biggies, I really feel we must get in there while we can. I've heard that J. Paul Getty wants the concession in the Saudi Arabia–Kuwait Neutral Zone and the surrounding territorial waters."

"Let him have it. He's personally a *billionaire*." Bosley scratched his head. "There are plenty of other areas we can tackle better. Remember, the desert is mainly undeveloped. Getty can afford to fortify his flanks and spend many millions in exploration, and if it takes years, he won't get hurt. We can be. Damn, if only it were ten years from now, when technology will be more sophisticated. The war set us back a decade. We should have had oil rigs in there while we were fighting the Japs and the Germans." He shook his head. "So far, however, there are only about three old-line companies solidly entrenched. The oldest, of course, is Aramco—the Arabian American Oil Company. Its concession, granted in nineteen-thirty-three, won't expire until nineteen-ninety-nine, and includes over one hundred and twenty-five thousand square miles of Saudi Arabia as well as offshore areas. Aramco is composed of Standard Oil of California, Texaco, and Standard of New Jersey, each with thirty percent. Mobil has only ten percent. The Bahrain Petroleum Company, Limited, owned jointly by Texaco and Standard of California, received its concession in nineteen-thirty-four, which doesn't expire until twenty-twenty-four!"

"Do we have enough information at our fingertips, Bos, to visit Muhammad Abn?"

Bosley nodded. "I think so, at least enough to begin the preliminary talks."

Luke drew in his breath gently. "He's a warm, caring individual. You know what I think cemented our relationship? Remember when he was here in nineteen-forty-five, and we invited him to the farm in Angel? He said it was a memorable experience for him. Of course, he had graduated *cum laude* from Cambridge and was familiar with the British way of life, but he told me that he had never been invited into an English household, can you imagine?" Luke shook his head. "He was very touched by our invitation."

"And how he enjoyed Letty's Angel cake!" Bosley pursed his lips. "She was so nervous, too, because she was afraid she'd make a wrong move and did not want to be forward."

Bernice knocked on the door, then came into the room quickly. "I'm sorry to disturb you, boss," she said, "but the mail just came, and I knew that you'd want to see this right away. It's marked 'personal.'" She placed the thin airmail letter on the conference table.

Luke recognized Luke Three's handwriting as he opened the letter. He sighed and read aloud:

Dear Dad:

I'm writing you at the office and not at home, because this is a business letter. I suppose you think I've been off on a wild goose chase, evading responsibility, and I suppose, in a way, I have. But, I've learned a lot about *people*, I mean people in general, and looking back on my childhood and everyone that I grew up with, I was locked into a kind of vacuum. I really never knew much about the way people thought or felt or how to cope with emotions. I've had a few shocks, as Grandma might say, but I'm doing okay.

I've got a job that I like and can handle with no sweat, and for the first time I'm learning to do for myself. I don't know how long I'll be here or what I'll eventually be doing. For the first time, I understand some of the things that Uncle Mitch must have gone through, when he spent all those years over here.

I'm not going to ask you to be patient, because that's one thing that you've never been with me—ever. If I want to rejoin Heron sometime in the future, and you don't want me back, that's okay, too. Right now, I think I'd be happy owning a little station somewhere in the States, pumping gas, doing a little mechanic work, and just surviving. If it's not a Heron station, that's all right, no big deal.

Right now, I've got so many things to work out that I don't really want to hear from anyone at home—maybe later, but not right now.

I'm sorry if I've been a disapointment to you, or especially Robert Desmond, who taught me so much and wanted me to really be a big man at Heron.

Tell the family—Grandma, especially—that I'm okay.

Luke T.

P.S. If I write again and you don't want to open the letter, that's okay, too. I should have written before, but I didn't have anything to say.

Luke pushed the letter aside, and he did not look at Bosley when he left the room. He barely made it into the hall before his eyes smarted, and he quickly went into the bathroom and threw water on his face. That god-damned, foolish kid! He'd been a disapointment from the beginning. Luke ran the revolving towel over his face and then savagely wiped his hands. Had he failed the boy? He did not like to think about failure; that particular word was not familiar to the Heron family. Yet, as he looked back over his own life, he realized that there were times when he should have been strong when he was weak, and yes, he might as well admit it, strong when he should have been weak. He must be careful not to make the same mistake with Murdock that he had evidently made with Luke Three. It wasn't the most complimentary idea in the world, that he had caused his son so much pain that he had to run away. Yet that was what Luke Three had done—run away, perhaps from society, but also from a father who hadn't really been a father.

Luke squared his shoulders and went back into the conference room. He shoved Luke Three's letter into his pocket and then turned to Bosley. "Well," he said brusquely, "now that we've been invited to visit Muhammad Abn again, when are we going to leave for the kingdom of Saudia Arabia?"

"It will depend, I expect, on Mr. Truman. There's going to be a lot more fuel needed in Korea, plus all the big by-products. We've got to alert Robert Desmond, because he'll actually be in charge of Heron when you're gone." He paused meaningfully. "I never thought I'd live to see another war, my boy."

Luke shook his head. "Neither did I, Bos, neither did I."

22

The Revelation

Clement Story and his Cherokee Swing Orchestra had finished a fortnight series of one-night stands in England's provinces and returned to London.

They were having a holiday before heading back to New York when an excited Max called from the Music Corporation of America's Chicago office. The line was plagued by static.

"I've just received 'The Cowboy Waltz.' What in the hell happened?" he sputtered.

"Just calm down, Max," Clement replied calmly. Eerie waves of sound perambulated across the Atlantic, and Max's voice was momentarily lost; then a few words came through: "... drawl ... wailing horn ... sweet strings ..."

The line cleared, and Clement went on hurriedly before they were cut off again. "Max, I can't make heads or tails out of this conversation. What's wrong with the recording?"

"You doublecrossed me!" Max shouted clearly. "Are you trying to ruin your reputation? Sometimes I don't know what gets into you, Clem. I think we've got everything worked out, and then something like this comes up. I don't know why you don't listen to me; after all, I've guided your career for over twenty years."

"Max," Clement replied quietly, "now, let me have it from the top again. This connection is terrible. What's wrong?"

Max's voice became the personification of patience. He enunciated each word as if he had just taken a course in elocution. " 'The Cowboy Waltz' will do nothing for your career. You sound folksy."

Suddenly, what Max was saying made sense. Panic rose in Clement's throat. "Max," he demanded, "before I have a heart attack, please tell me that the record you received was a demo."

"Demo, hell, it's the real thing! Seventy-five thousand records have already been shipped all across the country."

Suddenly Clement knew with a terrible certainty what had happened. "Max, it's not my fault. The band cut the record that you've just heard, but it was a reject. We brought the Storyettes out of retirement to do a new arrangement—soft and sweet. Obviously the disk wax masters got mixed up, and the wrong disk was mass reproduced. Christ, nowadays you've got to be on top of everything! What time is it there? What? Ten P.M.? Do you have George Pollafox's home telephone number? Yes, I'll wait until you find it."

Clement smiled grimly. He could see Max in his big office overlooking the Loop, at eleven at night, trying to find a telephone number in his secretary's Rolodex. Max, waited upon by a raft of secretaries, could not even dial a telephone correctly by himself. Eventually he returned. He had found the number in Connecticut. Clement was not certain if they had been cut off or if Max had angrily hung up on him, but the line was dead. He hoped, for his own peace of mind, that the fault was inherent in Mr. Fulton's Atlantic Cable.

Sarah was driving to a luncheon date at the Wyandotte Hotel and listening to Dave Marks, her favorite disk jockey. He played three Sinatra records in a row, and was quickly losing favor with her, when his excited voice came over the air again. "Folks, while you've been listening to Frankie Boy, I've been hearing the new Clement Story record, 'The Cowboy Waltz.' You've never heard anything like it before! It's a complete switch by the wily old maestro. Could it be that the master of swing is changing his image? You be the judge."

Perplexed, and puzzled, Sarah turned up the volume on the car radio just as the opening bars blared out of the small speaker. She pulled over to the curb, but left the motor running so that she could still hear the radio. She waited for Clem's vocal. How had this terrible demo reached Dave Marks' console? True, he was a renowned jokester, but this bit of business was really rank. In the past, he'd been an enthusiastic supporter of Clement, but to have him pull some stupid publicity stunt was truly unworthy of his audience. Too soon, it seemed, his cheerful voice came back over the airwaves. "Remember, folks, you heard it here first. Now a word about compact roofing tiles . . ."

Sarah angrily switched off the radio, got out of the car, and went into a gasoline station across the street. She looked up the number of the radio station in the telephone book and dialed, then asked for Dave Marks. The most reachable disk jockey in the Midwest, he either answered the telephone himself, while playing records, or returned the call after the show. "Yes?"

She disguised her voice. "Who really was responsible for that 'Cowboy Waltz' record?"

"Clement Story, ma'am," he answered politely, the bombast that he used for his radio audience absent from his soft voice.

"You attributed it to him on the air, I know, but who *really* made the recording?"

He laughed easily. "I just told you, ma'am. No kidding, it's Clement Story. Sorry, gotta go." The line went dead.

Sarah searched in her purse for more coins, and, finding only a few pennies, asked the operator to connect her with Max's number in Chicago and charge the call to her home telephone. A moment later, Max's hoarse voice came over the wire. "Hi, Sarah, I've been on the phone since early last night. No sleep, and I'm dead. I finally got Clement in London. No one knows how it happened. George Pollafox is blaming it on quality control, but there may be sabotage in there somewhere. Anyway, his company is trying to recall all the records which were shipped to the stores, but several thousand have already been distributed, and I'm told disk jockeys all over the country, who always get theirs first, are having a field day."

"That's where I heard it," Sarah replied, throat tight, "right here on the Dave Marks Show in Kansas City."

"I must go, I've got two other calls on hold," Max said. "At this point I don't know what will happen, but we've got to get the rest of those disks back pronto."

Max pushed a button, and George Pollafox's voice came over the wire. The connection was so clear that he could have been in the next room. George was a man of few words. "Where were you, Max," he growled, "when the shit hit the fan?"

George Pollafox, president of BCR Records, woke up at seven-thirty in the morning; his head buzzed and his throat felt as if he had swallowed sand. He eased up on his elbows, and the room swam. He lay down again and called weakly to his wife, who came in a moment later from the kitchen.

"Honey," she said persuasively, "you must get up if you're going to catch the 8:05. Since your car is in the garage, I'll drive you to the station and then pick you up this evening." She smiled, a pretty woman, even without makeup and with her dark hair in curlers.

"I'm sick," he said, "so I won't be going in today."

She shook her head. "When will you learn that you can't drink cocktails? You've got to stick to straight bourbon. Want some orange juice?"

He nodded his prematurely gray head. "Of *all* days in the world to be ill, it would be today! I've got to get my brain functioning, there're so many calls to make."

After he had taken two foaming tablets and had drunk two cups of coffee, he felt slightly better. With two pillows supporting his upper back and head, he discovered that the room stayed in focus if he did not make any abrupt movements. At seven-forty the telephone rang. "Yes?" he answered weakly.

It was Tim Dextor, the marketing manager, whom he had known since they both worked in the mailroom at BCR. "Thank God I got you before you left home," Tim said, excitement building in his voice. "There's a groundswell building on 'The Cowboy Waltz.' I had three field reps call me from the coast—midnight their time. One DJ in Los Angeles has played the number for three hours straight! Everyone smells a hit. With action like this, we've got to okay another pressing this morning. We need a biggie right now. The first quarter is way down, and this looks like what we've been looking for."

"Isn't it ironic?" George croaked. "You realize we pressed the wrong record—the scrapped version—don't you?"

"Well," Tim expounded happily, "who cares? It's going great guns." His voice became concerned. "By the way, you sound like hell."

"I'm sick as a dog. I won't be in today. In fact, I can't even get out of bed. What a day for a landslide!"

"Imagine Clem Story having a runaway record at this stage of the game. He'll be ecstatic. Do you want me to call him?"

"He's in London. I spoke to him last night. His agent had been on the phone, raising hell. The version that was supposed to be pressed featured the Storyettes—remember them?"

"Well, George, everyone in the field thinks it's the greatest novelty since 'Three Little Fishies.' And let's face it, Clem Story is an institution. No one has been around longer, except maybe Paul Whiteman. Clem's records always sell moderately well to the same people, but this new vocal will reach a new generation, those kids who were born in early 'thirties—too young to go into the service. They'll eat it up!" He laughed. "You know, I'm not the easiest guy in the world to please, but even I like it. My wife says it's 'corny,' and I agree, but it's fun. Darryl, my seventeen-year-old, was waltzing around the breakfast table. Imagine kids waltzing today! Our local station played the number first thing after the news." There was a long pause. "Are you still there, George?"

"I'm here," came the gritty reply, "but I'm feeling dizzy. Not only from what you've told me, but my head is beginning to spin. Do you have Max's home number, Tim?"

"It won't do any good to call him at home. He's still at the office—or was a half-hour ago. He sounds worse than you do. He's not sick, but so hoarse he sounds like death warmed over."

"I'll call him," George replied, "if I can get up enough strength to dial."

"Call you later if I have more world-shattering news," Tim replied cheerfully and hung up.

After dialing MCA's Chicago number five times in succession and getting a busy signal, George finally got through. "This is Max," came the growl.

"This is George," he growled back.

Max snorted. "I don't appreciate being imitated!"

"Who's imitating whom? I'm sick in bed."

There was a low chuckle on the other end of the line.

"Then let's cut the horseshit and save our respective voices," Max croaked. "Have you gone into another pressing yet?'

"No, but we will, as soon as I get some figures in from marketing this morning. The plant is going to be operating around the clock."

Max cleared his throat and rasped, "I've had a complete change of heart. I've heard that record eight or ten times already, and you know, it grows on you. It's pure satire, and I don't think he overdoes it at all. Has Clem called you?"

"No."

"Well, he will! He's afraid that the band will become identified with this new Western sound, and that scares the hell out of him. He's become too damned conservative in his old age. Ten years ago he'd have stood on his head to promote a hit record or go into any new sound that smacked of the controversial. But he's changed since he was missing."

"Well, I guess having your plane shot down and not knowing who in the hell you were for eight months would affect anyone," George answered quickly. He liked Clement Story.

"We've got to push this strictly as a one-shot novelty."

"By the way, who did the arrangement? Has Sonny taken a new lease on life?"

"It wasn't Sonny, but some mixed-blood Cherokee kid Clement discovered and sent to music school. He not only did the orchestrations, but he wrote both the music and the lyrics. It's one of those flukey things that comes along once in a coon's age ..." Max ended the sentence with a siege of coughing. "I've got to get off here. Hope you feel better."

"You, too." George hung up, and the phone rang immediately. "Yes?"

It was Tim again, sounding like a high school quarterback who'd just won a football game. "The record just got into the stores on Friday, and by Saturday night most stores had sold out. The reorders are trickling in big from all over the East. We'll be hearing from the eleven Western states as soon as the stores open at twelve our time. What'll we go for on the pressing?"

"A hundred and fifty thou," George replied. "That way we won't be stuck if the public goes sour."

"Now who's being conservative? I'd go for more," Tim put in enthusiastically. "L.A. alone should sell twenty-five, if the trend keeps up."

"But that's our biggest market. I don't want warehouses full if the record bottoms out. We can always press more if it continues to build."

"All right," Tim replied reluctantly, "but ..."

"What you have to worry about is getting the record shipped as soon as they cool down. Also, I've got to call the production manager at the plant. The last time we had an overnight hit quality control slipped badly. We had thousands of records go out to the field with crooked labels. Boy, did RCA Victor laugh about that."

"Yeah"—Tim laughed—"that miserable hound Nipper was just jealous he didn't have a hit right then! 'His Master's Voice' indeed!"

"Don't poke fun at Nipper," George replied. "I only wish our logo was that well known!" He swallowed quickly. "Now, I've got to take some aspirin and try to get over this hangover. One of the biggest days in our company's history, and wouldn't you know that I'd be stretched out in bed?'

"Better sick in bed than sick in the head!" Tim quipped.

"Hang up, you son-of-a-bitch!" George exclaimed affectionately, heard the click in his ear, then left the receiver off the hook.

There were five overseas telephone calls clocked while Clement and the orchestra transcribed a broadcast in the plush new BBC Studios, which had been bombed out during the war. He appreciated the talents of the British engineers, who had installed the latest recording equipment. In fact, he had worked with two of the boys when in England during the war; they had shared an aircraft shelter when several raids had interrupted broadcasting.

Clement looked over the list of callers: Sarah, William Nestor, George Pollafox, Max, Ray Cornwallis. He went into one of the small reception rooms used for artists and asked the overseas operator to get him Universal Studios in North Hollywood. He liked and admired Corny, who had recently been promoted to a producer, and who had been his superior officer during the war years. Surprisingly, the call came through at once; one advantage of using the recording studio's telephone. They found him on Stage Four. After the usual greetings, Clem asked, "So what's on your mind? I assume it doesn't have anything to do with money, since you didn't say to call you back collect!"

Corny laughed. "*Au contraire.* When do you have to be back in the States?"

"We've tickets for an early morning flight tomorrow."

"That's not what I asked. *When* do you have to be back?"

"We've got an appearance in Milwaukee on the fifteenth, but I'm so tired I'm going to spend five days at home in K.C. before then. Why?"

"We're shooting a picture at Ellstree, under the Edy plan."

"A musical?"

"No, a comedy-drama, *Jubilee,* and it's supposed to wrap tomorrow. I've seen a rough cut already here at the studio, and it's a corker! Anyway, the character actress who's doing the hep grandmother—I forget her name, she's the only one in the whole cast who's British— is just wonderful. It's the kind of role that can earn an Academy nomination and add a hundred thou to the picture's grosses. So we've come up with a smash idea for an additional scene for her. She goes to a nightspot in Piccadilly, has too much champagne, and ends up tight as a drum, making a fool of herself on the dance floor."

Corny paused. "Now, this is where you come in, Clem. I heard 'The Cowboy Waltz' on the car radio coming to work this morning, and it's sensational. I want you to sing it in the nightclub for the drunk number."

"Whoa, Corny!" Clement exclaimed. "You're hitting me with all of this at once. You've had time to think, I haven't. As far as doing the number for the movie, I'm not sure I want to get involved."

"Are you out of your mind? You've got what looks to be the biggest hit of your life, and you 'don't want to become involved'!"

"Everyone in the business knows that novelties die out quick, just as soon as the tune becomes tiresome. Besides, by the time *Jubilee* is released 'The Cowboy Waltz' will be a dead duck as far as the public is concerned, and you'll be stuck with a number that's old hat."

"Clem Story," came the patient reply, "I've never known you to be so negative before. This picture has taken months to shoot, and it's practically put together. It'll be ready for release in two months, and if I'm correct in my reasoning, in eight weeks 'The Cowboy Waltz' will be at the top of the hit parade and help the movie—not that it needs strengthening, of course."

Clement paused. "I'll have to talk to Max."

"I already have. He's asking an arm and a leg and special billing."

"Well," Clement replied slowly, "when do we shoot?"

"Day after tomorrow for three days. The production manager will be in touch. They'll film right on location in Piccadilly."

"Oh, Christ!" Clement exclaimed.

"What's wrong?"

"You'll have to send over a recording of the number for us to use as playback. I don't have any with me."

"I'll ship it over by air. By the way, who did the arrangement for 'The Cowboy Waltz?'"

"A twenty-three-year-old part-Cherokee, from Willawa, Oklahoma, who also wrote the music and the lyrics."

Corny whistled. "If all of his stuff is as inventive, he's got a helluva future. What else has he done for you?"

"It's a long story. He's just learned to read and write music."

"Got him under wraps, huh? I'd like to meet him."

"Oh, no, you don't, Corny. I found this kid, and I'm not going to have him end up working on arrangements for the studio orchestra. That would be slow death for this boy. He's got too much on the ball."

"Okay. Forget I asked. By the way, when are you coming out to Hollywood?"

"Not for a long time. I go into a series of one-night stands, then home to K.C., where I'll probably go to bed for a week!"

"With Sarah?"

"Amen. Frankly, I'm tired of going to bed with myself."

Sarah straightened the pillow in back of Clement's head. "How did the picture and the one-night stands go, darling?" she asked sleepily.

"A breeze," he replied, running his hand along her thigh. "But I have the feeling that all this hoopla isn't going to last very much longer. The business is changing all the time. Big nightclubs are closing everywhere, and those that are still around are charging an arm and a leg. If this keeps up, my pet, it'll get to the point where ordinary people won't be able to pay the tab, and big bands cost big money. If the hotel business ever falls off, we're going to be in big trouble. And if the ballrooms ever close up, we've had it." He laughed. "Of course, I shouldn't complain, because having a hit song doesn't hurt. Really, Sarah, you know I always did 'The Old Chisholm Trail' as my last number. Well, I end the show with 'The Cowboy Waltz' now, and the audience just explodes."

She rumpled his hair and looked up into his face. "You could have taken me along," she answered. "It's not much fun here in the house alone."

"You know," he remonstrated, "it's my policy not to allow wives on these one-nighters. Besides, there's no room on the bus—which, by the way, is getting a new paint job in Tulsa." He kissed her ankle as he always did, moving the light golden bracelet and the heart-shaped diamond with his teeth. The telephone rang, and he looked up apologetically. "I'm not going to answer it," he said, kissing the back of her knee.

There was another ring, and Sarah reached over to the nightstand and removed the receiver, then lay back on the pillow. "Clem! Clem!" Max Rabinovich's voice boomed out of the instrument.

Sarah looked at Clement and mouthed, "Should I hang up?"

He shook his head.

She sighed and picked up the receiver. "Hello, Max." She paused. "Yes, he's here. Just a moment."

Clement stretched out on his back beside Sarah and growled into the instrument, "Yes?"

"Howdy, Clem. How's the weather?"

Clement could visualize Max, slouched down in his big leather chair, the black Chicago skyline behind him, his feet on the desk, a cigar dangling between thumb and forefinger. "You should be shot at sunrise," he retorted, "if you called me up just to talk about the weather!"

Max laughed. "Well, actually, I did have something else in mind. Do you ever watch that audio-video set that I gave you for Christmas?"

"I would if there were any programs worth watching and if I was ever home long enough," Clement replied. "But once in a while I do like to make love to my wife."

There was a pause at the other end of the line. "Like now?" Max asked quietly.

"Yes," Clement replied in the same tone of voice.

"I *am* sorry. I'll call back."

"No, now that you're on the line, what's so terribly important?"

"Television. Seriously, do you ever watch it?"

Clement sighed audibly. "The programs are about as interesting as fourth-grade arithmetic. I have more important things to do."

"Like making love to Sarah, I know." Max countered smoothly, then paused a moment. "You know Ed Sullivan, don't you?"

"Sure," Clement replied, "he's a nice guy—for a columnist."

"He's done all right by you, hasn't he?"

"I guess so." He turned to Sarah. "You keep track of all the press clippings. Ed Sullivan's okay, isn't he?"

She leaned her chin on his shoulder, and her voice was very soft. "All those months that you were lost after your plane went down, he was the only columnist who raised doubts about your being dead. He mentioned you often in his 'Toast of the Town' column. I was always grateful to him for that."

"Max, Sarah says he's fine in her book. Now, why all this third degree?"

"Well, my boy, Sullivan is very big, believe me. He'd like you and the band to come on in a couple of weeks. He wants you to do 'Cowboy.'"

"You don't think this would conflict with my radio show, Max?"

"There is no clause in your contract that prohibits audio-video."

"How much is he willing to pay?"

Max cleared his throat. "Now, I don't think that's important."

Clement laughed. "That's the first time I've heard you make that statement, and you've handled me for twenty years!"

"Don't be sarcastic, you bastard," Max retorted humorously. "What's important is the exposure. It's like this, Clem," Max went on persuasively. "You're doing that crippled children's benefit in New Jersey on Saturday, the third, so you could easily do Ed's show on the Fourth of July."

"But I wanted to be home for the holiday. Luke's having the company plane pick me up in Newark and fly me to the farm in Angel. You should know by now that Mother and Bos always like to have the family home for the big days. The Fourth of July is always big in Oklahoma—lots of firecrackers."

There was a pause on the other end of the line, and Clement knew that Max was chewing his cigar. "This Sullivan appearance is a big opportunity, Clem," he said quietly. "The sooner you get exposure on audio-video, the better, because television, sooner or later, is going to cut into all forms of entertainment. As soon as cable can be stretched across the country, there'll be good programming, and millions of people will be glued to their sets. Do you know how much business taverns that have sets do? Get in on the ground floor." He went on persuasively, "Look, is it okay if I fix it up with the family?"

"No, Max, I'm going to be home for the Fourth of July. You can tell Ed ..." Clement ran his hand over the back of Sarah's head.

"Okay, Clem." Max's voice was cold, distant, no longer interested. He hung up, and Clem rested the instrument on the pillow, his mind racing.

"Remember me?" Sarah asked softly.

He looked down at her as if she were a stranger, then

smiled suddenly. "Sorry, Squaw, I was just thinking." He reached down and kissed her cheek. "I'm awfully hungry," he said. "Would you scramble me an egg or two?"

She nodded and got up slowly, and ten minutes later, when she came into the bedroom with the tray of food, he was asleep. She sat down on the bed and looked at his homely, lined face, and in that private moment she loved him even more. He was such a very special man, she would admire and respect him even if he were not her husband.

That night after dinner, when they were back in bed, the phone rang and when Sarah moved to answer it Clem shook his head. "I don't want to talk to anyone. It's probably Max."

She looked up apologetically. "Patricia Anne was supposed to call."

He nodded. "Okay. I *do* want to talk to her. Remember, I have a gig in Washington the second week in August, and I'd like Lars and her to come to the opening. That is, if he can tear himself away from the lab."

Sarah was on the line. "Of course, Mother." She glanced at Clement. "You're wanted, Hotshot."

He laughed and pinched her on the thigh. Letty's voice came over the wire strongly as he cradled the instrument between his neck and his head. He listened intently, lit a cigarette, took a puff, and blew the smoke out all at once. "But we were looking forward to seeing the family, Mama. Luke is giving me use of the company plane."

"You know, son," Letty was saying with conviction, "I've always made myself scarce as far as your career goes, but if Max thinks it's so important to perform on audio-video in New York, I think you should do it. Now, I'm going to hang up and you call that nice Mr. Max."

"Mama," Clement replied heatedly, "I don't appreciate Max involving himself in family affairs!"

"Good-bye, Mama," He hung up, and then dialed

Max's home telephone number in Oak Park, Illinois, but there was no answer. He threw the instrument in its cradle. "The bastard is not answering! He knows damn well I'm calling." He snubbed out his cigarette angrily. "Imagine, calling the family for support!"

"He's never done that before, Clem," Sarah put in gently. "Don't you think you should take a consensus from the members of the band? This television thing appears to be an important issue."

"I make the band decisions, no one else. To them, it's just another gig."

She placed her arm around his shoulders and lay on his pillow. "Is it, Clem? I read somewhere that they think that by nineteen-fifty-five there'll be three million sets all over the country."

He glanced at her, his brow furrowed. "So Max got to you, too!"

She broke away from him and did not reply.

"This is an absolute conspiracy!" Clement spat out. "You'd think I was Peck's Bad Boy. My God, I'm sick and tired of being badgered. Now, for certain, I'm not going to do the damned show!" He turned on his side, away from her. "Would you make me a cup of hot cocoa? It's about the only thing that works when I want to sleep. I'm exhausted. And once and for all, I'm not doing the 'Toast of the Town' show!"

The bus with the huge Clement Story banner headed up Thirty-ninth Street in Manhattan, then turned and parked behind the Maxine Elliott Theatre. It was twelve o'clock, an hour before dress rehearsal for the "Toast of the Town" show. The program had been blocked out and rehearsed the day before, and Clement and the band were scheduled for two numbers, "Lady Luck," which would be sung by the Storyettes, who had been reunited by Ed Sullivan for the appearance, and Clement was to sing "The Cowboy Waltz."

"I'd love for you to do more," Ed Sullivan had told Clement over the telephone the week before, "but it's difficult to feature an orchestra which is known primarily as a dance band in musical numbers. The audience will want to dance in the aisles."

"I understand perfectly. You're running what is, essentially, a vaudeville show," Clement had said, "and it's got to have pace. A lot of orchestra music, with no action, would kill the show. You know, Ed, I've made a lot of those filmed musical shorts. And the studios always thought that they were audience pleasers—and maybe they were—because they always received good applause. But, studying various movie crowds, I'd say that a good portion of all that handclapping was because the shorts were *over!*"

"You may be right." Sullivan had laughed. "I wish more people were as professional as you, Clem. When I cut their acts, most performers cry bloody murder."

In the dressing rooms, the boys in the band changed into cream-colored suits as Clement slipped into his dark suit; then they submitted to a quick wash of pancake makeup and took seats backstage. The Storyettes, wearing black-and-pale-blue evening gowns especially designed for the show because blue photographed white, stood nearby on leaning boards so that their skirts would not wrinkle. In a way, Clement thought, the hectic activity going on all around them was very much like a movie set, except for the unmistakable backstage odor of greasepaint, sweat, and musty scenery.

Ed Sullivan was announced, made his entrance, and was greeted with a wave of applause from the audience. He took his position at the left side of the stage. Clement was aware that there would be a new audience when the show was performed live that night at nine o'clock. For all intents and purposes, the "dress rehearsal" might not be the show finally televised. Max had told him that comedy routines might be cut several minutes if certain jokes did not go over, or acts reprogrammed to improve the pace of the show. As it now stood, the orchestra was to go on last, which was the star spot—not like vaudeville, where next-to-closing featured the headliner.

"Sullivan's tough as hell to work for," Max warned him on the telephone, "but remember that whole show rests on Old Stoneface's shoulders."

The audience was extremely appreciative, if not "hot," Clement thought, from the sound of the applause. But the show seemed interminable, and the acts long and drawn-out. The stage manager finally guided Clement, the Storyettes, and the band onstage, while a troup of jugglers performed in front of the curtain.

Clement waited for the stage manager's signal, and it seemed an eternity before he signaled "get ready." Ed Sullivan said, "Ladies and gentlemen, tonight marks a special occasion. For this performance only, the four girls who were featured with Clement Story and his Cherokee Swing Band have been reunited. Here are the Storyettes singing the band's signature tune, 'Lady Luck.' "

Clement gave the downbeat, Tracy Newcomb started the introduction on the piano, the gold curtain swished back, and the girls came forward to mild applause and sang the number, just as they had performed for the ten years that they had been with the band. After the applause, Ed Sullivan held up his hands. "Now, ladies and gentlemen, what you've been waiting for—Clement Story singing his hit song, 'The Cowboy Waltz.' "

Clement put on a ten-gallon hat, picked up his guitar, and walked to the microphone. To a clippity-clop beat from the orchestra, he sang, enunciating the lyric more clearly than on the recording. His face glowed, and he was almost handsome. The band came in with the chorus:

Teenage cats in Stetson hats,
College frats in sheepskin chaps,
Three-piece suits in roun'-tip boots,
Middle-aged curs in silver spurs,
Foreign dudes are havin' feuds,
All sippin' malts, discussin' faults
And doin'—the Cowboy, yes, doin' the COWBOY WALTZ*!*

He bowed from the waist, and Ed Sullivan bade the audience good night. The closing credits were run off quickly. A buzzer sounded, and the stage manager shouted, "That's it!"

Later, in the dressing room, Sullivan looked in quickly. "Only one change, Clem. We think it's better if Tracy starts the intro to 'Lady Luck' as I say: 'Here are the Storyettes, blah blah blah,' instead of when the curtain opens. This will prepare the audience. This afternoon's opening was too cold."

"Gotcha!" Clem said.

Ed Sullivan gave a rare smile. "By the way, that 'Cowboy Waltz' is a helluva tune!"

23

The Land of Hijaz

The newly polished 1934 black Cadillac limousine was parked on the street.

The chauffeur, a small sunburned man in a gray English uniform, which was somewhat faded and frayed so that it looked as if it could have come from a costumer, stood at the open door. Managing a rather good British salute, he bowed slightly and recited, "Greetings from Jeddah, dear and honored guests, enter, please, the automobile of Sheik Muhammad at-Ta'if Abn."

Luke nodded and replied politely, "Thank you. It is our pleasure to be escorted."

The interior of the car smelled strongly of incense, and the floor was carpeted with the fur of some short-haired dark animal. The chauffeur packed their suitcases in the trunk, saluted them again with his open palm at eye level, then slammed the door of the Cadillac sharply and proceeded down the narrow street at a pace of fifteen miles an hour. He continued the snail's pace until he passed a maze of small airport buildings, then stepped on the gasoline pedal suddenly as he turned into a wide thoroughfare. The limousine shot forward at sixty miles an hour.

Luke and Bosley tensed and grabbed the handstraps as the chauffeur swung the long car as if dodging objects on an obstacle course, barely missing pedestrians, camels, and the few automobiles, all of which seemed to be crisscrossing at every point along the route. He kept his foot on the gas pedal, his eyes on the road, and his hand on the horn.

"I'm afraid to look, and I'm afraid to close my eyes!" Bosley exclaimed, throwing Luke a quick glance. "Is your last will and testament up to date!"

"I only hope that Muhammad Abn lives near. I can feel my hair going white."

From what they could see of Jeddah, the town was a curious mixture of stark Western and elaborate Moorish architecture. Small wood and cement block buildings were being erected among five- and six-story "skyscrapers." Luckily, the traffic thinned, and while the driver did not slow down, there was less likelihood of an accident, although he had to brake suddenly when a group of white-clad men fanned across an unmarked intersection. They saw that the high walls that had once surrounded the city were being demolished.

The limousine was now traveling on a narrow, recently graveled road, sparsely lined with scrub trees, and all that could be heard was the sharp din of small pebbles being thrown up by the tires and cascading in a clatter against the sides of the car.

The chauffeur turned into a side road and parked neatly in front of a series of old buildings trimmed in mosiacs, which were separated by courtyards. "Do you have your phrases memorized?" Bosley asked.

Luke nodded. "Since it's morning, I had to learn a new set of greetings. When Muhammad was entertained by the State Department in Washington, the reception was held in the late afternoon, which required other formalities. By the way, Uncle Bos, don't inquire about his wife. It's considered bad form to mention women. In fact, we probably will not see the female members of the household."

"I wonder what Muhammad Abn thinks about the Western woman who takes her place in society beside her husband?"

"Since he went to school at Cambridge and has traveled a good deal, he's accustomed to our ways, of course, but I imagine it's quite a relief for him to return to his own country, where he only competes with other men. You know, I'm not so sure that the Middle Eastern way of life is all that old-fashioned. It is truly a male-dominated society." He laughed. "Sometimes when Jeanette's acting up, I'd love to say, 'Oh, shut up, woman'!"

"Well, don't you?"

"Yes, but of course she never does! Over here, she'd never think of crossing me in the first place!"

The chauffeur opened the door of the limousine, and they stepped out on an intricately patterned maroon-and-gold rug that led up to the huge door of the house. "You can't say we're not getting the royal carpet treatment," Luke whispered, nudging Bosley.

The door was opened by a smiling male servant dressed in a softly flowing white garment that wound down from the head. The small foyer was tiled, so their footfalls announced their presence as they followed the servant to another door, which he soundlessly pushed to disclose a large white room, devoid of furniture.

A tall man in robes, with his head covered with the traditional burnoose, rose from several enormous cushions. The floor was covered with several rugs woven with some of the most beautiful muted colors that Luke had ever seen.

Muhammad Abn bowed. *"is-salaam 'alaykum,"* he said formally.

Luke bowed. *"wa-'alaykum is-salaam."* He paused, and added, *"sabaah il-khayr,"* which was the traditional morning greeting.

"sabaah in-nuwr," Muhammad Abn replied courteously.

"kayf haalak?" Luke asked, which meant, "How are you?"

"tayyib, il-hamdu lillaah!" Muhammad Abn replied, meaning, "Fine, praise be to Allah."

There was a pause, and then it seemed that Muhammad Abn stepped into the twentieth century. Gone was his formal manner as he smiled and shook hands.

"My dear friend Luke," he said in his Cambridge accent, "welcome to the kingdom." He shook hands with Bosley. "Good to see you again, sir, it has been much too long." He clapped his hands once and spoke to the servant, who brought in two Western chairs. "Please sit down," he said, retiring to his high cushions on the floor.

Immediately another servant brought in steaming bowls of coffee flavored with cardamom. The taste was very exotic, and although Luke did not care for the mixture, he knew that they must have two cups or four cups, but not three, which was considered impolite.

"I hope that you had a pleasant journey," Muhammad Abn said, smoothing his black goatee.

Luke nodded. "I had forgotten from our trip here in nineteen-thirty-eight that you are located halfway around the world. I noticed many changes in Jeddah."

"Yes, while there is building now, there is much more to come as more petroleum is discovered and wealth comes into the kingdom. Our great problem is the dollar exchange. I must give you some background so that you can understand our predicament. Our finance minister in the early nineteen-thirties, 'Abd Allah as-Sulayman, was negotiating with Britisher Lloyd N. Hamilton concerning what has become the Arabian American Oil Company. The agreement stipulated that the kingdom was to receive four shillings of gold per ton of crude oil gathered."

Bosley nodded. "This was shortly before President

Franklin D. Roosevelt closed the banks and went off the gold standard." He sipped the coffee, making a small noise of appreciation.

"Gold, of course," the sheik continued, "is a universal exchange, the dollar or the pound sterling is not. So we are at the point now where we must exchange our dollars and our pounds for services and expertise from the outside." He placed the empty cup on a small table, and the servant offered more coffee which they all formally accepted.

"Do you know that at the present time we have only about fifty-two kilometers of paved roads in the entire kingdom? Everywhere there are improvements to be made, and we are a people not known for our cleverness in administration. Our leaders have much catching up to do, and very little money at the present time. Our only railroad, built by Aramco, from ad-Dammam on the gulf to our capital, Riyadh, a distance of some three hundred and seventy-five miles, will not be completed until later this year, and far from finished is Tapline, a giant oil pipeline which will eventually run seven hundred and fifty-four miles from Sidon to Qaisumah. Our airports are too small and must be enlarged. Jeddah, which is the gateway to our holy cities of Mecca and Medina, must be improved, the harbor expanded and dredged to accommodate large tankers. In the past, this was only a tourist city, because of pilgrims coming through to visit Mecca."

"Aren't most of the recent oil discoveries around the gulf?" Bosley asked.

"Yes, but there are other areas that we would like explored. We are now reviewing some of the concessions given out over the years, and plan to take back some of them. Tomorrow, if you like, we will take a truck into the Wadi Fatimah, a large watercourse to the south. It is a desolate area, almost as primitive as the

Wadi ad-Dawasir, which leads into the Rub' al-Khali, the immense sand dunes to the south."

"I've studied geological maps of the kingdom," Bosley said, "but they are far from complete."

The servant appeared and took away the cups of coffee, replacing them with cups of tea, which they sipped appreciatively before continuing the conversation.

"Little of the Red Sea area of our country has been mapped, because the Arabian Gulf offered its riches first."

When they had finished the tea, Muhammad Abn rose gracefully from his sitting position. "If you would like to rest, your rooms await. I have production reports for you both to peruse, and therefore I shall have luncheon sent to you. A bell will sound shortly after sunset, when we will have dinner."

Luke searched for the word for "thank you." *"mashkuwr,"* he said at last. There were two other words that also meant "thank you," *shukran* and *ashkurak,* but he did not know which was correct.

Muhammad Abn smiled. *"mamnuwn,"* he replied, which Luke knew meant "you're welcome."

As the servant led them down a wide hall to their quarters, Luke whispered to Bosley, "Do you think he is giving us the bum's rush?"

"No," Bosley whispered back, "he merely wants us to *work!*"

After a dinner of roast lamb, vegetables, and fruit for dessert, which was served at a low table brought in for the occasion, Muhammad Abn brushed his lips with his napkin and nodded. "We Orientals are accustomed to sitting on the floor, which I realize is not as easy for the Western bottom. Soon I will build a new house. I plan to achieve something extraordinary." He glanced from Luke to Bosley in expectation. "It is going to be a very large house, because I have many relatives, but there is going to be a section complete with Western furniture. Since the house will be electrified, I shall also display modern appliances. I wish my children to grow up with both cultures; then they will not have the difficulty I encountered when I first went to England to college." He bowed his head and went on proudly, "My sons and daughters will be educated abroad. The boys in the United States and the girls in Switzerland." He paused. "Your own childhood must have been extraordinary, Luke. I remember very fondly those days spent at your farm and the delicious food that was prepared for me by your mother. I hope she keeps well."

"She is fine," Luke replied, surprised that the sheik would speak of the female gender; yet it was logical, since he had spent time with them.

"There was a delicacy that I especially recall with respect. It was called . . . Heaven?"

"You mean *Angel*." Bosley smiled. "Angel cake."

"I wish my kitchen servant knew the formula."

"I've seen Letty make the cake many times. I know the recipe, although I don't know whether you have all of the ingredients. There are eggs . . ."

"We have poultry."

"Flour, white sugar, and baking powder." He paused thoughtfully. "If you don't have the latter, a local chemist could make a compound composed of sodium aluminum sulfate, calcium sulfate, and calcium acid phosphate, which are leavening ingredients, suspended in simple cornstarch—which I believe is sometimes used here in the Middle East as a dusting powder."

"Thank you, Bosley. Tell me, how is that distinctive shape acquired?"

"The batter is baked in a 'tube pan.' If your kitchen servant has an ordinary high pan, a tin can can be placed in the middle and the batter poured around it, and the same results will be achieved."

Muhammad Abn raised his hand in a gesture not

unlike that once used by George Story. "Normally I do not concern myself with domestic matters—but with such delightful food, the Prophet Muhammad himself would have inquired."

Luke leaned forward. "I hope that it is not impolite to ask what may be a strange question, but are you related to the holy man of whom you just spoke?" He had phrased his inquiry in such a way as not to use the prophet's name, if that was forbidden.

Muhammad Abn nodded gravely. "I am indeed fortunate to be a descendant. You are familiar with only part of my name, which is very long indeed. From Arabic names one can tell a great deal. It is possible to glean a person's forebears, the city in which he was born, and the father's or even sometimes the grandfather's name, as well as his title, if any. It is much the same as in your country, where the name Stone refers to one's ancestor who worked in stone, for instance, or the name of Heron, which is a rare and beautiful bird."

"It is very possible," Luke answered. "The name is the same?"

Muhammad Abn turned to Bosley. "Have you learned anything from the maps?"

Bosley smiled. The small talk was over; now the business would begin. "Yes, a very great deal. Since your country has many 'salt plugs,' there must also be salt domes. I'm familiar with the drilling methods used with this type of substructure because the giant Spindletop Dome in Beaumont, Texas, is very similar."

"There are sand dunes in Texas?"

"No, but the substructure underneath, so near the Gulf of Mexico, resembles the Arabian Gulf. In prehistoric times water extended up to Cairo and beyond, and when the lake receded down into Persia, where we are now, it left the Tigris and the Euphrates Rivers."

"Ah!" Muhammad Abn exclaimed. "Why have not I heard of this? The geologists I know never explain. They say, 'I suspect the oil is there,' or 'Let us drill in that location,' but they do not give reasons."

"If you are interested, I shall be pleased to give you more information when we explore the Wadi Fatimah."

After a breakfast of scrambled eggs, a farina-type mound that resembled mashed potatoes, and coffee, served in their rooms, a bell sounded, and when Luke and Bosley left their sanctuaries, Muhammad Abn greeted them at the door of the living room.

The house servants had packed food and water into a World War II jeep, burned incense in the cab, and arranged cushions in the back seat. They also set up a canvas over the top poles to keep out the sun.

Before climbing into the vehicle, Muhammad Abn presented Luke and Bosley with pith helmets and smiled. "These you will find more comfortable, I think, than a burnoose." He pointed to his headgear. "Both will reflect the sun. Even with all of our precautions, when the temperature climbs over one hundred degrees there are many cases of sunstroke." He laughed. "Many of our people are so brown from the sun, they look as if they were Ethiopians. When we spend much time abroad, our skin fades, and most of us are quite fair."

Luke had awakened during the night in a cold sweat, dreading the trip into the Wadi Fatimah. If the chauffeur had driven so badly in the city, what would he be like in open country? But it was a new man, not so polite as the first one but a much better driver, Luke thought. He headed the jeep into the small street by Muhammad Abn's house; he looked both ways, although there was no traffic anywhere, and continued to drive carefully and slowly, so that the bumps in the road were minimized.

Although it was very early in the morning, they passed several long caravans of buses, and finally the driver had to stop to allow passage. "Those are pilgrims on the way to the holy city," Muhammad Abn explained.

"As every Roman Catholic would like to go to the Vatican, so does every Muslim wish to visit the holy place. I will not trouble you with the rituals involved, but they are very complex indeed."

"How far *is* Mecca?" Bosley asked.

"Forty-six miles. But non-Muslims are not permitted within the holy city. The route, not too long ago, was traversed only by camel or on foot. The government has tried to make it easier for the foreign pilgrims, because our ways are strange to them also. There are guides called *mutawwifs,* who take charge of groups to be transported to the holy city and instruct them in *thram*— which is our holy state of purity—before they proceed to Mecca. Last year, over a quarter of a million pilgrims came through Jeddah."

The street had widened now as they reached a huge gate of stone and iron and stopped briefly to let a camel caravan pass. "This is the Mecca Gate," Muhammad Abri explained.

"What are the chants we hear?" Luke asked.

"They are exclaiming one word, *labbayka,* which means 'Here I am at Your service,' which sounds like a chant to you. They say this word many times on the way to Mecca."

Soon they were passing the walls of the city, which were being demolished. "What is all this work?" Bosley asked.

"Expansion!" Muhammad Abn replied enthusiastically. "The city has nowhere to grow, so we are making room for new additions. In a few short years, Jeddah will be a great seaport, but first, if the new giant tankers are to traverse the Red Sea, the Suez Canal must be deepened. Our petroleum reserves must be immense indeed to make this feasible."

They were in the open desert now, and the mountains in the background were noble and majestic and the sands pinkish-red, dotted with brush. Tiny pink-and-white flowers grew in small clusters. "It is always this way after a rain," Muhammad Abn remarked softly. "The seasons change every day of the year, it seems. The desert is poetic. There is every color of the rainbow, from the magnificent blue and purple mountains to the splendid Red Sea and sand."

"Which is caused from iron oxide stain," Bosley put in dryly.

"You take away all of the beauty," Luke said, "when you make a statement like that."

The sheik nodded. "Some people think this land is arid and dry and can see no beauty here, but we, who have lived here all of our lives, know otherwise. I love to see the greenery in Britain and the United States. It is most expeditious to have good rainfall throughout the year, but the poorest European country is more progressive than my own, yet when I come back to the kingdom after a trip abroad, it is as if I am returning to the true land of Allah."

Bosley drew in his breath, and a sigh escaped his throat. "I am glad to hear a young man speak like you do," he said. "I feel the same way about Oklahoma. After being in Washington in the company of important people, and seeing the sights, it's very nice to come home and watch the sun go down. In summer we have a long twilight that turns everything golden for a long time, and there's nothing quite like the first autumn chill. Yes, I know what you mean." He roused himself. "Let's stop up ahead on that flat slope."

Muhammad Abn spoke in quick Parsi to the driver, who selected a flat area on which to park, and Bosley unrolled a map.

"We are entering the Wadi Fatimah," Muhammad Abn explained, pointing to a huge ravine.

"With the watershed running down from those mountains," Bosley explained, "it's unlikely that an anticline runs underneath. The quickest and simplest way to find out the substructure is to use both a gravity meter and magnetmeter. Refraction surveying can also be utilized."

"What is *that*?" Muhammad Abn leaned forward.

"Charges placed below ground are set off, and the vibrations penetrating below are measured by an instrument called a seismograph." Bosley indicated the map on his lap. "This way, we can also determine the substructure, which gives a clue if there are oil sands."

Muhammad Abn shook his head. "No one has explained these things to me. This is one of the great problems." He pulled at his goatee and pushed his headgear back from his face. "We are much indebted to the foreign oil concerns, because, of course, we do not have the technology to drill for oil ourselves, but when we make arrangements so that they can have concessions—which is actually giving them *carte blanche*—they survey and explore and drill very expertly, but they do not explain how these things are done." He paused, and his face saddened. "Of course, most of my brothers are uneducated and would not understand even the simplest explanation, but there are others of us who feel we have a right to know. That is why you are so valuable, Bosley."

"Thank you," Bosley replied earnestly, "but I'm an old man, and while I know the *theory* behind what Heron is able to accomplish geologically, I am still not up on all of the new technologies. Remember, I am retired from Heron."

"You are altogether too modest, my friend," Muhammad Abn said. "You can give me the basic background that I need."

"Look," Luke said, "there is a camel caravan below in the wash."

Muhammad Abn nodded. "It is a group of Bedouins, actually, who will follow the camel caravan into the foothills, where they will separate and probably go northward. Soon, you will see flocks of sheep. About thirty-five or forty percent of our people are nomadic, and the percentage used to be much higher. But the cities are attracting some of the younger tribal members who do not want to herd animals as their fathers and their fathers' fathers have done. They want higher learning. Hopefully, in the future we will have universities at Riyadh, Dhahran, ad-Dammam, and possibly Jeddah. If Allah is willing, I will live to see these changes." He paused and gave directions to the driver, who negotiated a neat turn and started down a curved watercourse into the Wadi Fatimah proper.

The trio returned at ten o'clock next morning from a productive day of exploration into the Wadi Fatimah, tired and dusty, and went to their rooms to change. They had spent the night in a large, spacious tent erected in advance by a retinue of servants who had followed them in two World War II jeeps piled with bags of bedding, boxes of food, and an assortment of supplies—including a hubble-bubble pipe which Muhammad Abn had enjoyed after evening prayers the night before.

Their host had asked them to meet in the hall at two o'clock, and they were surprised to see him dressed in traditional robes. They were a few moments early, and Bosley, glancing out at the blue-tiled center courtyard, drew Luke's attention to a scene that surprised them both. Muhammad Abn was seated on the polished squares, reading to a large group of children, also dressed in white burnooses with white head coverings. Occasionally Muhammad Abn would glance up, and there was a beatific look on his face, a soft expression that neither Luke Three nor Bosley had ever seen before. They turned away because the setting was so private and personal that they felt like the intruders that they were.

They had just seated themselves in the Western chairs

when their host swept into the room. "I'm a few moments late because I was reading the Koran to my children and time slipped away. I try to spend as much time as I can with them; they are small such a short time, and it seems that adulthood comes much too quickly."

Since the sheik had brought up the subject of his children, and it would not seem that a question was out of order, Bosley asked, "How many do you have?"

Muhammad Abn smiled with paternal affection. "Seventeen."

Bosley kept his composure. "How many boys?"

"Allah was kind," was the reply, "twelve boys, only five girls." Then, sensing that perhaps there would be additional questions, he continued, "The journey is not far, but I believe we should start."

When they were ensconced in the limousine, he sighed gently and pulled at his beard. "I have just spoken with my father, and I should explain the routine of the afternoon to you. As you know, your presence has been requested at the meal . . ."

Muhammad Abn paused reflectively, and it was obvious that he was choosing his words with great care as he continued. "He is approaching his ninety-seventh birthday and is not well. I volunteered to act as host for him today, but he insists that he will be able to carry on." He frowned slightly and again smoothed his beard. "Also, he has requested that we return to the residence for coffee and dessert." He took Luke's arm and looked into his face. "This ceremony he believes to be Western, and from his association with the British many years ago, he was occasionally invited for tea." Muhammad Abn averted his eyes. "He is old, and his body is frail, as is sometimes his mind."

Luke nodded, aware of how difficult it was for Muhammad Abn to speak so confidentially. "I understand."

"He is a traditionalist, yet he has tried to modernize

his ways, but in reveries he is often in the time of his youth." As the limousine braked, Muhammad Abn roused. "Ah, here we are."

They were parked near a large grove of trees which featured a wide, sandy path that meandered through huge beds of cacti bearing large cerise blossoms. There was a heavy fragrance in the air, which Luke at first thought came from the flowers, until he realized that the pungent odor was the exotic aroma of incense wafting down the uncluttered pathway.

Two men dressed in white robes and flowing head-gear ambled out of the woods, and Luke and Bosley were startled to see holstered pistols attached to long belts slung over their shoulders. Muhammad Abn acknowledged the guards but did not explain their presence. It was the first time since they had been in Saudi Arabia that the sheik's personal protection had been obvious. Although there was certainly nothing menacing about the guards' presence, the firearms stood out starkly against their white garments.

As the trio walked slowly up to the clearing in the distance, the fine white sand underfoot deadening their footfalls, Muhammad Abn placed his hands behind his back and spoke in a low voice. "You will meet many family members this afternoon, too many to introduce by"—he chuckled—"name, rank, and serial number!" Having made his little joke, he went on, "Also, I will dispense with the traditional greetings for each person, with the exception of my father. Introductions, other than his, will be Western style. It will simplify the proceedings considerably; otherwise our afternoon picnic could turn into the evening meal!"

"Which reminds me," Luke said with some embarrassment, "I know the words for evening, but not afternoon."

"Oh," Muhammad Abn explained quickly, "*masaa' il-khayr* means either afternoon *or* evening."

They had now reached a clearing in the woods, which had been spread with the same fine white sand as the pathway. A twenty-five-foot hand-loomed rug with an intricate Persian design in blues, greens, and reds had been unrolled in the middle of the treeless space and the center spread with a long silver damask cloth, which gleamed in the sunlight filtered through the tree branches surrounding the clearing. It was a charming pastoral scene, made exotic only by the heavy smell of incense, which drifted upward from several small brass burners.

Muhammad Abn looked critically at the scene. "The incense is necessary," he elucidated, "because kitchen servants are nearby, cooking on braziers, and although food odors can be most pleasing on occasion, a sweet smell is preferable."

"Yes indeed." The remark, actually a loud whisper, was threaded with a heavy English accent and came from behind, yet they had not been aware of anyone approaching.

"I should like you to meet my father," Muhammad Abn said quietly, and they turned. At first Luke and Bosley were only aware of voluminous flowing robes; then it became apparent that there were actually three men, standing so close together that their robes seemed to be entwined. In the center was a man so ancient and frail that the skin on his face resembled rare parchment. His sparse mustache and beard were the color of pewter. Tiny eyes, encased in pale folds of skin, were piercing, darting nervously everywhere. They looked like small black jumping beans. His mouth was a thin slit, without lips. It was, Luke thought, a cruel face.

"*is-salaam 'alaykum.*" The universal Arab greeting was uttered in the low voice, seemingly summoned up from the depths of the man.

"*wa-'alaykum is-salaam,*" Luke replied.

"*masaa' il-khayr.*"

Luke nodded. "*masaa' in-nuwr.*"

"I should like you to meet my father, Luke Heron."

The men shook hands solemnly; then the old man turned to Bosley and the ceremonial greetings were repeated. Luke now saw that the men on either side of Muhammad Abn's father were actually supporting him, and when they moved on in toto it was not apparent that the old man was being assisted.

At once, then, it seemed that they were surrounded by a great many men, all dressed in white robes and headgear, and there were many introductions and many handshakes. Luke was amused because the "How do you dos" had obviously been rehearsed. The phrase was delivered in several almost unrecognizable accents, and the words were invariably run together. He wondered if his own phonetically learned Arab was also rendered so badly? The fact that the family members had taken the trouble to learn the phrase was an unexpected courtesy.

The gathering became more festive when a retinue of servants brought huge, steaming porcelain dishes, which they carefully placed on the damask cloth. Muhammad Abn's father, supported by bodyguards, stood at the right, at the head of the repast, and made little motioning gestures to the crowd. He indicated that Luke was to sit at the right of his son, and Bosley at the left.

After the guests had been seated on the strip of rug that surrounded the damask cloth, the old man stood unsteadily behind them, directing the servants. Bosley, folding his legs, tried to assume a position that would not look awkward to his Arabian hosts, but was not entirely satisfied that he had succeeded. His legs went promptly to sleep.

Servants continually brought side dishes, which the old sheik examined carefully before indicating that the food was proper to set before the guests. Twice he waved dishes away with furious glances at the servants.

Luke could only surmise what was going through his mind.

Luke and Bosley selected tender-looking pieces of lamb from the community serving dishes, carefully using only their left hands, aware as they had been since entering the kingdom that Muslims reserved their right hands for calls of nature and therefore considered them unclean. Luke did not speculate on what happened to those unfortunates born lefthanded!

Among the special dishes were small meat pies, roasted chicken with a lemony sauce, a green vegetable that resembled spinach, a variety of imported fruits, plain and stuffed dates, and a large plate of something that looked like a whole sheep's liver. They did not taste the delicious-looking pale yellow rice, because there were no eating utensils, and although the other guests helped themselves from dish to mouth with the dexterity of dervishes, Luke and Bosley did not wish to tempt fate.

While the guests enjoyed themselves, the old sheik remained standing, a bodyguard on either side. His face was impassive, yet he could not hide his fatigue; twice he would have fallen had not the bodyguards intervened, yet his black eyes constantly shifted over the assemblage.

The guests made many appreciative noises as they relished the food, and as much as Luke and Bosley enjoyed the food, they could not quite bring themselves to imitate the others. In Angel a belch was considered vulgar, and they were not going to change their eating habits in the kingdom of Saudi Arabia.

When the last of the fruits had been consumed, dark coffee was served; then the servants brought in small burners holding fragrant incense. Luke and Bosley watched with fascination as each man sniffed the piquant odor and waved the gray smoke into his beard and robes. Bosley took care not to sneeze when the burner was thrust at him, and since he did not have facial hair or robes, he swirled the vapors about his head and shoulders. But while the operation seemed silly to him, no one took notice except Luke, who was obviously taking mental notes as to what to do when his time came.

The guests rose all at once, good-byes were said, and the old sheik accompanied Luke and Bosley to the edge of the clearing, but not before administering handshakes, nods, bows, and smiles. Although seemingly on the verge of collapse, he summoned a strong voice. "We will meet in an hour at the house of my son."

"Your father is a remarkable man, Muhammad Abn," Luke said conversationally in the limousine on the return trip.

"Yes, he is that, yet we are opposed on many issues, which I suppose is natural, because we are of different generations. He has great fortitude and courage, although he is very frail. If his health were better, I would like to take him to the United States. He believes, as many who have never been abroad believe, that the sun rises and sets in our kingdom. We who have studied in other countries know that is not so."

Bosley nodded, feeling close to Muhammad Abn because he had been unusually candid, making comments that for others would most assuredly have been censored.

Forty minutes later, they met in the Western-style room, where a small folding table had been set up with plates, flatware, and glassware. The bodyguards had already seated the old sheik, who appeared to have gained strength, although his face held a yellowish cast.

A servant brought thick, spicy coffee, while another served pieces of light brown slices of dessert. "Why, it's Angel cake!" Bosley exclaimed, taking a bite of the light confection.

The old sheik smiled benevolently. "My son spoke of this extraordinary substance after visiting your country. I had a portion served to me before the picnic, and I must say that Allah would approve!"

They ate with relish, and the old sheik smacked his lips after each taste. As they sipped their coffee, he turned his black-bean eyes to Bosley. "I will make you a wager, sir, that you cannot do everything that I can do, here at table."

Bosley nodded. "I accept your wager." This was obviously a sort of game, and he did not wish to be impolite. "What are the stakes?" he asked pleasantly.

"Five hundred dollars, American."

"Father ..." Muhammad Abn put in, but was cut short by a curt phrase, uttered in Parsi.

The old sheik leaned forward. "You must do everything that I do," he announced, moving a water glass an inch to the right of his dessert plate and back to its original position.

Bosley nodded and moved his own glass an inch to the right of his plate and back again, and when his host took a sip of water and swallowed, so did he.

Luke and Muhammad Abn watched quietly as Bosley, following the old sheik's example, proceeded to move various cutlery back and forth and to the right and left, pausing every now and then to take a sip of water or coffee. He followed every direction exactly.

The game progressed for twenty minutes, the movements growing more and more complex, with the host folding his napkin in fourths and then in eighths, unfolding the square, and forming a triangle. Bosley copied the old sheik's action of taking a sip of water, swishing the liquid around in his mouth, and swallowing; then, after shifting the flatware around the table once more, Bosley followed directions by taking a sip of water.

The old sheik spat his mouthful of water into the glass and laughingly said, "You have lost the bet, sir!"

Bosley blushed to the roots of his hair. He had swallowed his mouthful of water. He looked at his host with open-mouthed surprise and admitted that he had indeed lost the wager. He opened his billfold and looked up with embarrassment. "I don't seem to have that much cash."

"Oh, a check will do, my friend," the old man replied smoothly. "I trust the House of Heron!"

"Father ..." Muhammad Abn interjected, but was cut off by a furious sidelong glance. His face was mottled red.

Bosley smiled wryly to himself. The old sheik had told him more about his character by setting up the wager than he knew; it was a lesson that he would never forget.

The next morning, the servants packed Luke's and Bosley's suitcases, which they placed in the back of the limousine. Muhammad Abn stood on the threshold, waiting to accompany them to the boat at the Jeddah port, where elaborate good-byes were eventually said. They waved from the deck as the limousine made its way carefully over the rough boards of the wharf; then Luke patted his coat pocket to be certain that the orders for six drilling rigs were safe.

24

The Verdict

Mitchell had taken Charlotte to the Criterion Theater to see Bright Leaf *with her favorite actor, Gary Cooper, on a Sunday matinee.*

They were driving to his house for dinner when she looked at him suddenly and said, "You know, Mitch, I just suddenly realized that you've got a very good-looking profile."

He grinned, but kept his eyes on the road. "After all these years, you've certainly seen various versions of it, because all the Herons have the same nose."

"But I never realized before that it's *sensitive*."

Mitchell laughed out loud and turned his Buick through the wooden gates of his small acreage. "That takes the cake—another regional expression. I've known you ever since I can remember, and at this late date you think I suddenly have sensitivity."

"I'm serious, you old goat," she said, half self-consciously, half humorously. "I've never really known you until this last year or so. As our next-door neighbor when we were kids, you roamed around by yourself and, let's face it, weren't very communicative. It was Clement I was mad about, or did you know?"

"You had a crush?"

"We'd talked about getting married."

"I didn't know that." He got out of the car and opened the door for her and helped her out of the front seat. "I was gone all those years. Would you like to see my rose garden?"

She looked into his eyes. "Please?"

He opened the gate to the back yard and escorted her through an arch of chinaberry trees and around a white mulberry. "Walk carefully," he said, indicating the ground covered with fallen fruit.

She grinned and took his hand. "Remember when we were kids and went barefoot in the summer and the mulberries would squish up between our toes?" She shuddered deliciously.

"Yes, or we'd stub our toes on a rock! I can still feel the burn."

"You had one more little toe than I did."

"I still do. When I was in the service during the First World War, the doctors wanted to operate, but I said no, because they were so small that I never had trouble finding shoes to fit." He paused. "Do you know, Charlotte, the funny thing is that the abnormality doesn't occur every generation. It skips around. My Uncle Luke, who got killed staking the claim at Angel, had a double toe, and his grandfather, too. Strange, isn't it? By the way, how did we get on such a silly subject?" They separated at the old water well; he went to the left, she to the right, and as they came together he said, "Bread and butter."

She giggled like a young girl and leaned back on the well. "It's all coming back, isn't it, Mitch?"

"What?"

"When I'm with you nowadays, it's like I've gone back, and then I look at you . . ."

"And what do you see? A middle-aged man with a funny kid crew haircut."

"I was going to ask you about that sometime."

Since he could not tell her the truth, he went on casually, "It's very comfortable and no care at all. I just run a brush through it twice a day." He turned to the rosebushes. "This is my pride and joy, a Cecil Bruenner, the best of the lot." He picked up a pair of shears that were hanging on the side of the garage and cut two short-stemmed red-orange roses and handed them to her.

"Thank you, Mitch, how very thoughtful."

"How about a drink?"

"Thank you, I'd like one very much. You know, I'm still getting used to being invited to people's houses in Angel and being asked if I'd like a drink, and suddenly realizing that they mean a drink of *water*. Twice when I've been asked that question, before I realized it, I said, 'Yes, Scotch and soda, please.' "

"And what was the reaction?"

"Oh, they think I'm peculiar anyway and laugh about it, but I'm certain that a few people like Cissie Baker really believe I'm an alcoholic." She studied her nails. "But they put up with me because I've got more money than they do. Isn't that hysterical, Mitch?"

He ushered her into the large paneled den, which featured a mahogany bar at the end. There was genuine leather furniture in the room, two sofas, several chairs, and even the two end tables were upholstered in shiny chocolate-brown hide. "Money does strange things all right," he agreed and mixed the drinks. "Let's have a toast to the Herons and the Dices?"

She held up her glass. "No Dice!" she said with a loud laugh at her own joke. "Just the Herons."

"Very well." He touched her glass with his own: "Here's to:

> *"The girl who lives over the hill,*
> *She won't ..."*

"... but her sister will!" Charlotte finished for him, and they laughed. She took a long pull from her glass, went to the rock ceiling-to-floor fireplace and examined the oil painting in the huge gilt frame over the rough mantel. "It's Paris, isn't it?"

He nodded. "The rue Dauphine. Just around the corner from the rue Christine, where some people I used to know lived. One's gone now; the other, I guess, is still there."

She turned to him. "Your voice was sad just then, Mitchell. Was there a romance?"

"Oh, no, Charlotte, nothing like that. Just two old maids who lived together. They were helpful to me a couple of times." He cleared his throat and changed the subject, "Let's go into the front room." He led the way through the hall to the living room, which was furnished in Queen Anne cherrywood, and she gasped with pleasure. "You have such excellent taste, Mitch."

"Well, thank you, but after all I'm in the business, remember?"

She examined the books in the polished wood shelves on the west wall. "Marcel Proust, Henry Wadsworth Longfellow, Pearl Buck, Robert E. Sherwood." She ran her hands over the richly bound volumes. "Quite a catholic taste."

"Yes," he kidded, "for a Methodist!"

She grinned and shook her head. "The day is full of surprises. You know that you're a much deeper man than I thought." She paused. "Not many people are invited here, right?"

"No one at Angel has been in this house, except Aunt Letty and Uncle Bosley."

"Why?" she asked gaily.

He gave her a long look. "I don't entertain for one thing. It's awkward because I don't have a ... hostess." He turned toward the kitchen. "Let's see what Mrs. Briggs of the Cabbage Patch has concocted for dinner."

He said it lightly, because he was on the verge of getting serious, and it was too early in the evening to become moonstruck, even though Charlotte's presence in the house was giving him goosebumps.

Mrs. Briggs had provided what she thought was an elegant dinner, he was certain, but he only picked at his food. The appetizer was muskmelon with white grapes in aspic, which was followed by iceberg lettuce with thousand island dressing, and a main course of sirloin tips and mashed potatoes, kept warm in the oven. As he served the food, refusing Charlotte's offer of assistance, he knew that Mrs. Briggs had picked a safe menu; she did not trust him to carve.

Mitchell served the coffee in the little cups that his mother had purchased the first year in Oklahoma in 1893, and ladled out rice pudding in the dishes that Aunt Letty had given him for a housewarming present. He took his seat opposite Charlotte, and over the second cup of coffee, took her hand across the table, looked into her eyes and said softly, "Don't you know that I've fallen in love with you?"

His voice was so matter-of-fact that he could have been asking her if she wanted another drink. She looked down at her hands, which were shaking, and got up from the table and went to the front window. Very quietly, without pretense, in a strange, little-girl voice, she said, "You won't believe this, Mitch, but do you know you're the first man who ever said that to me?" She glanced at him over her shoulder. "I've planned everything about my life up until the time that my folks died . . . and nothing since."

To her horror, she felt tears sting her eyes and they coursed down her cheeks; then she could not stop crying. He came up close behind her and placed his arms around her shoulders. He held her very tightly and placed the back of her head on his chest. She sobbed quietly, all defenses down, then turned in his arms and looked up into his face.

Mitchell felt her heartbeat gradually return to normal. It gave him an unaccustomed sense of power to know that, for the first time in his life, someone had turned to him emotionally. Charlotte was now a vulnerable, soft creature clinging to him. She was the first woman since Françoise, so long ago, to whom he felt protective, as if she would never let him go. He brushed away her tears and kissed her softly. Her lips were responsive, warm, alive, and suddenly he was shaking too. As he kissed her, she remained loosely in his arms.

She wanted to push her body up against his and hug him tightly, which she would have done had he been one of her Washington golden boys. But she did not need to press up against him to remind herself of his masculinity. She did not need to feel his immediate need for her, she found to her great surprise. Mitchell was not a panting, hungry boy who had to be satisfied instantly. He loomed above her, a living, breathing, pulsating force that she did not wish to control. It occurred to her, as they continued kissing, that this was an entirely new experience. Beyond sexuality, there was a new, and very much beloved, feeling of security and a knowledge that he was in complete charge.

He held her tightly, gave her a long, intimate kiss, and then released her quickly. "Let's go to bed," he said, and she found herself following him into the bedroom. No man had ever used that particular phrase to her, although, over the years, she had repeated the same words many times to a great many of the golden boys.

He pulled down the bedspread and sheet, then methodically began to take off his clothing. As she undressed, it occurred to her that she did not need to hide her body from him because he would not expect her to have the breasts of a young girl, a twenty-two-inch waist, or a flat stomach.

He was down to his underpants, and as he tugged at the elastic band he thought, *I'm undressing before little Charlotte Dice!* They could have been children playing house in the barn on the claim at Angel, feeling no shame at taking off their clothing or displaying their bodies to each other.

He lay down on the bed on his side and looked up at her, eyes shining. Smiling very softly, she whispered, "Be back in a moment." And she went into the bathroom. When she returned, her face was gleaming; she had removed her makeup and her skin glowed. Seeing her without anything on her face, he realized that she was very naturally a pretty woman, and she had inherited Fontine's marvelous complexion.

She lay down beside him, and he took her lightly in his arms and they kissed. She was totally relaxed. Not required to instigate the proceedings, she concentrated on being thrilled by his lips and exploring his body with her fingertips. Lean and naturally muscled, he had the body of a man of thirty.

Feeling and holding her soft body, he was pleased that she was not tiny and frail so he would have to treat her like one of those fragile figurines that he had sold so long ago in France. He also appreciated the fact that he was not on a strict schedule. There was no need to be conscious of time elapsing; no one was waiting in the hall to take his place in twenty minutes.

Slowly, luxuriously, with a sense of wonder, they grew accustomed to the feel of each other's bodies. They kissed and touched and traced exquisite patterns over responding flesh. She had never known this sort of foreplay; always before, what preliminaries were required were over very quickly. There was a young body that demanded attention, to be catered to and be satisfied. Her own wishes were always hanging somewhere out of reach, beyond ... always beyond that veil of instant demand.

Arms, legs, hands, thighs moved hither and yon on the bed; new positions were delightfully discovered and tactile pleasures were increased. Hot and cold vibrations ebbed and flowed, and, at last, time ceased to be time.

Very easily, effortlessly, they were together now; there was no feeling of supremacy, no sense of aggression, no anguish or distress—only a superlative tenderness as each sought to intensify the other's pleasure, which became more acute as they touched and moved and swayed in their passionate embrace.

She was totally possessed. They were so attuned now that the tiniest movement brought on waves of intense enjoyment, and these moments brought about convulsive inward stirrings, which in turn triggered other waves of feeling. After what seemed like a very long time they reached fulfillment, but the climax was different from what either one of them had ever experienced before.

So much time had been spent in an exquisite emotional buildup, when pleasure was constant, that the supreme moment was drawn out and augmented so that the final, chaotic rush was a sort of echoing *vibrato* of their bodies that left them almost senseless. Drugged by the total experience of the evening, they both fell into a deep, mind-releasing, energy-replenishing sleep. During the night, they roused now and then, conscious of each other's bodies and, half awake, caressed and kissed, then slept again.

He was the first to awaken, just after sunrise. He examined her face carefully, and she seemed dearer to him because he had known her all of her life. Many incidents from the past came up before his eyes, and he found this familiarity now enhanced the pleasure of her being next to him. At last he knew what strange electricity her body held for him, knew the touch of her flesh, the inward vibrations. Their muscular framework fit together with the ease of a wood puzzle, where every groove and each indentation must be expertly adjusted if the pieces are to be assembled in perfect order. They had solved the mystery.

Her eyelids fluttered, then snapped open. A look of panic washed over her face before she realized where she was. She smiled softly as the night came back, and reached out and touched his face with her fingers. "I love you, Mitch," she said softly, and although she had uttered the words carelessly many times during her life, the phrase took on new meaning now.

"And, I—love—you." It was a realization that he had only spoken that phrase once before with Françoise in Paris all those years ago. *He had not pronounced those words, in that particular order, in thirty years!* "Charlotte"— his voice was hesitant—"do you think that we have a chance of—making a go of it?"

"I've been wondering about that, too. I know that I feel more relaxed with you than with any man I've ever met." She paused meaningfully. "I really never thought that I'd meet a person that would be both a companion and a lover. Before, these qualities were always separate entities." She made a new indentation on the pillow with her fist.

"Yes, I understand, because I didn't think I'd ever find the right combination either."

She thought about all of those golden boys en masse, whose penises, if stretched end to end, would go from lower Manhattan to Central Park. "There are so many things about me that you don't know, Mitch."

"No, Charlotte, we don't need to know any more about each other." He thought of those years of wandering, his secret missions, that boy somewhere who might be his son, and he shook his head. "We've both lived quite a long while in this world. We've established ourselves and we've survived. I think we've kept our sanity. Let's not discuss any relationships that either of us has had before. They don't mean anything now, as far as you and I are concerned. I don't feel that I have to confess to you, and I don't want you to feel that you must confess to me." He brushed her hair back from her forehead. "For all intents and purposes, as far as emotions are concerned, we just met last night. Let's leave it at that."

Oh, my dearest, how wise you are! she thought. *And this is the joy of being the age that we are; neither of us has been virtuous. We've both been selfishly catering to ourselves all these years, doing what we wanted to do, behaving the way that our beliefs indicated, as we established our own identities.* "I agree," she said with finality. "We are what we are. Let's leave it at that."

It was at that moment that they heard a stirring in the kitchen and the sound of bacon sizzling in a pan. "Oh, my God," Mitchell said quietly, "I forgot about Mrs. Briggs!"

Charlotte drew in her breath. "What are we going to do?" She got up quickly and reached for her petticoat. He jumped out of bed and reached for his trousers, and then they both stopped dressing in midair. They had the same thought and started to laugh.

"Let's just calm down," he said when they had quieted. "This isn't the end of the world." He began to dress methodically.

"Is there a back way out?" she asked.

"Yes. But she's already seen the car parked in the driveway. I think we should get dressed and calmly have breakfast." He went into the bathroom, washed his face and hands, and combed his hair. "I'll be back in a moment," he said. At the door, he turned. "Are you embarrassed?"

"Not really, Mitch."

"Do you think you can do this breakfast business all right?"

"I can if you can."

He winked at her and then went into the kitchen.

"Good morning, Mrs. Briggs," he said cheerfully. "I have a houseguest, so there'll be two for breakfast."

When Charlotte came in a few moments later, he briefly made the introductions. The women nodded politely, and before Mrs. Briggs could say anything, Mitchell poured two cups of coffee. They sat in the nook at the end of the kitchen, where he always breakfasted, and continued a variety of casual small talk. He told her about the new store that he planned to open in Oklahoma City, and when the scrambled eggs and bacon were placed before them, they ate slowly and Charlotte asked his advice about contacting a landscape contractor, because the lawn was suffering from fungus.

When they finished eating, Charlotte thanked Mrs. Briggs for a delicious breakfast, and Mitchell walked her out to the car. They made a date for the following Saturday, when she suggested he come for dinner in Angel. He waved as she drove away.

He cut a few Cecil Bruenner roses, which he handed to Mrs. Briggs. She would not look at him. "They're really doing very well, don't you think?" he asked.

She placed them in the kitchen sink and reached for a vase in the back of a cabinet. "Much better than I am," she replied quietly. She filled the vase with water and slowly and methodically began to arrange the flowers. "I'll be leaving your employment at the end of the day," she said, her face still turned away, "so I'd be obliged if you'd give me a check."

"You won't believe this, Charlotte," Mitchell said that evening on the telephone, "but I just lost a housekeeper today."

"Because of what—happened this morning?"

"I guess so. Mrs. Briggs was vague, but she wouldn't look at me after you left."

"Oh, Mitch, I *am* sorry. But with you being a bachelor, surely she didn't think that you were entirely celibate!"

"It must have been a shock to her, because it's the first time that I've had someone stay overnight."

"In Washington, servants are servants, and unless one has an orgy in the living room and sells tickets, the affair going on 'upstairs' is no affair of those who live 'downstairs'! Are you going to place an ad in the *Enid Morning News*?"

"Yes, but for a houseman, if there is such a thing—either that or find a very liberal woman. In any case, if Mrs. Briggs was so puritanical, she didn't belong here in the first place." He paused. "That's not really the reason I called, however, Charlotte. I just wanted to reiterate my feelings. I've thought about you all day, and the more that I contemplate our situation, the more it appeals to me."

"Are you proposing to me, Mitch?" Charlotte's tone was light, but there was an undercurrent of excitement before she laughed.

"I've never proposed before, and I mean to do it properly, but I do want you to be prepared." He went on tenderly, "I can't wait to see you on Saturday."

"Well," she said warmly, "you can always drive over here to Angel."

"Yes," he replied, "I could, but I want to give you time to think. I also must have time, and then, too, I have to go to Guthrie tomorrow and listen to the manager's complaints. Half of my job is hand-holding. Now I must go before Nellie cuts in and volunteers to be your matron of honor! I love you."

"I love you," she repeated and placed the telephone back in its cradle.

She walked through the living room to the huge solarium, which was Fontine's favorite room. End-of-the-day sunlight shone through the windows, creating light patterns through the huge pots of leafy plants.

There was a peculiar silence in the room; the atmosphere seemed alive. "He's going to ask me to marry him," she said out loud. "Are you pleased, Mama? Are you pleased?"

25

The Passing Show

Louisa Tarbell opened the silver box from the Fifth Avenue shop and gasped with surprise.

"William, oh, William!" She brought the fur muff up to her face. Her eyes were brimming with tears. ". . . Beautiful, sinfully beautiful!"

"It's mink," he said quietly.

She threw her arms around him, and caressed his back, bringing the fur up to his neck. "Hey," he cried, "that tickles!"

She laughed. "A wonderful present, William, thank you, but it must have cost a fortune."

"It did." He pulled away gently. "But Christmas only comes once a year. I was window shopping this morning and it was so cold and I was shivering, and I noticed so many women were bundled up with their hands in their pockets, and I looked in the shop and saw this muff on a store dummy and she looked so warm and I . . ." He paused, and his voice became very serious. "It occurred to me that I'd never ever have been able to afford a present for you. Now that my royalty checks are coming in from 'The Cowboy Waltz,' I can afford to buy things that I've only seen in the movies."

She smiled at him fondly. "It's true that it appears the lean days are over, but you mustn't let success go to your head. 'The Cowboy Waltz' might have been a fluke; apparently so much about the music business has to do with timing. You very well may have to live on your salary, and I haven't spoken to Clement about that, so we don't know yet what will be coming in each month."

As she continued to speak about his future, pacing back and forth in front of the window in the Heron suite that overlooked snowy Central Park, he could scarcely believe that this beautifully dressed creature was the same plain schoolteacher who had taught him for so many years in Willawa. She had not been beautiful then, and she was not beautiful now, but she was so striking-looking that men glanced at her with more than passing interest. At first he had been jealous, but she seemed not to be aware of the attention that she was creating, and he had finally come to the conclusion that he had nothing to worry about. He was proud that she was always at his side.

They ordered dinner in the suite, then turned out the lights, switched on the radio to the "Hit Parade," and took chairs by the window overlooking the park. A glow from the lights on Fifth Avenue below highlighted the room, and when the program was almost over, he reached for her hand to share the precious moment that he knew would be forthcoming. There was a pause, and the announcer said, "... and for the eighteenth straight week in a row, the number one song in the nation is ..." There was another pause as excitement built. "... 'The Cowboy Waltz'!"

They leaned back in the chairs, still holding hands, as Clement's dry, perfectly controlled voice floated out over the airwaves. It was a perfect welding of material and performer; one complemented the other.

When the song was over, Louisa Tarbell squeezed William Nestor's hand. "Savor this moment, Billy," she said softly.

"I am," he replied, and then, after a pause, went on carefully, "You know, it just occurred to me, Lou, that of all the people I know, the only one that I really care about is you. You're the only one worth sharing moments like this. I've got the biggest hit of the year, and no one really cares, except you."

She did not reply, because she could not trust her voice. Suddenly all those wearisome years of teaching, with no money during the Depression, and the strain of the war years, and the trial of keeping her head up in a mean little town like Willawa, faded away. Out of those years her ultimate salvation had come about because of one boy, one lad whose talent was a wondrous, growing and living thing. She would protect him so that he would never know the perils of the outside world. Inwardly, she smiled wryly. The old maid schoolteacher would keep him safe . . . for herself.

The brown-stained envelope attracted Bernice's attention as she thumbed through the stack of morning mail. She drew it gingerly out of the pile of bills and circulars and blinked again. The handwriting was a penciled, childish scrawl, and the letters ran together. It was simply addressed to Luke Heron in care of the Heron Oil Company, Tulsa, Oklahoma, and the postmaster had thoughtfully forwarded it along with the usual packet. She was about to open the envelope, when she saw the word "personnel" in the lower left hand corner. Dutifully, she knocked on Luke's door twice, and then entered. "Excuse me, boss, but we really got a doozy this morning. It looks as if some kid got short-changed at one of the stations." She laughed and placed the letter on the edge of the desk.

Luke sighed and tore open the envelope and read the letter once and then reread it again.

21 March, '51

Dear sir: .

This here is Finney Nestor and I'm writing flat on my back because we ain't got any vittles in the house and my wife is sick next too me and we don't know how to writ to our Billy Boy cause we ain't got his address. It's been real rough sense you Heron people quit sending money and we shore need it right away because the doc won't come out here anymore without we pay him what we owe him right away. Shore hope you can send us a little something by return mail.

Fin

Luke looked up. "It's a private matter," he said to Bernice. "Would you please get me Louisa Tarbell on the telephone."

"Is she still in New York?"

"Yes. William is arranging an album for me. They've been there all winter. Keep trying until you get her. It's important."

The call came through immediately, and when Bernice buzzed the intercom, Luke picked up the telephone. "Miss Tarbell, I'm calling because I don't know where to reach Clement. I know he's in the East somewhere on tour, but you can probably help me. I have a letter from William's dad saying he's sick and he wants some money."

Louisa's voice caught in her throat. She had been a fool to think that she was free of the Nestors, but since their last encounter she had put them out of her mind. "I don't know quite what to say, Mr. Heron."

Luke read the letter aloud, and his distaste for the

man increased. "I don't understand what he means by we 'Heron people' not sending money. As far as I know, Clement never . . ."

Louisa cut in. "I'll take this in the bedroom," she said quietly, and a moment later she was back on the line. "I was hoping that this would never come up," she continued, her voice flat, and then she found herself telling him the entire story. When she had finished, there was a long pause at the other end of the line.

"Well," Luke said at last, "I've got to hand it to you, Miss Tarbell, I don't think I've ever heard of anything quite so extraordinary. I'll talk to Clem about this, but in the meantime I'll send Mr. Nestor a hundred dollars."

"You shouldn't send him a red cent!" Louisa exclaimed. "He's faking, just as he's always faked. There is nothing wrong with that man except laziness."

"I'm quite sure that you're right, Miss Tarbell, I remember the situation quite well, but just in case he is ill . . ."

"But he's *not*. I bet he's heard of William's success. He's just trying to cash in and . . ."

"Miss Tarbell," Luke said persuasively, "nevertheless, I'm going to send him a personal check for fifty dollars, just in case he and his wife are ill." He paused. "We'll be in touch."

Louisa looked at her pale face in the mirror, corrected her posture, and went into the living room. William, his face drained of color, sat in the wingback chair, still holding the telephone in his hand. He looked at her with a dazed expression. "You rented your house to get the money to continue the payments, didn't you?"

She nodded numbly. "I didn't mean for you ever to know," she said gently.

"My schooling meant that much to you?" He was still in a state of shock.

"Oh, yes, Billy, oh yes," she answered fervently, "that

and much more. Don't you see, you couldn't be stopped! No one could interfere with the opportunity that Clement Story was giving you."

"But, Lou, that was blackmail!"

She nodded. "Of course, but you were still technically under age, and I couldn't have your parents put up a barrier, and it was easier to buy them off. I don't think your mother would have put up a fuss, but your dad was mean enough to do anything. Talent to him meant nothing. To him, you were always a workhorse; he couldn't understand anyone wanting to better themselves." She paused and then went on more gently, "Besides, Billy, what did a few thousand dollars mean when the odds were so great?"

He looked at her curiously. "I was real lucky with 'The Cowboy Waltz.' What would have happened if I had flunked at Barrett?"

"But you didn't. Let's not think of what *might* have happened. You will learn, as you grow older, that there are times in life when you have to take chances. I believed in you, and I was right."

She paused, and the soft look that he loved came into her eyes. "Billy," she continued softly, "Life is made up of compromises." She moved toward him. "Our life together is a compromise of sorts. You probably don't look at it that way, but one day you'll see that I'm right."

He hugged her close. "I don't know what you're talking about, lady," he said lightly, "but right now I want to *compromise* you!"

Louisa giggled in spite of herself and flushed, suddenly feeling like a young girl again. She looked up into his young, unlined face and his limpid black eyes, and before she kissed him she thought that today he was looking very Cherokee, very Indian indeed.

* * *

Max glared at William and Louisa critically. He had flown in from Chicago for a conference. He took a puff of his big Havana cigar. "Let's put it this way," he said gruffly, "get your folks off your back. Give 'em a regular income every month to keep them quiet."

"But that's not fair," Louisa replied. "They're like leeches."

"Of course they are," Max agreed, waving the cigar, "but almost all famous people in show business are paying off in one way or the other. It's the way of life. Everyone has their hands out. There are Hollywood stars who are supporting every damn member of the family—mothers, fathers, sisters, brothers, aunts, uncles, dogs, cats.... It's all the same damn thing. You don't want to pick up a scandal sheet with headlines that read: FAMOUS SONGWRITER'S FOLKS DESTITUTE, do you? Of course not. Just be thankful that they're content with a hundred and fifty bucks a month; that's chickenfeed to what some famous people shell out."

Louisa nodded. "I suppose you're right, Max. What do you say, William?"

William's dark eyes were troubled. "If it was only my dad, I'd say to hell with it," he said with a sigh, "but Mama's different. She's had a hard life, especially being married to him. She was always on my side. Let's make it two hundred. I can afford that, can't I, Louisa?"

"Well, yes, I suppose you can." She paused. "Why don't you go downstairs for a cup of coffee, William?"

He grinned. "Are you trying to get rid of me?"

She smiled back. "As a matter of fact, yes, I want to talk to Max." She waited until he had left the room, then she looked directly across the desk at Max, who was carefully snubbing his cigar out in a huge ashtray formed in the shape of a pair of cowboy boots. "While we're speaking of money, Max, I need some advice. After all, you're an agent, you know about such things."

Before she opened her mouth, Max knew what she

was going to say; he had heard variations of the same sort of conversation many times over the years. "Yes?" he asked and lighted another Havana.

"You know, of course, that William doesn't have a written agreement with Clement Story, although something was vaguely mentioned when he started the arrangements for the new album. When he agreed to pay the tuition to the Barrett Conservatory of Music, it was agreed that he would become part of his staff, and it was left at that. To Clement, it was an investment that he hoped would pay off, but he didn't know that William would graduate or if he was as talented as he imagined."

Max sighed gently and took another puff of the cigar.

"Then, of course, he wrote 'The Cowboy Waltz,' which I believe in the trade is called 'a runaway hit,' right?"

Max nodded and glanced out of the window at the Central Park West skyline.

"If I'm right, then, about what I've heard of contracts, if William signs with Clement Story, everything that he writes will become the property of the orchestra."

"Yes"—Max frowned—"technically."

Louisa smiled thinly. "It's that 'technicality' that I want to discuss. What's right is right, and I want William to sign that contract with Clement, but there should be a clause that all of his writings are to be held separately and not included in his band duties."

Max laughed softly, and the laugh was not nice. "Have you discussed this with Clem?"

"Not yet, but since you're an agent . . ."

"Miss Tarbell, I am *Clem's* agent, not William's or yours."

"Then why did you recommend that we pay William's parents?"

"Because, dear lady," Max continued evenly, "I didn't want Clem to be embarrassed with unwanted publicity. He's always kept his nose clean, and I won't have a lot of crappy stories circulating that a member of his staff is letting his parents starve." He squinted his eyes at her and looked very formidable indeed. "And, while we're on the subject, I know that you brought William to Clem's attention, and that's admirable. You're probably set for the rest of your life as his business manager, which is okay, too, but beyond that, just what are you getting out of the relationship?"

Louisa kept her voice calm. "I have quite an investment in William," she replied quietly, "if you must know, a financial investment that I expect to pay off handsomely."

Max rolled the cigar from one side of his mouth to the other. "How much is the kid into you for?"

Louisa colored. "A few thousand dollars and about nine years of my life."

Max blew a perfect ring of smoke across the desk. "When I write up Clement's contract with William, I'll see that the clause you want is included." He paused. "By the way, Clement Story wouldn't have it any other way. Naturally, anything original that William Nestor writes is his own property." He leaned forward and continued evenly, "Also, Miss Tarbell, it's none of my business, but aside from having 'discovered' William and arranging his business affairs and looking after him, it must be clear to anyone with half a brain that you're not quite the self-sacrificing type altogether. It's also obvious that you're fucking the kid!"

Louisa turned beet-red and got up quickly from her chair and went to the door. She paused a moment, and when she turned around she had regained composure and the blush had faded from her face. The tone of her voice indicated that she had not heard his last remark. "I'll be expecting the contract in the mail," she said sweetly. "Send it to the Wyandotte Hotel in Kansas City; that's where the William Nestor corporate offices will be set up." She opened her blue eyes very wide. "Whenever you're in town, do drop by: tea will be served every afternoon promptly at four."

*   *   *

On June 24, 1951, Lerry took the twenty-five handwritten invitations to the post office, then stopped by the Red Bird Café. Belle Turne's eyes lighted up. "Why, Letty, it's been a coon's age since you've been in here! What's the occasion?"

Letty laughed. "I'm just getting tired of my own coffee, and I thought I'd try yours for a change."

"Thank God," Belle retorted with a laugh, "I thought you'd come to collect the interest on the mortgage!" She poured coffee from the large urn into a mug, which she placed on a paper napkin in front of Letty, who had sat down at the counter.

"You'll be getting an invitation in the mail tomorrow," Letty said, taking a sip of coffee and showing her approval with a gleam in her eye, "but I want to invite you personally to our Fourth of July picnic. We didn't have one last year, if you remember, Clement was on 'The Toast of the Town' television show and everyone else was busy."

Belle narrowed her eyes and patted her hennaed hair. "I didn't think outsiders were ever asked for the Fourth."

For a moment Letty looked flustered. "Well, it's different this year, I'm inviting a few people that are practically family. Luke Three won't be here, though. He's somewhere in England, I guess—at least, I got a birthday card from him for my eightieth, but there was no address."

"There wasn't a lazy bone in that boy's body, no matter what those articles in the paper used to say, calling him a playboy and all. Are Patricia Anne and Lars coming?"

Letty nodded. "Yes. He's still doing research, carrying on Sam's work. He gave an important paper in Vienna that stirred up a lot of controversy. I don't understand very much about it, although I read an abstract in a medical journal. It was something to do with helping people who have mental illness through drugs."

"What about Mitch?" Belle asked, and stopped wiping the counter. "Is he away again on one of those long trips?"

Letty shook her head. "No, but he'll be here." She paused, wondering whether she should go on or not, and then made a quick decision. "Belle . . ."

"Yes?"

"I know that you used to see a lot of Mitch in the old days, and . . . well, you'll be hearing it sooner or later, although he's trying to keep it quiet now. But it'll be in the *Enid Morning News* and the *Angel Wing,* and I'd rather you hear it from me. . . ."

Belle was making wide circles on the counter with the cloth. She didn't look up but kept on with the round motions. "He's going to marry *her,* isn't he?"

"It looks that way," Letty replied quietly.

"Well . . ." Belle sighed, shifting her gaze out the window to the station across the street. "There'll be one less old maid in Angel. Charlotte's wealthy and she's got good manners, and I'm sure that she'll make a good wife. It can't be easy for him marrying at this time of life." She sighed. "Charlotte, Mitch, and myself, we're all about the same age. I hope, for his sake, she's over the change. He'll have enough getting used to, without worrying about a menopausal woman."

She turned back to Letty. "I did love him, you know, but I got over him years ago. Remember that day when the new Angel library was dedicated, and we had the parade? Well, I hadn't seen Mitch in a very long time, and when the fire broke out, and I was standing here helplessly watching the old Red Bird go up in flames, I felt someone put an arm around me. I had to look over to see who it was! In the old days, if he came within ten feet of me, I'd have known!" She paused. "While it was a comforting feeling having him there, and I appreciated his concern, I didn't feel anything. Nothing at all. So I guess, Letty, all of our hot blood had run out a long time ago."

Letty nodded. "Isn't it strange, Belle, how every man conjures up different feelings? I truly loved my first husband, Luke, and when he died, I thought I'd fall apart, but I was pregnant with Luke Junior and somehow I got over my grief. Then I met George Story, and our relationship was different than what Luke and I had experienced. I suppose you'd say that George was my dream man, and when I lost him, I knew I'd never fall in love again."

"But then there was Bosley ..."

"Whom I didn't love when I married him. I told him so, but, Belle, I've grown to love him more than either Luke or George." She colored slightly. "I guess today is a day for confessions. I don't think I've ever told this to a living soul. But when you're eighty, I guess you're entitled. After all, Belle, if fate had ruled differently, you might have become my only niece-in-law." She got up slowly and reached for her purse, but Belle held up her hand.

"The coffee's on the house, Letty." She grinned. "And you can count on me for the picnic, I wouldn't miss it! Of course, when I get your invitation, I'll write a 'reply if you please' back, so you'll sure enough know that I'm coming. With you being so formal and all ..."

Letty laughed. "Don't make fun of me, Belle. If I want to write out personal invitations at my age, I'm going to do it, it's so much simpler than making all those telephone calls. Nellie is getting so deaf, you have to keep screaming the numbers into the mouthpiece until a person turns blue in the face!"

"Amen," Belle replied quietly, "amen."

Letty waved to her old friend, then walked home by way of the cemetery, where Luke Heron the First and George Story were buried close by Mitchell's parents,

Edward and Priscilla, and their little Betsy, who had died of the smallpox epidemic. Two plots over rested John and Fontine Dice. She shook her head and paused to catch her breath, holding on to the wrought-iron fence that surrounded God's Acres.

Letty wondered what Hattie had in mind for supper; then she smiled crookedly. She had forgotten that it was the maid's day off. If there was nothing special in the refrigerator, she would fry some potatoes with pieces of home-cured bacon, add an egg or two, and scramble the mixture. Bosley and she would have a feast. In the old days, before the Discovery Well came in, and they were short of cash money, many times all the family had to eat was that dish known as Johnny Hen Fruits! It was a recipe that Fontine Dice had brought up from Santone.

Letty went in the back door as always and spoke to Bosley, who was still sitting in the big chair in the living room, the latest issue of the *Petroleum World* propped up on his knees. When he did not answer, she lovingly touched his shoulder. He pitched forward onto the floor, and she screamed. "Bos!" she cried brokenly. "Bos!" She knelt by his side and took his head in her arms. It was then that she saw that he was dead. His face was ashen, and his eyes stared straight ahead. She was overcome, not only with grief, but with horror. She gasped in a great, nameless pain, because once again she was back on the prairie, cradling Luke's head in her arms. He had died with his lips forming the words "I love you." Now that same look of wonder was mirrored in Bosley's face, and it was as if he, too, had been surprised by death.

The telephone rang insistently in the station, and Luke Three cursed as he slid out from under the Citroën. It had been a hectic morning. While his helper, Leo, was busy at the pumps, he had changed three tires, replaced a transmission, and blown out a gas line. He wiped his hands on a blue towel, so as not to soil his new blue uniform, and picked up the receiver. "British Heron Station Four."

"Gene Holiday?"

"Yes." He had long become used to the name.

"Just a moment, please," came the clipped female voice, which sounded vaguely familiar.

Luke Three recognized Sir Eric Huxley-Drummond's voice at once. "Yes, Sir Eric, what can I do for you?" It was the first time since he had come to the station four years before that the old man had contacted him.

"Luke Three"—Eric Huxley-Drummond's voice was very weak on the line—"I have some very bad news. Bosley Trenton had a massive stroke yesterday. Death was instantaneous. The funeral will be held Sunday, the thirtieth at the Methodist Church in Angel."

"Oh, my God," Luke replied brokenly. "Poor Grandma!"

"I have been on the transcontinental telephone all morning. I am taking a flight tomorrow at ten A.M. for New York. I can easily book two seats."

Luke Three's mind whirled. He had long ago put the idea of returning to the States out of his mind, but now . . . "I have to think," he replied slowly. "May I call you back, Sir Eric?"

"Yes," came the prompt reply. "But I must know by one o'clock to get tomorrow's flight. By the by, the Heron company plane will be waiting at Newark Airport."

After he had hung up, Luke Three finished tightening the bolts on the engine of the Citroën, put an "out to lunch" sign over the garage door, waved to his helper, and took the pathway that led down to the beach at Eastbourne. The quay was crowded this time of year, and since he wanted to be alone, he took the graveled path that led to a series of huge rocks, where there would be no bathers.

The sea was beautifully calm, contrasting with the

emotions that stirred inside him. Tears filled his eyes. Bosley had been his great ally before he had become his grandfather, and he had always treasured his friendship as well as his love. Bosley had always understood him, he felt, had taken time to get to know him as a person, something that his father had never bothered to do. . . .

Luke Three thought of Angel, a town that he had no wish to visit; yet one could not deny his roots. If he could only see Bosley once more, without the family being present, without all of those accusing eyes staring at him. No, he would tell Sir Eric to go without him. He straightened his back and looked out to sea again; a breeze was blowing in gently now, causing the waves to rise up in small whitecaps. He was on his own, doing well with a job that he could handle superbly. For the first time he had identity: he was Gene Holiday, the best mechanic in Eastbourne.

He retraced his steps to the station and stood for a moment across the street, and suddenly the scene faded before his eyes and he saw the familiar Heron station on Main Street in Angel, and Belle Trune standing in front of the Red Bird Café. He saw the Heron clapboard with the lilac bushes blooming by the porch, and tears filled his eyes again. When he looked up, he was back in Eastbourne, and the contrast was so marked that he was overcome with nostalgia. It was then that he knew it was time to go home.

It was raining on the day of the funeral service, and the mourners, three hundred strong, were scattered over God's Acres. As Letty looked out from her position among the family under the awning that had been stretched over the grave, all that she could see was a sea of black umbrellas; below, where the throng stood, was a sea of red mud. She had not known, until the will was read, that Bosley had not wanted a formal funeral, and a notice had appeared in the newspapers that the service was to be held at the Methodist Church. But, as is the custom in small towns like Angel, word had spread that there were to be only a few lines recited at God's Acres. The new minister was late, but as the crowd waited patiently, Letty thought of the cryptic paragraph that had ended Bosley's will:

> There are those who do not believe in God, but I am not one of them, but I do join those who feel that funerals are barbaric. I do not want a man, however chosen and holy, to preach over me. I do not want masses of flowers. I do not want anyone to gaze down on me. Being a geologist, I am familiar with the "dust to dust" theory and I subscribe to it; therefore instruct Mitchell Heron to have built for me a box of sugar pine, stained with creosote. If there are to be words said, let them be the ten lines from *Paradise Lost,* by John Milton, that start out: "To slumber here, as in the Vales of Heav'n?" They are lofty lines; yet they fit me.

Reverend Miller drove up in his old coupe, took off his tan raincoat, drew his black lapels up around his neck, and walked quickly through the light rain to the protective awning. He paused a moment, nodding to Letty and the rest of the family, then, placing his hands behind his back, he stepped to the microphone that Clement had set up. He looked out at the white faces under the black umbrellas and, without looking at the book he held, said: *"To slumber here, as in the Vales of Heav'n? Or in this abject posture have ye sworn ..."*

My God, thought Luke, what in the hell was that young twerp reciting? He couldn't be making it up as he went along! He ceased to listen to the words, and he thought of Bosley. He would miss him as a stepfather, surely, but more than that, his wise counsel. At the moment, Luke was feeling very tired for his fifty-seven years. Perhaps it was time to take it easier at Heron. He glanced over at Robert Desmond, with whom he had had his differences, yet the man was brilliant. Now, with Bosley out of the picture, it might be a wise choice to have a talk with the board of directors. Bob would make a fine president of Heron, and with Luke himself, as chairman of the board, he would still be in charge. Yes, he was certain that was the answer. He was distracted by nine-year-old Murdock, who was standing beside him. "Stop fidgeting!" he commanded under his breath.

"To adore the Conqueror? who now beholds Cherub and Seraph rolling in the flood ..." Jeanette smiled wryly to herself. Bosley had obviously chosen what was to be said over his grave, but when he had made out the will he could not possibly have known that it was going to be raining the day of his funeral. Or did he? One could never tell what Bosley was thinking; perhaps he'd had a premonition. Truthfully, she would miss the old man, although they were never that close.

"With scattered Arms and Ensigns, till anon ..." Mitchell reached for Charlotte's hand, which he held tightly. Bosley had been like a father to him when he was a young boy, and had never condemned him for spending all those years in Europe as a failure. And during the Depression, when he'd come back to Angel to look after his mother's farm, Bosley had loaned him money. After his furniture stores were a success, and he had returned from France and Germany on those missions for the government, he had wanted to confide in Bosley, and one or two times had almost done so. He wished now that he had.

"His swift pursuers from Heav'n Gates discern ..." Charlotte squeezed Mitchell's hand and slyly glanced at the Dice tombstones, which were located in a nearby plot, where she herself would one day rest. "Jaundice and Fourteen," she said to herself, using the familiar names that they had called each other every day of their lives. "Mitchell Heron and I are going to be married on

August fifteenth, nineteen-fifty-one. I could legitimately have a white wedding, because I've never been married, but really my heart wouldn't be in it, and I'm certainly not a virgin!" She thought about all the years with the golden boys, and she was glad that she had waited for Mitch. "You'll both be there in spirit, when the Justice of the Peace says those magic words that'll make me respectable— in your eyes. For all intents and purposes, there'll be no one in Enid there, except the J.P.; his witness, who'll probably be his wife; Mitch, of course; and me—and Jaundice and Fourteen." She squeezed Mitch's hand again.

"The advantage, and descending tread us down ..." Clement shook his head. What was the man saying? The words seemed to make no sense whatsoever. It suddenly occurred to him that he was tired, bone-weary, actually. He must have a serious talk with Max about future bookings. He wanted to take it easier.

"Thus drooping, or with linked Thunderbolts ..." Sarah drew in her breath and swallowed a sneeze. Was she catching cold? Well, the service would be over soon, and everyone would go to the basement of the Methodist Church, where the Altar Ladies would have laid out a buffet, which would include, of course, chicken and noodles, which was always served after funerals. Her attention wandered. Was that really an English knight who had come all the way from London to pay homage to Bosley? She thought she had heard someone call him Sir Eric. Well, she reflected, he wasn't the only VIP present. Standing in back of Letty were the Governor of Oklahoma, two senators, one member of the House of Representatives, and a man from Kansas City who was reputed to be a cousin of Harry Truman. Standing beside Bella Chenovick were Belle and Darlene Trune, and Sarah could not tell if those where tears on Belle's cheeks or rain.... Next to Darlene were perhaps the oddest couple present, William Nestor and Louisa Tarbell.

Was that a sable collar on the silk faille raincoat? How ostentatious! And Billy was looking very Indian, she saw, in a pearl-gray cashmere suit—in June? In front of Torgo Chenovick, who was bundled up in his wheelchair, stood Nellie, cupping her hand to her right ear to catch the words of the minister—not, thought Sarah, that they made any sense.

"Transfix us to the bottom of this Gulf ..." Patricia Anne swallowed the lump in her throat. Although she was present to pay her respects to Bosley, she was more concerned at the moment with Lars. The plane trip from Washington, D.C., had been very difficult for him. Three times now, since they had returned from Vienna, he had sustained experiences when he had *not* taken the mushroom compound; he had been thrown into a lapse more serious than the others, from which he returned without memory. Some of these experiences lasted for several minutes and had occurred in the most awkward places—once on a bus, again in the waiting room of the hospital, and most recently on the plane. Each time he seemed to be crawling out of a pit, and his unblinking eyes held a terror that was awful to see. She had told the perturbed stewardess on the plane that her husband was having chest pains—indigestion— although she wasn't at all certain that she had been believed. These "throwback" experiences were side effects that Lars had not counted upon, and he was now rewriting his treatise. It was possible, he had conceded to his psychiatrist friends, that the properties in the mushrooms might have a more deleterious than beneficial effect in the long run, especially if the substance was eliminated from the body so slowly, or perhaps not at all. His own recurring episodes were truly frightening, she knew.

"Awake, arise, or be forever fallen." Letty sighed gently as the minister bowed his head, and at that moment the rain ceased, and just before the minister asked everyone

to silently pray there was a giant mass movement that shuddered through the crowd as umbrellas were folded, and everyone bowed his head. Letty repeated the Lord's Prayer silently, and when she raised her eyes she saw a familiar figure that stood a head taller than those on the left. As the crowd began to disperse, the figure came toward her, enveloped her in his arms.

"Oh, Grandma," Luke Three whispered. "Oh, Grandma!"

It was then that she saw that his uniform was not the ordinary Heron blue trimmed in white, but was dark green. She touched his arm and looked up into his face. "What is *this*, Luke Three?"

"I reenlisted two days ago, Grandma. Being in the Marine Corps is the answer for me now. I'll be useful, and when this mess in Korea is over and I come back, maybe Dad will take me back into the company—who knows?"

Letty nodded. Korea was so far away, much more distant, it seemed, than the East China Sea, where he had been stationed before.

Luke Three looked over Letty's shoulder and saw Darlene Trune standing beside her mother. He patted his grandmother's arm and held his hand out to Darlene. The moment their palms met, an electric shock went through his body, and he was glad that he was bundled up in a tight uniform. His celibacy rose up to mock him. He suddenly realized that he had always loved her. *I've broken the family ties,* he thought, *and perhaps we can resume our relationship.* She could never resist him when he turned on the charm. "Hi, Darlene," he said with a slow grin, and looked into her eyes, which were very wide.

"Hi, Luke Three," she replied softly; then she turned to her right and looked up into the face of an awkward young man. "I think you know my fiancé, Robert Baker?"

The men shook hands. "Congratulations to both of you," Luke Three managed to say without too much hesitation. So she was going to marry little Bobby Baker, who still looked sixteen years old! In twenty years, when he was over forty, he would still look cherubic, only his face would be covered with wrinkles.

Then someone near the gate to God's Acres pointed to the sky and cried, "Looky there!" The sun had come out. And as a hush fell over the cemetery, the gathering turned eyes heavenward.

Mitchell Heror smiled softly and exchanged glances with Charlotte. She squeezed his hand. "You've done your part for Bosley, darling," she said, "and, as usual, your timing is perfect. It's a work of art."

High above the town of Angel, suspended, it seemed, in midair, an enormous cigar-shaped blimp vibrated in the wind. The emblem of the famous blue heron in flight, emblazoned on its sides, sparkled in the sunlight.

The Windhaven Saga
by Marie de Jourlet

AMERICA'S #1 PLANTATION SAGA

OVER 7 MILLION COPIES IN PRINT!